Telpher

a novel of parallel destinies

Steven Eckroad

Copyright

Dedication

For Barbara. I could not have done this without you.

Table of Contents

Chapter 1. Exeter

March 7, 2376 (Greenwich Earth Standard – GES). En route to Adonis System, Sagittarius Sector S5, Orion Spur.

The vidlink was quiescent until Rolfo entered the *ISS Exeter's* navigation compartment. Sensing his presence, holographic readouts sprang into view in the confined space. First Mate on the *Exeter*, Master Sergeant Rolfo Hardy had drawn tachcon duty during the sleep shift for the next four day-cycles. He hummed a half-forgotten tune to himself as he sorted through the holographic images, checking vectors and values from the transit beacons against the ship's posted flight plan. Well-rehearsed routines marched before his mind's eye without invitation as he meticulously carried out the required shift check. "'Course, I don't need a blinking' flight plan," he said to himself. "I've been on this route so many times before I know it by heart. And everyone knows, ya' don' need to do these manual checks, what with all the backup systems. This ol' bucket, she can practically fly herself." At that point in his soliloquy he was overlooking the fact that the vessel he once knew as *Trident* was a new class of starship. *ISS Trident* spent three months in a lunar orbiting dry dock while being retrofitted with the newest version of InterStellar Dynamic's Frankel-Spinoza warp drive. As well, she had a new navigation system that used the latest tachyonic technology to come out of I-S's research labs on Verde. Renamed *ISS Exeter*, this trip to Verde from Earth was her maiden voyage with the new drive and navigation system. This was Rolfo's first tour of duty on what would become known as an *Exeter*-class starship.

A slight tremor in the ship interrupted Rolfo's musings for a moment. He glanced with mild apprehension at the engine readouts displayed on 3D screens in front of him. Normally, the Frankel-Spinoza Drive produced a ride so smooth that, in his view, you could play Space Marbles without a single marble moving even a millimeter from its position in the weak magnetic field of the game matrix. As a space liner commissioned to transport both humans as well as freight to distant reaches of space, passenger comfort was an important selling point. If InterStellar was about anything, Rolfo thought, it was about selling, and profits for the company were still shaky since the crash of '67. Investors were nervous. The *Exeter*-class ship, with its luxurious appointments, was the company's newest inducement to vacationers to make the weeks long trip to distant star systems. With the *Exeter*-class InterStellar hoped to add tourism as a significant component of its revenue sources along with the ever-reliable commercial freight business.

A second tremor, greater than the first, almost put him into a panic. Rolfo was an old hand at space travel and he quickly regained a professional patience. While the tremors were unusual, he remained confident there was an answer to this situation. He could remember the early days, as well as stories his father and uncle told him about the first century of interstellar travel. There were some pretty rough tumbles when the warp drive was first being perfected. Rolfo thought back on some of the stories he had heard sitting at his uncle's feet. Within the warp bubble there were always the uncertainties with your exact location in local space, given the coarse tuning of the first tachyon transponders. But the biggest problem in those days was exiting hyperspace. Re-entering normal space had to do with what the science-types alluded to as the "unfolding of the spacetime envelope." Rolfo, with but a trade directorate education, did not understand that stuff. However, he experienced it when, as a young man, he first entered space flight service. That was quite a few years ago and no longer a serious problem. Rolfo put an end to his musing with one of his usual epithets, spoken aloud to no one in particular: "*Exeter* ... well, she's a class act!"

Nevertheless, Rolfo knew the regs and he would have to run the diagnostics. Class act or not, there was no known reason for that kind of tremor. Painstakingly, he went through all the flight plan checks again. Finding nothing untoward, he entered the code for engine diagnostics and began the long process of checking expected subroutine values against actual metrics. Rolfo could be a little casual sometimes, but he was a quality first mate and he knew his stuff. When push came to shove, as his uncle used to say, it paid to be methodical. It took an hour to go through the engine parameters and he found nothing out of normal. The next check would be the navigation diagnostics. Rolfo was a little less confident in that realm, being an engine man, not a navigator. But, he knew his trade and entered the appropriate codes.

While the holograms were coming up Rolfo eased into the adjoining break alcove to get a bulb of coffee. The only child of English immigrants to the planet Verde a half-century earlier, Rolfo was a middle-aged man of average height and weight with well-developed muscles due to his rigorous use of the shipboard weight room. Nevertheless, owing to the sedentary nature of his job there was the beginning of a slight bulge at his waist. He was good looking without being what you would call handsome and often had a twinkle in his eye – particularly in the presence of a beautiful woman. He had never married.

With a glance at the virtual refreshment panel and mental assent, he was rewarded with fresh brewed java just as he liked it – black and hot. Like seamen of old, a stimulating beverage was a welcome relief in times of tension. His uncle used to say about space flight, "some things never change." Rolfo thought of his recent visit to the Space and Galaxy Museum back on Earth in KCMetro, the capital of the North American Federation. One of the exhibits there was an antique version of today's coffee vendor – an actual machine that was connected to water, had coffee beans it ground up and buttons you pushed with your finger to get the brew you wanted. Push-button panels such as those had long since been replaced by the cyber-organic, sub-cutaneous implant he bore. Thought assisted surveillance and control, aka TASC, the implant allowed a person to communicate with and control just about any kind of machine or cybertronic device. There were various grades of TASC implants, with different levels of control and communication capabilities. Rolfo's TASC was pretty basic, his folks not having been able to afford a more advanced unit when he was born. Of course, being crew now on an InterStellar Dynamics vessel and unmarried with no family to support Rolfo could have upgraded. He just never got around to it and old habits were hard to break.

No more coffee beans either! The *Exeter's* beverage dispenser could perform a complex molecular synthesis for just about any concoction you wished – legal concoctions that is! So, Rolfo guessed, some things had changed. Though, truth to tell, when he was at that museum in KCMetro he had ordered so-called "real" coffee made with real coffee beans. It was different – maybe even better, he had to admit to himself.

A half hour later Rolfo was engrossed in running diagnostics on the navigation routines. He went over in his mind some basic facts that he knew, at least superficially. The F-S Drive achieved super-luminal travel between distant regions of space without the ship itself moving in its "local" space. Though he did not understand the physics of it, Rolfo knew that during the hyperspace portion of the journey you could not communicate outside your local space bubble with ordinary means. That's where the tachyons came in – particles that travelled faster than light – allowing communication with the navigation beacons that were set up on Earth and in the destination solar system. There were navigation beacons in other star systems as well, those colonized from Earth in the last hundred years.

Rolfo knew that tachyons had been discovered some three hundred years ago. But, development of a practical tachyon-based communication system came much later. Until the development of drives for interstellar travel, you did not need tachyons for anything. They were just interesting curiosities in an otherwise well-understood universe. Or so Rolfo thought. Anyway, for galactic space travel you needed a functioning and accurate "tachcon," as starship crews called the tachyon-based interstellar navigation and control system. The tachcon, or HyperNav as it was known officially, was key to the practicality of the F-S Drive. Until its invention by one of the founders of InterStellar Dynamics, there had been no known way to "steer" a starship traveling inside a spacetime bubble. Without it, you could end up just about anywhere. Or, anywhen, Rolfo mused, though the thought seemed so weird it passed into and out of his consciousness in a moment.

Then he found something that wasn't right. Definitely not right. He paused the routine, made a note of the databank identifier and immediately put in a call to Anders, the Chief Navigator.

"What's up, Rolfo," answered the *Exeter's* navigator. "I am right in the middle of an old North American Western. It's the good part where the hero is about to rescue his girl from the Indians. I hope you've got a good reason to interrupt me."

Rolfo knew Anders was pulling his leg. Yeah, he knew she did watch those old vids ("movies" she called them), but he figured Jana did it more as a joke on herself than out of real interest. Jana Anders was well educated, with multiple degrees in celestial mechanics and astrophysics. Cowboys and Indians, he guessed, was just a means of relaxing her highly tuned brain.

"Did you feel those tremors a while back?"

"Yes, actually I did. But, the Indians were raiding the settler's encampment and I guess I was preoccupied."

Rolfo wasn't sure whether she was still joking or not. "Well, I thought it was unusual so I started running the engine and navigation diagnostics. And ..."

"And well you should have, Rolfo," Jana interrupted. "I always feel better when you are on duty."

Rolfo felt a small blush come to his face at this. Jana was a striking blond with naturally straight hair and finely combed bangs that all but covered a high forehead. Her blue-grey eyes fascinated the likes of Rolfo. Aware of her attractiveness, he knew she was nevertheless out of his class. Still, she was presently unattached ...

"Well, you know how we do get a bit of turbulence sometimes when we re-enter. But, we aren't due to pop into Verde space for another week – right?"

"That's right. So, what did you find?"

Rolfo told her and Jana Anders was transported instantly from 19th century America to the now of the 24th century. "Say again, please!"

"I said, 'the tachcon is showing an approximate 300-year plus time displacement vector on the departure beacon, as if the Earth signal originated way in the future.'"

"I'll be right down. No, first I'll alert Captain Tang. In the meantime, pull up the module that houses the rotation tensor algorithm. You know how, right?" She did not wait for Rolfo to answer, dropping the call and putting in an emergency summons to Tang. Jana had felt all along that prototype trials of the new HyperNav system, the Gen-4, were not as thorough as she would have liked and she had not been convinced that the new system was

5

space worthy. It was one thing to prove out the system in the relatively benign environment of InterStellar's planet-bound lab on Verde, where gravitational effects on spacetime were well understood. It was quite another to be assured that it would function correctly in the uncharted regions of space. Where, for example, anomalies in the gravitational field could potentially distort the communications paths between ship and planet-based navigation beacons. Shipboard transponders were sophisticated enough to detect and report local anomalies. But, navigation accuracy depended upon those signals being captured and analyzed by an elaborate network of galactic navigation centers. The planetary control centers continuously communicated with shipboard equipment to ensure fidelity to the flight plan. Jana worried that the improved sensitivity of the new HyperNav might make it more susceptible to very strong gravitational fields. She had been outspoken to management in her beliefs, to no avail. The company was under pressure from stockholders and she was told that they needed to push into the new market as swiftly as possible. The new navigation system would cut interstellar transit times almost in half. More direct routes to the destination were possible by reducing the allowed separation between the ship's warp bubble and the steep gravitational wells caused by large stars.

* * *

March 7, 2376 GES, Orbiting Earth

Comfortably couched in the navigation pod of IFSS #5, Lukos Manteel had just begun his shift. Inter-Federation Space Station Five was one of several geosynchronous satellites orbiting Earth. There, space flight controllers monitored all space travel – both within Sol's system and without. The "warp room," as the navigation pod was known, was where the trained tachyon flight controllers were stationed. From there they could monitor the regular pings from interstellar ships as they traveled in hyperspace from Earth's sector of the galaxy to other distant regions. Like old-fashioned radarscopes, controllers could "see" the progress in interstellar space of all outbound and inbound traffic. Tonight, Lukos was assigned to monitor the sector of space in which that newest class of space liner, the *Exeter*, was making her maiden voyage. Lukos felt important to be assigned this role.

ISS Exeter had entered hyperspace about two weeks ago, Earth time, and was due into local space around Verde in six days. Her progress in hyperspace had been without note and there was not anything to worry about. The geosynchronous satellite system provided continuous communication with land-based supercomputers. At an altitude of some 6-1/2 earth radii above the planet the satellites could monitor the celestial routes of all interstellar traffic in all directions of travel outbound from Earth. Routing and starship locations were analyzed with microparsec accuracy. A redundancy of such satellites allowed the several Federation client states around the world to have their own communication link. More importantly it provided 100% coverage for even the small portion of space blocked from the view of any one satellite at any one time as the Earth rotated, as well as backup in case communication systems aboard a satellite failed. Officially named Terra Control Nexus, it was complemented by similar arrays of planet orbiting or surface-based control centers in each of Earth's sovereign federations in distant star systems. The complex, intra-galactic assembly of control centers guaranteed the safety of interstellar travel. The Inter-Federation Astronautical Commission coordinated policy and operations to produce a smoothly functioning pan-galactic agency. Since IFAC's establishment the management of space traffic had become routine.

While booting the system under his own login ID, Lukos reflected that, of course, there were some unfortunate incidents in the early days. Spaceships had gone off course or even gotten "lost" for a while. But no lives were lost and the early pioneers of interstellar travel persevered through the formative stages of space travel. Now, in the year 2376, interstellar jumps were routine.

Communicating with the HyperNav control interface with his specially purposed TASC, Lukos brought up the Narrow Field Array that showed the region of space within 5 parsecs of *Exeter*. At this point in its journey *Exeter* was supposed to be "passing" within about 0.5 parsecs of a large blue supergiant of about 10 solar masses. That was significantly closer than the older starships were allowed to get to such a large gravitating mass. But, the new navigation system had been proven to permit this. At least, that's what management told them. Lukos had memorized *Exeter's* flight plan (a skill for which he was justifiably proud as well as commended by his superiors) and knew that this was the closest she would pass to a large star system. You did have to be careful to not get too close to a massive star when in warp drive since the curvature of spacetime near such an object could potentially interfere with the tachyon navigation beacons. A blinking green triangle represented *Exeter* in the display, mimicking the periodic transponder signals. Lukos watched the blinking icon with a mixture of satisfaction and ennui. Then it was gone.

Lukos just stared at the screen, mouth ajar. "That just doesn't happen," he mumbled aloud to himself. Assuming it to be a vid-rack failure, he activated the secondary vid-screen. There was no blinking green triangle on that one either. With a rising sense of panic, Lukos manually switched to the backup monitor, a piece of hardware from earlier days that was still considered by old timers as more reliable than the TASC-directed scanners. Many of the newer flight controllers preferred the implant scanners since it kept their hands free to play old fashioned vid-games. Lukos scorned the opinion. Hands for old school vid-games, he thought to himself, but not for old school (yet proven!) monitors – give me a break!

Adjusting the backup monitor with a few key strokes to *Exeter's* flight plan and last-recorded position, Lukos found the blue supergiant star and zoomed in on a region 2 parsecs in diameter around the star. There was no *Exeter*. He zoomed in closer, but still no *Exeter*. In a state of disbelief and rising tension, Lukos nevertheless knew the drill at this point. He first initiated a traffic control transfer to IFFS #2, the Pan-Pacific Federation satellite, and requested confirmation of the readings he was getting. These were confirmed. With backup systems reporting all Earth-based systems functional the next step was to elevate the event to control central. Selecting the central comm link, Lukos announced, "Priority alert! Potential space liner navigation failure! *ISS Exeter* X156 has stopped responding to nav pings"

The Nexus chief of staff came back in a few moments, "Acknowledged. Send last known coordinates *Exeter* X156 to Lunar Nexus 2"

"Aye, aye," intoned Lukos as he keyed in the communications code for the backup navigational beacon array on Luna. Nav-Luna was a remote site operated by the privately funded Space Travel Association as a backup in case the IFSS Control Nexus went down or had problems – something that never happened. Lukos keyed in the last reported coordinates of *Exeter* and waited for Nav-Luna to respond. Thirty seconds later Nav-Luna sent back a hologram image of *Exeter* local space. There was the blue supergiant, but there was no sign of *Exeter*.

On the comm link again Lukos announced, "Chief, Nav-Luna query negative. STA reports *Exeter* off the beacon."

"Roger that. Commence emergency polling. I'll report up the chain."

"Aye, aye." Lukos felt like he was in a dream.

The low murmur that always formed the audible background of the Control Nexus had disappeared. There was complete silence as Lukos' fellow space-flight controllers gathered around the Nav-Luna display that now showed empty space where there should have been a starship – the starship *Exeter*.

* * *

March 7, 2376 GES. Location: Unknown

Captain Arun Tang was a square-faced, solidly built man whose outward hard appearance belied a pacific temperament and a keen insight. In his early sixties now, he had piloted interstellar space liners for over thirty years. Married, but recently widowed, and with two grown children – one of whom was accompanying him on this journey – he was not easily ruffled. Nevertheless, listening to his Chief Navigator's report on the apparent failure of the tachcon, Tang was troubled. *Anders does not get rattled easily,* Tang thought, as Anders' voice seemed to rise and fall unexpectedly. He smoothed back a lock of graying hair and absently fingered one of his bushy eyebrows as Jana continued, her voice now rising again in a note of hopefulness.

"The tachcon does not appear to have failed. It still seems to be pinging something, unless it is just an echo."

"Then how do you explain the time coordinate shift?" Tang lifted an eyebrow, favoring his chief navigator with a piercing glance. From long association with her, Tang was not misled by the seeming image of innocence Anders sometimes affected, aided by an almost childish face and hair that she wore unfashionably long to her shoulders. Anders, who was taller than many women, possessed an acute intelligence and an unerring ability to exercise command when and if needed.

"I can't," Commander Anders almost whispered through generous, yet barely parted lips. She fixed Tang with a thoughtful yet troubled gaze. Tang was disturbed by her uncharacteristic response.

"Well, let's try a different tack. Where do you think we are?"

"What do you mean? We're in a spacetime envelope – as you well know."

"No, I mean where in galactic space are we? I believe that our flight plan would put us in the vicinity of Bellatrix. If we dropped out of warp drive would we expect to see the star?"

"Of course we would, Captain. How could we be anywhere else?"

Lieutenant Joss Sommers, *Exeter's* Pilot, listened silently to this exchange. She unconsciously wrapped an unruly curl of black hair at the back of her neck around her little finger. Her petite and limber frame permitted a very informal, almost contorted posture in the pilot's couch. Anders and Tang had convened this emergency meeting on the Bridge and had instructed Sommers to join them. Now she confirmed Anders' statement, "The last reading from the HyperNav showed that we were 33 AU from Bellatrix and travelling at a speed of 4800c relative to local Bellatrix space." Glancing at her ship's chronometer, she continued, "Assuming we were at the point of closest approach to the star at the last tachcon reading before the coordinate shift, and given that this was about 45 minutes ago, we should be about 0.14 parsecs away if we drop into normal space at this point. Bellatrix is a Class B2 blue giant with a luminosity of about 1100 times Sol and a radius of about 6 times Sol. So, let's see…" Scanning the virtual console projected on her retina she focused on one of the readouts and reported, "At that distance it should appear to us over 600 times brighter than Venus and around 6 times the angular size of Betelgeuse, as viewed from Earth. That star should be quite visible. A large – and pretty – blue diamond in the sky," she added, with a wry look of amusement on her caramel face. Nevertheless, her normally smiling black eyes were silent.

Tang wondered to himself why Sommers assumed they were at the point of closest approach when the tachcon went haywire. Was she thinking the same thing he was? Aloud he announced, "Well, why don't we drop out of warp and find out if we are?" Sommers and Anders simultaneously turned to face him, with questioning looks.

Tang had a reason for suggesting this. He wondered how thoroughly Anders had thought through the possibilities. Their nearness to that star as they passed was beginning to trouble him. It was possible that spacetime curvature was greater than expected and was interfering with the new navigation system. Perhaps by dropping into normal space they could re-establish communication with Earth or with Verde, their destination. The ship's negative mass power source had sufficient fuel to leave and re-enter hyperspace multiple times, so that was not a concern. Tang looked at Jana. Like most men, Tang sometimes felt the allure of her wide-set, credulous eyes, but did not believe or credit the scuttle often heard in certain ranks of I-S fleet personnel about her ability to bewitch a man with them. Nevertheless, a beautiful woman, he thought, wistful at the remembrance of Maddy when she (and he) were Jana's age.

Jana's countenance brightened. "I see where you're going," she said, her eyes resuming their customary sparkle. "We drop into normal space where tachyon transmission is not befuddled by strong spacetime curvature."

"Exactly," Tang's confidence in Anders' high intelligence was again rewarded.

"Then, we re-establish contact and request Earth-based diagnostics. Earth-sat routines should be able to locate the anomaly and, if it is onboard software, even possibly transmit a recalibration signal, if necessary." Jana knew she was grasping at straws a bit in that last statement. But, what was the harm in hoping that would be the fix?

"Should we do a ship-wide announcement?" Sommers asked.

"No, that might cause panic – or at least give the stewards a handful of problems." Tang thought of his unusual manifest. Besides the usual commercial passengers, there was a large contingent of "new-world" colonists – folks fleeing the complexity and congestion of Earth to begin a new life on a new planet. Thinking of them, he observed further, "Of course, astute passengers will figure out that we have gone normal. I will instruct the chief steward in what we are going to do and let him handle any nervous people. Watskil is good at that."

Captain Tang sent out an all hands call to the crew, as Commander Anders took up her position at the central navigation console. Lieutenant Sommers engaged the helm, rearranging her diminutive frame into a more formal position in the pilot's cushioned chair. Her physical size and delicate features belied an acute intelligence and capability for intense concentration. She began to set up the codes for shutting down the warp drive. There was some danger in this maneuver, Tang knew. There was at least a strong possibility of turbulence since they were still near that big star. But, that could not be helped and he could think of no better way to crack this egg. Anders' concurrence, once she saw where he was going, gave him added confidence. If there was anything that could jeopardize the ship in the maneuver they were about to try, she would have spotted it and spoken up. He glanced over at her, noting the somewhat strange but nevertheless peaceful expression on her face.

"On my mark!" Tang spoke the command. "Three, two, one, … initialize!"

Sommers executed the envelope reversal routine and the ship surfaced smoothly into normal spacetime. Holographic displays leapt into view over the command console giving them a stunning three-dimensional view of their local surroundings. The Milky Way presented a majestic vista across the lower portion of the display. Just to the center right was a large bright disc. It could not have been more than 200 million kilometers away, about the distance of Mars from Sol. A star, certainly. But decidedly not the brilliant blue diamond they expected to see. And, it was much closer.

Other than Tang's mumbled "What the …?" there was a stunned silence on the *Exeter* Bridge as they all viewed the orange-red star in the viewer. Despite the jarring turn of events, Anders was busy querying the tachcon. Tang shot her a questioning glance.

"No, Captain, there is no change in the tachcon. I think it must be in some kind of internal loop. "I will reboot it but I am beginning to suspect it is non-functional."

"Sommers?" queried Tang.

"I'm running a scan on that star right now."

The growing tension became evident in their voices, threatening to destroy protocol.

"Jana, any idea where we are?" Tang almost shouted as he paced about the Bridge.

"I've performed a search of the stellar neighborhood looking for known star configurations – constellations, if you will. It looks like we are in a location, as seen from Earth, on the border between the Constellations Pisces and Andromeda. That's quite far from where we should be. But, it gets worse. There is something wrong with some of the star positions. I've got the computer running a relative motion profile."

That puzzled Tang. "Why?"

"Just a hunch." She did not want to say more. More long minutes passed.

Then Sommers announced, "Captain, it's a K0, young main sequence star, a little cooler than Sol. It masses as 0.76 Sol and appears to have a slight variable output in the visible region. Might even have habitable planets," she added, with a quizzical expression that accented her small facial features and piercing black eyes. "I am inputting the exact spectral characteristics into the Federation Stellar Database to see if there is a match with any known stars."

The Bridge of the *Exeter* settled into an uncomfortable silence, as Tang's crew continued to study the nearby star and its neighborhood. Tang got on the intercom with Watskil to find out how the passengers were doing and was reassured that all was relative calm. Sergeant Rolfo Hardy requested admission to the Bridge, which was granted. Jana was glad for his silent presence, noting with favor his firm stance, with feet slightly apart and hands clasped behind his back. Smiling at him, Jana felt a momentary sense of hope. He smiled back at her through admiring brown eyes.

Tang stared at the grapefruit sized star in the viewer, almost transfixed, his thoughts a jumble of possibilities, none of which he wanted to give credence to. Long minutes passed. His troubled reverie was broken by Sommers and Anders, both speaking at once.

"I've got a match," announced Joss.

"Bingo!" exclaimed Jana at the same moment. But the sinking feeling in the pit of her stomach did not match the brief exultancy she felt at finding her hunch to be correct.

"Joss, you first." For some reason he was afraid of what Jana was going to say.

"Well, Captain, it's a star cataloged as 54 Piscium. About 36 light-years from Earth and about 6th magnitude from there. However, strangely, it has not yet been explored by Earth federations."

"And," Jana now interjected, "The star is in the position relative to Earth that it occupied in about the year 2029 GES." Her normally soft voice was clipped, hard, emotionless.

Tang jerked around to face her. "Meaning …" he began, but couldn't finish.

"Meaning that beside having travelled to a location in space far from our intended destination, we have also apparently travelled back in time some 350 years – 347 to be exact." Jana let those last words drop like mill weights into the deadly pool of silence that mirrored an eternity in their midst.

Long moments passed. Then Tang spoke: "How … how did that happen? I mean, if it is true?" He did not believe it, could not believe it. He looked at Jana, at Joss, at Rolfo. They simply stared back at him, the enormity of this development still fascinating their thoughts like a meteor shower. Then Jana spoke up.

"I think the HyperNav encountered some kind of bug in the module that continuously calculates the Alcubierre Metric. That then led to a spatio-temporal dislocation which propagated into the F-S Warp Drive."

"Translation, please!" demanded Tang.

"Translation: We created some kind of spacetime rip or rift, a "gateway" – or wormhole, if you like – and travelled through it, coming out the other side in a far-removed spacetime." Jana's voice was still rather mechanical. She continued, "And it is likely that the gate was unstable and collapsed after we went through." After a pause she added, "Meaning, we cannot go back through it as it does not exist anymore."

Chapter 2. Sonja

Late May, 2052 (Common Era – CE). Toronto, North American Federation.

Sonja felt her Lynk signaling an incoming call and knew it was Sergei even before looking at the display. She could almost hear him saying, "Want to do dinner?" Not tonight, she thought. She just could not spend another evening with him when all they talked about was his research, his ideas, his dreams – even if his dreams of space travel did inspire her. That was the main attraction of this strange man for her – his bold ideas of travel to the stars. Although Sergei was not particularly handsome, Sonja unfortunately hadn't understood the attraction in the other direction. Unwisely, she had let the relationship go beyond the platonic and her face flushed as she remembered some of the nights they had spent together. At first she excused herself that it was hard to find guys with more than just sex on their minds, even in grad school. Sergei, with his brilliant intellect and ready ability to discuss far out concepts, was a welcome exception. However, it eventually become apparent that Sergei had only one obsession – himself. Now, because of her earlier indiscretions, Sergei had a different view of their relationship than she did.

But not this night, she told herself again. This night was to be a celebration of Sonja, for she had just heard from CETL that her application for a post-doc position there was accepted. Yes, Sonja thought, I would have liked to celebrate this with a fellow scientist – even Sergei, if he could be counted upon to share my success instead of just his own. But, I know better! He'll just mumble "congrats" or something non-committal and then launch into his own latest pet ideas. So, Sergei, you're going to have to spend the evening by yourself.

Had Sonja known Sergei's call was about passing his orals she might have relented, owing to the sympathetic side of her nature inherited from her Spaniard father. But tonight her Irish heritage would reign supreme and reward her with the rich accolades of self-congratulations that were her due. Kudos that she otherwise would not get from men like Sergei.

With the appointment to CETL, Sonja felt her life was just beginning. The *Center for Extraterrestrial Life*! Sonja reflected on her good fortune to get the post doc position there. CETL was part of the University of North America and located adjacent to the UNA main campus in Kansas City. She would be assisting Dr. Eleanor Spitzer, noted astrobiologist and program director at CETL, on a new project for which CETL had just obtained a grant from the Federation Science Foundation. They would be developing psychogenesis models to investigate the potential origin and evolution of mental processes in intelligent species that might be found on known exoplanets. It was speculative work given that very little was known about the geological makeup and atmosphere of these extra-Solar worlds, among other factors that might influence the emergence of intelligent life.

An even more speculative aspect was a subtask of the main FSF grant that involved exploring new methods for detecting signals from intelligent societies on those planets. Surely, with the billions of stars in even our own galaxy, it was reasoned they must exist. Sonja's most fervent dream was to be able to travel to the stars herself, not just hear from them. However, if travel to the stars was out of reach – Sergei notwithstanding! – then Sonja would be satisfied with communicating with their putative yet enigmatic denizens. That is where Sonja would be focusing her efforts at CETL.

Pausing at the hallway mirror before leaving her apartment, Sonja removed the band that held her rich auburn hair in a ponytail, and tossed her head to free the gentle curls. Parted in the middle without bangs, it fell in generous waves to her shoulders. She had a delicate, almost aquiline nose with just a slight upturn and soft emerald eyes wide set under arched eyebrows. Friends told her she had a perpetual, laughing smile. Sonja hummed a tune she had heard that afternoon in the Toronto Museum of Language and Culture. There was an interesting exhibit at the museum on the history of "popular" music with the opportunity to put on earpieces and listen to various samples from different eras. One struck her with particular relevance. Though the song had been written some 100 years ago, the words were so fitting for her new life: *"I'm goin' to Kansas City, Kansas City here I come..."* She thumbed her Lynk to page Grace Reason, a neighbor in her apartment complex who was a singer in a local hop-pop band. Grace, she was sure, would know how to have a good time tonight – without any self-important men to distract them!

* * *

Sergei Levkov was elated. He had just been informed that he had passed his orals at the Toronto Technology Institute with flying colors and was cleared to begin his thesis work in earnest. The questions on exotic matter and possible practical applications were a cinch, as he knew they would be. With a kind of smug chuckle aloud, he recalled the expressions of near disbelief on the faces of a couple of the committee members as he laid out the basic concepts for an exotic matter engine. He knew they were thinking: where does he get such ideas? Well, he thought somewhat ruefully, it was not where but what to do with those ideas that was important to him now. That would come soon enough, he hoped. He always had a plan and even this detour in Toronto would not deter him from final victory.

Pulling his Lynk from a pouch in his tunic he keyed a message to Sonja. He hoped she would answer, he wanted to see her tonight. Most of the people in this university – students and professors alike – were boring and lacked any genuine intellectual talent. Talent that he could respect, in any event. And outside of the university, in the society at large, there was genuine distaste for people with an intellectual bent. That foolish World Cyber War had all but destroyed the human will to push the boundaries of intellect and discovery. But Sonja Bellesario was different. She was bright, intuitive in a way that Sergei wished he could emulate, and innovative. Her daring ideas about space exploration and extraterrestrial life – so unusual in this place – appealed to Sergei's own brand of recklessness. Then too, she was good-looking. Despite his own tendency to self-absorption, Sergei was enthralled with her beauty. Alas, mused Sergei, what started out heatedly had now

17

cooled significantly. He did not know why.

Perhaps, now that he could start on his thesis research in earnest, he could devote more attention to her. He knew she appreciated intelligence, and his planned research topic was bound to excite her interest. Sergei knew that Sonja liked listening to his ideas on building a so-called faster than light space ship engine – a hyperspace drive. She was one of those rare people who genuinely had an itch to go out into space. Most of the world was still trying to recover a sense of normalcy after the devastating war. Sergei knew he could make her dream come true. He was sure of it. What Sergei did not appreciate was the inevitability of Sonja's growing ambivalence toward him. Even the breakthrough in interstellar space travel that he planned to bring forth would not win back her affection.

His Lynk remained silent and Sergei had to give up for the moment his plans for the evening. He pocketed the unit and walked out of the Space Physics Department building. The downtown Toronto sky scape spread out before him, the CN Tower dominating the city's architectural profile. Leaving the campus compound, he walked the three blocks to his apartment where he showered and changed into some more comfortable tunic and slacks. A second try to reach Sonja was unsuccessful so Sergei resigned himself to a solo dinner at his favorite pub, the Clock and Candle. He would see her tomorrow, he knew, at the post-Commencement convocation. Sonja was graduating, with honors, with a doctorate in astrobiology – well deserved, Sergei faintly acknowledged to himself.

That brought back a persistent worry. Sonja would likely be leaving Toronto. She had applied for several post-doc positions, only one of which was in Toronto. That one was her least favorite, he knew. Dare he hope that she would take the Toronto appointment? Well, he thought, if she didn't then he would have to follow his planned course without her.

* * *

As the last strains of the Commencement postlude ended, and the graduates mingled with family and friends, Sergei spotted Sonja conversing with two of her girlfriends. He began to push his way through the crowd. Sonja turned his way and saw him. She spoke something to her friends and started toward him with a happy expression on her face. Sergei was relieved. As she came within earshot they both spoke at once.

"Oh, Sergei, I'm so happy, I got ..."

"I tried to call you last night ..."

Confused smiles and embarrassed sentence fragments ensued as each tried to recover the momentum. Sonja got the upper hand.

"Sergei, I got the post doc position at CETL!" She put her hand on his and smiled warmly. "I'm so excited – it means I'll be able to pursue my ideas on exploring the use of radio-enhanced telepathy as a tool to contact extraterrestrial civilizations. If any exist, that is ... Anyway, I'm gonna' accept the post-doc position. I leave for Kansas City in just a few days." Sonja put as much spunk in her voice as possible. She still hoped Sergei would crawl out of himself into the real world and congratulate her.

"Hey, that's great Sonja." Sergei did try hard to sound enthusiastic, his normally downturned, thin lips attempting a wider smile. But, his heart fell and in moments he had switched emotional tracks. His mission surged into the vacuum being left by Sonja. Aloud, and with a little more honesty, he repeated, "Sonja, I *am* happy for you. But, you're going to miss the big event: I passed my orals and I get to start on my hyperdrive research project right away! I think I can finish my dissertation in less than two years."

"Hey Sergei – that's good news too! Well, we can always keep each other informed on our research through the blogosphere, or email. I do wish you success, you know."

"Yeah, I know. But, I'm really going to have to dig into this and I won't have much time for a personal life anyway."

"Oh Sergei, don't be such a stick in the mud. C'mon, let's go celebrate – for both of us!" This was Sonja's nice side speaking. Anyway, she thought, this would probably be the last time they would see each other. It was time to make the break official.

"Well, okay. Where do you think ...?

"How about the CN Tower? Have you ever been to the top? You get a great view of the City from there. And, there is a super 360-degree revolving restaurant."

"I guess that'd be fun – I've never been up to the top. Uh, can we go Dutch on dinner?" Sergei wasn't short on money but there were some big expenses coming up for his research and he wanted to save as much as possible on ordinary expenses.

Suppressing a frown Sonja replied, "Yeah, okay ... Come by my place at 7 and we can take the free tram." If he was going to be such a tight wad, then she could play that game as well. The tram would take twice as long as a taxi, but it would be too loud with excited city-goers to have a conversation. She would be spared a little while from Sergei's inevitable monologue.

The tram, it turned out, wasn't too noisy for conversation, and Sergei asked Sonja about her planned research into radio-telepathy. Then he even listened to her. So, Sonja was in a pretty good frame of mind as they stepped off the tram and walked the half block to the entrance of the Tower. The air was fresh and there was a faint fishy smell this near the lake. Even with the sunshine that day – after several days of rain – the early May air was cool. Sonja pulled her jacket close as they walked along.

"Hey, I just noticed: the tower isn't lit up as it often is."

"I think it has to do with bird migrations," Sonja replied. "I read that with the recent storms making bad weather for flying, a lot of migratory birds headed for parts further north have been lying low at Thompson Park. The news link quoted a park official saying that with the clearing weather today once nightfall hits a lot of birds will pick up and head north again. So, they probably have doused the lights to help the birds out. Too bad, though, since the city lights are fabulous from the observation decks."

"Well, we'll be too busy talking anyway. I want to tell you about my latest discovery. Uh ... and, hear more about your research." Sonja grimaced and said nothing. She had her chance to talk on the tram so she guessed it was his turn. She would put up with one more evening of Sergei's soliloquy. She planned to make a definite break with him by the end of the evening.

They purchased lift tickets and took the elevator up 115 stories to the restaurant level. As they ascended in the glass windowed elevator car, the city's skyscrapers fanned out below them on the left; the Inner Harbour filled their view to the right. Sonja pointed out the skinny, needle-like shadow of the Tower cast by the late afternoon sun. The image aligned almost perfectly with the ribbon of rail lines that condensed into a single line in a northeast direction as they left Union Station below. The din of downtown commerce and traffic could not be heard.

Sonja had called ahead for reservations so they were seated almost immediately. They had good seats, on the outer perimeter next to the glass windows. There weren't too many people in the restaurant this night and they were in a section where there were still some vacant tables. It was quiet and for a moment neither spoke. They each were caught up with the stupendous view as the restaurant slowly rotated, repainting the view moment by moment. It was a clear evening and the sun was setting to the west. Even with the supposed voluntary Fatal Light Awareness Program there were a few non-conforming downtown skyscrapers beginning to sparkle in the twilight. They ordered drinks and made small talk for a while.

Sonja studied Sergei's face. It was narrow, with deep-set, furtive black eyes that tended to squint under angular eyebrows. He had a determined chin, long narrow nose, and small ears that were almost unnoticeable. His curly brown hair was unkempt in appearance, though not by intention she was sure. Sergei's shabby appearance belied his great intelligence. She wondered how she had fallen for him in the first place, and how she was going to manage her plan to break off the relationship tonight.

After ordering their meal Sergei launched into his latest idea. Sonja noted with relief that his typically dour countenance reverted to a more open expression, as often happened when he was describing something of significant importance or interest to him.

"You know that I have been studying the principles around the Alcubierre hyperdrive, right?"

"Yes, you told me all about that last week. I mean," she corrected her tone, "I remember the cool idea about warping space in front of and behind a space ship." As an astrobiologist, Sonja was not as keen on the how to get to planets orbiting other star systems so much as what you would find upon arrival.

Sergei didn't notice her implied weariness. "Yes! Well, there is a problem with communication with the outside when you are in the local space bubble created by the drive. That is, ordinary electromagnetic signals travel only at the speed of light so any communication with planets at your points of origin or destination would take many light-years whereas the ship could travel between interstellar locations in a matter of weeks."

"Well, how does the space ship know where it is then? How does it stay on course?"

"That's exactly the point of my research. Ever since Wells and Sullivan perfected their technique two years ago to send information via tachyons I have been wondering how to use their ideas to achieve hyperspace navigation. Yesterday I came up with something that I think will make a breakthrough."

"What?" Sonja couldn't help getting interested. She so earnestly wanted to go to the stars someday, as far off as that seemed to be. Maybe Sergei was smart enough to do it. She had once overheard two of his professors remarking on his intellectual prowess and the rather miraculous knowledge he seemed to have.

"Oh, that's a secret!" Sergei suppressed a chuckle. "But, I'll let you in on part of it. Anyway, I don't have it all figured out. But, it has to do with creating a local wormhole through which ordinary matter or energy can pass."

"A wormhole! How do you create a wormhole? I thought those were things that existed at the center of black holes and that no light could escape them once it entered."

"Yeah, wormholes were once thought to occur at the center of a black hole. But, the consensus now is that in some sense they may be all around you. Some physicists even as far back as the 20th century speculated that there could be sub-sub-microscopic wormholes everywhere. You've heard of quantum gravity and quantum foam, haven't you?"

"Yes-ss. But you know cosmology is certainly not my area of specialty. As an undergraduate I took a survey course that included a section on general relativity and quantum theory. I remember the gist was that the 4-dimensional spacetime of human experience is in fact a membrane, or "brane-world," in a higher dimensional spacetime and that gravity can spread out into a higher dimension making it appear relatively weak in our sensory world. I also remember learning that around the time I was born experiments with the VLHC in Geneva discovered the graviton. My professor pointed out that although Einstein's General Relativity theory required the graviton to be a massless particle, if its motion were constrained to a higher dimension it would appear to us on the brane to have mass. And that is exactly what they found with the VLHC, gravitons with mass."

"That's right, Sonja. Good memory! Discovery of the graviton revealed a higher dimensionality to spacetime and showed that the so-called Planck length was much larger than would be predicted by the weakness of gravity on the brane. There are still competing theories to fully explain quantum gravity but all of them show that spacetime is quantized, resulting in the indeterminacy associated with quantum mechanics. Anyway, at the Planck length the geometry and topology of spacetime becomes probabilistic. I suppose that this indeterminacy led to the moniker 'quantum foam.' There would be a kind of surging sea of geometric discontinuities, each occurring with different probabilities. These could include "local" discontinuities in spacetime through which passages from one part of the spacetime matrix to a "distant" one could spontaneously form. These could, in fact, traverse a higher spatial dimension and would be similar to what we would call a wormhole. The passages, of course, would still be quantum scale in size. But, what if you could reach down and capture such a wormhole and bring it up to classical size? Bring it up to a size corresponding to the wavelength of normal electromagnetic communications?"

"Can you do that?" Sonja couldn't help being impressed. Then, remembering how the conversation had started, she asked, "What about the tachyons? What do they have to do with it?"

Sergei was pleased that he had caught Sonja's full attention. "Wow, Sonja, you're sharp! Most of the others just don't seem to understand. You've hit on the secret!" He asserted this last with an innocent simplicity that belied his age. He was some ten years or more older than Sonja – another puzzling fact about him in Sonja's eyes. Why had it taken him so long to get to this stage of his academic career, she wondered? She had never felt comfortable asking that. Sergei went on, "My theory is that, rather than being a faster-than-light particle, tachyons are some kind of ordinary boson that either creates or latches on to quantum-scale wormholes. To us, at classical scale levels, we think they are travelling at superluminal speeds over large distances. In reality they are normal, light-speed particles that capture and ride through quantum wormholes that extend over what to us appear to be great distances. But, in fact, the tachyons are just taking a short cut through a higher dimension. Anyway, that is what my research project is going to be about. If I am successful, you will be the first to know."

Sergei did not want to say more, and fortunately at that point their dinner arrived. The restaurant had rotated around by this time to give a magnificent view of Lake Ontario that shone dully in the light of the rising moon – it was just past full that evening. They both stared silently at the glass-encased view while the waiter laid out their food.

After dinner ended while they waited for their checks, Sonja tried to direct Sergei away from his pet theme. "Hey, you wanna' go out on the observation deck? It's pretty amazing – there is a glass floor that you can walk on and look all the way down to the ground."

"Okay," Sergei responded, without much conviction. He wanted to continue their discussion but he could tell Sonja was getting restless.

After paying, they took the elevator down a level and walked out onto the observation deck. There was a mixture of people there, some of them oohing and aahing at the views. Others walked slowly around the tower deck, their thoughts unexpressed. Tourists with children, senior citizens, a couple of students like themselves, here and there a lone man or woman who probably didn't want to be there but were anyway because they had no one to be with and this is what people did when they were lonely. While Sergei dawdled, taking in the sights and sounds that were so different from the restaurant above them, Sonja walked briskly around the perimeter.

"Sergei, come along," she motioned. "I want you to see the glass floor." Sergei pushed his way past a couple of oblivious teenagers and joined Sonja at the edge of what initially seemed to be a gridded floor, with nothing between the grids. He was so caught up with his thoughts that he did not hear her description. He gasped, as she stepped right out onto what at first seemed clear air. Then he realized his mistaken perception, seeing the glass floor for what it was. Still, he hesitated momentarily before joining Sonja in the middle of the clear expanse. There was a fleeting sensation of vertigo as Sergei adjusted his vision to focus on the ground over a thousand feet below. Off to the right was a large stadium, its garish lights flooding a green field on which moved tiny, ant-like figures. Sonja explained that it was Rogers Centre, home to the Toronto Blue Jays. It was a night game, just getting started. Not being a baseball fan, Sergei hadn't clue who was playing.

Sonja did. "It's the Blue Jays playing the Royals! Tonight's game is the last of a four-day series and the Jays are poised to sweep the Royals!" Sonja was almost gushing with enthusiasm, Sergei noted. She was obviously a dedicated fan. "But," she went on, "in division play they aren't doing so well. Anyway, I better start switching loyalties and root for the Royals tonight. You know ... I'm going to Kansas City next week." Her voice dropped as she looked up at Sergei and she wished she hadn't rubbed it in. The strains of that old blues song began to run through her mind again. "*Goin to – Kansas City ...*" She recovered herself, realizing that this was as good a segue as any into what she needed to say to Sergei tonight.

Sergei walked to the parapet and looked out through the glass observation windows to the city and the waterfront. Sonja followed him and stood beside him. "Sergei," she hesitated, but then continued firmly. "Sergei, you're a good friend and colleague in scientific research ... but that's all. I have appreciated the relationship as far as it has gone. But I think you may be more serious about this than I am, and I just don't want to continue down that road. We both have our research to pursue and I, for one, am not ready for any complicating emotional entanglements." She hesitated. "Do you understand?"

"Yeah, I get it. I knew you felt that way anyway. I was just hoping ..."

"Look, we're in similar fields," she cut in. "I hope we see each other occasionally at conferences or symposia. I am interested in your research and I wish you great success. Even a little selfishly. There's nothing I'd like better than to have a chance in my lifetime to get off this planet!" With that Sonja hoped to change the subject.

"Yeah, I do agree with that. It would be really great to get off this planet!" Sergei turned to her and forced a smile. "You ..."

He did not finish his sentence. There was a loud boom, followed by several sharp staccato cracking sounds. The deck floor seemed to jump several inches and then the whole structure was swaying back and forth. The lights blinked off, then flickered on again. Sergei saw pieces of some kind of material, ceiling perhaps, flying down around the people near him. One elderly gentleman was struck and fell to his knees. There were screams and even curses, and someone shouted "Earthquake!" The lights went out, blinked on again momentarily, and then went out and stayed out. There was the sound of running water somewhere.

Sergei looked for Sonja but she was nowhere to be seen in the darkened area around him. An eerie blue glow from the baseball game suffused upward through the glass floor a few meters away from him. Was the game still going on? The tower continued to sway in periodic motion. The glass observation window behind him cracked, then split open. A rushing wind from outside caused him to stagger forward toward the glass floor. Sergei saw people on the floor instinctively trying to move away when suddenly an entire panel of glass fell out of the floor, plummeting toward the ground. There was a child, a girl no more than 10, slipping ominously toward the failed floor, trying to get her footing. Sergei watched, thinking to himself how foolish the girl was to not just get up and run. The wind from behind him seemed to escape the violent movements of the structure by rushing through the ruined floor, trying to take the child with it.

The tower continued to sway back and forth. It seemed to go on forever. Another lurch and bump threw Sergei toward the floor, and toward the little girl. Without knowing why, he reached out and grabbed her ankle just as she was about to go through the break. At the same time a large metal panel fell beside him, a piece of it coming loose and striking him a glancing blow across the side of his head. The last thing he remembered was hearing someone shout, "You saved her!" and then feeling rough hands on his own legs pulling him backwards. Something wet flooded into his eyes and he blacked out.

* * *

Sergei awoke. There was something on the side of his head. He turned his head to see what it was but something restrained his movement. Then he realized he was in a bed. Everything was white. White ceiling. He was on his back, looking up. White walls and white sheets, at least as much as he could see. He felt woozy, felt like lapsing back into listlessness. Instead, a surge of determination took possession and his thoughts coalesced. Someone approached.

"Where am I?" Sergei croaked more than spoke.

"You're in a hospital," said a voice in white.

"Why?"

"There was an earthquake. You got a concussion. The rescuers brought you here. You and a hundred others. Hospitals all over town have taken in folks who were in the Tower." The nurse spoke in matter of fact, punctuated tones – as if she (or was it he?) were an automated medical attendant. "Some weren't so lucky as you …"

Then the events atop the CN Tower began to come back to Sergei. "There was a friend with me," he blurted out. "Is she …?"

"You mean Sonja?" The nurse winked at him. She leaned over

so that Sergei saw her amused face clearly and saw that she was not a machine after all.

"No! I mean yes!" He meant, no she is not that kind of friend that deserved the wink, but yes she was a friend, a colleague. He remembered the whole painful conversation with Sonja just before the earthquake. "Yes," he said. "Sonja Bellesario, a fellow grad student – scientist – from the university. Is she all right?"

"Yes, she is fine – very fine," and she winked again. To Sergei this nurse just wouldn't give up. Maybe she had a nervous eye. The nurse continued, "Your Sonja was here this morning to check in on you. She's been coming every day for the last three days. Today she was a little concerned because she must leave town tomorrow and she was worried you would not wake up before she left. Actually, I think she was worried you were not going to wake up at all." Another wink. "You've been out for three days, you know."

"You mean she was not injured in the earthquake?" A pause. "Out for three days?" Then, again, "How did I get here?" Sergei still could not quite grasp what had happened. He had never experienced an earthquake. Lurid images winked in and out of his mind as he remembered the breaking glass, the staggering people, the rushing wind ... that terrible, sucking wind! Then he remembered the little girl. Why on earth did he try to grab her? He could have fallen through the broken floor himself by doing that. Confused thoughts threaded themselves through his mind, obscuring the thin patch of consciousness in front of him, which was threatening to slip away. He could no longer form words, and only stared at the nurse.

The nurse started to speak, but thought better of it. "You need to rest now. I've given you a sedative in your IV. Sonja said she would stop in again tomorrow morning. I'm sure you two will be able to visit a little while then." With that the nurse disappeared from Sergei's sight. Fortunately, she did not wink with that last statement. He let go of his racing thoughts and sank back into a dreamless sleep.

Morning came and Sergei felt a lot better. At least until he had a basic breakfast of porridge and apple juice. A minor spell of nausea at that point threatened to ruin what otherwise appeared to be a sunny, bright day. His room sported a window looking out to a green lawn and shade trees that were just finishing putting on their summer finery. The nausea passed. There was a knock at his door.

Sonja had already been informed that Sergei awakened from his coma the evening before.

"Sergei!" she exclaimed. "Welcome back to the land of the living. How do you feel?"

"Well, okay I guess. Considering, anyway, that I have no idea what happened to me. I mean, I know there was an earthquake … But, what happened to you? You're okay, I guess? How did I get here?" Sergei's energy level was not up to normal and his thoughts were still a bit random.

Sonja chuckled. "One question at a time. But, first, can I get you anything? Something to drink?" She noticed the dryness in his voice.

"Yeah, I could use a drink. The glass on the table there is empty," he motioned with his eyes. The neck and head brace had been loosened somewhat but still pretty much constrained his movement. Sonja disappeared for a moment and then brought back from the nurse's station a full tumbler of ice water with a straw in it. She handed the glass to Sergei and sat down beside the hospital bed.

"Sergei," she said, "you're a bit of a hero. You rescued a little girl from falling to her death through the broken glass floor. I saw what happened, but I was too far away from you and her to do anything. Some people were not so lucky." Her face fell as she remembered the terrible sight of a man falling from the wide ledge above the Tower's main pod, the so-called Edge Walk. Normally harnessed, there was no danger to patrons from falling, but they must have been in the process of unhooking someone when the earthquake hit. Or maybe a strap broke from the force of it. She shuddered at the thought of falling 1200 feet to your death.

"Hero, huh? I guess I'm just lucky to be alive. What happened to you?"

"Really, Sergei! You're a local hero. It's on all the news links. Her family wants to come to the hospital to thank you but they haven't let them so far – until you are better." Sergei groaned: all the news links? That was not good. Aloud, he said, "I don't really want to see them. It was nothing. I think she just sort of fell into my hands and I grabbed her. That's all."

"Well, I'm sure you'll think better of it after a few more days of recovery. As for me, I guess I was lucky too. That first jolt knocked me to the floor and I just started scrambling away from the parapet as fast as I could, on my hands and knees. Stuff was falling from the ceiling but it missed me. I saw the piece that came down and hit you. It was a good thing because it fell across the place in the glass floor that broke open and blocked anyone else from falling through. Then, the next thing I knew was that someone was pulling me toward an inner room where some others were huddled. I got under a table and waited it out.

"So much of what happened the rest of that night is still a blur. The rescuers came and I did not know where you were. I was unhurt, so after a paramedic examined me in a temporary triage center at the base of the Tower, I was released. I asked where you might be but, of course, no one knew. All was confusion. The next day, after calling around, I found where they took you."

There was an uncomfortable silence between them. Sergei tried to adjust the bandage on his head. Sonja looked at her watch. Finally, she spoke again. "Sergei, you know I was supposed to leave for Kansas City today. I was going to take the Maglev, but they have shut down the route from Toronto to Chicago until they can inspect all the right of way for damage. So, I'm going to fly. My plane leaves this afternoon at four."

"Yeah, I know. Good luck in KC." He stared out the window at the shaded lawn, lost in thought. There was an awkward silence. But Sonja had made up her mind.

"Well, I better get moving. I still have some packing to do and transportation to the airport is still iffy with all the damage to some of the highways. It was a 6.2 earthquake – about the largest ever here." Sonja stood and shook his hand in a friendly goodbye gesture. "Let's keep in touch," she said without much conviction. What else could she say at this point? The earthquake had somehow punctuated her disavowal of a few nights before and that was the end of it. She turned and left.

Chapter 3. CETL

Early June, 2052 CE. Kansas City, North American Federation.

"Hi, Janet? It's Sonja!" Sonja cradled her Lynk between shoulder and ear as she finished buttoning a summer blouse. It was going to be hot today and Kansas City weather was quite a bit warmer than Toronto.

"Sonja! Hey, awesome to hear your voice. Uh, where are you …?"

"I'm in Kansas City. Just arrived."

"Awesome! I mean, I wondered when or, gosh, even IF you would get here. I mean, what with the earthquake and all. What happened? Are you all right? Well, I guess you are or you wouldn't be here. You'll have to …"

"Tell you all about it," finished Sonja. Sometimes you just needed to cut in on Janet. Once she took off she didn't seem to know how to land. "Yes," she repeated, "I'll tell you and I bet you won't believe it. When can we get together? I'm still unpacking and I've got to go out and get some things for my apartment."

"Oh, right way girl, right away. But, uh oh, no can't be tonight. I've got a heavy date … Uh … Well, you'll just love Bart. I only just met him and, well more of that later. So, not tonight, and tomorrow night is my book club – we're reading Franklin's "To the Stars". Hey, you'd like that book, have you read it already? It's fascinating what they think we are going to do in the next 50 years. But, it's fiction, not real life. Anyway, how about day after tomorrow? It's some war holiday and I have the day off. We could meet at this new coffee shop in the old Union Station and catch up on stuff."

"That would be great, Janet. I can't wait to see you. Union Station is just down the street from my apartment complex. What time, then? Say, 12 noon?"

"Yeah, that works fine. I'll catch the tram downtown. I live out in the suburbs you know."

"Okay, see you then."

"Bye."

The line went dead on the other end and Sonja pocketed her Lynk. Janet could talk your ear off, but Sonja needed some irrelevant distractions to help her get settled. Janet was just what she needed. The intensity of her departure from Toronto, and Sergei, still weighed upon her. And on Monday she would have her first day at the Center, starting with a meeting with her advisor and mentor-to-be for the next two years, Dr. Spitzer.

CETL was located on the former site of the Liberty Memorial that had been dedicated in 1926 to the men and women who served in World War I. In the turbulent years following the 2037 war, neo-anarchists had dynamited the memorial and WWI museum, claiming that it was a symbol of the false hope of peace among all nations, as was demonstrated once again in the recent war. The University subsequently purchased the grounds and remaining structures to house the new CETL facilities as well as the Center for Space Flight.

Walking now from her apartment, located near the CETL facilities, Sonja passed by the remains of the Memorial on her way to the small shopping mall at the old Union Station. All that was left was the lower half of the tower atop the Memorial, which had supported an artificial flame, and one of the buildings at its base. It was ironic that the Great Frieze situated behind the Memorial on the north side and below the tower had, for the most part, also escaped the anarchists' anger. It was a series of bas-relief sculptured panels depicting the journey of the then United States from war to peace in the early 20th century.

On a whim, Sonja angled to her left and walked up the sloping sidewalk to where the frieze portion of the Memorial still reminded folks of war's horrors and the beauty of the peace that was to come. It has yet to come, she mused rather sourly, as she surveyed the sculpted, limestone panels. A huge center panel portrayed Liberty, who symbolized peace and understanding. A series of panels flanked

Liberty to the left and the right. On the left were scenes of war's destruction and misery, patriotism and sacrifice, and those who did not return. To the right of Liberty the panorama continued, now with a more hopeful message. The first one depicted men turning the instruments of war into those of peace. Then came various panels setting forth a confidence in the virtues of home, the abundance of nature, and a coming prosperity. Above the panels were four biblical inscriptions, from left to right, describing the inevitability of war, the promise of peace, the obligation upon mankind to secure that peace, and the ultimate certainty of blessing and abundance. Above all that, running the full length of the 150-meter long entablature, was the inscription: *"These have dared bear the torches of sacrifice and service. Their bodies return to dust but their work liveth evermore. Let us strive on to do all which may achieve and cherish a just and lasting peace among ourselves and with all nations."*

Well, Sonja thought with no small degree of skepticism, it's been 130 years since this memorial was erected and the world since then has endured a half dozen major world wars or large-scale conflicts, to say nothing of the multitude of regional hostilities. She wondered whether it was brave hope or hopeless ignorance that motivated people to build memorials such as this one. Maybe both. She recalled the ironic words from a song that she had heard in the Toronto Museum of Language and Culture, just before leaving to come to Kansas City. The museum placard indicated the recording was by a long-ago 20th century folk singer by the name of Joan Baez. To Sonja her voice had a haunting presence that seemed to still speak almost a century later:

> The First World War, boys
> It came and it went
> The reason for fighting
> I never did get
> But I learned to accept it
> Accept it with pride
> For you don't count the dead
> When God's on your side.

Sonja wondered whether God was that engaged in the affairs of mankind. For her part, she was experiencing a heightened social conscience as she slowly emerged from the sterile halls of academia and the intense focus of graduate studies. A nascent moral sense in her was beginning to protest the depredations of mankind upon both itself and nature. Personal relationships as well as events in the world at large were shaping her maturing views. She thought of Sergei Levkov. He seemed to typify the greedy, self-seeking attitudes that had landed the world in such a mess. A momentary pang of conscience surfaced within her as she remembered how she had encouraged him in his dreams of building a ship to go to the stars, for her own selfish reasons. Why did she want to go to the stars, anyway? Was it just boredom with her life or was there some deeper meaning to this compulsion? Yes, there was a growing sense of despair regarding the future of the planet. She wondered if the best hope for humanity might be to start anew – on a new planet orbiting a new star, far from Earth and its travails. Of course, she thought, I'm not so naïve as to think that merely transporting men and women to a new world would by itself be a solution. That's been tried before on this very continent, and without notable success. However, perhaps humanity has progressed to the point now where a brand new and virgin world would at least "clear the air" and give people a chance to take stock of themselves and of what did and did not work.

But, no! That was not it, or at least not all of it. She had been drawn to the stars in her dreams and phantasies ever since she was old enough to know what she was looking at when she gazed into the numinous night sky. There was life out there, a life for her, though what this half-believed conviction meant or would lead to she did not know. But to hang her hopes for this on Sergei? Surely that was a fool's errand! Sometimes she thought his selfishness and avarice would end up destroying his obvious genius, bringing down to Earth both himself and the hope of space travel. The thought of it seemed to tarnish the bright hope of her childhood aspirations.

The third biblical inscription over the frieze arrested her attention momentarily: *"What doth the Lord require of thee but to do justly, and to love mercy, and to walk humbly with thy God."* Not a religious person, Sonja nevertheless felt an agreement within her own soul to this sentiment. She wondered if she could carry out this dictum in the competitive and sometimes self-serving world of scientific research that she was about to enter.

* * *

Sonja hurried to complete the notes from her latest experimental run. She had been at the Center for three months now, and things were going rather well. She cautioned herself to not be too optimistic, however. While she felt good about her research she knew that from external appearances she still had little to show. Unhappy with her seemingly slow progress, Sonja knew she still must prove herself, both to her colleagues and to her superior. She had a meeting with the Director in ten minutes and it would be unwise to be late. Director Eleanor Spitzer was a brilliant scientist with little patience for mediocrity and sloth. Being late for a meeting was to invite suspicion of one or even both qualities in those who depended upon her good favor, as did Sonja. Closing and locking the door, Sonja turned and hurried down the hall. She paused outside Dr. Spitzer's office. A fake wood plaque below the frosted window of the glass-paneled door read: "Communications Laboratory" in large black letters, and underneath in smaller capitals, "Center for Extraterrestrial Life." And, under these words in yet smaller capitals, "North American University."

CETL was established in 2048, toward the end of a decade-long turbulent aftermath to the World Cyber War. The War lasted only a year with no clear winner. But it resulted in turning the general populace against technology and its alleged benefits. Before the War the "Internet of Things" – once hailed as the ultimate vehicle for achieving sustainable life on the planet – was now seen by many as not much more than an avenue for international espionage and destruction of the means of livelihood that they had come to depend upon. Much damage had been done to critical infrastructures impacting every sphere of normal life – finance, medical services, communications, transportation and even food delivery in some cases. A world-wide recession followed, lasting almost a decade. Even at this time, some fifteen years after the war, many of the conveniences they once enjoyed were not available. Now 24, Sonja was a child when the war started, but she remembered the driverless car that her father had in Spain. Nowadays it was almost impossible to get one, and the common people still looked upon them with great suspicion. However, one good outcome of the war was the formation of a pan-federation union, the Euro-North-American Union – ENU. The ENU set about to rebuild the electronic and informational infrastructures that would hopefully help restore the prosperity with which the century began.

The formation of CETL was one of the more promising developments of the new era – an era that perhaps would see the advance of humanity into maturity. The North American Federation, a post-war political consolidation of the United States, Mexico and Canada, was now financing academic research institutions, after tending to the more basic needs of a war-injured technological society. Sonja, a child growing up in Spain before the war, attended university in Canada, first with an undergraduate degree in communications and then a doctorate in astrobiology. While Sonja was finishing her work in Toronto she heard of a brand-new department, Astropsychology, being formed at CETL. She applied for one of two research positions and, surprisingly to her, was accepted. It seemed to her only yesterday that she had left Toronto.

A stenciled label on the glass panel read in gold letters: Eleanor M. Spitzer, PhD, Director. Underneath her name the glass announced what Dr. Spitzer was director of: Department of Astropsychology, CETL. Sonja hesitated before knocking lightly.

"Come in Sonja. You're right on time."

Sonja breathed a sigh of relief and pushed the door open. "Good morning Dr. Spitzer."

"Eleanor. Please call me Eleanor. When it comes to science we're all equal colleagues here."

"Yes, Dr. Spitzer … uh, I mean Eleanor. Thank you."

Dr. Spitzer had recently begun to insist on the first name basis with Sonja and it was still difficult for her to accept. For one thing, Dr. Spitzer – Eleanor – was a very large woman, and she was many years older as evidenced by the slight crow's feet beginning to form around her eyes. Her short and straight mannish hair style reinforced the sense of distance Sonja felt in her presence. By comparison, Sonja was a little slip of a girl in her own mind, with a streak of Irish pluck inherited from her mother's side. That side of her personality seemed often at war with the other side, the polite and self-effacing modesty of a Spaniard father. Despite impeccable manners, Don Roberto Bellesario had been an astute and brilliant industrialist. Though Sonja received her above average IQ from her father, she felt her mother's influence assuaging her fears as she entered Dr. Spitzer's office.

Spitzer appraised the young woman in front of her. In spite of being barely into her twenties, Sonja Bellesario had an intuitive, finely tuned intelligence graciously complemented by a plain but disarming beauty. Spitzer decided that Sonja was somewhat oblivious to the effect she might have on those of the opposite sex. This was good, she knew, for now in her life Sonja needed to focus on establishing her career.

"So, how's the research on ET communication patterns going?" Dr. Spitzer reached for Sonja's notes as she handed them to her. She sat tentatively on the edge of a chair beside Dr. Spitzer's desk.

"Great! At least I think so," replied Sonja hopefully. "Communication Patterns in Extraterrestrial Societies." That was her research project and it was all about how the social and communications structures of extraterrestrial societies would be impacted by differences in planetary and solar environments. That is, if there were extraterrestrial societies anywhere in the galaxy. That was still a big if, she knew, and it sometimes amazed her that the Federation Science Foundation would fund this type of research. Particularly since a component of her research, still unrealized, involved attempting to hear or receive communications from outer space. Sonja was working on a prosthetic device, which she wore like a helmet, which could enhance reception of such signals when used in conjunction with a radio telescope. So far she had only tested a prototype of her prosthesis using the university's ten-meter dish. It wasn't large enough to resolve an expected signal source, and Dr. Spitzer had recommended trying to get observation time at research facilities with larger telescopes.

"Well, I'll look at this tonight. But, right now I've great news for you. We've been given time on Green Bank!"

"Time on Green Bank!" Sonja was breathless. The National Radio Astronomy Observatory in Green Bank, West Virginia, was one of the largest radio telescopes in the world. She and Dr. Spitzer had applied to NRAO two months ago, but Sonja had little hope of success. Her proposed project was … well, to put it in the vernacular, it was a bit wacky. "That's … that's hard to believe," Sonja gave a weak smile to Dr. Spitzer, who returned it with a broad grin and thumbs up signs with both hands.

"Look, Sonja, I know you feel a little outclassed here and that your research ideas are somewhat out of the mainstream. But, so-called "mental telepathy" is no longer considered pseudo-science. Not since Alliander's discovery that ULF radio waves are correlated with thought transmission between humans. Probably animals, too, but we haven't figured out yet how to talk to animals to find out." She smiled, a bit crookedly. "Admittedly, there is still much we don't understand about the so-called psi force or how the human brain can generate and receive electromagnetic signals that become the medium for thought and image transfer. But, that it does – at least in some people – has become clear. Your idea that "thought waves" from advanced civilizations could be transmitted over galactic distances by radio waves is just a logical extension of this discovery. Besides, remember Penzias and Wilson who accidentally established the existence of the long suspected cosmic microwave background while trying to build a satellite communications telescope. You might end up discovering something you don't expect!"

* * *

Early Fall, 2052 CE. Kansas City, North American Federation.

Sonja disembarked from the Union Station Maglev and walked slowly down the ramp to street level. Summer was over; it was cool and rainy. She headed for the bus that would take her the short distance to her apartment. She was dejected, and thoroughly embarrassed. Green Bank had been a bust, an out and out flop! Yes, the scenery, the cool mountain air even in summer and the lush smells were all wonderfully different than the Great Plains atmosphere of Kansas City. And amazing things like fireflies, so abundant in the mountain meadows of West Virginia. But, so what? Her experiment produced nothing and she had sensed the condescending attitudes of some of the other researchers there. They were celebrating discoveries nightly while Sonja had nothing. She was probably being too hard on herself, she knew, and Dr. Spitzer might have some encouraging words for her tomorrow. Well, she thought, at least the equipment I ordered came and I set up the headgear.

Sonja's plan was to use a miniaturized functional MRI machine that would image her own thoughts, together with an ordinary radio receiver interfaced through suitable band pass filters to the output of the Green Bank radio telescope. The part of this that was her own idea was the headgear that enclosed the fMRI coils and which provided a snug fit to her temples. It was a bit unwieldy because the superconducting magnet coils required an external cryogenic cooling system. This was developed for her by a friend in the campus materials science lab, and it was small enough to carry in a backpack. But the gear worked and that was what counted. Using a computer-based neural network with the fMRI, Sonja had developed a concept dictionary based on her own brain waves. The entries in the dictionary were simple concepts, things like prime numbers, pi, and stick figures of living beings with arms and legs. She did not hope to understand the language of an alien race, but such concepts should or could be universal. Her theory was that the ultra-low frequency radio waves would carry thought patterns of presumed sentient-being societies to the large NRAO dish and thence to her headgear where they would be associated in real-time with her own thought patterns via the neural network software. This much about her experimental apparatus and the theory behind it Dr. Spitzer knew.

What Dr. Spitzer did not know, and what Sonja was determined she not find out, was Sonja's own native telepathic ability. A "gift" some might call it, though at best a burdensome one. While she could not prove it, nor even discuss it with her colleagues, she believed that her telepathic ability could enhance mental recognition of rational thought patterns that were captured by the telescope and impressed upon her brain by the innovative headgear. It was disconcerting to realize that even if she were successful in her plan, full disclosure of her methodology was not advisable, however much she yearned to do so. She had good reason, she believed, to be concerned about such a disclosure – notwithstanding the seminal work of Alliander. Sometimes she wished she'd never been so "gifted" and wondered why.

Since her earliest memories of childhood Sonja had been aware that the thoughts she sometimes had were not her own. There were times when thoughts came to her that seemed very much outside of her – yet they were right inside her head. It was with her mother that she first began to realize that the strange thoughts were those of another. She and her mother were very close in those days. As a child, she would sometimes hear an almost audible voice speaking inside her as her mother entered her playroom. The voice would always say the same thing: *You are such a sweet, bubbly little angel!* Then, amazingly, her mother would take her up in her arms and whisper into her ear, "You are such a sweet, bubbly little angel!" By the time she was six she "heard" her mother "say" other things – sometimes things that she instinctively knew she was not supposed to hear. So, she hid this strange ability from her parents and from her younger brother, Tony. Strangely, she never heard anything that would seem to have come from others in the family. Only with her mom.

But, in school, there were others. A few others, whom she realized she could eavesdrop on. This did not make her happy, for it seemed "wrong." She could do nothing about that, however, and the thoughts of others were often painful or brought up things she could not understand. As Sonja neared adolescence the periodic intrusion of foreign thoughts began to plague her, especially since they would get in the way of friendships. Friendships were important and she did not want to know things that friends thought unless they told her directly. In a clumsy attempt to get help, Sonja decided to confide in her best friend her "ability" in the hope that her friend could help her deal with her difficulty. One of the reasons that Susanne was her best friend, in fact, was that she could not read Susanne's thoughts. It was a real friendship, or so she thought. One day at lunch the teacher sent the class out to the academy lawn to eat. Sonja and Susanne found a place under a large spreading cork tree and sat down in its shade. Earlier that day there had been a spat between two of the girls in their class, Teresa and Sophie. Sonja was nearby and could not help overhearing. She also knew what Teresa was thinking but not saying out loud. Teresa was one of those few people with whom Sonja had a "connection" though she was not a particular friend. The spat was about a boy, of course, and Teresa was telling Sophie that Brad did not care for her and that she, Teresa, was going to go out with Brad instead. Sophie blew up at this (she was pretty hot-tempered) and slapped Teresa, saying that it was not true and that Brad was going out with her. It turned into a scratching and screaming fight that took two teachers to break it up. But, the thing that was most unsettling to Sonja was that she had been able to read Teresa's thoughts and she understood that Teresa was lying to Sophie and had deliberately done so to get back at her for getting a better grade in history. So silly, Sonja now thought, thinking back on her adolescence.

It was what happened next that set the course for Sonja for the rest of her life up to now, her resolve to never disclose to anyone her ability. For, during that lunch period under the cork tree she had confided to Susanne her ability and she had gone so far as to tell her that she had known that Teresa was lying to Sophie. Susanne didn't believe her and said she was just making it up. She got up and started to walk away. At first, Sonja misunderstood her friend's reaction. But as Susanne got up words came unbidden into Sonja's mind. *Oh, pooh, I forgot to bring a bottle of water.* Sonja had "known" that Susanne was going to get a drink from the fountain across the lawn – though she had not said so. "Susanne," she said, "You can have my bottle of water – I am not thirsty." She said this without even thinking. Susanne had turned then and stared at her at first speechless, mouth agape.

"You …" Susanne stuttered, "You can do it! You read my thoughts! How did you know I was going to get a drink? I didn't tell you that."

Sonja couldn't reply. She was almost as amazed as Susanne, since never before had she been able to read Susanne's thoughts.

Susanne's surprise then turned to pique. "You're my best friend. Best friends should not do that to each other! I can't read your thoughts. It's not fair." Then came the crushing blow: "I don't want to be your friend anymore. Stay out of my thoughts!" With that Susanne turned and ran across the lawn leaving the remains of her lunch next to a large, exposed root. The loss of her best friend, however, was not the worst of it. Susanne then told Sophie about Teresa's deception and told her how she knew. By the time it was over, all three of them had ganged up on Sonja and had made life miserable for her for the rest of the term. It was fortunate there were only a few weeks left before summer holidays and she begged her mother to send her to a different school the following year.

It wasn't until Sonja went to university in Toronto that she could make a semblance of peace with herself about her telepathy, and even to begin to see it in a positive light. It was Herman Alliander's work in paranormal psychology that helped turn the tide of Sonja's own sense of worth. His, and other researchers as well. University had opened an entirely new world to Sonja with its easy culture of scientific discourse and intellectual freedom. Sonja devoured the current literature on parapsychology and even went to hear Alliander speak once. Reflecting on Dr. Spitzer's mention of Alliander's work, Sonja suspected she knew far more about the subject than Dr. Spitzer. And, while she did not fully understand the connection of low frequency radio waves to mental telepathy, she knew that the latter was real and that she did not need special coils to enable her to read thoughts. To her, the low frequency radio apparatus was a means of amplifying the feeble signals of mental thought waves that she conceived might come from other, and possibly more advanced civilizations in another part of the galaxy. So far it was just theory that the fMRI and neural network would enhance communication. But, if the headset she designed would amplify a "signal" that was there, she was confident she would be able to "read" it.

Besides, she thought, with my apparatus I could use my ability to benefit mankind without risk of exposure and the consequent pain of rejection that I experienced when I was young. This, at last, will be what makes it acceptable. If there are advanced civilizations out there and if I could contact them perhaps I could help bring to mankind knowledge that would bring lasting peace between belligerent nations. Or, knowledge that would grant humans the key to interstellar travel so that those who are tired of the fighting (as I am) could get off the planet and go somewhere else. One side of Sonja's mind knew this was naïve and simplistic, but she persisted. That was why she was initially attracted to Sergei – because of his ideas about space travel. He was so sure about it that at times it seemed as if he had already managed it. But Sergei misunderstood her interest and she had for a while yielded to a different relationship before finally breaking it off.

As she walked down the ramp from the KC Central Maglev station and thought of Sergei, she wondered how he was doing. Then she remembered that conversation with him in the restaurant atop the CN Tower. What was it he had said about quantum wormholes and electromagnetic signals passing through them? Could she somehow adapt her apparatus to capture signals that came through quantum wormholes? She decided to send Sergei a note when she got back to her apartment.

Chapter 4. Colony

Planet Mycenae, Apollo System. Local Date: Circ 1, Late Summer.

Cunningham was livid. Tang had promised to send down two more of the ship's micro-fusion power supplies. That was two months ago, and still nothing! He resolved to go back up to the *Exeter* and confront Tang, as much as he disliked the journey from the planet's surface to the orbiting starship. While taking an aircar to the space dock from New Athens City, Roger Cunningham thought back on the rapid events of the last six months. Six months Earth time that is. Their new home had an orbital period around its star that was almost exactly two-thirds that of Earth around Sol. They would have to figure out a new calendar and periods that worked in the new world. But, that would come in time. In general Cunningham was satisfied with the progress they had achieved in beginning this world's colonization. It wasn't the planet or the star system they originally intended. Or, the time period either he thought, a bit ruefully. But, so what! They wanted to distance themselves from Earth and its potpourri of mutually distrustful federations, political positioning, and constant threat of war or economic bust. Of course, a few tens of light-years was not a sufficient barrier with modern star travel technology – they would never be able to isolate themselves the way they had wanted to. But, three hundred odd years separation, that was a different story! If it was true, he thought. Such concepts as time travel were difficult for him, an economist by training and a politician at heart.

After his people recovered from the initial shock (and anger at

Captain Tang and his cantankerous crew) most of them were quite pleased. Yes, there were a few of the colonists who continued to weep over the fact that they would never see loved ones on Earth again. Hardly! Their loved ones hadn't even been born yet. He paused to mull that one over. Cunningham was a pragmatist. Nevertheless, he had to admit that it was hard even for him to fully get a hold on how to adjust to this new reality – colonizing a world only 36 light-years from Earth during a period on Earth before space travel had even been achieved. One thing for sure: besides not having to hear about Earth's troubles in the 24th century (which hadn't happened yet) they wouldn't be receiving any help or supplies from the Earth of this era either. Or any other era. They were on their own! And that was where Roger Cunningham would find his greatness, his place in history! For, if he was anything at all he was a consummate survivalist.

His aircar arrived at the crudely constructed space dock and he leveraged his bulky frame out of the car and onto the deck. He paused to check his appearance in the reflection of the aircar glass, noting with satisfaction this morning's trim on his mustache. Part of his reason for the mustache, he admitted to himself, was to offer a distraction from his rather large Roman nose and otherwise plain face. His wife, bless her heart, sometimes teased him about this. Smoothing his carefully tailored tunic, Cunningham straightened his 5-foot, 8-inch frame and set out toward the waiting vessel.

The space dock was an aerogel/metal foam platform about 30 meters square with a small control house beside it. The ship-to-surface passenger and freight vehicle vessel rested in its cradle. They were loading food supplies to go up to the *Exeter*. How foolish this was in Cunningham's opinion – supplying food grown on this wonderful new world for a few holdouts that insisted on staying shipside. Why did Tang and his crew hang on to the idea that they were going to be rescued? By whom? Or, that somehow they would figure out a way to re-open the gate, or whatever it was that had dropped them here, and return to 24th century Earth. They just needed to accept the facts and go with the flow. Cunningham and his people had everything they needed to tame a new world. Or, almost everything anyway. And that was why he was making this trip up to the *Exeter*. Manufacturing power supplies and certain other advanced machinery were going to be a problem for a few generations. But, how fortuitous and even providential that most of the passenger manifest of *Exeter* consisted of would-be colonists, and that the ship's freight consisted in 90 percent of what they would need on the virgin planet they had been heading for. However, Tang absolutely must give him those micro-fusion sets. What did he need them for? Even if they did figure out how to return to the 24th century they would have no need for them there. Cunningham was overlooking the fact that the tractor beam that would lift the ship-to-surface vehicle required micro-fusion power. In spite of the degree of self-sufficiency they had already achieved, the colonists still needed some advanced infrastructure support capabilities, such as weather reconnaissance and geo-mapping, which were on the *Exeter*. *Exeter's* science officer and executive medical officer were also useful to the colonists who were short-handed in some disciplines. As long as they stayed aboard, there would have to be continued communication from the ship to the planet surface, and vice-versa. But that could not last, Cunningham knew, for reasons that both he and Tang knew.

* * *

Jana was in a funk. Every angle she thought of, every software algorithm she checked, every jury-rigged control sequence she tried — they all produced exactly nothing. In the meantime, they investigated other actions, such as setting up a special distress beacon. This was Rolfo's idea and she had to humor him a bit. There was no way this would work. They were 36 light-years from Earth. A normal, light-speed transmission would take 36 years to get to Earth. It would arrive around the year 2065, which was before interstellar space flight had been achieved. So, even if Earth received their SOS what could they do about it? Send back a "We're sorry!" message? Jana recognized the hint of despair in that last thought and repented of it. She knew that survival, and certainly emotional survival, depended upon keeping a positive attitude.

They next thought to somehow modify the tachyonic navigation system to send a faster-than-light message back. Rather, to send it forward, for they were stuck in the past. That was the major obstacle. She thought she could modify the tachyonics to use as an SOS generator. But, how in the world did you aim it to the right place in the galaxy in the right century? She had no clue. Yet, she felt certain that the key to that puzzle lay in the same part of the navigation system that had produced the spacetime dislocation to begin with.

The more she thought about it, the more she became convinced that the gate through which they had passed was opened up via the tachyonic navigation control mechanism. Once opened, possibly on even a quantum dimension scale, the energy from the *Exeter's* negative mass accumulators had widened this tiny rift in spacetime and sent them hurtling down (or up?) a fifth-dimensional canyon into another ... "Another what?" Jana wondered aloud to herself. "A parallel universe, perhaps?" she said aloud. And that was somehow even worse than the thought that they had merely gone back in time. Her scientific training recoiled at the idea of time travel to the past. Rather, it must have been a branching of histories, occasioned at the quantum-scale level by probabilistic behavior in a corrupted navigation system. Had the designers of that system inadvertently set up a situation wherein certain choices by its creators would cause the wave function of their existence to collapse into an undesired state? Collapse into an alternate reality? That was truly scary.

"What did you say, Jana?" It was Rolfo. He had just entered the close confines of the navigation equipment cubicle, carefully balancing two bulbs of coffee, one of which he offered in a feigned matter-of-factness. He was always in awe of this beautiful and brilliant woman. Jana felt, and was comforted by, his strong masculine presence and enduring optimism. Her avowed celibacy since her husband had died was beginning to feel outdated. She was warming to a growing intimacy of trust and friendship with Rolfo – if not something more. She turned to him and smiled.

"Oh, just mumbling to myself about the cowboys and the Indians. The Indians have us surrounded, you know, and we're running out of ammunition." It was a standing joke between them. Her leisure time taste for old Westerns was a source of fun for Rolfo who, she realized, could not understand how someone with the kind of education she had would go for stuff like that. Rolfo had intimated that this kind of entertainment was more in keeping with his station in life than hers. But Jana pushed such reasoning aside. Rolfo was a dear man and she did not think of him as any less capable or resourceful than she was, despite any differences in education. Like her brother, Jana had very egalitarian ideals and Rolfo was, if nothing else, a colleague on equal grounds. Especially now, considering the straits they were in. Thoughts of her brother caused a sharp pain, which she hid from Rolfo.

"Seriously, though," she placed her hand on his arm, "I was thinking about the tachyonic communication problem. I confess, I fell into a bit of a funk about it. But I'll snap out of it, if for no other reason than that you are here now." She winked at Rolfo in a way that brought an immediate flush of red to his face, taking a bit of private pleasure in her power.

Rolfo cleared his throat, missing the obvious flirtation, "Well, that's kind of you … Jana. I don't know that there's anything so special about me, but if you say so I'll latch onto it. We ain't got a whole lotta hope or options just now, so all the good feelin's that we can muster will go a long way." He was glad they had gotten to the stage of calling each other by first names, even while on duty. It was still hard to look straight into those crystal eyes, however.

"Well said, Rolfo. Come, let's leave this stifling warren of wires and widgets and take a little air, so to speak, topside. About this time dusk will be arriving to New Athens and we can watch the terminator sweep across this lovely new planet."

"You sound like you might want to live there, Jana."

She paused as they entered the corridor and looked at him sweetly. "Rolfo, do you really think, in your heart of hearts, that we are going to get away from here? Come on, let's go topside." With that, she took his arm and led him down the corridor to the elevator shaft that would take them to the command level of the *Exeter*, and thence to the observation deck. As they entered the elevator car, none other than Roger Cunningham, the mayor of New Athens, joined them.

"Why, hello, Mr. Cunningham," said Jana good-naturedly. "Or, *Mayor* Cunningham," putting the emphasis on the title. "Here to preach the gospel of colonization again, are you?" There was no rancor in her voice, though certainly some of the things Cunningham had said to the *Exeter* crew in the past about their so-called foolishness passed through her mind. But Jana's vow of optimism held and she smiled at him as he answered.

"No, I am not. I am here, against my better judgment, to get Tang, Captain Tang that is, to make good on his promise of the power supplies we need. I really do not like having to come to him, hat in hand this way. But we are in desperate need for those supplies and I cannot see why you folks here need them."

Jana surprised him at that point, interjecting before he could continue, "I'll have a word with Captain Tang myself. I think I agree with you that we do not need all of them." She looked down on him with a kindly smile.

Cunningham was speechless, and he looked from Jana to Rolfo and back to Jana in surprise. Jana winked at Rolfo as Cunningham looked away, studying the progressive series of lights indicating the passing decks. A clumsy silence ensued until they reached the executive deck where Cunningham departed. As he left the car he said, genuinely, "Thank you Commander Anders. I would appreciate it." With that, he turned crisply and left Jana and Rolfo to their journey topside.

* * *

"Please inform Captain Tang that Roger Cunningham is here to see him." Cunningham spoke to the orderly. He had thought to announce himself as "Mayor Cunningham" (recently elected), but after that warm-hearted remark from Commander Anders he thought better of it. Tang certainly knew he had been elected and he likely knew why Cunningham was here as well. So, he thought, I'll try a softer approach, and lead into my concern with a report on how well things are going. As he was finishing this mental preparation the stateroom door opened and the orderly motioned him inside.

"Good afternoon Captain Tang," he said in as positive a tone he could muster. He almost said "... at least it is afternoon on the planet surface, in New Athens that is." But, he caught himself in time, preserving his newfound strategy.

"Hello Roger. Good to see you again." Arun Tang always tried to use the familiar greeting, the name he knew people most liked to go by. He had long since learned that Roger Cunningham liked to be addressed by his first name, even by people with whom he was not closely connected. Motioning Cunningham to sit in one of two cushioned chairs that faced each other on either side of a simulated oak side table, and seating himself in the other, he continued, "By the way, Roger, congratulations on your election. You're just the man for the job. I would have voted for you myself had I been, uh, part of the community. But, you know ..."

"Yes, I understand Captain Tang," Cunningham cut him off politely. "You don't have to explain. The colonists have set up a charter to govern themselves and I know that you understand the need to establish certain rules such as voting rights. Once you are a member of the community, however, you'll be free to vote. That is," he paused and gave Tang a non-committal look, "if you decide to become a member of the community." He hurried on, not wishing to dwell on this. For already the conversation was veering in a direction he did not want, nor think productive. "I'd like to give you a progress report and to thank you for your help so far. I also want to say how pleased I am that the community has been able to export, so to speak, food grown ourselves on the new world to serve you and your crew's needs." Cunningham surprised himself with these words. Surely Jana Anders' behavior in the elevator must be working its magic on even him. He had heard that she had a way about her that bewitched people, notwithstanding her bewitching beauty, which was not inconsiderable. If he was not happily married himself he would readily court the commander. Though, he suspected he would not have gotten very far. Anders was a purposeful, even driven executive scientist who clearly knew what she wanted and how to get it. Like me, he prided himself, though without the science bit, which he did not in the least understand. Two people with similar drive, he realized, would probably not do well together. Even, or especially, in the challenging circumstances of building a new world on an uninhabited planet.

"Yes, we have enjoyed the fresh vegetables," Tang was saying.

"Well, yes, and that is not all," Cunningham resumed. "We have located deposits of bauxite in the alluvial plain north of New Athens and have begun mining operations there. We are fabricating a small aluminum smelter. The aluminum together with the powdered titanium hydride we brought with us will enable us to fabricate all the metal foam panels we need for building and infrastructure. Housing and building construction will be wood at first, of necessity, but in time we will have more modern structures with better building materials. Plastics, too, are in our plans, as you know."

Cunningham continued, warming to his task. "Two separate groups of our colonists have decided to launch out and found cities, or towns, in two different locations some distance from New Athens. One group has settled Mycenae City just north of New Athens, where there are gorgeously forested valleys with rich mineral deposits and good farming land. The other group is going to the seacoast, on the northwest corner of the continent, some one thousand kilometers away. They hope to establish fishing and forestry industries there.

They have decided to call their city Cyclades, after a Mediterranean island famous for fishing."

At this, Captain Tang broke into a large grin. Cunningham wasn't sure why. "What's so funny about that Captain," he asked.

"Not funny, certainly. No offense, Roger. I just think it is amusing how all of your cities and place names are taken from ancient Greek civilization. I understand that you have renamed this star, cataloged in the Federation database as 54 Piscium. You're calling is 'Apollo,' I believe?" Cunningham nodded, stiffly. "Good choice, I might add. Much better than its official star catalog name."

"Well," Cunningham relaxed a bit, "I readily admit that my wife, Persis, is something of an extreme philhellene. She already has a little Greek culture interest group going, in fact, and has quite an influence on our growing society. I guess some of it is catching on with many others." Cunningham was proud of his wife's leadership in New Athens society. She was an able partner to his political ambitions. "Although the Greek naming is a bit of a trifle, I do think it gives the colonists a sense of adventure and uniqueness about their endeavors. It helps with the hardships, you know."

He continued, "Which brings me to another issue." Keeping his voice soft, so as to not destroy the somewhat collegial atmosphere, Cunningham brought up the matter of the power supplies. Outlining the need again, he now added a new dimension. "With the two pioneer cities being formed there will be a need for communications. We could use old fashioned, shortwave radio. Your Science Officer informs us that the ionosphere of Mycenae is adequate for that. But laser comms are so much more convenient, and easier to use. Unfortunately, they require considerably more power. With the two groups moving off to remote locations, we do not have enough micro-fusion power plants to send one with each of them." Here, he paused and looked Tang in the eye.

Tang was silent for a moment, then began, "Roger, I know and appreciate the need. And I think, I hope, that you appreciate the need on our end as well. As long as *Exeter* is in orbit, we need the power supplies we have for basic services. If we rely on the ship's normal space propulsion systems we risk burning up needed fuel. Fuel that would be needed for re-entry and transit to a destination planet. That is, if we ever get a chance to try that." Here he looked hard at Cunningham, seeing the rising skepticism in his facial features and body language. "Yes, I know that you think that is foolish. And, I know that there is something else that you have figured out. We are coming to a decision point. *Exeter* cannot stay indefinitely in this orbit – we have to use fuel to make continuous orbital corrections. By staying close enough to the planet surface to utilize the tractor beam for ship-to-surface transit we experience significant atmospheric drag over time. To move further out would help that, but then we would cut ourselves off from supplies from you. So, we are in a no-win situation. However, and I tell you this in confidence and in the hope that you will not take advantage. The crew is split on whether to persevere in the hope for rescue or a navigational fix, or whether to come down and join the colony, giving up all hope of returning to Earth or Verde or wherever their loved ones and families are." Tang paused, letting what he said sink in. "Yes," he said, "There is that difference between them and you all. You have brought your families with you and you never intended to return to Earth or go to any of its far-flung settlements. We, however, had not done so. We have families who are awaiting our return – or, most of us do. Nevertheless, the reality of our situation is sinking in. Soon, I think, we all will join you. But it isn't time yet. So, bear with us, if you will, and be patient. And continue in the good work down there so that when we do join you we will have some of the comforts of home already waiting for us." With this he smiled and stood, signaling that their meeting was over. As Tang ushered Cunningham to the door, he added, "Let me consult with my chief engineer and see what we can do about the power supplies. I think we may be able to do something."

* * *

A week later, Captain Tang assembled the crew on the *Exeter's* mess deck. He had worked on his speech for two days but still felt inadequate to the task. A weariness was setting in, threatening his resolve. Still, he had to give it a go and let the chips fall as they may. "Ladies and gentlemen," he began. "You all know the events over the past six months or so that have led to our present situation, orbiting the planet Mycenae – as the colonists have named it. So, I do not need to rehearse those. It is important, however, to bring you up to date on our present circumstances. Not to put too severe a face upon the situation, it is nevertheless serious. I would even say desperate. We have not been able to fix the *Exeter's* navigation system concerning the bug or malfunction that dropped us into another, and very distant region of spacetime. Nor have we figured out how to communicate with InterStellar officials or anyone else in the 24th century from whence we came. We have run out of rations that were stored on the ship and are now dependent upon food provided by the growing colonies on the planet surface. In order to receive those food shipments we must maintain a fairly low altitude. This, however, requires continued use of precious fuel for orbit corrections, and we are now running low on fuel. We could go to a higher orbit but at the price of cutting off our food supply." Here Tang paused for long seconds, to let the facts sink in.

"At this point," he then continued, "I find no other way to state the obvious but to be blunt: If we are to survive we must abandon the *Exeter* and join the colonists. There is really no other recourse. I know that some of you are ready to do this, yet others are not. I urge you all to speak with one another over the next few days and to try to come to a unified consent in this. Because," he continued with a hopeful note in his voice, "If you act as a single body, each one holding with his or her neighbor, it will give you all the strength you need to live out your life in a manner and location that you never would have thought possible a year ago." Tang concluded with some words of praise for various members of his crew over recent accomplishments, and then opened the meeting for questions. There were a few.

"Captain." It was Tyrone Weld, the quartermaster. He was one of those who already was willing to go down. "Captain, when do we go? That is, do you have a plan for disembarking or a deadline of any sort?"

"Good question, Sergeant Weld. There is a plan and it involves a phased departure from the ship, in order to keep things operational. I will post the schedule at 0800 tomorrow. I will be the last to leave. However, I will say this, if anyone disagrees with the order I post I am open to rearranging things – as long as I can do so without endangering safety of you all and of the ship as long as anyone is aboard."

"Captain Tang," Serene Jackson, the ship's medical officer, spoke up. She had a husband and young children on Verde. It had been very hard on her and she was still on the verge of a nervous breakdown. "What is the possibility of retracing our path and going

back through the wormhole, or whatever it was, to the 24th Century?
I understand that the problem may have been that we travelled too
close to a large star. Could we perhaps try to duplicate this in a
reverse sort of way?"

Tang responded, "I think I will let Commander Anders answer
that. Commander?"

"Okay, sure. Serene, and all of you as well, I know how much
you wish that such could be possible. In fact, it is the first thing I
thought of when we understood what had happened. I will admit
that whatever is the malfunction in the navigation system it is quite
possible that were we to attempt transit into a hyperspace bubble
near a large mass object something similar could happen. The
problem with that is, we would have no control whatsoever as to
where we would end up. That is because I believe the error in the
coding modules of the new Gen-4 HyperNav is random in its effect.
Without understanding the source of that error and fixing it, we
could end up anywhere or anywhen, and be in a far worse state for it.
Therefore, it is not an option – at least until and if I can find and fix
the error." Then, she added, "Rolfo and I are still working on the
HyperNav and will do so until the day of departure planned. I do
not hold out much hope, but we will continue as long as we are
able."

There were a couple more questions of a minor nature, about
this or that detail associated with disembarkation. Tang handled
these smoothly and then dismissed the meeting. There was little
discussion among the men and women as they quietly went back to
their stations or other activities. Tang was thankful that no one came
up to him and that the session was over. He retired to his cabin and
sat down with a sigh of relief. Ordering a drink from the cabin
dispenser, he pondered the future – a future on a new world. He was
a widower and his two children were grown, but with no children of
their own. And, one of the two was here and had already joined the
colonists, with an incipient romance in the offing he noted. Tang,
therefore, could face the future on Mycenae more equably than some
in his crew. Moreover, he was not feeling well. The stress of the
recent months had affected his health and he was now experiencing
worrying symptoms. He had put it off until now, but he must go see
Serene and let her examine him. He resolved to do that first thing in
the morning – after posting the embarkation schedule. This he now

turned to, to complete the draft that he had already begun.

As he was finishing the schedule a knock came on his door. "Enter," he answered, pushing the finished schedule aside. It was Jana. "Hello Jana," he said, and then asked, "How do you think it went? Please be honest."

"It went well enough, I guess. Everyone knows the score – has known it for some time, in fact. Word gets around, you know. Your meeting was just to put an official face on the ghost that has been haunting the ship for weeks. Uh, sorry, for the allusion, sir ..." Jana realized that her imagery had been inappropriate.

"That's all right. I guess it is something of a ghost. Maybe it will cease to look that way now that we've put an official face on it, as you say. Anyway, you didn't come to talk about ghosts. Have a seat and tell me what's on your mind."

Jana sat across from him, the writing table between them. She rested her forearms on the table, folding her hands comfortably. "Well, it's the idea of a distress beacon, sir. You may remember that Rolfo brought this up at one of our meetings awhile back, but we put it off as we were still hopeful for a fix in the system. Now, however, it would seem to be more of an imperative."

"What kind of a distress beacon? And why?" Tang wanted to know.

"Not using the tachyonics – we don't know how to aim such a signal across a 350-year chronological divide. Rather, a regular light-speed form of communication, using a frequency and content that could be detected and be understood by Earth. Earth of the 21st century that is. The century in which we find ourselves," she added unnecessarily.

Tang sat up then, with greater alertness. They both knew such a beacon could not be received on Earth for 36 years and a response, if it came at all, would exceed their own life spans in all likelihood. In any event, what would the good citizens of pre-space-travel Earth do with such an SOS? So, he jumped past the obvious point: "And you hope to gain by this, not a rescue as such but, but a ...what?"

"A warning perhaps. A warning that, when they do develop interstellar space travel on Earth that they should take it slow. That they should be careful as to who or what controls the development of technology." Here Jana was alluding to something that she had previously confided to him, that of her dissatisfaction over the way that InterStellar controlled the trade secrets to space travel and prevented true competition in this arena. Competition, she believed, would result in better products, safer systems, checks and balances. Their present predicament might have been avoided had that been the case in their own 24th century.

Tang was not so easily persuaded. "What about potential chronology problems for 21st century Earth? What would a message from the future – for that is what it would be, in essence – what would or could such a message do to the future course of events for those on Earth? Is it even possible that this would constitute some sort of time paradox in which news from a future Earth-based civilization could effectively prevent the formation of that future civilization, leaving us in a logical limbo of sorts?"

"Yes," Jana hesitated momentarily. "Yes, I've thought of that."

"And …?"

"And, I have an answer. An answer of sorts."

"Go on," Tang's curiosity was kicking in. Jana was smart, very smart, and he trusted her thinking process.

"To be blunt, Arun," she used his first name, a rare condescension to their intellectual fraternity. She continued, "An alternate reality, a parallel world."

"A what?"

"When we went through the gate, I believe that we may not have just gone to another place in spacetime. We may have entered a parallel universe. A universe with just a very slight offset from our own, but a different one nonetheless. If so, that will protect us from the time paradox you suggest. We may be in a different universe from the one we started this journey in." Drawing a breath, for her words now tumbled out, Jana continued. "That means the universe that we now inhabit is one in which the descendants of those in the 21st century who receive our distress signal will go forth into space with the knowledge that humans had already been there – humans from an Earth of a different, parallel universe, that is. They may be able to recognize that a people from a future, but alternate spacetime, had gotten trapped in their own universe through misapplication of the benefits of science. It may also be that when they do achieve interstellar space travel capability they will seek out the originators of those signals. That's us. Except, we, you and I and all the crew and passengers of *Exeter*, will be long gone. It will be our descendants they find. If they survive, that is. And … *if* there is a distress beacon to call attention to us. If all that happens – and, I know that's a lot of ifs – but if that happens then they may be more cautious with the unchecked development of technology."

"Whew, that is a galaxyfull!" Tang exclaimed. "How in space did you come up with that?"

"Well, first, please know that it is just speculation. I have no proof of this. We do not know, cannot know." She paused, and then continued, "Anyway, a simpler solution to the time paradox you suggest is to go ahead and try to put up the beacon. If we are successful in doing so – that is if some weird or unexpected series of events does not prevent us from doing so – then we may rest assured that our past, in whatever universe it exists, is one in which we must have – in the future – sent signals back." Tang gave her a puzzled look. Jana went on, "I believe a 20th century physicist by the name of Stephen Hawking proposed such a "chronology protection" feature of the universe. Events that could create time paradoxes cannot, or will not, happen in any real universe. If putting up the beacon would cause a time paradox we will, in some way, be unsuccessful in trying to do so. Or, there will be no success in receiving or acting on our message on the other end."

Tang was a space jockey, not a physicist. So in the end, even though he failed to fully follow Jana's logic, he assented to the mounting of a high gain antenna on the hull of *Exeter* and the assembly of a powerful radio transmitter from parts that Rolfo had been able to find. He did suggest, however, that besides a 20th century coded signal they also include a modern code – that is, a signal that used 24th century astronavigation conventions. Not really believing Jana's parallel universe theory, he knew that at some point InterStellar would send a rescue mission and that such a mission might indeed find them, or rather their descendants. If they came to this star system, the modern beacon code would guide them to the colony. Of course, the grim reality was that were a rescue mission dispatched to this star system from the century from which they had come, such a mission would arrive here some 350 years from now. If that were the case, and if the beacon could somehow be kept operational for three and a half centuries, the rescue mission would possibly be able to find their descendants. That was a long shot, of course. A lot could happen to a human colony in that period of time.

In fact, and he brightened momentarily at this thought, their descendants might even go to the stars themselves. Would they meet themselves, so to speak, in the 24th Century? He doubted it, but decided to pose that to Jana the next time they spoke of such things.

The distress beacon was successfully deployed, powered by one of *Exeter's* remaining micro-fusion power supplies. Rolfo added to the two coded messages a personal touch: a short musical piece from his favorite band. Jana laughed at that and happily included it in a rotating sequence with the two coded signals.

Exeter's orbit would begin decaying more severely now that they had reduced boosting. Jana calculated that she would probably last only five or six weeks before succumbing to Mycenae's atmospheric drag. Their plan, therefore, was to remove the transmitter and antenna after about one month and take it planet side. That meant that Jana's plan to "warn" Earthlings about mishandling advanced technology would amount to a signal lasting one month or so, and very likely might not even be noticed. The signal from the planet's surface would not be as strong. In the first place, the planet's ionosphere would reflect some of the signal. Moreover, the micro-fusion power supply could not be expected to last more than a century or so – unless the colonists developed means to separate deuterium from the seawater. In any event, the pressure coming from the likes of Cunningham meant that once on the planet surface, the micro-fusion power supply would get "appropriated" for more "urgent" needs. Anticipating such a scenario, Rolfo's plan was to convert the power source of the transmitter to solar once it was set up on the planet. A solar powered transmitter wouldn't be powerful enough to reach Earth with a coherent beam, but it would create a signal that a rescue party could pick up in local space. Current solar cell technology was based on multi-layered, perovskite fullerenes that were room-temperature superconductors with high efficiency power conversion. The flexible, power-generating sheets would last almost forever. Rolfo and Jana suspected that whatever befell the new civilization on Mycenae, the solar panels would remain operational without human intervention.

Chapter 5. Jame

February 22, 2376 GES. Departing Adonis System for Earth.

As the starship *Draconis* accelerated into the outer reaches of the Adonis System prior to warp engagement, Jame tried to console himself with the sudden complications in his life. Jame Anders, Founder 1st Degree, recently appointed Chief Scientific Officer of InterStellar Dynamics, was making an unexpected trip to Earth. As a confirmed bachelor, he liked to methodically arrange his life into well-defined sections of work and leisure. In his mid-40s, like his twin sister, Jana, he was blond, tall and well proportioned. He had a slightly more angular face and firmer jawline. The same blue-grey eyes were more narrowly spaced contrasting with a large, infectious smile. Jame possessed the athletic physique and good looks that many men wished for and many of the opposite sex were naturally drawn to. He had been the object of interest of more than one lady at one time or another. If he thought much about his marital status, however, he figured he was probably just too picky. Jame adjusted his seat restraints to better accommodate the brief zero G portion of the trip just before warp.

Sinking back into the chair, he reflected upon some new realities: He now was directly responsible for development work on the next version of InterStellar's Frankel-Spinoza Drive since Hald Forsen resigned. Forsen had resigned while on vacation on Earth. Forsen, that inscrutable genius, thought Jame. Forsen was the inventor of key components that made the F-S Drive commercially feasible – in particular, the navigation system. He was, or had been, thought Jame wryly, a key person in the hoped for rise of InterStellar's stock. Now Jame would have to add Forsen's duties to his own until a replacement could be found. If a replacement could be found, he corrected himself. There were few men or women with the kind of intellect owned by Hald Forsen.

Jame activated the star field viewer for one last view before the *Draconis* entered hyperspace. For a few moments he forgot Hald Forsen and his own new responsibilities. The view was magnificent – it never ceased to enthrall him. There was his home star, at this distance a fair-sized golden smudge against the ebony curtain of space. Stretching across the bottom of the viewer the crystalline backdrop of the Milky Way feigned a blazing field of native starflowers. Jame adjusted the magnification, wondering if he might spot the fifth planet – Verde, his home – transiting Adonis. It was late summer in the southern hemisphere of Verde. From the direction of their departure from the planetary system, the planet should be on this side of its star. It might just be possible to spot the dark spot that the transiting planet would present. He recalled that this was how the planet was first observed centuries years ago when Earth's scientists were focusing light measuring telescopes on distant suns in the effort to discover extrasolar planets. Periodic reductions in his home star's luminosity had tipped off astronomers to the probable existence of planets orbiting the star.

Verde was the fifth planet of a K2-Class star some 300 light-years distant from Earth. It was named "Kepler 1213e" when first discovered, a name it retained until men landed on its surface 100 years ago. From the beginning Earth-based astronomers knew it was the right size and distance from its star to host life – the "Goldilocks" zone. It was one of the first such to be found around a K-class star. Many rocky, Earth-sized planets had already been discovered orbiting M-Class stars, some positioned to be suitable for organic life. At the same time these were not thought likely candidates for human settlement since in most cases they were close enough to be tidally locked, leading to atmospheric extremes. Decades later, further observations of Kepler 1213e and its star added to the initial excitement. More sophisticated instruments aboard Earth-orbiting platforms peering into the blackness of space eventually showed the presence of water on its surface as well as an oxygen-rich atmosphere. In time, many more Earth-like planets were discovered during that century of discovery. Without a means to get to them, however, interest waned. Earth's nations had more urgent problems to deal with in the intervening years, as Jame remembered from the mandatory history classes of his early schooling. The World Cyber War in 2037 dealt a severe blow to the growing commerce in mining asteroids and nearly doomed the colony on Mars. The ensuing antagonism in the general populace to all things technical had moreover dampened the drive to conquer space in all but a few daring souls. The real problem, however, was not the urge but the means to go further out.

Jame's reflections continued as he gazed at the star field. Mankind's irrepressible urge to explore waited impatiently on the edge of the Solar System. The dream was held captive. Men lacked the technology to take the next step – to the stars. Yes, the theory was there – even some decades before the confirmed existence of exoplanets. Reputable science suggested the possibility of travel to the stars without taking centuries to do so, and even the possible existence of a necessary enabler: exotic matter, or negative mass. Not only mainstream science, but science fiction as well, a literary genre of that era, had popularized the concept in the form of so-called "warp drives." The name was derived from the mechanism by which travel through vast regions of galactic space at superluminal speeds could occur. As often happened with that particular genre of literature, fiction began to look like it might become fact. When explained in the complex terms of Einstein's general relativity by Alcubierre and others at the end of the 20th century some began to believe in the possibility of warping space. It was a term so embedded in the vernacular of the time that when interstellar travel became a reality the term just stuck.

While the warping of space was thought theoretically possible, the hitch was the need for a class of matter unknown to science of the day – negative mass. The existence of such exotic matter, as it was called, was pure speculation at the time. Then, in the third decade of the 21st century the mystery of so-called dark matter was resolved with the discovery of the long-sought axion particle as one of a suite of self-interacting "dark" particles and atoms. Experiments with high-energy accelerators exploring the properties of "dark matter" led some researchers to postulate the existence of a parallel universe in which mass would be negative. It remained an open question at the time, however, whether or not one could achieve mass inversion. In other words, would it be possible to somehow "capture" or accumulate negative mass particles from the parallel universe via conjoint geodesics? Surprising to some it did turn out to be possible, though the theory behind it was poorly formulated – if at all. The first negative mass accumulator, so called, was invented by researchers at Novatron in 2032. The Novatron device was initially just a laboratory curiosity. Due to the sketchy understanding of its principle, no one could figure out how to scale it up. A macro-scale engine, an actual machine that would make interstellar travel possible, remained out of man's grasp. Until Frankel and Spinoza.

That is where, for Jame, dry history became personal. Jame's ancestor Kim Robis had been a member of the Frankel - Spinoza team that developed the first interstellar starship engine late in the 21st century. Then Jame's parents were among the first colonists on a starship bound for the fifth planet of Adonis – aka Kepler 1213e. The colonists named the planet Verde for its muted green appearance from space and its abundant vegetation. Verde did not have the large oceans that, on Earth, contributed to its blue color from space. It did have abundant water but the many bodies of water were small and widely distributed.

Jame, born on Verde but educated on Earth, followed his ancestor's footsteps becoming a space flight engineer. He placed high enough in his classes at the North American Space Institute to earn a Founders – the highest degree attainable for an engineer. Taking employment right out of school with InterStellar Dynamics, Jame's quick intelligence combined with a boyish enthusiasm and a way with people led to a rapid rise within the company. He was known as a competent trouble-shooter. He had often proven his mettle as the company struggled to make newer versions of the F-S Drive profitable. As a reward Jame now occupied an executive suite, though he often missed the hands-on aspects of space flight engineering from his younger days.

Jame smiled to himself as he thought about the early conception of warp drives, which were described as propelling the starship at velocities that violated Einstein's famous, and still-valid postulate. In fact, the ship hardly moved at all in local space but accomplished its galaxy-spanning trajectory by changing the shape of spacetime – taking a short cut from one star system to another. In effect, the starship drive created a ripple in the fabric of space, compressing it in front of the ship and expanding it behind. So, although the name warp drive was accurate, it was somewhat misunderstood by the average layman of the day.

Jame's reverie returned to the present. His trouble-shooting skills were why management had called him back to Earth. Initially it was because there were production difficulties with the newest version of the Drive – the "S Class" Drive. In addition to a more efficient negative mass accumulator, or "NMA," the new drive utilized an improved navigation system from Forsen's lab on Verde. The new S Class promised to at last bring the company into solid financial health. Hald Forsen had promised management to solve the problems with the new engine, but his sudden resignation – still puzzling to Jame – stalled the project. Forsen went to Earth a month ago for an extended vacation but then had resigned. So Jame moved up his planned trip to Earth in order to both debrief Forsen and consult with corporation executives on how to recover the lost momentum. Running his fingers through the soft bristles of his hair, he stared resolutely into holographic projected space.

The warning light for imminent transition to hyperspace came on. Jame checked his restraint system and relaxed into the soft folds of the bucket seat. He felt the soft vibrations in the deck as the ship's NMAs were engaged and focused to a point slightly ahead of the vessel. There was a brief moment of zero G as the accumulators reached full power, creating a gravitational wave down which they would "surf" as they entered the warp bubble. Then the star field viewer went blank and *Draconis* slipped into hyperspace. The transition was smooth – as it always was – and in a few minutes the transition light extinguished. Normal gravity returned. Jame tried to settle himself for the long journey ahead. Light would take some 300 years to make the journey in ordinary spacetime that Jame and his fellow passengers were about to accomplish in only two weeks, local shipboard time. With all the concerns of recent developments on his mind and his itch to tackle the problems and find a fix, Jame was impatient with even two weeks of idleness. But there was nothing substantive to do until he got to Earth. Tachyonics allowed sufficient superluminal communications for hyperspace navigation and elementary two-way communication in emergencies. Due to high bandwidth requirements, however, a full-orbed audio-video messaging system on a practical scale was still out of reach. During the warp portion of the trip Jame was in a virtual blackout: no company holos, no newscasts, no chatting with friends, nothing. So, what to do, he wondered.

His twin sister, Jana, was a junkie of 20th century Earth "Westerns" that she voraciously consumed while navigating starships for the same company Jame worked for. Somehow she got Jame interested in pre-galactic-era Earth culture as well. He had brought along some of his sister's vids but this did not appeal just now. Thinking again of his forebears and their role in the origin of interstellar space travel, Jame hit upon the idea of researching company archives on the history of the F-S Drive. Walking across his private cabin to the desk and built in media console, Jame toggled his TASC to audio mode and spoke aloud.

"Access *Draconis'* InterStellar Corporate Archives, please – audio format."

Draconis' AVI responded in an authentic librarian-like nasal voice in Jame's ear implant: "Access complete. What topic?"

"Frankel-Spinoza Drive."

"What sub-topic?"

"Early development history,"

"Text or AV?"

"Text." Jame felt like reading instead of viewing a graphically enhanced narrative. The text was projected by corneal implants onto the retina of his eyes, appearing as a virtual image in front of his face at just the right distance for reading. He sat down and began to read.

Scanning the document at first briskly, Jame reviewed some things he already knew. Even though the original drive concept had been invented some 300 years ago, essentially the same company still owned the trade secrets of the Drive. The original company name in the late 21st century was Venture Star. The archives indicated that Venture Star was a startup that was formed by some wealthy businessmen to capitalize on the ideas of two brilliant physicists, Jonas Frankel and Edwin Spinoza. According to the archives, interstellar space travel was thought to be outside the realm of possibility by most scientists of the day. The genius as well as the original foresight of Venture Star and its founders, Frankel and Spinoza, proved the majority wrong.

A sketchy biography of the two men provided Jame with some

previously unknown details. The bio indicated that Frankel and Spinoza previously worked for a company named Aerospace Specialties. There they made noteworthy contributions to the Mars exploration program – particularly in conventional fusion rocket drives. The archives did not give details on how they came up with the basic concepts for both the exotic matter Drive and its tachyonic navigation system. The silence of the archives on that point indicated that they must have come to Venture Star with that understanding already developed in their minds. Jame guessed they made their discoveries while at Aerospace Specialties, or were helped by others there. Since exotic matter engines were totally different from fusion rockets, the latter was probably correct. So, they were fusion rocket experts who somehow learned about exotic matter drives at Aerospace Specialties. Then they left Aerospace to start their own company using the intellectual property belonging to their former employer. That kind of thing was unheard of in Jame's day, though he knew such things happened back then. Unfortunately, some of the spirit of those beginnings still characterized InterStellar's business model.

The archives went on to document the development of the F-S Drive and the beginning of interstellar exploration and colonization – all of it centered in Venture Star's trade secret drive technology. About 100 years ago there was a major shakeup at the company and after the dust settled a new company, the present InterStellar Dynamics, was formed. The assets and intellectual property of Venture Star passed without public disclosure to the new company. The protected technology of the F-S Drive had survived accidental disclosure over the centuries and no one had been able to invent an alternative drive. InterStellar owned a virtual lock on interstellar space travel and strenuously enforced it. Sometimes ruthlessly, Jame reflected, and in truth he was uncomfortable with some of the actions his company took to prevent disclosure of technology secrets. He wondered if company politics were a factor in Forsen's sudden departure. And he continued to marvel over this new knowledge about Frankel and Spinoza. Jame had always thought that those two invented the Drive while at Venture Star, but the archives seemed to indicate otherwise.

Chapter 6. Forsen

March 7, 2376 GES. Arriving Earth, Sol System.

The two-week journey to Earth from Verde was almost uneventful. Jame spent much of the time either laying out a plan for debriefing Forsen or reading up on the history of InterStellar Dynamics. While the company had not officially announced Forsen's resignation, it would not be long before the rank and file found out. To forestall rumors and maintain morale, company executives asked that Jame expedite a plan to replace him and to continue the crucial work he was overseeing. Jame now felt prepared, as much as possible, to begin implementation of that plan.

There had been one unusual event during his journey, just prior to their dropping out of warp drive to take up orbit around Earth. Jame was relaxing in the Media Bay, watching one of Jana's "Westerns" when there was a rather severe bump. At first Jame thought the couch he was reclining in had slipped out of its mooring. Upon enquiry with the ship's pilot, whom he knew, Jame found out that the bump had affected the entire ship. The pilot was equally mystified and had ordered a check of the hyperdrive engines and navigation system. All was reported to be normal and a few hours later the warning light came on announcing imminent return to normal space. The *Draconis* entered the Solar System without further incident.

After the ship settled in arrival orbit, Jame took the a-grav shuttle to the spaceport south of Chicago City. Then, by aircar, he accomplished the modest distance to KCMetro, the Earth-side corporate home of InterStellar Dynamics and the capital of the North American Federation. He was supposed to meet with Forsen the next day, but events proved otherwise. As the new day dawned the stunning announcement came of the disappearance of an InterStellar Dynamics starship bound for Verde – the Starship *Exeter*. Jame had just entered the executive suites when the news broke. The company's scrambling, press conferences and tense top-secret meetings that took place in the next few days all but overshadowed the original purpose of his trip. Jame, however, was upset about the disappearance of the ship for more personal reasons: his twin sister Jana was *Exeter's* Chief Navigator.

He finally got his debrief session with Forsen, but it was a bust too. Now less than a week later, between concern for his sister and irritation with having come all this way for almost nothing, Jame sat at the hotel bar nursing a scotch and soda, thinking back over the useless days just past. He was going back to Verde with more questions than answers. As the liquor began to dampen his anxious feelings, Jame went over in his mind the details of the abortive interview. He thought of how Forsen seemed to have aged since he had last seen him, which was not more than a few months. Not as tall as Jame, but much broader of frame, Hald was maybe fifteen years older than Jame, graying and losing hair around the temples and at the top of his roundish head. His chocolate colored eyes, though still very alert, seemed to have receded even further under once-black eyebrows. The nervous tic he sometimes displayed came more frequently.

Things went well on the first two days, though Forsen at first was nervous about this interview with his former boss. Jame avoided asking personal questions or even trying to probe Forsen's reasons for resigning. He wanted to keep everything on a technical, factual level. So, on the first day they covered things that Jame mostly knew already: the latest progress on the S-Class drive and the new pico-gravitic containment system for the negative mass particles, and so forth. The second day was taken up with details on plans for the new production facility. The day's session was cut short however by another top-level meeting on the *Exeter* disappearance.

Then on the third day they were to discuss his research on a new hyperspatial navigation and interstellar communication system that Forsen was carrying out in the company lab on Verde. Things started out smoothly enough as Forsen described some of the new concepts. Jame had not been keeping up on all that Hald had been doing. He was amazed that the traditional tachyon-based ranging and location system could be enhanced in Forsen's project to permit audio and visual contact between the starship and planet-based navigation centers.

Hald asserted that they had developed a new device – he called it a trans-galactic information transport system, or "Telpher," for short. The Telpher would make possible starship-based audio and visual communications while on an interstellar voyage. Communication could take place with anyone anywhere who had a suitable transmitter/receiver. Jame asked how they had achieved this. Forsen, after exacting from Jame promises of no further disclosure to others, told him that it was based on the ability they had worked out for scaling up quantum wormholes to act as carriers for high bandwidth information. A communication "packet" technology was used, hence the name Telpher. The term referred to an ancient method of transporting a car, or carrier, suspended from cables in an aerial transportation system. The wormhole was the "suspension cable" in this case. They had invoked a naturally occurring, so-called chronology protection mechanism that would ensure the necessary avoidance of causal paradoxes. At least that was what he and his associate conjectured. It sounded to Jame as though some of this was highly speculative and he wondered just how far they had gone. However, he marveled at Hald's creative naming conventions. Hald was quite a history buff, like Jame's sister in some respects. Jame pushed the thought of Jana out of his mind.

Forsen had been rather sketchy on the details around the Telpher. He cautioned Jame that this was "ears only" top secret and that Jame was now the only executive within the company to know the nature of the mechanism. Maintaining information on a "need to know" basis was essentially in line with company policy that helped to protect trade secrets, though disclosure to superiors was generally expected. The technology was also not yet mature enough, Hald maintained, to let others in the company know. Jame was not so sure about that. He was torn by conflicting emotions of company loyalty on the one hand and a realistic appraisal on the other hand of the sometimes-vicious company politics around internal dissemination of technical information. Jame did not want to get in the middle of that in this instance, and promised Hald that for the time being he would honor his friend's request.

Jame then inquired about how this research could proceed to a successful outcome with Hald's retirement. At that point Forsen became somewhat fidgety and allowed only that his associate in the lab on Verde would be able to continue the work. Jame tried unsuccessfully to pry more information out of him but about all he would say was that all the notes on his research were in the lab database. It was clear that Jame's probing was causing discomfort and straining their communication. It wasn't long after that their discussion turned decidedly south.

They were sitting in a company conference room, a table between them strewn with flex-screen drawings and production schedules – along with coffee bulbs and leftovers from a vended lunch. They had opted to not go out to eat and were both showing the effects of the long sessions. Right in the middle of his description of his research on the Telpher, Forsen dropped a comment about a possible problem with the current navigation module of the F-S Drive – the HyperNav. Most of InterStellar's fleet used the G-Class drive with the third generation HyperNav. It had been in service for almost 30 years and had never shown any problems – certainly not with its navigational capabilities anyway. The new, *Exeter*-class star ship used a more modern V-Class drive and an upgraded HyperNav – the fourth generation, or Gen-4 HyperNav. This was also slated to be used in the new S-Class drive. Jame wasn't sure how long the Gen-4 had been in service or whether there had been problems, but he did know that the *Exeter*, his sister's ship, was using the Gen-4. Jame also did not understand the connection between the Gen-4 HyperNav and the new communication system – the Telpher – that Hald was working on. At first he thought the two systems were based on different concepts but Hald's descriptions of the Telpher, though vague, made it clear they both used some of the same technology. After all, the HyperNav itself was a sort of closed circuit communication loop using tachyons that worked to establish and/or confirm celestial coordinates. The new piece that distinguished both the Gen-4 HyperNav and the Telpher was connected with what Forsen referred to as "scaling up" quantum wormholes. Later, he had an uncomfortable thought about this in view of what happened next in their discussion.

"So," Jame said, ignoring the comment about the HyperNav and trying to get the conversation back on track, "You think you can develop an interstellar communication system that is wideband, allowing audio-video communication? Am I hearing you right? Because that would be revolutionary, as you well know."

"I think so ..." Forsen's tone of voice suggested ambiguity and a nervous tic caused his left eye to flutter. "But, I am still trying to find the error in the hyperspace metric that is also used by the Gen-4 HyperNav. I mean, in the algorithm that solves the Alcubierre metric tensor for the planned journey trajectory."

Jame shot back, "What are you talking about? What bug?" That there was a possible bug in the navigation module, at least in Forsen's mind, utterly floored him. It was the first he had ever heard of such a thing. Forsen was no longer looking at him, and in fact seemed to be speaking to himself as much as to him, eyes directed somewhere over Jame's left shoulder. And Jame had no idea what he was talking about.

With growing excitement, even agitation, he continued, "You know how the HyperNav penetrates the distorted spacetime fabric surrounding the ship using a tachyon signal that links navigation beacons in both the embarkation and destination ports?"

Jame nodded in the affirmative, somewhat tentatively. He was rather weak on the physics of tachyons. He wondered where all of this was going.

Forsen launched into a long and mostly over Jame's head explanation of how the tachyon-based navigation system worked, his southern continent regional drawl becoming more apparent and making it even harder for Jame to understand what he was talking about. Finally, his speech seemed to clear up a bit, and he looked directly at Jame. The words were rushing out now, and Forsen's voice resumed its usual crystal clear and professorial quality so familiar to Jame, as if a new theory of hyperspace travel were about to be pronounced.

"The Gen-4 HyperNav is different from previous embodiments of tachyon-based communication systems. In fact, it capitalizes on a new understanding of the actual mechanism of tachyon transmission that we also implemented in the Telpher – a quantum phenomenon that was postulated in the 21st century but never proven. Until now.

We modified the Gen-3 HyperNav to take advantage of this new formulation – producing the Gen-4. However, I recently found a potential computational scenario within the Telpher guidance system, which might also be present in the adaptation for the Gen-4 HyperNav. This could affect control procedures that under certain trajectories could lead to unexpected results. I have been trying to catalogue all the subroutines that feed the principal projection trajectory and find out if one of these might be giving an incorrect result. If that could happen it would change the chronological sequencing. And, if that …" Jame interrupted. Later, he would regret having done so.

"What on earth are you talking about? What is 'chronological sequencing'? I don't know what that means. Please explain." Jame felt something ominous in those two words.

Forsen stared at Jame. His mouth worked, but nothing came out. Abruptly, he stood up with such force that the chair supporting his largish frame was thrust violently rearward, floating noiselessly across the glassine floor until it collided with the wall with a large thump. Without a word and without looking at Jame, he turned and strode across the room toward the door.

"Hald, what are you doing? Where are you going? Come back! What did I say that upset you?"

Jame used Forsen's first name, for their friendship went back many years and he had never seen Forsen so agitated. He had always been the epitome of the cool and collected scientist, methodical and certain in his deductions.

But Hald Forsen continued walking without looking back. He paused to allow the room sentry to open the door, and then was gone.

Jame rose from the table in frustration, trying to decide what to do. Conflicting emotions crowded Jame's ability to think, his own expectations concerning professional behavior colliding with personal affection for Hald. Then, assuming that Forsen was simply tired and would rejoin him the next day, he decided to not go after him. Some minutes later, Jack Ibsen, IS's Executive VP for Operations, and Jame's boss, called to invite him to dinner that night. Exhausted and puzzled as he was Jame wanted to be alone, so he politely declined. Before closing the comm channel, Jack mumbled some sympathetic words to Jame about Jana, that he was sorry and that he was sure they would find the missing ship, and so forth. Jame appreciated that – Jack was a good friend, as well as being his superior. But the words meant very little. He didn't think the company had a clue as to what happened or where to look. He had gone back to the hotel and sat in the bar, drinking too much and thinking about Jana, worrying about something he could do nothing about. Going up to his room he lay down on the contour field without removing his clothing and fell into a troubled and dreamless sleep.

Morning came with a hangover that Jame exorcised with a cold-water shower (a rare extravagance!) and a neuro-statin. Freshened and with a new resolve to finish the thing with Forsen, he walked the short distance back to company HQ. The sun was just coming up above the ancient buildings that housed the North American Space Institute situated just behind InterStellar's office complex. Originally named the North American University, the Institute had changed its name sometime during the dawn of interstellar travel. Jame's research on the origins of InterStellar had informed him that in its very early days, while still known as Venture Star, the company was co-located with the famous university. After all, why not? The university had produced the fathers of interstellar space travel, including Frankel and Spinoza. Jame had received his education at the Institute as well, and the sight of those weathered stone buildings brought back some much-needed pleasant memories.

Jame took the lift tube to the executive level after greeting the receptionist and submitting to the security scan. He entered the conference room with two bulbs of fresh coffee, one for himself and one for Hald. The room was empty, except for the production documents lying strewn about on the table where they had been left the day before. Jame sat down to wait, but Forsen did not show up. Attempts to reach him at his hotel were to no avail. Nor was he located in the days following. He had just disappeared.

The continuing furor over the disappearance of the *Exeter* thoroughly trumped Forsen's disappearance, and company management seemed unconcerned with Forsen. The events of the week put everyone in the company on edge, including Jame. He thought that this "accident" should have caused InterStellar to shut down all hyperspace travel – or at least all commercial travel. But no, corporate attorneys smoothly explained to the public in slick publicity releases that the disappearance was an anomaly that would not happen again. Moreover, company minions went on to explain to the press that the "location" of the missing starship would be identified and a "rescue" operation mounted. Answers would be forthcoming when simulation analyses were completed in the company's laboratory on Verde. Forsen's laboratory, to be precise. But, thought Jame bitterly, there were no simulations going on in Forsen's laboratory, for Forsen was nowhere to be found. Now Jame would have to go back to Verde and would probably have to explore that laboratory. Without Forsen the only alternative was evidence that he may have left behind, though Jame knew in advance that he hadn't a clue where to start.

* * *

April 5, 2376 GES. Verde City.

The journey back to Verde seemed quick, as Jame pored over every scrap of information that Forsen had given him about his research. Much of it concerned the new exotic matter drive. But Jame was more interested in the matter of a presumed bug in the HyperNav algorithms. And for that there was very little information, though Jame did turn up some notes and calculations that Forsen had made. He did not, in actual and painful fact, understand them.

After settling some personal affairs and checking his holos, Jame decided to visit Forsen's labs. There were two: a downtown lab that was part of corporate complex in Verde City, and a more or less secret mountain top lab some kilometers outside of the city. Since Jame's office was also in headquarters downtown, he decided to visit the city lab first.

Stepping up to the auto sentry, Jame centered his face in front of the scanner. Hidden sensors at the sides of the portal found and recognized the subcutaneous implant in his neck. In a brief moment the door to Forsen's lab slid open soundlessly. He stepped in, palming the door closed and secured as he passed through the portal. No sense in having any nosy neighbor inquiries, he thought – at least until he could figure out what Forsen had been up to.

Jame walked tentatively between oddly half-familiar machinery, coming to Forsen's worktable in the back. As he surveyed the large and complexly arranged laboratory, Jame thought back on his own career. Memories surfaced of being completely alone for days on end as he happily carried out prototype testing on components for an earlier version of the HyperNav guidance system. It had been a long time – too long, thought Jame – since he had been in a lab, since he had been doing hands on stuff. Elevation some years ago to a lower executive level position in the company all but prevented him from working on real hardware or software, and he never looked back. Now he missed it. He surveyed Forsen's world of 3D printers and laser-lathes alongside starship cockpit simulators and opto-neurological guidance headgear worn by starship pilots. What was he doing with pilots' gear? Jame wondered. Had Forsen been working on something that could explain the ship's disappearance? Surely not, for that disappearance happened after Forsen resigned. Still, there was that bit Forsen mentioned about the HyperNav bug and "chronological sequencing" – whatever that meant. Did Forsen stumble onto something that would turn out to be connected to the *Exeter's* disappearance?

Forsen had an associate, Jame recalled. He knew little about him except his name, Pavel. Company rumors said that Pavel had been in line some years back for the Director of Research position that Forsen got instead. That was before Jame was appointed VP of Development and became Forsen's boss. The company rumor mill had it that Pavel nursed a bitter resentment over the slight. Jame had met Pavel once or twice and recalled a man with a somewhat morose countenance. But if he was resentful of Forsen's ascendancy he hid it quite well, at least in Jame's eyes whenever the three of them were together. Jame recalled that Pavel was also quite young, probably not much more than thirty. He must have had a lot on the ball to have been considered for so high a position as research director. In fact, Forsen had described Pavel to Jame as very bright, but also reckless. Jame felt hopeful. More than he had been in weeks. Pavel would know what was going on. It was as if a great burden began to be lifted.

Buoyantly, wondering where Pavel could be found, Jame connected to an interoffice communicator and paged Forsen's administrative assistant, Allene. "Hey Allene, it's Jame. I'm in Hald's lab here in the City. I guess that's no surprise, huh?"

"Oh Jame, I'm so sad about *Exeter* and what happened ... you must be really hurting right now. I've been thinking about – and praying ..."

That was Allene – a very sympathetic and compassionate

woman. More concerned about Jame than about the total upset to her own life caused by Forsen's sudden resignation. As Forsen's administrative assistant, Allene was one of the few people who had been officially informed of Forsen's departure. "Thanks, Allene, for your thoughts. But, there's not much we can do. The company has mounted some kind of search effort, but I am not too hopeful on that end of it. I am hoping that I can find some clues to the *Exeter* in what Forsen was working on."

"Really? You mean Hald was working on something related to the …?" She did not want to say explosion or wreck or anything like that, even though that is what she (and everyone else in her mind) figured. She felt so bad for Jame. Jana was such a precocious and beautiful child. Allene was in her seventies, so people the age of Jame and Jana seemed to be children – not grownups at all.

"No, I don't think so. Or, maybe he was. It just isn't clear. When I interviewed him Earth side at one point he became almost incoherent and started talking about something that could be related to the … Well, anyway, its just an idea I had." Jame did not want to go into details with Allene. She did not need to hear technical details and he wanted to keep his speculations private. "Say, is Forsen's associate around? You know, Pavel something or other? Where is he?"

"Pavel. His name is just Pavel – we never got a second name for him." Her voice turned sour. "Haven't you heard – he's disappeared too!" Jame marveled at her choice of words: "disappeared." Evidently the company rumor mill was working quite well – even over light-years of spacetime. In spite of their general lack of interest in Forsen at the moment, company execs nevertheless made a point of covering up his sudden disappearance. Coming on top of the *Exeter* disappearance, that would not play well with the public. Jame was angry at their hypocrisy.

Turning back to their conversation he asked, "What do you mean, disappeared? When did that happen?" His heart was sinking at this news, but maybe he had misunderstood her.

"Well, maybe I shouldn't say disappeared. The fact is he said he was going to take a few weeks off to go visit his brother in Port Robis, but he hasn't been back since. I didn't even know he had a brother, but Pavel said his brother was ill and he had to go see him. But Port Robis? That's clear on the other side of the continent …"

"Allene!" Jame cut her off. "When did Pavel leave?"

"Well, let's see. I guess it was just before the, uh, the incident with the *Exeter* – I recall he told me the Friday of that week that he would be gone for a while." She looked at her calendar and said, "Yes, it was Friday, March 5. Sort of a strange coincidence, I guess. Pavel leaves and right after that the *Exeter* goes missing. Not that we knew it then as it takes a couple of weeks for news to arrive from Earth. Oh, I am so so …"

Again cutting her off, Jame asked, "So that means he has been gone for about a month, right?" Jame was anxiously figuring out dates in his head.

"Yes, that seems right"

Jame had a sudden thought, "Wait a minute – weren't they also working in the mountain top lab, outside the city? Maybe, Pavel is up there and just hasn't come into town in a while."

Allene acknowledged that this was possible, though she was sorry to say that she doubted it. She felt Jame's disappointment on learning that Pavel was gone and could sympathize with his apparent hope in Pavel's ability to solve the problem he was working on. But, in her opinion, Pavel was a loser – poor man – even if his brother was sick. Allene saw Pavel as someone who always seemed to have some other agenda than the good of the company they both worked for. If it weren't for Jame, she would have said good riddance, or something like that. Or, at least admit to herself that she thought it. Instead she said, "Well, Jame, you should just go up to Mount Saturn and find out if Pavel is there. I'm sure he could help you," she added on a note of sympathy.

Two days later Jame took an aircar out of the city to Mount Saturn – named after a 20th century booster rocket used to launch heavy payloads to Earth orbit and beyond. The Saturn rocket was named in honor of the Roman god of antiquity, who was known for his power. That was before space elevators and, later, anti-gravity generators that made escape from a planet's gravity field a process as simple as riding an elevator. Saturn was also the name of Forsen's lab atop the mountain. Jame had not yet been out to this lab, though he should have been as befitting his recent appointment. His R&D budget certainly had significant line-item expenditures for it.

Approaching the lab from the air, Jame could see that it was quite substantial. From the looks of the out-buildings and fenced areas it was obvious that the lab had its own off-grid power source and private communication facilities. There were several concrete bunkers and what appeared to be an outdoor launch area. There was also what looked like a large radio-telescope antenna. Jame knew, however, that much of the lab's facilities were buried in the mountainside. Landing in the park quad, Jame stepped out of the car. The air was brisk this morning, as Verde's winter was approaching in the southern hemisphere. Some of Earth's extraterrestrial settlements, including Verde, used the North American Federation calendar. So, while it was early April on Earth in KCMetro, on Verde it was the Earth equivalent of, say, October in the northern hemisphere. Verde's 370-day year made the synchronism almost perfect, with "lag" years inserted at appropriate intervals.

The first matter of business was to locate Pavel in this sprawling complex, though Jame had a sinking feeling that he wasn't there. Allene's disclosures, while obviously opinionated, were troubling. Activating his company ID he entered what appeared to be the main entrance. There was no one around and no one challenged him. Not that he could be challenged. As VP of Development and Chief Science Officer, he had recently approved another billion or so for further upgrades to this facility. He marveled that he had never visited it until now.

Passing through the double security portal, he came into a modest but artistically appointed lobby. Curving plasticene walls arched around each side of the lobby, ascending to an apex directly overhead from which hung a huge stylized light fixture. The fixture portrayed the outline of a starship by fancifully shaping and positioning the letters "I" and "S" of InterStellar Dynamic's corporate logo. It slowly rotated, casting indirect beams of laser light upon two slender, matte-finished strips of metal that ran along each side of the convex walls. From these, ingeniously engineered, the beams were reflected and splashed onto the floor creating patterns that looked like spiral galaxies that moved slowly across the obsidian-like surface. Jame could not help but be impressed.

Directly in front of him was a round reception desk with nothing but a communicator on its surface. No one sat behind the desk. There were two backless couches to his right, with black imitation leather covered cushions. These were obviously intended for visitors waiting for their host to receive them or, more likely, someone sent to escort them. Jame imagined that not many visitors came to this facility and that the visitor lobby was more decorative than functional. He surveyed the rest of the lobby.

On the right, illumined by unseen lights, there was a large painting that looked like a field of stars above an ancient village. It was vaguely familiar to Jame, from his early school days but at first he could not place it. Then it came to him: It was called "The Starry Night" and had been painted by a 19th century impressionist. Van Gogh, he thought, was the name. He recalled that Forsen was something of an art connoisseur as well as a history buff, and he recognized the appropriateness of the painting here in the lobby of a laboratory dedicated to advancing the technology of star travel. Then he remembered that Van Gogh had committed himself to an asylum near the end of his life, and that this painting portrayed the view from his asylum window. The conjunction of this thought with the reason he was here was disturbing.

Jame strode resolutely across the glassine floor, which sparkled with simulated starlight as he walked toward the only door in view. Entry required identification again but was easily accomplished for Jame. He was gratified that the architects of the security system for this opulent building at least knew who paid for it. He entered a long hallway, with doors that periodically punctuated its mute sterility. His day boots made soft noises on rubberized floor tiles as he passed doors marked with some indication of the contents of the room behind them, or sometimes the name of someone responsible for it. There was no regularity in the spacing of the doors. The light was constant. The hall seemed endlessly long.

Walking slowly down the hallway, Jame thought again of Forsen's Van Gogh mural in the lobby, musing about how some of the people closest to him had an affectation for things long gone. His sister, Jana, enjoyed ancient "movies" as she called them. Forsen had named his lab after an ancient god and he often wore those odd "Google glasses" from the 21st century instead of having corneal implants like everyone else. He wondered if there was any significance to these yearnings for the past. He, himself, certainly had no interest in what had gone before unless it could somehow directly influence the future direction of mankind. Yet, as a scientist he was all too aware that whatever the past could teach us, it could not restore the universe to the lower state of entropy to which those movies and Google glasses had belonged. The "forward march" of humanity was somewhat futile in that regard, though not a futility that would be easily discerned in the ordinary lifetime of a single human being. Maybe this interest in lives lived long ago was a way of avoiding the relentless, unidirectional thrust of time. Jame pushed further thoughts of time from his mind as he approached the end of the empty hallway.

Jame studied a layout plan of the lab before coming and knew that Forsen's main lab was somewhere toward the back and down several levels. He came to a lift tube and entered. A tiny hologram of the building floors presented itself to the right of the tube portal, with a flashing triangular icon next to the floor he was on – the top floor. Motioning with his finger, Jame caused the icon to move to the lowest level, five floors below him. The symbol beside this floor indicated its purpose with only a miniature diagram of a starship inside a space warp. The portal closed and he descended.

Reaching the lowest floor, the lift tube carriage opened into an antechamber and another short hallway at the end of which was another security portal. He passed through and found himself in a huge, high ceilinged lab with small office cubicles on either side. Surely, he thought, this is where Pavel will be found.

"Hello! Anyone here?" He called out.

Silence. He called again and again received no reply. Then a voice seemed to crackle from out of nowhere. "This is security. Do you need help?"

Jame looked around but could not locate the source. Some kind of hidden PA system he guessed. Then a holovid of a man appeared in front of him -- obviously the security guard, located somewhere else on the premises. Maybe even a servbot implemented with a realistic animation and AI, thought Jame. He looked closely at the man in the holovid but could not tell if he was looking at a real man or a sim.

"Yes. I am Jame Anders, InterStellar CSO. I am here to inspect the laboratories. In particular, I am looking for an assistant to Dr. Hald Forsen whose name is Pavel. Do you know where he is?"

"Just a minute, sir." There was a clicking noise in the background. The holovid spoke back to him. "Security scan ascertains that Assistant Director Pavel is not currently in this facility.

His last recorded entrance was on March 7, 2376 GES, or 7.3.104, local Verde at 0700 hours. There is no record of his exit."

What the dickens did that mean, Jame asked himself. No record of his exit and yet not here? Jame knew that the security scan cited by the guard holovid (he was pretty sure now it was a computer he was talking to, and not a live person) would have searched the facility for Pavel's TASC signature. Verde laws forbade government or private "tracking" of citizens via their TASC signature, but companies were permitted a low level of presence monitoring inside their own facilities. InterStellar required its employees to sign a waiver to that effect. So, if Pavel were here, he was either shielded from the scan or … or dead. No, he thought, the TASC would continue to transmit a baseline signature even after a person died, at least for a few months until the power source failed for lack of a recharge.

"… reported a power outage to main data archive at 1730 hours, 7.3.104 local Verde." The guard holovid had continued to speak. Distracted by his internal questions, Jame had missed the first part of that. The guard continued, "Power was restored to critical systems instantly but systems check reveals damage to the main data archive for the period 1730 to 2130 hours, 7.3.104 local Verde. Is there any other information you require, sir?"

So, that explains it, Jame thought to himself. There was a power outage and emergency generators switched on immediately. But, the database that keeps records of comings and goings to the facility was damaged by the power surge, and the self-healing system didn't bring it back on line for several hours. Obviously, Pavel must have left sometime after the power outage yet before the data archive was restored. Meaning he isn't here now and no one at the company has seen him since. Allene hadn't known the address in Port Robis for Pavel's brother, so there was little hope finding him until he decided to return. Jame was deflated and looked around with a sigh of exasperation. Then, the question that had been at the back of his mind since he arrived at the lab surfaced. Where was everybody? He asked the holovid guard and received the answer he should have come up with by himself. Today was the annual celebration of the founding of Verde City, 104 Verde years before. All business shut down on that day. In his preoccupation with the problems presented by Forsen, and now Pavel, Jame had totally forgotten it.

Jame was discouraged, but not about to give up. He decided to search through the laboratory to try to find out where Forsen and Pavel were carrying out research on the new communication system, the Telpher, as Hald called it. For one thing, he had an obligation to the company to see if Forsen's research could be continued. At the same time, Jame felt that maybe Forsen's research held a clue to the disappearance of the *Exeter*. It was when the Telpher became the subject on the third day of the debriefing that Forsen started talking (almost raving) about a bug in the HyperNav. Jame had become convinced that Forsen's supposed discovery of the HyperNav bug had something to do with the disappearance of the *Exeter* – and of his sister. Somehow, and this was a further stretch Jame knew, the HyperNav bug and the Telpher were also connected.

Jame was anxious to find out what had happened to *Exeter*, but even more desperate to find Jana. Being twins, they had always been close. Even marriage had not separated them. When Jana got married Jame became best friends with Logan. After only three years of their contract, Logan had died in a tragic accident off the west coast of North America, on Earth. Jana did not remarry, and Jame had never married. He was not really a confirmed bachelor – he just had not found the right mate. So, Jana was the closest human being to Jame, and he missed her.

Chapter 7. Mycenae

Planet Mycenae, Apollo System. Local Date: Circ 520, Fifth Twelve-Day.

Shawna pretended sleep when her ma looked in on her. She figured her pa and ma would likely be talking about the events of Pa's trip to Mycenae City. Her pa and her brother Kyl had come back that afternoon, after having been gone some days longer than expected. Her ma tried to hide her worry from the children, but Shawna was not deceived. Then Pa and Kyl appeared, to everyone's great relief, and everything seemed normal again. But it wasn't. Shawna knew that something had happened to them while they were gone. She tried to worm it out of Kyl but he refused to talk. Shawna figured that her Pa probably laid a pretty heavy punishment threat upon Kyl for spilling what had happened – at least before Pa was ready to tell the rest of the kids. Or else Kyl was just being contrary, and that was probably it, she decided.

Now that all the children were put to bed, Marco felt he had the freedom to speak with his wife about the amazing events in Mycenae City. He would tell the other children tomorrow, he figured, because he knew Kyl couldn't keep his mouth shut any longer anyway. Marco first wanted to rehearse all that happened with Kara. He still wasn't sure he believed it all himself.

Shawna heard the low voices and crept out of her bed. She stood just behind the curtain separating the sleeping room from the main room. They were sitting by the wood stove. As Shawna hoped, Pa was recounting what had happened that made them a few days late.

"… it was a large flying machine of some kind, come right down out of the sky," her Pa was saying. "The folk in the city square all dove for cover, thinking they was gonna get hit!"

Shawna heard her mother gasp and imagined her hand reaching to Pa as she exclaimed quietly but with obvious worry in her voice, "You and Kyl – were you alright … weren't you?"

"Well, we're here, ain't we," he chuckled a bit. "Yeah, we was fine. Anyway, we was off to the side o' the square a bit and I think we seen it comin' so we wasn't caught off guard like some of them."

"But, what was it?"

"Told you. A flying machine. And when it landed guess what happened?" Shawna's Pa was a jokester and loved pulling Ma's leg sometimes. Shawna was as much taken in by the suspense as she imagined her Ma was.

"I can't guess, Marco, you know that. I wasn't there … Don't be difficult – tell me!"

"Why, a hatch in the thing opened and four men got out! What did you think?" Again there was a slight chuckle. But then her Pa's voice turned serious.

"Actually, we was all pretty scared like and they was dressed funny – uniforms it looked like. It was some kind of symbol on the left shoulder: a star, zigzag arrow, and the letters "IS". The leader of the group, I guess he was anyway, come up to us and started speakin. I had gone up for a close look, so I heard him clearly. But his language was strange, hard to understand. I had thought these were guys from Athens City and had gotten one of those old machines working again – you know, like is in the cave under Ask Mountain – and had come to scare the wits outta us. A joke or something. You know how those folk in Athens think they're better'n us, anyway?" He did not pause for her to answer, but plunged right on. "So, at first we couldn't understand a word he was a sayin. But old Conrad's a wise one, ya know, seems to have hung onta much of the learnin of the old ones, and he piped up that they was speaking an old dialect of Universal. He started interpretin' and slowly the rest of us begun to understand. It turned out to be just a weird twistin' of our own tongue that they was speakin."

"Well what did they say? Where had they come from? What did they want, anyway?" Kara wanted to know everything at once. She had considerably more education than Marco, and an intelligent mind. But, she loved him nonetheless. He was a hard worker and she figured she was fortunate to have such a man during these difficult times.

"Just hold yer horses, woman. I'll get there soon enough. The leader, his name was Blair – Lieutenant Blair his mates called him – asked us right off to tell him where to find a Captain Tang. None of us knew of any Captain Tang and we said so. That puzzled them and one of the others started talkin about some kind of distress signal from a 'starship,' whatever that is, – they called it the 'Exeter,' a funny name – and that they had traced the origin of the signal to this city. Well, that got old Conrad excited and he started tellin them 'bout that old pre-plague bunch of buildings on the north side of the city. You know what I'm talkin about, right?" Kara nodded yes and Marco continued. Shawna, unbeknownst to her folks, was still listening raptly and beginning to get an idea about these strange visitors.

"Well, ya know no one any more goes out to the "old city" as folks call it. 'Cept Conrad – he goes out there from time to time, for whatever reason I don't fetch. Most folks don't like to be reminded of the terrible plague that happened back in grandpa's day." Marco still remembered the stories his grandpa had told him about the devastating illness that had struck the human population of Mycenae, wiping out almost 90 percent and forcing the survivors into a mostly agrarian culture. His grandpa had been only a child about Shawna's age when that had happened – probably almost 160 circs back since his grandpa was over 100 circs old when Marco had been born. His grandpa used to regale the children with stories about the former days that were so fantastic they hardly credited them.

"You remember Gramp, don't you," Marco continued, "the yarns he told?" Kara nodded again, an idea floating in the back of her mind that she could not quite get hold of. "Stories, come to think of it now," Marco was saying, "About how they used to travel from one city on Mycenae to another in machines that flew through the air similar to the one that we seen come down in the plaza this past 12-day. Things like how they could talk to folks in distant cities and even see them by looking into window machines – 'radios' and 'vidlinks' he called them. And Gramp had even more fantastic yarns about how the people of Mycenae had all come to this planet on a 'starship' that came from another planet, 'Earth' he called it, that travelled around a star named 'Sol'. You know we never put much stock in those stories, though some folk still believe there was a place called Earth that we all came from."

Shawna listened with fascination to Pa's recounting of his Gramp's stories. Of course she'd heard him repeat some of them to her and Kyl (Stace was too young) once or twice herself and did not know quite what to make of them. The legend that the people originally came from a place called Earth she'd also heard about from a couple of the kids in school. Now, at the mention of Earth being a planet revolving around another star, and a starship that carried people from Earth to Mycenae, Shawna caught her breath. Suddenly, she knew. She guessed it! That "star" she had seen in the evening sky while Pa and Kyl were gone was in reality a starship, orbiting their planet. It came from somewhere else, another star system, maybe the mythical 'Earth' itself!. And the flying machine that had come to the city square was from that ship. Space travellers from Earth had come to visit them! Her folks did not understand things like this, she knew. Well, maybe her Ma did, a little. But the teacher she had in school did. He was young and had just come out to the country from Athens City where there was supposed to be some kind of 'university' he called it. He was trying to get some of the kids interested in things he called 'science' and 'technology'. That was why they must learn quadratic equations, he said, and astronomy. He had some old electronic tablet-like things with complex information on them that he wanted them to learn some day. That was, in fact, how Shawna understood things like planets orbiting around stars. Her teacher had drawn pictures of this on the writing board.

Her teacher also spoke a lot about the so-called old days, before the plague. Shortly after coming to Mycenae City he got to know Conrad. He told Shawna that he had even gone out to the old city with Conrad to explore around, and had seen some old equipment there that was still powered by what he called solar cells. One was a device that he called a radio beacon. Conrad told him that it had been set up by his own great-great grandparents, though Conrad wasn't sure why. Shawna wondered what her teacher would say about the old stuff she and her brother had found in the cave under Ask Mountain. She resolved to tell him about it next school day. Something exciting was happening in her world, though Shawna wasn't quite sure what it all meant.

Chapter 8. Search for *Exeter*

InterStellar HQ, KCMetro, Earth. April 15, 2376 GES

Jack Ibsen looked up from the vidtext and sat back in his chair in his executive suite at the top of InterStellar Towers in KCMetro. It was early morning. Jack stared out a window that faced west, barely noticing the sharply etched shadows marching out from the city's skyscrapers toward the western prairie and the flashes from nearby building windows as the sun rose and reflected itself back to him from one location and another. He was stunned at the news, contained in a top-secret report just passed to him from InterStellar's Security Chief, Patrick Mons. InterStellar's communications jocks had been analyzing the last HyperNav signals from the *Exeter*. By a form of hyperspace triangulation, using Nexus stations on Earth, Earth's Moon, and Mars, they located the sector of space they thought the ship went to. Though how it got there they hadn't a clue, and some on the team believed their triangulation efforts had given them bogus results. Nevertheless, InterStellar immediately launched a "rescue" mission to that sector, using a fast military corsair. The *Eagle*, skippered by Captain Bennet Wrain, reached the identified star system, which was some 36 light-years from Earth, in just under three days, Earth time. Upon entering the sector they found a K-Class star with several planets, one of which was orbiting in the habitable zone. But, there was no sign of the *Exeter*, even though it should have been emitting homing signals if still functioning.

According to the secret InterStellar report, the captain of the

Eagle had decided to orbit the planet to determine if by some chance the occupants of the *Exeter* had been able to land on the planet. (There was no explanation of where the *Exeter* might have been.) The planet showed an atmosphere of 19 percent oxygen and about 60 percent nitrogen. There were no toxic gases noted and carbon dioxide was at a safe level. It had almost the same diameter but only about 0.8 Earth mass. The planet was mostly land, with two major oceans, smaller than those of Earth. With that much land mass and without an electromagnetic signal coming from the planet, assuming it was inhabited, a search for the crew and passengers of the *Exeter* would have been practically impossible in the amount of time the *Eagle* had. That is, assuming there were any survivors of the *Exeter* on the planet.

* * *

Captain Wrain's Exec was arguing that they just got a bum steer on the triangulation. "Cap'n," said Lieutenant Blair, "If there's no homing signal coming from the *Exeter*, it probably means she isn't here. We don't have fuel or provisions to orbit for long, or to conduct a reasonable search throughout this star system."

"I know, Blair. I'm tempted to agree with you and head home for new instructions. We can't communicate with Earth until we get back to Sol System, except broadcast our tachcon location signal. But, I've just got a funny feeling. Something strange is going on here."

"Well," shrugged Blair, "You're the skipper. I guess we can hang around for a while. I'll tell Reconnaissance to continue scanning all the comm channels that *Exeter* uses."

"Tell them to scan the channels of the older starships as well. We don't know what *Exeter* may still have, or still able to use if something happened. This planet has the same length day as does Earth, but revolves around its star somewhat faster than Earth revolves around Sol. CD computer shows it to have a sidereal year of just two thirds of Earth's year – about 243 days. We'll put the *Eagle* in a polar orbit at about 1600 km above the planet surface, giving us an orbital period of about three and a half hours. That will allow us to survey a new swath of the planet surface each pass. In this orbit we should be able to do a full survey of the planet in about two weeks, while having plenty of time to focus high gain antennas at all the land masses."

"Two weeks!" Blair started to object, but hastily zipped it. "Aye, aye, Skipper." He turned and was gone.

But after two weeks, the search for any kind of communication signal indicating the presence of life yielded nothing. Wrain was just about to call it quits when Rudy Ost, the *Eagle*'s competent communications officer, came to him with a strange suggestion.

"Captain, why not use the old Earth-based shortwave radio waves instead of the solid-state laser frequencies we use nowadays. I did some reading on our way here on the *Exeter*'s manifest. She carried mostly colonists outbound for a new star system, along with much of the supplies and equipment to establish a new colony. *Exeter* was going to stop on Verde to transfer most of her materiel and passengers to a colony ship. The people who were on *Exeter* would have been fully prepared to establish a new colony on this planet."

"So, what's the connection with short-wave radio," asked Wrain. He was nevertheless impressed with Ost's diligence and intrigued by his potential insights.

"Just this, Captain. In the early days of an extraterrestrial colony, energy is a rare commodity and communications are important. Laser comms take a lot of energy and sophisticated infrastructure. Shortwave radio is easy by comparison, and with a reasonable ionosphere on the planet, it can be very useful. Perhaps the *Exeter*'s laser comms were disabled and they are using shortwave radio to communicate between the ship and the planet surface. If so, those signals should be detectable."

"Well," said Wrain, "That's great. But, I'm sure we do not have any of that old-school type of comm equipment aboard the *Eagle*."

Ost suppressed a small cough. "Actually, Captain, we do." Ost was a little nervous at so saying, because the reason they did is that he had brought it along – purely on a hunch, of course. He hoped the Captain would understand.

It took a little doing and some EVA to set up a dish antenna array on the hull of the *Eagle* that could be tuned across a spectrum from 2 to 20 meters, the bands that Ost thought might be in use. They jury-rigged Ost's shortwave receiver/transmitter into the ships comm system and fired it up. Ost began to tune through the various frequencies but found only bands of noise that appeared to come from the planet's star, or from one of the gas giant planets they had observed further out in this system. Then, as Ost tuned through the 406 MHz band, the noise level dropped to zero indicating presence of a coherent signal of some kind. The directional antennas indicated that the source was on the largest of the two land masses, over which the *Eagle* was currently passing. As the tuner reached exactly 406 MHz they unexpectedly heard music! Captain Wrain and those crowded into the Comm Bay were stunned.

"Music?" exclaimed Wrain. "Ost, I hope this isn't some kind of joke."

"Captain, I assure you it is not. I am just as surprised as the rest of you. But also, if I can say so, I am very pleased. We may have found *Exeter's* crew and passengers on the planet surface. Though it does puzzle me why we did not pick up anything from the ship itself. Unless, the ship has been destroyed ..." He did not want to go down that path any further. No one did.

Then, while they were speaking to each other the music stopped. A moment later a different signal started, repeating a pattern of beeps over and over. To everyone except Ost this was a mystery.

"Holy novas!" exclaimed Ost, staring at the receiver in unbelief.

"Ost, what is it?" commanded Wrain.

"That is an international distress signal in a mode last used in the 20th century! SOS. It's Morse Code."

Before the others could ask Ost what was Morse Code, the audio output of the receiver changed again. This time it was a signal they were all familiar with, a distress beacon established by the Planetary Distress and Safety Commission – a PDSC locator beacon. This beacon was one of a set of communication protocols established by the PDSC when interplanetary space travel had become common. This particular beacon was used to identify the location of disabled space vehicles. Every crewmember on the ship knew this one by heart.

Blair made the connection. "Isn't 406 MHz one of beacon frequencies set up by PDSC for the early star ships?" he asked.

"Yes," replied Ost. "And, as you may be wondering, Morse Code was a similar distress signal used in the 20th century. It was replaced in the 21st century by various safety and communication protocols that eventually evolved into those established by PDSC about 100 years ago."

As he spoke, the signal switched back to music again. As they continued to listen in wonderment the signal cycled through the same pattern, at roughly half a minute for each portion. Blair expressed the discouragement that was beginning to sweep over all of them, deflating their initial hopes when they heard the music. He said, "It's just an automated beacon—repetitive. There may not be anyone alive behind it."

"Nevertheless, we need to trace it and find out exactly where on the planet's surface it's coming from. Then we go down and have a look around." Wrain was a man of action and he had heard enough speculation at this point. "In the meantime, Ost, try broadcasting our own message." Ost followed Wrain's instructions to put the message in Morse Code and also in the current code lexicon of the PDSC. He then started broadcasting: "Interplanetary Federation Rescue Cruiser *Eagle*, responding to *Exeter* distress code. Acknowledge."

While Ost was setting this up, a comm tech began correlating signal strength information from their dish antennas as the planet continued to slip by underneath them. It might take a couple of planetary rotations before they could identify the exact area, from which the signal came. After four rotations, and growing impatience from Wrain, the tech came to him with the results.

"Captain Wrain, the signal is coming from mid-latitude in the southern hemisphere of the planet, from a place near the coast of one of the large bodies of water. We have ascertained its location to inside a circle of some 1,000 klicks in diameter. I've checked with the landing logistics guys and we could probably bolt an extra micro-fusion power pack onto one of our EVA pods to give it extra range and use it for a lower altitude survey. Even land if necessary, using the a-grav units. They think we could cover that large of an area in about 4 hours and find the exact location of that signal. Fitting the pod with a smaller version of our radio antennas would greatly help."

"All right, see if you can set up the antenna and prepare to join the landing party. That is all, sergeant." Wrain turned to Ost. "Any response to our hailing?"

"None, Sir," replied Ost. "Of course, it's a long shot. We don't have many watts coming out of this hobby-style, amplitude modulated transmitter I was able to cobble together. They might also be using FM down there, which is less susceptible to atmospheric noise, but we do not have anything on board this ship that I could use to construct an FM transmitter. Just laser comms and advanced photonics." Ost was a genius, but quick to humbly acknowledge his limitations.

"Thanks, Ost." Turning to his exec he said, "Blair, I'm going to assign you to take a landing party down there. Besides Sergeant Mill, pick three others. Put together a plan for my review and approval, at 0300 tonight. We can't afford to hang around here much longer due to fuel and provisions, as you know. As much as I would like to go planet side myself, regulations require I stay here on the ship. But keep in touch and stick to the plan – that's an order!" Wrain knew how tempted Blair often was to go his own way and always seemed to find very reasonable excuses for having done so when found out.

Blair turned with only a salute and left the Bridge. Wrain turned once again to Ost to engage him in more speculation about what may have happened. Now that there was (or would be) a plan of action, Wrain was not above trying out ideas – especially with Ost. The man was a storehouse of odd information and unusual skills.

* * *

Ibsen finished reading Security's report on the findings of *Eagle* and reflected back on what he had learned. The conclusions were beyond belief. But they were inescapable. Wrain's landing party had come back to the ship with incredible stories about a people living in small cities and rural areas with a culture that resembled 19th century Earth, but with odd, out-of-place artifacts like radios, and memories of a time when a far more advanced civilization had existed there. There had been a plague of planetary proportions some 100 years earlier that had claimed the lives of most of the human population. This explained the strange mixture of a mostly agrarian society with remnants of advanced technology. But who were these people, Wrain at first wondered. What connection, if any did they have with *Exeter*? Was this a colony established sometime earlier in the 24th century by a renegade galactic exploration company that had somehow stolen InterStellar's F-S Drive and built its own star ships? That seemed the only explanation, but the timing just did not work out.

At first Wrain reasoned that if this were some renegade group, they could not have been on the planet that long. Earth had been colonizing other star systems for just over 100 years, yet the stories coming from these people on Mycenae (that was what they called their planet) indicated a much longer history there. Centuries, in fact. Then had come the bombshell discovery. Wrain had sent down another exploratory team under Blair to find out more about the people there and to see if he could make some connection with *Exeter*. Perhaps *Exeter* had visited there before going on. But that was not what they found out.

A school teacher from one of their regional schools had come to the city where Blair's party first landed. He had information he was sure would interest Blair and convinced Blair to come with him to a village some 10 klicks from the city. One of the teacher's students, a bright young girl named Shawna, had shown the teacher a cave in a mountainside just outside the village. The teacher wanted Shawna to lead them there and show them what was inside. It was her discovery and she deserved the credit, the teacher reasoned. He was proud of Shawna and the connections she was making between the recent events and the history of Mycenae.

The trove of equipment Blair found in the cave was astounding. There were laser communication equipment, astrophysical navigation computers, spare parts for micro-fusion power packs, and tools of various sorts – all of the latest 24th century manufacture. And most astoundingly of all, a digital Ship's Log, clearly marked *"ISS Exeter."* The Log identified the ship's captain as Captain Arun Tang, along with the others who had made up the *Exeter* crew the day she had left Earth a few months earlier. But the equipment and electronic discs in the cave had the appearance of great age and were not well preserved.

Following this discovery, further interviews with the current inhabitants of Mycenae produced family names of great-great grandparents that resembled names in the passenger manifest of *Exeter*. The only conclusion was the impossible one: the *Exeter* had landed on Mycenae many centuries before, Mycenae time, even though in Earth time it had only been a few months since she had disappeared. The present inhabitants were their descendants, as farfetched as it seemed.

With a heavy heart, Ibsen closed the report and dictated the one communication he knew he had to make. This revelation would remain – had to remain – a company secret for some time to come, perhaps for a long time to come. Only a close circle of the most senior company executives could know about it. But Ibsen knew he must tell one other officer, and that he must do so immediately. He completed the transmittal and marked it company confidential, to be opened only by Jame Anders. The subject line said, simply, "Jana."

Chapter 9. Saturn Lab

Verde City. May 6, 2376 GES

Jame was stunned. He closed the company missive from Ibsen and stared out the crystalline window framing a panoramic view of the green hills surrounding the city. He brushed a tear from his eye as he searched the far horizon for some meaning, some answer. Jana! Gone! Yet not gone in his own time. Gone in another time, an alien time. In spite of his education and training, Jame just could not get his head around the story. Somehow, according to Ibsen's report, Jana had lived and died and perhaps had borne descendants that were alive today. Descendants who meant nothing to Jame! People on a benighted planet living in the past. Would Jame travel there to see, to learn, to find out if he had distant nephews and nieces? Hardly, he thought. Rather, to somehow change the past was his fervent desire. Yet he knew he could not.

Opening the other communique, marked Confidential as well, Jame read that the company would be shutting down all interstellar passenger travel. The wording of the announcement was predictably vague and sparked a brief, unreasoned surge of anger within him. Nevertheless, Jame was gratified that the company had taken this step. They needed to find out what went wrong before exposing others to a similar fate as his sister's.

Jame decided to return to Forsen's lab, with a new determination to find out what caused the *Exeter* anomaly. If only to appease his loss of Jana, he thought. But scientific curiosity was growing in his mind. It had been a long time since he had done hands on stuff and his visit to the lab the other day had whetted his appetite. There had been a strange device at the rear of the main room that Jame noticed on his first visit a month earlier that he had not inspected. Now he wanted to take a closer look.

Prior to making the trip out to Saturn Lab, Jame consulted the lab personnel registry to see who might be able to help him. He supposed that Forsen and Pavel must have had technicians helping them, and he was rewarded in his guess. A list of projects underway in the company portfolio included the Telpher, under which were listed the Saturn staff assigned to it, and heading that list after Forsen and Pavel was the name of the Senior Technician, one Friedel Ruder. From his office downtown, Jame input Ruder's extension on the company comlink. In a few moments a hologram image sprang to life in front of Jame. Mr. Ruder, obviously a little discomfited at the prospect of receiving a call from someone as high in the company as Jame, spoke with polite deliberation – oddly old-fashioned.

"This is Friedel Ruder. How do you do, Dr. Anders?"

"Mr. Ruder, nice to meet you, at least remotely. However, tomorrow I would like to meet you face to face out there at Saturn. As you know, Hald Forsen has resigned and I have not yet found a replacement for him. You must also know that his chief assistant, Pavel, was called away by a family emergency and has been delayed in returning. In the meantime, due to company production schedules, we must try to pick up the work that they were doing and I am counting on your help to do so." Jame did not want to tell Ruder the other agenda he had in coming to the lab, at least not over the comlink, which recorded all communications.

"Dr. Anders, you can count on me for full cooperation. I am ready to help out in any way I can."

"Good! I will see you around mid-morning tomorrow as I will be taking an aircar from my home in the Eastern Sector." The Eastern Sector of Verde City was a comfortable middle-class suburb, not one of the high rent districts that highly paid executives typically inhabited. Jame had a modest lifestyle and he wanted Ruder to know this and to remove any possible class barriers that might influence the collaboration that Jame planned. Jame had researched Ruder's background and achievements and immediately imagined that he was both underutilized and underpaid, a situation Jame would rectify once he confirmed his suspicions. Thus, developing a close working relationship with Ruder was going to be crucial to the achievement of his goals. Goals that included not just the re-invigoration of the S-Class Drive program but also finding out what happened to *Exeter* – and Jana.

At this, Ruder responded with a little more enthusiasm and Jame concluded the call. The holovid of Friedel Ruder winked out.

The next day, Ruder was at the main entrance to Saturn Lab when Jame arrived.

"Glad to see you sir," exclaimed Ruder, standing to attention and proffering a rather formal salute. "How can I be of service ... sir?"

"At ease, Ruder. This isn't the military, you know. I hope to be able to build a collegial relationship with you over the next few days. I think it is going to take us both putting our heads together to figure out what Pavel and Forsen were up to, and getting it moving again. So, you can drop the "sir" and let's be friendly colleagues. Okay?"

"Right, sir ... I mean Dr. Anders"

"Jame."

"Jame, it is, sir ... uh, I mean Jame." Flustered, Ruder motioned for Jame to follow him, unaware that Jame had just the other day been out to Saturn on his own. Chatting about the weather and other trivia, they strolled across the museum-like entrance foyer, with its floor-bound galactic display, and down the long, white hallway to the elevator that would take them down to the lower levels. Disembarking from the elevator on the lowest level, Jame shifted the focus of the conversation, quizzing Ruder on how much he knew about Forsen's work. He suspected, correctly as it turned out, a fair amount of secrecy on the project – even within the project team – and he wanted to gauge its extent.

"Well," responded Ruder, "Of course I was personally involved with the Director and the Assistant Director in the development of the enhanced communication system – Telpher, we called it. Mostly I just followed their instructions, ordering equipment, assembling pieces, helping set it up, and the like. And I was pledged to secrecy since it was still a prototype and they wanted to work out all the kinks before letting the rest of the company know." He looked nervously at Jame at this admission, knowing that such secrecy might not be appreciated, particularly by Forsen's own boss.

"That's all right, Ruder. Forsen told me about the secrecy and gave me the same reasoning. Can't say that I agree with him, however. Anyway, go on. What do you know about any connection between Telpher and the Gen-4 HyperNav?"

Ruder looked at Jame in surprise. "Connection, sir? I didn't know there was any connection. Gen-4 was just a tune-up so to speak of the Gen-3 system – updated coding techniques, some new hardware and such."

"Oh? I thought that aspects of the principle guiding Telpher – some kind of quantum effect – were adapted to serve in the new version of the HyperNav."

"Not that I knew, sir."

"Jame, please."

"Right. Jame. Anyway, I never heard of such a connection. In fact, I don't think I was even aware they also worked on the Gen-4 HyperNav – it came out before I was assigned to the Telpher team. And, that's another thing I should tell you."

"What is that?" Jame stopped as they approached the lab door and auto sentry.

"Well …" Ruder paused to let the auto sentry clear him and open the lab door before continuing. Choosing his words carefully, Ruder went on. "Well, they didn't let me in on everything they were looking into. They often came down here after hours. I know because I returned late one night to get a document I left and had promised my lady to make a copy of." He paused, with a nervous look at Jame. "Hope you don't mind, sir, using company copiers and such."

"That's all right, Friedel, I do it myself." Jame used Ruder's first name, hoping to encourage a more egalitarian relationship between them. "So, go on … please."

"Yes. Well. Anyway, I came here kinda late since we had gone out for the evening and the lady was asking for the copy. I left her in the aircar in the park quad and hurried down here to get the copy. There they were, at the machine, working away. It was all lit up like I had never seen it up to that point, glowing the color of Verde grapes. So I knew right away a couple of things." Ruder stopped and looked at Jame.

"And …?"

"Well, I knew right then and there that they were hiding from me their true progress on the machine. And, of course, I found out that they were working off hours as well. Out of curiosity, the next day I went into the lab occupancy logs and saw they often spent many evenings in the lab."

This revelation was news to Jame, but not entirely surprising. Forsen had acted very strange when the subject of the enhanced navigation system was being discussed and there was his strange reference to "chronological sequencing" that still puzzled Jame. He was tempted to mention this now to Ruder, but decided against it. Best to not push the envelope too fast with him, Jame thought. He did want to develop a close working relationship, but he needed to find out first how much Ruder knew. He also decided to not let on, at least for the time being, that he had been out to the lab already and had seen the Telpher device. At least he thought that is what he saw on his first visit. Aloud, Jame asked, "Friedel, where is this device?"

"In the back of the lab, sir ... uh, Jame. Follow me." Together they weaved around lab benches and pieces of machinery with no clear purpose, and approached the strange assemblage of equipment that Jame had previously noted.

Aspects of the device resembled the navigation system of an F-S Drive. At least to the extent that there was a navigator's seat and console. The navigation console in front of the seat was recognizable as a navigation interface, though considerably simpler in scope and instrumentation than those on starships. So much for relatively understandable equipment, Jame thought. But there was also an elaborate headset suspended over the seat and beside the console a large, cubical cage-like structure with what looked like air raid horns in each of the cube's eight vertices. These were pointed to the center of the cube.

"Friedel, can you explain what I am looking at?" Friedel went over the obvious aspects that Jame had already noted, and then continued.

"As you can see, next to the navigator's seat and console is a holoviewer."

"Do you mean this odd three-dimensional array of components that resemble a sort of cage?" Jame interjected. "I suppose that it has something to do with the visual communication capability?"

"Yes, and yes," Friedel responded. "During communication a hologram of the person with whom you are communicating is supposed to appear in the center of this cage, just like our common vidlinks. Only in this case the other end can be very distant, like in another star system for example. At least, that is what Forsen and Pavel claimed."

"Amazing! Does it work? I mean, is this a functioning prototype?"

Friedel looked uncomfortable as he responded, "I, uh ... in truth I don't know. What I mean is that Forsen let on that the device was still under development and was not functional. But, as I said, one night I was down here and they didn't know it. I saw it all lit up and heard it humming. I'd never seen it operating that way before, nor have I seen it so since then. I've gotta conclude they were hiding something about its state of readiness."

Jame pondered this as he continued to survey the set up. Pointing to what looked like a miniature field condenser array behind the cage of the type used for aggregating and containing negative mass, he asked, "Is that what I think it is?"

"You mean, a negative mass accumulator? Yes, it is." Friedel was again looking uncomfortable, but for a different reason it turned out.

"What can that have to do with tachyon communications?" Jame asked.

"I'm sorry, sir ... uh, Jame. I confess I don't fully understand." Ruder wanted Jame to accept him and value his expertise as they worked together. But there were limits to his knowledge of what Forsen and Pavel were doing. He just could not do anything about that.

"What I heard them discuss at one point," he ventured, "is that the mechanism employed by the communication device is based on using Planck-scale wormholes somehow. And the negative mass generator seems to have something to do with the wormholes."

Hearing this, Jame recalled his conversation with Forsen on Earth a few weeks ago. At the time he was so puzzled by Forsen's behavior that he had forgotten his mention of quantum wormholes in conjunction with the Telpher. Now, with renewed perspective, Jame remembered that one theoretical explanation for the existence of tachyons – never satisfactorily proven and not accepted by the scientific community at large – was that tachyons were not really faster than light particles. Rather, they were ordinary boson-like, massless particles that traversed Planck-scale wormholes at ordinary light speed. The appearance of superluminal speeds across galactic distances was rather due to their taking a shortcut through a higher dimensional space. As far as Jame knew, this was more speculation than solid theory. Jame wondered if Forsen had built something that would bring credibility to the theory. If so, he would be in for a Nobel-Severain Prize, for sure.

"Of course," Jame continued aloud, "Negative mass accumulators are also a key component of the F-S Drive, since the principle of the drive requires the extreme warping of space in the vicinity of the spaceship. The NMAs are used to manipulate the gravitational fields within a finite region of space surrounding the starship. But, I have never seen one this size and I wonder what its relationship is to the other components here. Also, I don't see how negative mass can be related to exploiting quantum-scale wormholes. Unless …"

Here Jame broke off speaking, unable to properly verbalize his thoughts. They ran something along the line of wondering whether an appropriately focused beam of negative mass particles could be made to thread a quantum wormhole and create a stable bridge to another location in spacetime. Or, possibly enlarge the wormhole to enable transit through a fifth (or higher?) space dimension. Could that be what happened to *Exeter* he wondered? But surely not! *Exeter* did not have this kind of equipment on board. Or did it? Jame had to admit to himself that he did not know much about the new Gen-4 HyperNav navigation system. All he truly knew is that his sister, Jana, had sent a holo to him before leaving on her ill-fated journey in which she expressed concerns about it. He made a mental note to look up the design specs for the Gen-4 as soon as possible.

Aware that Ruder was staring at him, Jame spoke up again. "Sorry, Friedel. I just began wondering what connection all of this may have had with the *Exeter*. My sister, Jana, was … you know, she was the *Exeter's* navigator." He faltered and could not go on.

"Yes, sir, I knew that. I'm sorry …"

There was an awkward pause; then Jame spoke. "It's all right. Thanks for your concern. I'll get over it. Let's get back to this unusual contraption that Forsen has built. Do you know how to turn it on? I suppose not …"

"No … Sorry. They never turned it on in my presence and, like I said, I think I was meant to believe it wasn't yet operational. But there should be a write up somewhere on its operation. It must be complicated enough that they wouldn't rely on memory to go through an activation sequence."

"Excellent point, Friedel! Let's look. You can access the lab server, right? So see if you can log into directories that are connected with Telpher, while I look around the lab for any other form of documentation."

While Friedel busied himself at the main computer console, Jame rummaged through a stack of flex-screen notebooks on a nearby bench. A half an hour passed in fruitless efforts. Their search had found nothing that seemed to mention the device behind him. Stumped, Jame sat down in the navigator's seat and tried to imagine what one would do to turn the thing on. Since Friedel had seen it "lit up" there was certainly a way to do so. But, for fear of breaking something, he did not want to just start throwing switches or pushing buttons. And, anyway, one did not carelessly fool around with negative mass accumulators. You could be in big trouble if one malfunctioned – even a small one like the innocent looking black box beside him.

Then, as he surveyed the navigation console from his seated perspective, Jame spotted a half-hidden shelf under the console. Leaning forward, he found a portable transcribing device called a mempad. It was of the kind used by laboratory technicians to record experiment results.

"Friedel, I found something! I think this may be what we are looking for."

As Friedel joined him, Jame switched on the mempad. They were confronted with notes that referred to something resembling Forsen's device. The notes were cryptic and did not clearly disclose the purpose of the device. They provided, however, enough information for activating the machine. The mempad outlined a sequence of steps involving a power supply in an adjacent laboratory bay and several switches on the console. Going through the startup sequence carefully, and pressing the final button, the cage to his left emitted a low vibrating noise and lit up all around its perimeter with a faint purple glow. Inside the cage there appeared a small holographic projection of a planet orbiting a star. Upon closer inspection, Jame realized that the hologram was of Earth orbiting the Sun. For long moments they just stared at the image. Then Jame spoke.

"Well, what do you know? It does work! A tachyon based audio-visual navigation and communication system. The headset must somehow be related to navigation control and the cage-like structure with the hologram must be a prototype visualization aid for starship navigators. Amazing!"

Friedel was doubtful. "Is this thing truly communicating with a station on Earth? I don't think they had time to build a sister unit and send it to Earth."

"You've got me, Friedel. I don't know. Seems to me you would at least have to have a locator beacon, or something, to home in on." Jame fell silent as he pondered the mystery. Then it dawned on him. "Hey, maybe the machine tunes in to IFAC's navigation satellites – you know, the ones that track all interstellar traffic via the HyperNav tachyon communication system."

"Maybe ..." Friedel was still uncertain. He had an uncomfortable feeling about this apparatus but he could not put his finger on it.

"Okay," conceded Jame. "Maybe I'm getting ahead of the game a bit. We need to study the notes on this mempad more and see what else we can learn. One thing I am puzzled about is the size of the power supply. It is big enough to produce in excess of 100 megawatts, but I don't think we are using nearly that much power to light up the cage this way and produce the hologram we see. Anyway, let's call it a day and come back to this tomorrow."

"Probably a good idea, Jame. But, ..." he hesitated, then continued, "I am due for vacation starting tomorrow and my lady and I already made plans to travel to Port Robis. If that is all right I mean ..."

"Absolutely, Friedel. You have been extremely helpful as it is. Take your vacation – you deserve it. I can get along here by myself and when you return perhaps I will have something concrete to show you."

Chapter 10. Signals from Space

Toronto, North American Federation. May 2054, CE

Sergei packed his bags, ready to leave for Kansas City and his new job. He had obtained a post doc position at the Center for Space Flight at North American University where a research lab had been built to explore development of space travel technology. There Sergei would join a team that was developing fusion drives for space travel as well as exploring new concepts. Because of his thesis research, which established a theoretical basis for achieving spacetime warp using exotic matter "accumulators," Sergei had been invited to head a team to attempt development of a hyperspace engine. He had bigger plans, but this was a start.

He also hoped to renew his acquaintance with Sonja, though he was not too optimistic about that. At least in a personal dimension. But, there was a professional connection because NMU also housed the Center for Extraterrestrial Life, CETL, and Sonja had sent him an email describing some of her research and asking for help in designing her equipment. Her fascination in the possibilities for space travel was a start, and he thought that maybe he would have another opportunity to convince her to join him in his quest.

Putting away her misgivings, Sonja met Sergei at the KC Central Maglev station. She had vague hopes that he had changed, but wasn't going to let herself be drawn in as she had in Toronto. In the two years since she left Toronto she had gained a new perspective on Sergei, one that was unsettling. Nevertheless, she had sent him a note asking for his help in designing equipment to aid her research in the search for extraterrestrial life. As Sergei descended the ramp from the station he grinned and waved to Sonja.

"We meet again," Sonja spoke equably, holding out her hand in greeting.

"And, under more favorable circumstances," returned Sergei, remembering the last time he saw her – from a hospital bed.

"How was your trip?" Sonja wanted to move on, and not relive those days in Toronto.

"It was good – went pretty fast in fact. I was making notes on some new ideas for the equipment you wanted to build."

"Oh Sergei, that's great! It's kind of you to want to help me." Sonja was impressed by this show of interest in someone else's problems. But, her positive thoughts about Sergei were short-lived.

"Well, the equipment you want to build is just an application of the communication principle I formulated during these past two years at Toronto. NMU has given me a position to further my research into something practical. Your project may be just the thing I need to demonstrate a prototype of the principle. That's my hope, anyway."

"Well, okay Sergei," Sonja said, repressing the desire to tell him he hadn't changed. "Where are you staying? I can give you a lift if you like; I borrowed a friend's EV. Later, I'd like to show you my lab and what I've developed so far -- that is, if you're interested in seeing it."

"That's perfect, Sonja. I'm staying in grad student housing – Perkins Hall, to be exact. And, yeah, I'd like to see your lab but I need to get over to the new Center for Space Flight as soon as possible."

"Okay, whenever," said Sonja as she led the way to the parking lot behind Union Station. They drove the short distance to the University in silence, when Sergei again spoke up.

"Uh, Sonja, how about dinner tonight?"

Sonja expected this and was prepared. She had already arranged to have dinner with Midge that evening. Midge had a new boyfriend whom she was excited about and Sonja wanted to meet him. His name was Randall.

"Sorry, Sergei," she said. "I'm going out with a couple of friends tonight. Maybe, some other time." Sonja used the tone of voice that on the surface indicated interest but underneath telegraphed a message that it would not happen anytime soon.

"Hey, Sonja. I understand. Look, how about I come around to your lab first thing next week and you can show me what you've done and how the equipment you want me to help you with fits in?"

Sonja nodded okay as she pulled into the Perkins Hall parking lot. Sergei got his bags and waved goodbye. Sonja was relieved, and on the whole felt positive about their reunion. Sergei, she was confident, would help her with her apparatus. She, for her part, had drawn the lines of their ongoing relationship as being professional rather than personal.

And that was how it continued. She and Sergei saw each other occasionally at University colloquia, or at the infrequent international conferences on space exploration. Sergei grew to be quite a rising star in the space flight field, having finished his post-doctoral research with singular achievements in both tachyon-based navigation systems and star drive mechanics. After a stint as an adjunct professor at NU, he was invited to join a core team of researchers in a company that was spun off from the Center for Space Flight, a company named HyperDrive. The startup would develop some of Sergei's ideas into a working star drive. Sonja continued to follow his work, always nursing the hope that success would come before she was too old to volunteer to be among those first to go to the stars. She also continued to hold out hope for a message from one of those stars, one that in the best of all possible worlds she could visit herself.

* * *

Kansas City, North American University. September 2065, CE.

The years passed for Sonja with little solid results in her research. She took up other research projects in order to maintain the flow of grant money that was a major part of her income. The university system in North America had changed from before the War days. Now, a tenured teaching position did not pay enough to support even a frugal lifestyle like hers and one needed to rely on other sources of income. Thus, other grants related to extraterrestrial life origins, exobiology, planetary biogenesis, and so forth filled Sonja's days. She had been given a research associate position at CETL after completing her post-doc and publishing certain aspects of her research on contacting alien races. Sadly there had been nothing more to report. In between her other projects she continued to pursue her favorite idea, that of using her innate abilities for mental telepathy to contact advanced civilizations in remote regions of the Galaxy.

At first she had high hopes for the headset that Sergei helped her to design – one that used the principles of tachyonic transmission of information packets. This technique was Sergei's invention. He did the formative research on it while at Toronto, and then perfected a prototype while a post-doc at North American University. Sonja admired Sergei for his genius, and was sad to see that his arrogance and self-centeredness often negated his professional achievements in the eyes of his peers. He had no friends at all, except Sonja. And she could not sincerely call herself his friend either, at least not in the normal sense. It was all one-way and had been from the first time they had met some dozen years ago in Toronto. She was just glad that Sergei was not one of those people with whom she had a telepathic "connection," as she liked to call it. She was sometimes fearful at what she might "hear."

Sonja had continued to keep her telepathic abilities hidden, even from her best friends. There were a couple of them with whom she had a connection, people whose minds she could read. She developed a kind of mental screening exercise by which she could continue a normal relationship with them for the most part. It was difficult, however, because sometimes there were just some embarrassing or even critical things that she became aware of with her friends and she carefully moderated or conditioned her behavior while knowing something that she was not supposed to know. She just wished she could do something useful with this so-called "gift." Else, why have it? There had been that incident a couple of years ago when Midge, one of her friends with whom she had the mental linkup, got pregnant with her boyfriend. Midge was a very traditional sort of woman and was embarrassed that this happened to her. Randall wanted her to get an abortion and she was considering it, though with much uncertainty. Midge did not confide her predicament to anyone, but Sonja had known. Sonja believed very strongly in the sanctity of life and hoped Midge would keep the baby, Randall or no Randall. Life was precious and should be given every opportunity. This was central to Sonja's belief system, extending even to her search for extraterrestrial life.

Sonja could not directly approach Midge on the subject of abortion without revealing her "ability." She tried roundabout approaches such as telling Midge one day that she, Sonja, did not think she would ever get married. Midge had said to her, "What about Sergei?" Sonja was at first put off, but the wink in Midge's eye and her thoughts, easily read, told her that Midge was teasing. They both sniggered at that. Then Sonja said, "What about you, Midge? Are you and Randall going to get married and, you know, settle down and have children?" It was an obvious attempt at opening the door for Midge to confess her condition. But it didn't work. Midge's reply was non-committal and the question had stirred up anguished thoughts and self-recriminations that pummeled Sonja's sensitive mind. She was instantly sorry she had brought it up, as much for herself and the bruising mental torrent, as for the distress produced in Midge.

In the end Sonja had a hand in helping Midge resolve her inner conflict, but not by design. They had gone to the Missouri Museum of Anthropology where there was a special exhibit on what extraterrestrial life might look like. Sonja's friends suggested this as a means of lifting her own spirits because they knew she was discouraged about her own research. The museum exhibit was fascinating, if a little bit exaggerated, but on the way out they passed a parlor where there was another special exhibit by a local photographer and professor of anthropology at the University. Sonja was astounded to note that included in his works were very realistic photos of a developing fetus, taken in utero with special catheter cameras. The photos of the later stages of fetal development left no doubt about the humanity and even the nascent personality of the growing baby. Sonja called attention to the exhibit and said she wanted to have a look. Midge, along with her other friends, followed her. Once Midge saw the pictures the tide of battle within her turned. Apparently she won over Randall as well, for a month later they announced their plans for marriage. The baby, a beautiful girl, turned two last month, and Sonja had been invited to the birthday party.

* * *

Then the tide turned for Sonja — or so it seemed. The news was trumpeted in every media outlet: "Intelligent Signals from Outer Space." Sonja had been working in her lab at CETL. One of her students, Latya, a girl from the European Federation, was using their own ten-meter dish to do a conventional scan for intelligent radio signals from space. One morning, at 3 o'clock, Latya was startled out of an unintentional slumber by the sound of music coming from the speakers monitoring the output of the radio telescope. At first she was indignant, thinking that one of her fellow students was playing a joke. But there was no one around. The music ceased and was followed by a strange pattern of sounds that was vaguely familiar. These shifted to another, unfamiliar pattern. Then there was a brief selection of music, followed again by the coded signal patterns. It kept repeating over and over and Latya was beside herself with joy. She immediately called Dr. Bellesario and in less than half an hour Sonja was hearing the same spectacular sounds that Latya had first heard.

Sonja was skeptical however, and determined to carefully check out the phenomenon before going public. The signals were coming from an area of the sky near the boundary between the Constellations Pisces and Aquarius, a few degrees north of the ecliptic. Due to the small diameter of their dish they were unable to resolve a distinct star system source. She contacted two colleagues, whom she trusted, who also worked in the field and had access to larger radio telescopes. One of them was in the German Province of the ENU and the other in Australia. She transmitted to them the galactic coordinates for the apparent source (R.A. 00h 42m 52s, Dec. +21° 36' 52.2") and the frequency band, which was a common one: 406 MHz.

Meanwhile, Sonja and Latya tried to decipher the signals. The music was strange, unearthly and something they had never heard before. The second set of coded beeps was also strange and undecipherable. But the first set of coded beeps was unmistakable to Sonja. Latya had not picked up on it but Sonja knew there was no question – it was Morse Code. It was an SOS distress signal in Morse Code. This was troubling. Surely an advanced civilization would not have developed the same Morse Code as Earthlings had. That left only two possibilities, one of which Sonja was desperate that it not be true. It was possible that the alien civilization had intercepted Earth communications and, not knowing the meaning of the code, had simply parroted it back. The other possibility was that it was a hoax, perpetrated by a hacker or some other miscreant. That possibility, were it to turn out true, would be the ruin of Sonja and her research efforts, she was sure.

However, in spite of their attempts to cloak the discovery until it could be verified by responsible colleagues around the world, the news had slipped out. Sonja suspected one of her students, a friend of Latya's, but she could not prove it. Anyway, it didn't matter. All over the world professionals and laymen alike were rejoicing that we were not alone in the universe, and that proof was at last at hand! The communications office of the University was bombarded daily with requests for interviews and information. Sonja prepared a non-committal press release, not revealing the exact content of the communication from space. She refused to grant an interview. She had to slip out of the lab at night by a back door to avoid being accosted by paparazzi.

What if it was just a scam? This was her constant concern. What if, for example, someone somewhere on the planet figured out a way to generate a so-called message and relay it from a hidden Earth transmitter to an uncharted satellite launched by one of the rogue federations still outside the civilized world? From the satellite the signal might be made to appear to come from outer space. Then, when everyone was sucked in, the perpetrator would go public, bringing humiliation to the North American Federation. They had searched the skies and found no such satellite, but it might have been too small to detect. Moreover, there was a small Doppler shift associated with the signal suggesting origin from a planet orbiting a star rather than an Earth-based source. Her colleagues in the EU and in Australia had also confirmed the signal, and they were able to resolve its point of origin. The signals originated in the vicinity of a K-Class star there, catalogued 54 Piscium. The star was about 36 light-years distant. To date there was no astronomical evidence of planets orbiting the star, however. In any event these astronomers were equally skeptical, particularly given the message content.

Attempts to decode the other set of sounds failed and most people thought the music was phony. What had at first been a vindication for Sonja turned into an embarrassment. To make matters worse, the signals lasted for a month and then ceased. This only added to Sonja's chagrin. At first they thought that they might have lost the signal because the Sun was transiting the sector of the heavens from which the signals originated. Two months later, however, the signal had not returned and the scientific community turned its attention elsewhere. While let down in a way, Sonja was relieved. Nevertheless, the whole episode had heightened her anxiety about her future.

Yet, Sonja thought, I do believe those were real signals. Somehow, she thought, they were real. She just could not figure out how to explain them to anyone else.

* * *

Kansas City, North American University. April 2066, CE.

The next year the possible existence of extraterrestrial civilizations again got the attention of not just the scientific community but the public at large. Not that Sonja or her team had anything to do with it, nor the idea that aliens were perhaps trying to signal Earthlings. Rather, it had to do with the hope that humans themselves could instead travel to the stars and directly interact with other denizens of the universe. And that was something that Sonja was deeply interested in, and even something with which she had a tenuous personal connection. Her colleague Sergei Levkov was about to become the first man to attempt interstellar space travel, or at least demonstrate a new technology that would make such travel possible.

Under the direction of Levkov, HyperDrive had succeeded in building a prototype engine that could traverse interstellar distances in less time than required by light. The engine was designed according to principles first conjectured by late 20th century physicists. Though a tight secrecy was maintained around the details of the engine, HyperDrive had publically announced the success of laboratory trials of a device capable of "taking a shortcut through space" as it was expressed in the press releases. The releases only vaguely outlined the experimental methods, suggesting that clocks were used as "proof specimens" without saying how these were evidence of success. However, the perceptive reader as well as scientists familiar with the theoretical aspects of the subject could reasonably guess that Levkov and his associates had succeeded in creating a device capable of compressing and expanding local spacetime. Of course, it was also well known by those who followed such things that in order to create an Alcubierre-type drive you had to accumulate sufficient quantities of negative mass and to harness its power. It was conjectured that the HyperDrive team had harnessed the Casimir Effect to harvest negative mass particles. How they did it was unknown, and how this was incorporated into a warp drive was also a mystery.

Among the followers was Sonja, who desperately wanted to leave planet Earth and become a colonist on a habitable planet in some far away star system. That this was a bit of a wish fulfillment fantasy on her part, she acknowledged to both herself and her close friends. Planet Earth was becoming increasingly intolerable to Sonja. The constant regional armed skirmishes between competing federations, the overcrowding in the cities with little regard for the environment, and the increasing intolerance among races and religions were a plague on humanity in Sonja's eyes. Not that enlightened principles of life were not known or advocated – ones that embraced eco-sensitive government policies and universal toleration of human and social differences. It was just that people said one thing and did another – particularly the politicians, who nevertheless were voted into and retained in office by a public that seemed oblivious to their own contradictory lifestyles. Sonya felt (and often stated to others) that the best thing for humanity would be to go to another planet and start over. This did not win her many friends, particularly among colleagues who thought that education and good public policy would ultimately solve all of man's problems. Sonja doubted it.

Chapter 11. Pasadena

Late Summer 2066, CE.

Later that year Sonja was invited to a colloquium on planetary biogenesis at Caltech in Pasadena. Desiring to get away from the lab for more than a couple of days, she took the Maglev instead of flying from Kansas City to LA. It was an 8-hour trip by train, but she stopped over in Flagstaff to take a side trip to the Grand Canyon. She arrived at the Pasadena Hilton four days after leaving her apartment and got a good night's sleep before the colloquium.

It was a little over a mile from the hotel and the colloquium convened at 8 am. The early morning air was crisp, even in late August, so Sonja decided to walk to the Caltech campus. The Jacaranda trees were still in bloom as she walked across campus toward the Beckman Institute building where her session was being convened. Due to the continuing change of climate across North America for the last century, southern California was progressively returning to the dessert it had originally been. Ongoing battles over the past few decades with the descendants of the early 20th century "water barons" of the Imperial Valley, who still controlled much of the Colorado River water, had won significant water for the thirsty cities of the southland, notably LA, but there was still not enough. Too many golf courses in Palm Springs for the rich! And too many people in cities with too little regard for conservation, thought Sonja. The War had resulted in a general disdain for technocracy, and there was somehow an unchecked urge to the simple profligacy associated with wasting water – water parks and green lawns despite laws restricting both.

Responding to the growing crisis, the Caltech authorities obtained permission to utilize recycled water to keep the vegetation of the campus flourishing. Changes were made to campus plantings to emphasize drought tolerant species. Fortunately, the glorious Jacaranda trees were drought tolerant. This tree, a native of Central and South America, also flourished in her birth home of Andalucía, and Sonja was heartened as she walked beneath their lavender-blue panicles, remembering her childhood. The architectural theme of older portions of the campus – Spanish-revival with churrigueresque ornamentation – reinforced Sonja's sense of belonging in this place, just now. Burdens associated with disappointments in her research and an uncertainty about life's future began to lift.

It was still summer break for most students and Sonja was almost alone as she approached the Beckman Auditorium from the south, walking around it and then along the reflecting pool – the so-called "Gene Pool" from the yellow and brown tiles forming a double helix against the background of its blue-tiled bottom. She marveled that the pool still had water in it, though the fountains were not operational anymore. In this she was disappointed, for she had read that the garden fountains of the Generalife outside the Alhambra in Spain had inspired the fountains that were installed in the Gene Pool at the Beckman Institute. Sonja recalled her childhood when at the age of eight her father had taken her to see the Alhambra. Gentle memories of her father, and those happy days, replaced discouraging thoughts about the inability of mankind to manage natural resources that threatened to ruin this peaceful morning.

Sonja strolled purposefully along the oblong pool, approaching the building where the colloquium was to be held. A marble-engraved name spanned the central third of the building façade above the third floor, set off by a shell-like sculpture between the words Beckman and Institute. Passing the polyhedral granite fountain at the end of the pool, she entered between ivy-festooned arches into the arcade between the East and West wings of the large building. A digital placard on an easel directed her to the left, or West wing. Ascending the steps, she walked into the lobby and crossed the red-tiled floor. On her left, in a tile-enclosed alcove, the sculpted busts of Arnold and Mabel Beckman were enshrined, honoring their philanthropy that had benefited Caltech over the years. Beckman, the inventor of the pH meter, went on in his career to develop instrumentation for a large variety of applications and industries, founding many successful companies. It pleased Sonja to learn that he had also been a pioneer in combatting smog in the Los Angeles basin where he lived and worked.

Sonja found the conference room where her session would take place. She was approached by one of the room monitors for an electronic copy of her slides. Her talk, titled *The Biological Origins of Life on Planetary Systems of Sun-Like Stars*, was first on the agenda after the welcoming keynote. A summary of some of the basic aspects of the subject, her presentation wasn't a particularly deep treatment of the topic. The colloquium organizers had wanted something basic to introduce the more esoteric papers planned. Sonja had agreed, somewhat relieved that they did not want something from her for which she was better known (or, rather notorious!). It had not been that long since the debacle related to the supposed signals from 54 Piscium. She still believed those signals were real but kept this opinion to herself.

The first day's sessions ended promptly at 5 pm, somewhat surprisingly. The papers were interesting but Sonja was too distracted to get engaged in the animated question and answer session at the end of the day (distraught was a better word, though she was not yet willing to admit it to herself). The late afternoon sun threw pools of light through the arched openings to the inner courtyard as she left the Beckman building, her back to the Sun's direction, and walked through the shadows now eclipsing the Gene Pool. The round, canopied Beckman Auditorium, a venue for musical and theatrical productions, stood silent before her. It would host no event this evening. Sonja wasn't ready to return to the sterile environment of the hotel, and she had turned down two invitations to dinner that evening. One was with a colleague she hadn't seen in several years and she knew they would have a lot to talk about. Not sure why she was feeling so anti-social now, Sonja wandered about the campus, savoring the many varieties of tree on the campus, from the Jacaranda, to the ubiquitous palms and cypress, while ignoring some of the more utilitarian architecture of the modernist period of construction at Caltech. The nearby San Gabriel mountains to the north were stark against an azure sky, the sun mottling their craggy faces and sere attire with lighter facets among more predominant dark patches. She finally admitted to herself that she was lonely, and moreover at a seeming dead-end in her career – if not her life.

As she approached the end of Moore Walk, she spied a huge Sequoia tree on the other side of South Holliston Avenue. It seemed a sentinel of promise, somehow. Off to her right were a few café tables and chairs, a shaded place where students would congregate over espressos and exam results. No one was there. Angling from the Walk, she sat down at the nearest table, facing the stately Sequoia, and let her mind wander. The silent mountains, peeking through the trees and over the tops of distant buildings, bespoke another world – one that, just like those mountains, Sonja seemed unable to reach. Unwillingly, she dozed.

"Excuse me … Dr. Bellesario?" An aged voice startled Sonja out of her somnolence.

"What! Oh, yes, I'm Sonja Bellesario. You startled me – I guess I had dozed off."

"Sorry! I did not mean to disturb your … your, ah, reverie. But I did want to speak with you before you left."

He was a thin man, with angular features and gnarled fingers with veins that stood out on hands spotted from age. Yet, in otherwise perfect health it seemed, for his movements as he approached her table were energetic and firm footed. Bushy, gray eyebrows and silver streaked, black hair accented a face that upon closer inspection suggested a wisdom she had not seen in a man since her father. In fact, this stranger somehow reminded her of her father. He continued his self-introduction with a friendly urgency.

"I am Xander Abraham, Dr. Xander Abraham, I suppose – for those who care for titles. May I sit down? I would like to have the honor of having a brief chat with the daughter of an old friend as well as the famous discoverer of the first intelligent signals from outer space."

Sonja was floored by this man's announcement of a familiarity with her when she had no idea who he was. But, despite the combination of embarrassment and a bit of pique at his directness, she managed to say, "Of course, please have a seat. And, forgive my rudeness!"

At this invitation, he sat, but said nothing more, offering Sonja but a friendly yet somewhat quizzical smile. An inkling of recognition was trying to gain access to Sonja's conscious mind, but she still could not place the man. There was something about his name, a rather unusual one at that. She was sure she had never set eyes upon him. Yet she somehow felt she knew him. Then it came to her.

"You're Xander Abraham!"

"Yes, that is what I said," he returned.

"I mean, you're the Xander Abraham, the astrophysicist who perfected the plasma fusion drive that has given us interplanetary travel! I'm so sorry I did not recognize you at first."

"Please, no need to apologize. Like you, I get tired of notoriety."

Sonja straightened herself in her chair from the slouch into which she had fallen and gazed with intense interest into the aged face of this space pioneer. It was a kindly face, yet with black eyes that, had she allowed it, would have pierced her anguished soul. Yet, upon his countenance there was no demand or even polite request for such entry. Apart from those eyes, he seemed just a friendly old man.

"Well," Sonja continued, "I've read so much about your work. And, I am interested in space travel, even though my field is astrobiology. But, how is it that you know me? And, how did you find me here?"

"Plainly put, I saw the notice in the Tech about today's colloquium – yes, even at my age I browse student publications. And I saw your name, so I decided to attend the session to hear what you would say. And, frankly, I was disappointed!" He winked, letting Sonja know that this was not to be interpreted as a criticism of her performance or even of the value of her material. She vowed to ask him what he meant by that in a moment, but first she needed to clear something up. That bit about her father was still ringing in her ears.

"But, you didn't know my name just because I was listed as a speaker in the conference, did you? You have implied that you knew my father, that he was an old friend. What's that about? I may know your name from professional associations, but I don't recall my father ever mentioning you."

"No, Sonja, you would not have." Abraham frowned at this and his eyes lost some of their keen aspect. "It was before you were born that we were friends. Before Roberto met and married your mother."

Sonja was astounded. This man not only had known her father but also referred to him by his first name, speaking of him as 'Roberto' rather than 'Don Roberto.' They must have been good friends, indeed, for she had never heard anyone who knew her father call him Roberto – except her mother, of course.

Abraham continued, sensing her predicament, "Yes, we were very good friends – in college, back before the War, of course, and back in Spain. *He ovidado mucho de mi espanol, lo siento.*" He smiled, and went on. "You see, after public school my family sent me to the Continent, to widen my horizons. I enrolled in the *Universidad de Sevilla*, mostly just for kicks. That's where your father and I met, in a first-year physics class, in fact. We had a jolly good time that freshman year! It's a wonder we survived the academics. Or, at least that I survived. Your father, brilliant man that he was, seemed to have no trouble partying on the weekends and getting good marks midweek. I transferred the next year to Oxford and finished my studies, getting serious about education. Nevertheless, we often saw each other during vacations and at other times. I was ever the dreamer while your father was ever the practical one. I wanted to go to the stars. He wanted to build factories. Our different destinies ultimately separated us, as I emigrated to North America and he went on to build his companies in the south of Spain."

Sonja started to interrupt, but he seemed to know what she was thinking. "Yes, I know that it did not work out for him and that after the, uh ... well the unpleasantness of the worker uprising in his factories over the devalued Peseta and resulting layoffs, he fled to Canada with you and your mother. I never tried to renew our friendship in that time, but I always followed news of him whenever it surfaced. And, yes, I mourned his early passing." Here, he paused, resuming his keen inspection of Sonja's face.

"I see," Sonja began, but could not finish the thought. An awkward silence ensued for long moments. Abraham seemed lost in thought somewhere far away. Sonja was remembering her life in Canada, her coming of age and decision to pursue astrobiology as a career. Manned missions to Mars had become frequent and a permanent habitation of the planet was underway. The confirmation of subsurface saline water and Abraham's plasma fusion drive were two major factors in what seemed sure to become mankind's first permanent step into space.

"What about Mars, Sonja?" Abraham seemed to have read her mind. Yet, for her part, Sonja felt no "connection" with him. The sensation was all the stronger for the fact that he had put emphasis on the second word: 'What *about* Mars, Sonja?'

Confused, she replied, "I don't know what you mean, sir."

"Well, I mean that you could consider joining up, volunteering to be one of the first colonists of another planet. A moment ago you professed your interest in space travel. Why not give it a go? I'd go myself, but I'm too old I'm afraid. But you – you are still young. And you are disenchanted, aren't you? So, why not join the advance of humanity in its next big leap?"

Flustered, Sonja tried to answer more than one question at once. Ignoring for the moment the comment about her disenchantment, she answered, "Oh, Mars is no fun! They'll live in little huts on a barren world with barely enough gravity. It will be at least a century before they create enough of an atmosphere to grow things outside and more centuries before they can go out and smell the fresh air – if ever. No, I want to go to a planet like Earth. I don't mean like Earth is today – messed up with too many people and too little planning. A fresh planet, Earth-like, where we can start over."

Abraham looked at her, withholding comment. Sonja continued, changing the subject, "And how do you know I'm disenchanted? You seem to know more about me than I know myself!" She stopped, retreating from a tone of voice that was turning sore. "I'm sorry. I'm forgetting my manners. I was brought up to respect my elders. It's just ... just that, well yes I *am* disenchanted." She paused, reflecting on what was happening to her. This man had opened a corridor in her consciousness, a passage that promised to lead to a new perspective on things. A passage nonetheless fraught with danger that she feared to tread. After a few moments she spoke again, "You said just now that when you were young you wanted to go to the stars. I also want to go to the stars – to other solar systems."

"I know – it's why I knew that you would say "no" to Mars. And, it's why I felt compelled to speak with you."

"How do you know these things?" she asked, wondering if in fact he was telepathic like her.

"Just suffice it to say that I know. However, it may interest you to know that ever since your father's untimely passing I have followed the fortunes of his scientist daughter. Oh, from a distance, to be sure. I never wanted to intrude. Your career since leaving Toronto has been noteworthy and would have made your father proud." He paused, seeming to look inward, then continued. "As to why I did so, I guess I felt guilty for not having kept up our friendship. I had good intentions and when your family moved to Canada I knew I must get in touch, being a few miles away in New York. But he passed away soon after your arrival in Canada and I had no chance. So, you became the substitute for my desire to renew friendship. Yet, I did not know you, nor you me, and it always seemed rather awkward. Anyway, I'm an adjunct professor here at Caltech now and your arrival on campus today was an opportunity I could no longer ignore. Besides, I felt I must see you if for no other reason than to encourage you."

"Encourage me about what?" Sonja inquired.

"Why, about your desire for the stars of course!" His eyes didn't quite twinkle at this. It was more of a gleam of deep ebony.

"Yes, well it's not going to happen – not in my lifetime at least." This was spoken as more of a retort than a statement of fact. Sonja's disappointment was bitter. The falling out with Sergei came crashing back into her consciousness, though she had up to this point successfully put it out of her mind.

"You're referring to Sergei Levkov, of course."

"How ... how do you know about him?" Sonja demanded, irritation again creeping into her voice.

"Well, I read the newspapers. And, I have followed your research efforts. I know you were both at Toronto Institute at about the same time. And, I know you are now both at North American University, so you must have some contact with each other. I may be old now, but I can still put two and two together to get four."

More than a little miffed at this seeming intrusion into her private life, her Irish temper rising to the fore, Sonja did not try to hide her disdain. "So, exactly what is it that you have figured out?"

"Well, let's see," Abraham continued calmly with no sign of offense. "The latest news is the big flap between Dr. Levkov and his fellow company founders, about who is going to get to test the new star drive. It appears that Levkov has insisted that he alone be the first human to experience warping space to span light-years in moments of time. Moreover, it appears that he won that battle, having threatened to take elsewhere certain secrets about the technology that only he possesses if they did not accede to his demands. Am I correct so far?"

"Yes, you are. But that's no great feat since, as you say, this was all reported in the news. What about me in all of this? I don't work with Sergei nor do I have anything to do with the development of the star drive." In saying so, Sonja was technically correct, but she was somewhat avoiding certain related facts. It still troubled her, the decision she had made. Yet, unhappy as she was about it, she still felt that it had been the right decision. She just wished that she had someone she could confide in, someone who would help her come to peace with the failed directions in her life.

"Well," Abraham continued, "The next bit is based on some public knowledge about you as well as, perhaps, some wild speculation. Let's see how it sounds." At this he smiled warmly at Sonja, trying to overcome the deserved mistrust he had invited. "Not many people believed you about the signals from 54 Piscium, as you know. But, I was not one of them."

Sonja interrupted him, "How do you know it was 54 Piscium? We never published that."

Ignoring her question, Abraham went on, "Sonja, you may not believe it but I have always admired your talent and your achievements, to the extent at least that they were public knowledge. You are your father's child and he was a brilliant man. You have inherited his genius, if not his down to earth practicality. And, please, do not think that I have tried to pry into your private life. As I have said, I have only been following the professional achievements and assumed aspirations of an old friend's daughter out of some sense of obligation. Please do not be offended."

At this Sonja relaxed a bit. "Okay, then please go on."

"Well, I knew there was something to those signals from space but to this day I have not been able to understand them. Nevertheless, and putting myself into your shoes, I figured that if I were you I would want very much to go to that star and find out. That is, I would want to do it if I thought it were possible. Then, here comes this Levkov fellow and his supposed invention of the means to do so – a person whom you just happen to know. And, this is where the speculation comes in: Because of your past acquaintance with Dr. Levkov – Sergei, as you have just now referred to him, by the way – I guessed that there may have been some discussion about you going along with him on his first ride. Was I right?"

Sonja caught her breath. There it was, and from a total stranger! He had touched the very thorn that still pierced her heart. It was true: Sergei had offered to take her with him on his first trial of the hyperdrive. More than offered. She thought back now to that afternoon he had showed up in her lab uninvited and had tried to talk her into going with him. It was all so crazy! The dream of a lifetime held out for her, only to take it. The chance to validate her research and find the source of the message, maybe even find the reason for her telepathic ability. Yet she could not, would not. There was something wrong about it. Something that he said, maybe, or just his insistent manner. Warning bells had drowned out the delight. The memory of all the old incidences of his self-aggrandizement, of his never being truly interested in anyone but himself had pressed in upon her as he paced about her lab, fingering one piece of equipment after another, never asking what this was for or how she was succeeding with that bit. Sergei had never changed, and now at the pinnacle of his selfish career, a pinnacle that he had publicly refused to share with coworkers who had to be given at least some credit for his success – now, he had come in secret to her, a relative nobody, and offered her a spot beside him! She had so much wanted to say yes to something that seemed so wrong. So, she said no, and he left.

The torment of this decision erupted again into Sonja's mind and heart, under the soft but penetrating gaze of this man from her unknown past. Yet, something else happened: a peace began to emerge beneath the torment and slowly yet surely swallowed it up. Sonja looked at Abraham and he smiled. At last she knew it had been the right decision.

"Yes," she said to him, "You were right." Breathing a great sigh of relief, she went on to tell him of most of the details of that encounter, as well as all the background of her relationship with Sergei. It was good to get it all out with someone who had no apparent stake in anything she said, yet who offered complete confidence in her.

When she finished, Xander took her hands in his. Smiling and looking deeply into her eyes he spoke softly. "Sonja, I'm not one to say whether you made the right decision or not, though I think you know by now. I do feel strongly, though I don't know why, that you will go to the stars one day. Your turn will come, and when it does there will be a mission for you to fulfill. Of that I am sure!"

At that, he rose to leave. Favoring her with a radiant smile he spoke, "Good-bye, Sonja. It has been such a pleasure to meet you in person — and to settle an old debt! I do hope we will meet again. But, if not, God be with you!"

"Thank you Dr. Abraham ... Xander! Thank you for helping me sort it all out."

As he walked away in the direction of the Sequoia, Abraham turned and said, "Sonja, the story of the stars is not yet over. Don't forget that! Remember 54 Piscium!" With that, he was gone.

Chapter 12. Star Drive

Kansas City. May 7, 2067, CE

A sizable segment of the literate population of Earth was taking the day off. Or at least part of it. Every broadcast outlet was vying for the most viewers to please their sponsors. Everyone who was anyone had their television or netviewer tuned to at least one of those outlets. It was a big event, whether or not you believed in the social benefit of science and technology. Mankind, or at least one man, was about to travel into hyperspace and usher humanity into the next phase of civilization. A galactic community was on the verge of reification. An interplanetary plasma fusion powered space ship, one that had seen routine service shuttling between Earth and Mars, had now been retrofitted with HyperDrive's new engine. It was an engine that was reported to be able to warp space and transport the ship many light-years distant in a relatively brief moment of local time.

For this first test, however, Sergei Levkov would travel only out to the near edge of the Oort Cloud, some 150 billion kilometers (1,000 AU), and then back. At the speeds achievable by current interplanetary craft, such as the one retrofitted with Levkov's warp drive, a journey to the Oort Cloud and back would take three decades or more. At light speed such a journey would take almost six days – one way. The HyperDrive was supposed to make such a journey in less than one thousandth of light speed local time. The round trip, assuming he turned around shortly after arriving, would thus be viewed on Earth as having taken about 20 minutes! Then, about six days later, radio signals sent by him from the halfway point of the trip, would arrive "proving" that he had, in fact, travelled to the Oort Cloud and back.

It was a neat scheme and now that it was all packaged up and about to happen, even Levkov's bruised partners at HyperDrive were excited. The anticipation was palpable at HyperDrive Mission Control in Kansas City. Coffee and sleepless nights were the order of the day, as each of many techs and systems operators carried out his or her functions to assure a safe launch and to monitor the ongoing status. Most had forgotten the bitter feud that predated the final victory for Levkov in becoming the sole human being to attempt the gravity-defying feat. Frankel and Spinoza, Levkov's two principal assistants, were among those who could have been the most disappointed, but they were not. These two, more than any others at HyperDrive, had supported Sergei in the development of the Drive. But they knew, if others did not fully appreciate it, that although the achievement about to be proven today was a team effort, the genius and the key theoretical insights had come from one man alone: Levkov.

Levkov had prevailed in his controversy with HyperDrive colleagues and was the only human being on board the ship. He assured them that a solo mission on his part would in no manner affect the future development of interstellar space travel, and that others would soon follow his footsteps. They bought into his arguments and the plan was set. At this moment, Levkov was already well beyond Earth's orbit, some 2 AU from the Sun. It was important, according to calculations he made but that had not been made public, not to be too near a large gravitating mass like the Sun. Otherwise, the course of the ship could be adversely affected.

Along with most of the inhabitants of Earth who had access to television, Sonja was watching as Levkov began the final maneuvers that would cause his ship to blink out of visual existence to those on Earth. Some 20 minutes later it was expected to blink back into view. This tended to make the approaching event all the more mysterious, if not downright scary, to the millions watching. It also tended to make the test, at least as seen from Earth, something of a non-event. One moment he would be there, and then next he would not be.

The final 30-minute countdown began. In thirty minutes Sergei would make history. Actually, Sonja corrected herself, it would be in about 15 minutes for it would take some 15 minutes for radio and light transmission to reach Earth from Sergei's location. Yet, for the sake of Earth's audience, Mission Control was using a countdown based on events as they would be recorded by Earth-based observers.

Once again, as she waited for the countdown to complete, Sonja rehearsed the main outlines of events in her own life that had touched upon Sergei's. She now realized that from the first acquaintance at Toronto some 15 years ago she had been both fascinated and repulsed by him, though the repulsion had not prevented an unwise liaison. A genius, no doubt, well beyond any of his peers, yet insufferable in his attitudes toward the achievements and needs of others upon whom he nevertheless depended in some measure. Yes, he had somewhat helped her develop her own career and he helped to keep alive in her the hope for exploration of space beyond the frontiers of the solar system in her own time. Yet his help always seemed to have a caveat, a hook, a hidden agenda. She still did not know what that agenda was. Then, this latest betrayal, the crowning insult to their relationship: his invitation to her to accompany him, alone, on this journey he was about to take. An invitation that should have gone to his team members. An invitation that in consistency to everything about his interaction with her carried with it something hidden, which she could not fathom. Oh, she had gotten over the hurt of it. Xander helped her do that, bless his heart. But still she wondered what she was missing.

The countdown reached zero and there was a bright flash on every video device on the planet. There was not supposed to be a flash. Rather, just a disappearance followed by a reappearance about twenty minutes later. There was considerable buzz as broadcast announcers tried to interpret for their public what was going on. Sonja had a sinking feeling in the pit of her stomach. But maybe they all had misinterpreted what it would look like for a space ship to create then enter what was essentially a sharp fold or rip in spacetime. She waited the twenty minutes. Everyone on the planet waited the twenty minutes. HyperDrive Mission Control waited the twenty minutes. They ventured no comment, though they at least must have known the significance of what everyone had seen.

Twenty minutes came – and passed. Then thirty minutes, forty minutes, an hour. There was no sign of the spaceship returning, no sign that the journey had even taken place. Mission Control went silent and the media outlets floundered for soothing words, technical explanation, anything that would break the fall of Earth's millions who wanted to go to the stars or, probably more realistically, see someone else go. Sonja turned her vidlink off, put on a light jacket and walked outside. She needed some fresh air, and not just the natural fresh air of the outdoors. It was possible that Sergei had made it to the Oort Cloud but for some reason could not return. They would all have to wait the six days to fully confirm that. Sonja knew in her heart already the answer that would come to that question. Sergei was gone. The ship had exploded upon actuation of the hyperdrive – she was sure of it. He was gone, died in an attempt to take mankind to the stars. And she was still here! The enormity of what had just happened and the realization that she could have died with him, but hadn't, settled upon her like a cloak of chain mail.

* * *

A week passed, then two. Finally, the official announcement from HyperDrive: Levkov's ship had evidently detonated due to a breach in the negative mass bottle that occurred just as the jump to hyperspace took place. A week later, the company announced that it was filing for bankruptcy protection. Many, though not all, mourned not only the loss of a great scientist, but also the apparent failure of the hope for interstellar travel.

Months passed. Sonja began to experience bouts of depression. At first it was the loss of the star drive technology that weighed heavily on her. Had Sergei been successful there would still have been hope for her. His company would have gone on to commercialize the drive, and perhaps still before she was too old, she would have had an opportunity to join a mission to the stars. But that was not to be, for with Sergei's death there would now almost certainly be no mission in her lifetime. Incredible as it seemed (to all but Sonja, anyway), it was learned that Sergei had destroyed all records of key aspects of the drive technology before he left. It was as if he had planned the whole thing. But to what end wondered Sonja? Was he so egotistical as to think that if not him, then no one? Despite his self-aggrandizing personality, Sonja knew Sergei well enough to doubt this extreme of him. Greedy for attention and professional recognition, yes, but not a martyr to get it.

Although Levkov's chief assistants vowed to continue the work, trying to recover the lost research results somehow, there were significant financial challenges to be overcome as well. There was little appetite in the investor community for continued research at this point. Frankel and Spinoza had only the documentation for the portion of the work that they had undertaken directly under Levkov's supervision, the development of the navigation system. And at that, the design details they had were for an earlier version. Sergei had made changes to it at the last, changes for which they had no record. In any event, it would be many years before attempts could be made to build another warp drive.

However, the worst part for Sonja was not the disappointment of the failed vision of interstellar travel in her lifetime. A blackness began to consume her over the fact that she could have been on that ship with him, but instead survived. What if she had agreed to go with him? Perhaps she could have slowed him down in his rush to prove his invention, slowed him down enough to allow him or others to discover the fatal flaw in the negative mass containment system. She began to blame herself for his failure. She could have maintained a closer friendship with him all those years and helped to prevent this tragedy somehow. In moments of clarity, interspersed with such black spells, Sonja knew that such speculations were idle, not true. She knew she wasn't to blame. But something inside her seemed to reach up and grab her attention away from the rational part of her being. Knowing that these feelings were just lies didn't seem to help. She began to have nightmares in which she would be walking along a gravel road in the middle of a dessert at night when suddenly the stars overhead would stream together to a bright point, which then winked out leaving her in complete darkness. She awoke in sweats. Day by day she was sinking into a deeper and deeper pit, the times of clarity becoming further and further apart.

During one of those rare moments of clarity an email arrived. It was from Xander Abraham, who must have guessed what Sonja was going through. There were just three words in the email: "Remember 54 Piscium." Something snapped in Sonja when she read those words. Hope flamed anew and the black bands of guilt dissolved in the light of the realization of her own self-worth. There was the key to her destiny! Once again: 54 Piscium. It was for her, perhaps her alone. Somehow, someday she would know why. It did not matter that the world did not believe her about the signals from that star, because they were for her and were an emblem that her own life was yet valuable to mankind. Sergei did not matter. Interstellar travel did not matter. From that day she turned a corner, entering a wide avenue of discovery that would lead her to unexpected destinations. It would not be without its trials and disappointments, but it would be forever free of bondage to Sergei Levkov.

Chapter 13. Pavel

InterStellar's Saturn Lab, outside Verde City. January, 2376 GES

Aleksandr Pavel was not a happy camper. As he disembarked from his aircar in the Saturn Lab park quad, he loosened his tunic to get a little more ventilation. It was going to be a hot day. However, this was not what was heating up Pavel. It was Hald Forsen, Pavel told himself, and his continual insistence on going slow. They had made a big breakthrough on the Telpher last week, getting it to produce a hologram of the intended target location. Pavel wanted to exploit it. He wanted to test his hypothesis about what they had discovered. But Forsen was too careful. More to the point, thought Pavel, Forsen was jealous – jealous of him, the great Pavel. (Pavel hated his given name, Aleksandr, and never used it; no one in the company even knew it.) Pavel made the key discovery that showed that what they had created was far more than a superluminal audio-visual communication system. It was Pavel who asked the right questions. It was Pavel who found the clue. It was Pavel who realized the truth. It was Pavel who proved the hypothesis. But, would Pavel get the credit, he asked himself. No! Forsen would get the credit, as he always did. Ever since losing out the directorship for the IS Saturn Lab to Hald Forsen the slights to Pavel's genius and capabilities had only multiplied.

But Pavel had a plan, a plan to get back at Forsen and the company, and to regain the recognition he deserved. And monetary gain as well. He smiled at the thought of riches beyond what even his rapacious appetite could imagine. For, if Forsen and the

Company did not want to go forward with what he had discovered, then Pavel knew of others who would. All they needed were some of the precious trade secrets of InterStellar Dynamics along with the workings of the machine that he had developed. These others would have to give Pavel the position in a new company that he wanted as well as satisfy his demands for remuneration. Otherwise, no deal. But when they found out what he knew – and was now ready to test, were it not for Forsen's intransigence – there would be a deal. He was sure of it.

As he entered the Lab and navigated the hallways and lifts down to the secluded chamber in the depth of the mountain where the Telpher awaited him and his momentous decision, Pavel thought back over the last few months. They had been months of intense activity as he and Forsen struggled to satisfy corporate demands for a more effective starship navigation system, including the capability for a starship to have direct and instantaneous audio and visual contact with distant space stations while it was in the warp bubble.

* * *

It was late October or early November the previous year that he had joined Forsen in the project that came to be known as Telpher. Together they began work on what was at first an F-S Drive navigation simulator. They had constructed a full-scale starship navigation console, complete with tachyon-based communications with Earth-based navigation systems and a full, working version of the latest HyperNav, Gen 4. There was also a small negative mass accumulator and a warp field transmitter to simulate conditions that a starship would experience inside the warp bubble. They constructed a cage-like structure inside of which a small region of local space could be warped. That, in fact, was the trickiest part. As it turned out, it was also the aspect of the apparatus that Pavel had realized was more than what it seemed to be.

The goal was to produce a means of visual communication to normal space from within hyperspace. The existing tachyon technology only allowed a kind of radar beacon that required constant monitoring by planetary control centers. The scale model warp drive and navigation system he and Forsen built permitted experimentation with a hyperspace holographic projector that would allow the visual communication they were seeking. The experimental setup was in the company's semi-secret laboratory sequestered in the mountains outside the principal city on Verde. There was also a technician helping them in the Saturn lab, whom Pavel kept ignorant of the details of their work.

Their plan had been to first attempt a visual communication with the city lab from the mountain top lab before the more ambitious goal of communicating with Earth, some 300 light-years distant. In that phase of the plan they would use the existing interstellar beacon navigation system. It wasn't enough to find a way for ordinary electromagnetic waves generated inside the artificial warp bubble they had created in the underground Saturn lab to escape and be received in the city lab. Even if such means of transmission to ordinary space were found, signals from an actual starship would take light-years to transit the large interstellar distances. Instead, and this had been Pavel's contribution, they attempted to exploit a little-known theory that sought to explain tachyons as a quantum phenomenon involving the transit of ordinary, subluminal particles through tiny rips or folds in spacetime. Pavel had done the literature review that led to his uncovering a Space Physics Journal paper published in the 22nd century by an obscure astrophysicist named Emit Hooper. The paper outlined the theory in considerable detail and, upon discovering the paper, Pavel wondered why the man's idea had not been accepted at the time. The idea had been forgotten and Pavel supposed that this was due to the advent of the First Interplanetary War in 2136. In any event, Pavel was enamored of the idea and had done some further calculation based on what modern science now knew about the ability to warp space with negative mass particle beams. His calculations showed that they might be able to harness quantum-scale wormholes in their quest. He suggested this approach to Forsen and went on to elucidate the theory for enlarging the bandwidth of the tiny spacetime discontinuities by utilizing tightly focused beams of exotic matter – the same that was used in the F-S Drive. Pavel admitted to himself with some reluctance that it was Forsen's astronautical engineering genius that had enabled them to build a prototype machine. But the idea had been Pavel's.

Enlarging the bandwidth and stabilizing signal transmission turned out to be a matter of building a large (by lab standards) negative mass accumulator and the associated power supply to energize it. That had been achieved without significant difficulties.

The more challenging trick was to make connection with the remote receiver through a spacetime discontinuity. This latter problem was solved, again at Pavel's suggestion but with Forsen's engineering skills, by homing in on the signal from a HyperNav navigation beacon such as was used in the existing HyperNav navigation system. Once convinced, Forsen built the cage-like focusing device to achieve this. It was only Pavel's resentment over the company's treatment of him that tragically blinded him from realizing what a great team he and Forsen made.

Forsen himself was not unaware of their potential as a team, and at first graciously put up with Pavel's occasional displays of resentment. After some trial and error they were successful in creating a holographic image of the downtown lab, homing in on a navigation beacon originating from there. The next step, far more ambitious, was to link up with Earth using navigation beacons. But that achievement only came after the discovery of the true potential of what they had. Oddly, in the flush of excitement over the successful transmission to the city lab, the obvious did not occur to them. What they did not at first realize was that the supposed holographic image inside the warp field projector was in fact a small hypersphere. One could insert far more than simple electromagnetic waves into that opening. It was Pavel who realized this through an odd twist of events.

Thinking back on the events of those fateful days a few months before, he rehearsed again to himself the amazing events that had opened a whole new future for him. They were in the Saturn Lab, doing some fine-tuning on part of the Telpher that produced the hologram – in the center of the cubical framework that was used to focus exotic matter beams. Hald had asked, "Pavel, have you seen my glasses? I think I may have dropped them on floor when I crawled into the viewer frame. But, I cannot see them anywhere."

"No, I haven't." He did not disguise his grumpy reply. To Pavel, Forsen's eccentricities were just another annoyance. Among these was his "old-fashioned" habit of wearing glasses instead of retinal implants. The glasses had similar capabilities as retinal implants in that they were network connected and provided optical scanning for control of appliances, etc. But surely, Pavel thought, they could not be as convenient as the more modern implants.

"You probably put them down on a workbench for some reason

and they got covered up by something else," continued Pavel.

"No, I don't think so. I am sure I had them on as I began adjusting the vernier on the visual receiver."

With a sigh of resignation Pavel walked over to the view frame and looked around. The holographic view of the downtown lab shone brightly inside the frame. He looked all around but saw nothing. "Sorry, Hald. They are not here. Why don't you look over on the bench?" With that he turned back to the task he was absorbed with. The exact mechanism of the focusing apparatus they had built, that allowed them to locate the other end of the Telpher communication channel, was still somewhat of a puzzle to Pavel.

"Tomorrow I am going to the city lab to check and make measurements on the energy levels of the navigation beacon there," he announced.

"That's fine. Give my regards to Allene and the staff there. It seems ages since I have been down there."

With a grunt of acceptance, Pavel picked up one of his mempads and started to leave. In a rather uncharacteristic burst of charity, he looked over his shoulder and asked, "Sure you're okay bouncing around the lab here without your glasses?"

"Yeah, I'll be okay. I've got an older set over there in my cubicle."

"Humph!" Pavel expostulated under his breath. "What foolishness."

The next day, Pavel left his apartment in the City about mid-morning. He treated himself to a leisurely morning ion shower, robo-massage, and a rich breakfast. Arriving at InterStellar's Verde city headquarters, Pavel took the tube to the lab level, and used a back passage to avoid having to greet Allene. She was just too nosy and he did not feel like making small talk. He went at once into the room where the navigation beacon sat. In a similar view frame as that in the mountaintop lab was an identical version of the holographic receiver. Pavel bent down to connect the leads of the energy spectrum analyzer he had brought from Saturn. Out of the corner of his eye he caught sight of a glint. There on the floor, under the holographic display, were Hald's glasses! Apparently Forsen had come to the lab earlier that morning and, foolish man that he was, once again dropped his glasses. He supposed Hald was in an adjoining lab, and was about to call out to him when the full realization of what had happened cascaded down upon him. "Hald!" he called out, just to be sure. But, there was no answer, as he knew there would not be. In that moment Pavel realized that what they had succeeded in constructing was no mere visual communication device. No, not at all. It was a type of teleportation device using quantum spatial discontinuities! Hald had somehow dropped his glasses "into" the hologram in the Saturn lab and they had been transported to the City Lab. The holograms in each lab were the hypersphere openings of a stable wormhole!

This was a discovery worth the highest scientific prize in the Galaxy, accompanied by significant fame ... and fortune? Not likely, thought Pavel. At least not for him as recent company history had shown. Forsen would get the credit, he figured, and what of himself? Fueled thus by his resentment and greed, Pavel decided to withhold this discovery from Forsen. He would look for an opportunity to leave the company and start his own with the knowledge of the invention. Meanwhile, he must prevent Forsen from discovering the real function of the device. First, he would bring the glasses back to the Saturn Lab and set them on a desk in a nearby room where Hald would find them and conclude that he must have left them there. Then Pavel would have to perform some kind of fix on their "viewer" when Forsen was not present so that its true function would be disguised. That would not be easy, he knew, but it had to be done. Forsen might be slow and methodical, but in time he would find out. Pavel had to buy enough time to perfect his understanding of the device to be able to recreate it for his imagined clients.

Pavel returned to Saturn Lab and smuggled the glasses to a room that Hald sometimes used. The ruse worked. The next day Forsen had his glasses back none the wiser it seemed, and they continued their research efforts on the Telpher to bring it to a commercial prototype stage. But Pavel started coming in on the weekends to experiment with the device when Hald was not around. He started small, moving little objects between the two labs. The City Lab setup was in a secure section that only he and Forsen had access to. It would not do for someone there to see items mysteriously appear. Pavel progressed to larger and larger items with continued success. He also learned how to control the size of the wormhole mouths at each end. The view frame and warp field generator could expand the hypersphere to about 50 centimeters in diameter, though in their initial experiments they had never increased its size that much. The eventual conclusion from these experiments was inevitable. Pavel began to wonder if a person could be transported. But even if that were possible, the hypersphere would need to be much larger and that would require more power to the negative mass accumulator.

Meanwhile, Forsen was not as slow as Pavel thought he was. He had continued to puzzle over how he had "lost" his glasses and then "found" them again in an adjacent office. Since the glasses had GPS functionality via their net connectivity he hit upon the idea of querying the central data bank at the lab to determine if it had records sufficient to track where the glasses had been on the day he lost them. Indeed it did, he found, and discovered that they were located in the City Lab for a day before again being located again in Saturn Lab on the mountain. Thanks to the neurochip implants that everyone had, he also found out that Pavel had been in the same location as the glasses on their "journey back" to Saturn Lab. It was time to speak to Pavel about this. Though he could hardly credit it to himself, the same realization that had occurred to Pavel some weeks earlier was forcing itself upon Hald's own, more peripatetic mind. Though he was slow by some standards, he was thorough. The germ of an idea eventually sprouted into full-blown understanding and then it was time to speak.

"Pavel, I have a question for you." They were working together to improve the focus of the image at the receiving end of the Telpher.

"Yes, what?" he answered somewhat crankily. Pavel was not in the best of moods that day owing to his inability to figure out how to get Forsen to agree to a larger power supply.

"My glasses. Remember that day I lost my glasses?"

Pavel was suddenly alert. "Yeah, so what?"

"Did you take them to the City Lab instead of giving them to me?" He knew that this could not have been the case since the data records showed them located in the City Lab at about the same time Hald had missed them. Pavel was still with him at Saturn Lab at that point. The truth was all but inescapable. But, he wanted to be sure. He wanted to know what Pavel knew and why he had hidden his knowledge from Forsen.

"I don't know what you're talking about."

"And why did you bring them back here the next day without

telling me what happened?" He ignored Pavel's attempted evasion.

Pavel began to fidget and looked away. Forsen obviously knew something but what did he know and how? He turned back, and attempted a half-truth. "I saw them on the floor and just put them in your office figuring that it wasn't important how I found them."

"Yes, I believe you did see them on the floor." Pavel let out a small sigh of relief. Forsen continued. "But, it wasn't the floor in this lab. It was the floor of the City Lab. Wasn't it?" He looked directly into Pavel's eyes, his anger mounting at Pavel's refusal to own up. At the same time his excitement about the discovery was growing.

Pavel blew up and stomped away, flinging back over his shoulder, "Holy shit, so you figured it out, didn't you? Smart guy, huh? But, who was it that discovered it? It was me, right? And who developed the key concepts? But will I get the credit? Certainly not!"

"Calm down, Pavel. No one is going to deny you credit. Though in truth this device is the creation of both of us. But I have no problem with sharing credit with you and even making you the lead inventor." Forsen's personality would not let him remain angry long. The implications of the stupendous discovery were swamping his irritation with Pavel. "Forget your petty grievances and think about this discovery. The magnitude of it is world shattering!"

At this point Pavel recovered his equilibrium enough to capitalize on the opening that Forsen was giving him. If he played it right, he could still prevent him from understanding what he planned. "Okay, fine," he said, speaking back in a softer tone. "I just wanted to be sure I got the credit, and I didn't know how you would react. I guess I made a tactical blunder."

"That's okay. Forget it. Let's move on. We need to figure out how to incorporate this development into something that will benefit the company."

Pavel rankled inside at this, but nodded with a shrug of apparent approval. Then, seizing the opportunity, he said, "We need more power to stabilize the wormhole. I've designed and estimated the cost of a larger power supply. What do you think, should I order it? I think Anders would approve it."

"How do you know it needs stabilizing?" asked Forsen, again suspicious.

"Okay, I'll admit I have been experimenting with it." How hard it was to humble himself to this man, but he had to do it to preserve his cover. "If you put objects larger than, say, your glasses, sometimes the wormhole collapses. We need more negative mass and that will take a larger power supply." He did not mention that this would also enable the device to create a larger hypersphere – one large enough for a man to enter.

Predictably, Forsen was angered at Pavel's admissions and said so. Pavel apologized and just waited for him to cool off again. He was gaining a better understanding of Forsen through all of this and learning to adjust his behavior in order to deceive him. As smart as Forsen was, he had a blind spot. Forsen could not see what was driving Pavel and he missed the clues as to what he was planning.

A new, and larger power supply was ordered and delivered. They continued to work together amicably for a while. They built a larger version of the warp field frame to move larger objects between the two labs. They also conducted further experiments to improve its stability. After about a month they had a device that could project a hypersphere about 1 meter in diameter.

Forsen was under pressure from company management to report progress on the hyperspace visual communication device they were working on, but the discovery of its teleporting capabilities had complicated things. Forsen was a perfectionist and wanted to be sure that what they had found was practical before disclosing the discovery to management. InterStellar policies around internal scientific research allowed considerable latitude with respect to disclosure of innovations. The policy was deliberate, as it promoted an atmosphere of secrecy as a means of protecting trade secrets. It also gave Forsen time to decide what to disclose and when to disclose it.

There were still occasional instances of wormhole collapse at unexpected times. These were often associated with attempts to move a more massive object than had been previously attempted. Fine-tuning the Alcubierre metric algorithm typically resolved these problems, but in a way that neither of them fully understood. It was more of an art than a science to get the device to accept more massive transports. More worrisome, however, were what appeared to be temporal anomalies.

Forsen was troubled by the incident with his glasses because he had noted a small chronological mismatch in the lab database time stamp versus that resident in the small memory chip in the glasses. He brought this issue to Pavel's attention one day but Pavel merely dismissed it with an insinuation that the microcomputer in Hald's glasses was at fault somehow. However, Forsen continued to investigate the source of these inconsistencies and found that they were associated with a sub-module of the HyperNav starship navigation system that they were using to position the other end of the wormhole in the City Lab. This was the more troubling because the same sub-module was deployed in the Generation 4 HyperNav that was used in the new, *Exeter*-class starships. That sub-module had been ported over from earlier versions of the HyperNav and had never before exhibited consistencies. Forsen suspected that the problem might be correlated with the larger mass of the objects they were teleporting, but his efforts to unravel the mystery were unsuccessful.

They got to a point that the one-meter diameter wormhole would remain stable regardless of what they put through it. Forsen was almost ready to make a cautious report to company management, when Pavel dropped another bombshell.

"Hald," announced Pavel one day, "We are consistently transporting masses of up to 80 kilograms. That's about how much I weigh. Why don't we see if we can transport a person?"

Forsen was stunned. "Absolutely not!"

"Why not? Think of it, Hald! It would revolutionize transportation, even space travel itself if we could build a powerful enough transmitter to transport people."

"You don't know what you are saying, Pavel. We have no idea what could happen to living organisms going through a spacetime discontinuity. That's crazy! Transporting goods and packages is okay. But not human beings!"

"Where is your spirit of adventure, Hald? How about we start out by putting an animal through the wormhole?"

"No, Pavel. I won't hear of it. Besides we have gone too far as it is without notifying management. I am concerned with the possible repercussions when they learn about what we have discovered, how far we have gone, and ask why we didn't notify them sooner. I am preparing a summary report now and I had hoped to finish it before going on my planned vacation. Unfortunately, I cannot finish it until I get back. In the meantime, you can continue to investigate the chronological problem and maybe by the time I get back you will have it figured out. If you do, that would be another feather in your cap."

Forsen hoped that this would motivate Pavel to forget his wild ideas of transporting people. Instead, it provided Pavel with just the opening he'd been looking for. He kicked himself for not remembering Hald's planned vacation. But, all was not lost. Adopting a subservient expression, he said, "Okay, fine. You know I don't think much of the supposed chronological problem, but since you are going to be gone for a while I guess I can consider it."

Forsen was relieved at this and proceeded to give Pavel some additional instructions for things to tidy up while he was gone. He wanted his report to management to be complete, with no loose ends hanging about. Pavel could help by documenting some of the more minor aspects of what they had learned as well as by cleaning up the lab area – there were assorted subassemblies lying about that had been tried at one point and later discarded. It would be good to have some clean photos of the device for his report. Assigning Pavel to oversee this would take his mind off his wilder ideas, Forsen hoped. However, just in case and out of a lingering distrust of his motives, he forbade Pavel from further experimentation. To enforce his proscription, Forsen locked the power supply for the accumulator with his own code. Pavel could still operate the HyperNav and investigate the chronological issue, but would not be able to transport anything.

* * *

Saturn Lab. Late February, 2376 GES

Despite Forsen's admonitions and precautions, Pavel was not to be thwarted from pursuing his own plans. Forsen's vacation gave him the time he needed to determine whether their device could transport people. It was something of a challenge, but he soon succeeded in breaking the code that locked the power supply. In an uncharacteristic step, Pavel took to heart Forsen's concern about the impact on living organisms. He tried a couple of experiments with animals before committing his own life to his project. Going out to the Greenwood Forest beside the lab, he trapped a grubbel, a small rodent-like denizen of the woodland that had not enough sense to avoid humans. He also got a lizard. The first attempt was with the lizard. Since it would no doubt scamper away upon landing in the City Lab, Pavel put it into a cage and then unceremoniously dropped it, cage and all, into the hypersphere opening. Looking into the hypersphere opening, the distorted image of the City Lab floor revealed to him that the cage had landed there on the floor – just like Hald's glasses some months before. But it was impossible to tell if anything serious had happened to the lizard. So, Pavel made a quick trip into town and brought the lizard back to the mountain. It appeared to be just fine. The next step was the grubbel, which he also placed in a cage. This time he put some padding in the cage as well to prevent physical injury to the hapless animal that might result from its falling to the floor of the lab from the open wormhole port. He first tested this by deliberately pushing the cage and grubbel off a lab bench in his own lab and satisfied himself that the resulting shock to the animal was not injurious. This experiment was also successful, the final proof being the grubbel's response after having been transported. When Pavel released it back into the forest it happily hopped away as if none the wiser that it had been the first warm-blooded creature to travel instantaneously through a spacetime rift.

With these experiments done and a couple of weeks remaining before Hald was scheduled to return, it was time for the crucial experiment. Pavel went into the City and placed mats on the floor beneath the hypersphere opening there. He was not sure how he might land when he went through it and obviously did not want to hurt himself. He also left a vehicle in the company aircar shelter for his trip back to the mountaintop lab. Back at Saturn lab he ramped up the power of the accumulator and widened the hypersphere to its maximum. Then, with the briefest of stomach flutters, he crawled into the opening. As expected, he fell onto the floor of the City Lab, where the thick pads he had prepared absorbed the energy of his fall. There was a momentary disorientation and a feeling of needing to vomit that lingered a few moments. That was all. He was there in the City Lab. Looking up and behind him, there was the hypersphere opening of the wormhole and in it a distorted image of the Saturn Lab from whence he had just come. Pavel was overjoyed.

As he drove back to Saturn Lab, the wheels were spinning in Pavel's head. He would try this transit to the City Lab another time or two. Then he would try for a longer distance – to Port Robis, some twenty-five hundred kilometers away. The company had an office there and he figured he could set up a tachcon beacon there without generating too much suspicion. This would allow him to position the other end of the wormhole. Yes, he thought to himself, Port Robis will be the next step but that is not the end of my experimentation. He wondered what Forsen would say when he returned and found out that Pavel was on Earth, instead of Verde, not having booked passage on a starship nor even having had time for the journey.

As with his teleportation between the mountaintop lab and the lab in the city, Pavel's journey through the wormhole to Port Robis was successful. It had taken some back and forth travel to set up a tachcon beacon in an unused storage locker in the company's Port Robis facility. Then, it took more time fiddling with the HyperNav to get a stable connection to the remote site. At the end of a week Pavel was ready to try the extended journey and was rewarded once again with only the minor discomfort of a short "fall" and brief stomach queasiness.

Now he was ready for the big one – a trip to InterStellar's headquarters on Earth. This would present yet new challenges, for there was no tachcon beacon at InterStellar headquarters in KCMetro and no opportunity to set one up. Instead, Pavel used the interstellar navigation system to obtain spacetime coordinates for Earth and from these and the Earth-based GPS system he obtained coordinates for the company lab. Satellite imagery provided him with knowledge of a flat-roofed building in the company complex. This was a good spot for an inconspicuous landing, he hoped. There appeared to be a rooftop entrance to the building below, which should assure passage to the ground level. It proved to be somewhat difficult to establish the other end of the wormhole in this fashion but eventually he succeeded in doing so. To prevent injury, he tried to position the remote hypersphere as close to the rooftop as possible. He also wore pads on his knees and elbows to help prevent serious injury. He would time things, he hoped, so that he would arrive at night and arrive unobserved. However, in truth, he was not sure exactly how he would do that. He was not so foolish as to ignore possible relativistic effects over so great a distance, but his recklessness and greed had all but overcome any real sense of caution at this point.

Whether or not Forsen would accept his next great discovery, Pavel was certain that his future was all but assured.

He succeeded in "imaging" his destination on Earth but the largest size of the hypersphere that he could obtain was 20 centimeters. Apparently, this was a restriction imposed by the much greater spatial distance involved. To overcome it he needed to increase the power to the warp field generator. That took some modifications to the negative mass accumulators, and he had to re-route power from one of the lab's emergency generators. After reconfiguring the power supply and increasing the size of the power cables he produced a one meter hypersphere, as before. The image of the other end was somewhat fuzzy, and seemed to change contents in a slowly revolving panorama that resembled a slow-motion vid of a building being constructed on an open field. Soon the image stabilized in what he presumed was a view of his desired destination. A wormhole between Verde and Earth was now achievable.

* * *

Saturn Lab. March 7, 2376 GES

There was no time to lose. Forsen was due back in a matter of days, Pavel thought, and he needed to take this last step to convince him of his aspirations. On Friday he had made necessary arrangements for being gone for a while, including informing Allene in the City office that he had to visit a sick relative in Port Robis. It was late Sunday afternoon on Verde when Pavel completed his preparations at Saturn Lab for the big journey. After verifying the focusing of the hypersphere on the Telpher, he toggled the power to the accumulators and watched the hypersphere expand to a glowing portal into the future – his future! With scarcely a thought of consequences at this point, other than his own grandiose plans, Pavel crawled into the opening in the Verde laboratory and disappeared.

Chapter 14. Telpher

InterStellar Corporate HQ, Verde City. May 7, 2376 GES

Ruder, Forsen's assistant, was on vacation but Jame had planned to go out to the Saturn Lab anyway to continue investigating the strange device that Forsen and Pavel built. It seemed they had succeeded in creating an audio-visual navigation device that could transcend the Einstein-imposed limit on the speed of electromagnetic communications by taking a shortcut through a higher dimension. Jame was torn between returning to Saturn Lab and his other obsession: finding out what had happened to *Exeter*. Deciding on the latter, at least for today, Jame went to his office downtown. He would just have to divide his time between searching for clues to the apparent failure of the *Exeter's* warp drive navigation system and tinkering with the Telpher device in Forsen's lab.

The news, unbelievable and still not public, that somehow *Exeter* was transported back in time, led Jame to further investigate the design details of the F-S Drive. Perhaps something there, he thought, would suggest a direction to pursue in ferreting out the apparent flaw. The company library was the first place to start, and Jame began to search the design documentation stored there to get a better handle on the engineering specifications for the Drive.

Library archives contained semi-detailed descriptions of the exotic matter engine and the tachyon guidance system that seemed to further establish the fact that the F-S Drive had changed very little in concept at least in the three centuries since it was developed. There was less detail on the navigation system than for the engine. Jame chalked that up to the fact that investors from the rocket engine business, who had little interest or expertise in tachyon communications, had founded VentureStar. Nevertheless, it seemed strange that neither Frankel nor Spinoza were expert in tachyonics.

As he delved deeper into the design documents for the Drive, Jame came across a footnoted reference ascribing the origin of the tachyonic navigation system to a physicist named Sergei Levkov who had worked for a company called HyperDrive. "So that's it," he thought. "This is the missing link to the origin of the tachyonic navigation system." But having said so, Jame was nevertheless perplexed. He thought back to his recent trip to Earth during which he had read up on the history of the Drive on board *Draconis*. He was certain that the shipboard history archives had made no mention of someone named Levkov or of a company called HyperDrive. Deciding to double-check this, Jame put in a request to the central computing system located in the Verde HQ building. He asked for company history records, believing that these would be the same ones he had accessed while on board ship, since shipboard media were routinely kept up to date by downloads from the company's central database. What he found deepened his disquiet about the fate of *Exeter*.

The corporate library records quite clearly documented that VentureStar's assets and intellectual property had been secured from a company named HyperDrive. They also noted that a prototype of both the Drive itself and the tachyonic navigation system had been developed by a brilliant physicist named Sergei Levkov who had worked for HyperDrive until his untimely death in the explosion of that first prototype. The records further stated that after Levkov's death, details on the design of the drive and navigation system had been lost. However, two bright assistants of Levkov's, Jonas Frankel and Edwin Spinoza, continued the work and within two decades were able to reconstruct most of what they had learned under Levkov. These two made refinements to the negative mass generator that Levkov developed, believing that this was the source of the explosion that killed him. They also determined that his tachyon guidance system was still very serviceable and therefore incorporated Levkov's guidance and communication system code.

From that point on, the history was what Jame had previously understood it to be. Frankel and Spinoza were the fathers of the F-S

Drive that was still in use today, the only odd thing being that someone named Sergei Levkov had mentored them. That aspect of things had not been in the shipboard records Jame perused on his trip to Earth in February. Jame was puzzled and resolved to check the archival records on the library of the ship at his first opportunity. He also wondered that he had never heard of, until now, one Sergei Levkov – especially since the development of the F-S Drive had involved his death. That was not something that folks would forget, even over the space of three centuries! Obviously company historians had not gotten something right.

Frustrated with his exploration of Drive design particulars Jame returned to Forsen's lab the next day. He was anxious to continue exploring the Telpher, and had a growing sense that there was more to it than met the eye. He and Ruder had succeeded in turning it on before Ruder left on vacation. They had been amazed to see a hologram of the home planet, Earth, in the middle of the cage structure. But, the hologram had been small, 20 centimeters or so wide. Yet, the cage itself was two meters in height and width. Jame wondered why.

It was a Saturday so Jame had the lab to himself. It was possible, he thought, that since the Telpher appeared to achieve hyper-spatial audio-visual communications with Earth based control centers while in warp drive, components of the device might have been included in the Gen-4 HyperNav used by *Exeter*. Perhaps, he thought, this device would help him solve the *Exeter's* navigation system anomaly. Upon further reading of the mempad "instructions" he discovered what appeared to be two modes of operation for the device. The brief notes seemed to indicate that each mode was associated with the up or down orientation of a funnel-shaped icon in a crystalline vidscreen on the navigation console. Jame activated the device in the manner that he and Ruder had discovered a few days ago.

The cube lit up, and now Jame observed that there was a funnel icon on the vidscreen pointing down. The hologram showing the Earth appeared in the middle of the cube, as before. Moving his finger over the crystal, he found that he could reorient the funnel icon to a position pointing up. At that, the hologram disappeared. Now, however, tiny lights on what he assumed to be the navigator's headset came on with a steady green glow. Jame reoriented the funnel icon again to the down position and noted that the headset lights, which he had not noticed before, were now flashing orange. The hologram of Earth reappeared in the cage. "Well," he said aloud to himself, "I suppose that is some sort of progress. But, I wonder how to get the device to image other known navigation centers in the galaxy?" The mempad instructions didn't seem to address that. He decided that Forsen and Pavel must not have implemented communication links with other centers yet.

Referring back and forth between the mempad instructions and the control console itself Jame was able to make changes to the holographic display. Manipulating one of those controls Jame found that he could zoom into very small areas on the Earth's surface. As he did so he realized that the device was "focused" on a portion of the North American continent, but he had no control as to the center of focus. He could only zoom in closer, and as he did so he recognized that the focus point was centered on the location of KCMetro in North America Federation, the Earth headquarters of InterStellar. So that's it, he thought. They have another receiver at headquarters and have been testing the device that way. He wondered that Forsen had not mentioned this when he was with him a few weeks ago.

Thinking just then of Forsen and that strange interview, happening as it did on the heels of the stunning news of the disappearance of *Exeter*, plunged Jame into a funk. He got up and paced the lab a bit, wishing to himself that he had never gone to Earth, and that he had never been there to hear the bad news. That was silly, of course, for anywhere else he would still have learned of the ill-fated mission. He turned off the machine and left the lab. He needed some fresh air and a change of pace. Boarding his aircar, he instructed it to take him to the Blend Center in downtown Verde. It was Saturday night and there would be music and dancing and people having a good time. One of his favorite bars was just paces away from the central plaza where he knew there would be plenty of action to distract him tonight.

* * *

As his car approached the City he could see the iconic green and blue floating globes above the Blend Center Plaza. They were of various sizes and hues – greens and blues mostly with a burgundy or rust orange globe mixed in here or there. Ambient temperature superconducting magnets levitated these and on weekend evenings they were lit up from within by powerful gallium arsenide LEDs. Both the superconductors and the LEDs received their power from microwave antennas stationed atop the high buildings surrounding the plaza. The largest of these globes was two or three meters in diameter and viewed from below on the plaza they made a dazzling spectacle as they rotated and cast tinted beams of refracted light in all directions.

The Blend Center, so named because it was dedicated to the enjoyment of people of all ethnos, ages, and social stations, was unique in the Galaxy. No other city or planet had such a large variety of entertainment, shopping, and intellectual stimulation all in one place. Moreover, Verde was further distinguished from most other planetary societies in its heterogeneous mixture of humankind. Many of the planets that humans had colonized in the last two hundred years tended to be monolithic, mostly because financing for those colonies was government money from sympathetic nation-states on Earth. Verde had been one of the first colonies and was established before the wars and social disruptions on Earth in the latter part of the 22nd Century. These had divided the already fractured planet into hardened zones of religious or cultural persuasion. The earlier mission to Verde had been undertaken under the direction of a more enlightened humanity, one that was still able to mount international efforts to explore the frontiers of space. No more, Jame sadly reflected. The North American Federation itself was still something of a melting pot, but Verde was the shining jewel of that multiethnic exodus of earlier times. The other populated regions of Galaxy, for the most part, were havens for one or another crusade or opinion. Of course, mankind had barely landed on galactic shores. Its penetration amounted to just a few hundred parsecs from Earth-home whereas there were tens of thousands of star systems yet to be explored many light-years distant from Earth. Perhaps a new generation of explorers from a planet like Verde would turn the tide and spread a more enlightened humanity into the uncharted regions.

Jame landed his aircar at one of the public park quads. A parkbot glided up as he exited the car. Jame surrendered the car's control chip to the automated unit, receiving in turn an identification wafer for when he returned. He strode to the elevator tube and stepped onto the moving platform. Sensing his presence, the platform accelerated to a comfortable downward speed and Jame was soon at ground level. The jangled sounds of competing music venues and excited conversations greeted him as he exited the conveyance onto the great central plaza, amid groups large and small of happy celebrants. The wondrous globes overhead welcomed him into a world of sensation and forgetfulness. Tonight, he thought, he would cast all his cares aside and just enjoy himself – something he had not done in a long time.

Jame elbowed his way across the crowded plaza and turned down a side street. There at the end of a short block was his bar, the Oort Cloud. It was a corny name for a bar, but they served a good daiquiri with the juice of a Verde-grown lipon. The rum, however, was imported from the Caribbean region on Earth and that made all the difference. The bar also was home for many Verde singles, like himself, and he knew he would likely run into one or another of his lady friends there. It had been a while since he had enjoyed a soft-spoken and uncomplicated interlude with someone of the opposite sex and he was looking forward to it.

* * *

On Monday Jame returned to the lab, refreshed and with a new resolve to understand how the Telpher worked and what connection, if any, it might have with the *Exeter*. He slowly went through the startup procedure, following the mempad instructions. The hologram of earth appeared in the center of the large cubical frame next to the navigation seat. Using what he had learned the day before, Jame zoomed in on what he supposed were company headquarters on Earth. He was also able to enlarge the hologram a little so that he could make out some of the details. Expecting to see the communications center at I-S he was somewhat surprised to see that the view was of a laboratory. This took him aback because he had thought the Telpher would allow him to contact a spaceflight control center – perhaps one on Earth since the hologram inside the cage showed Earth in miniature. But it was clearly a laboratory, not a spaceflight control center. There was someone walking around in the lab, a woman it appeared. She had on a white garment of some kind. A lab coat? The details in the laboratory were strange to him but there was not enough clarity in the image to understand all that he was seeing.

Jame attempted to improve the image, adjusting first one control then another, with little success. At one point he succeeded in extinguishing the holographic image altogether, and it took two hours to regain it. The controls on the Telpher were difficult to understand. Moreover, the device had an instability, which manifested itself at random moments.

As he perfected the focusing of the hologram he began to wonder if he might be able to speak to the woman who appeared in the lab. He assumed that was what the navigator's headset was for and put it on. Its lights were flashing orange, as before. He tried speaking into the voice boom and watched the image of the woman for some sign of recognition. There was nothing. Then he remembered that the headset lights turned green when the funnel icon was oriented up. Reaching to the vidscreen, Jame selected the up position. As he did so a strong sense of vertigo washed over him and he blacked out momentarily. What happened next he was never quite sure.

What Jame experienced he could only describe to himself as looking through a spherical window into another world, like almost being there. The window had replaced the hologram in the cage and had increased in size to almost a meter in diameter. The image was distorted as if he were looking into a polished sphere. Except, instead of seeing his own image, he saw the same woman he had seen in the small hologram in the middle of the device cage. The laboratory looked antiquated and Jame was confused about that. Nevertheless, thinking that he had established contact with someone in the InterStellar labs on Earth, Jame spoke into the headset's voice boom.

"Hello, this is Jame Anders, CSO InterStellar, calling from Saturn Lab on Verde. Do you read me?" The woman in the spherical window seemed startled and looked toward him. Her mouth moved but Jame heard nothing. Jame thought there might be something wrong with the settings on the audio portion of the device and looked for an obvious control. But there was nothing. He spoke into the headset microphone again, still to no avail. Frustrated, he reached for the control knob that had enlarged the hologram. With caution he advanced the control. The spheroid began to expand until it almost filled the cage, some two meters in diameter. The image of the woman was quite distinct, though distorted at the edges. Just at that point, however, the Telpher became unstable and the hologram collapsed. Exasperated, Jame gave up on his efforts and went back to his apartment in the city.

* * *

Throughout the week, with repeated visits to the Lab, Jame progressed in his understanding of how to control the image projected by the Telpher. By the weekend he had succeeded in achieving a stable image. So he once again attempted to establish communication with the woman in the lab. With the navigator's headset on he expanded the spherical hologram to its full extent of two meters. Again he spoke into the voice boom but heard nothing. However, this time the woman turned, and her image in the spherical window enlarged. He spoke again but she did not seem to hear. Then he saw that the funnel-like icon was now in the down position. He flipped it up and immediately wished he hadn't.

There was a loud slam of a large relay closing and a rising, almost violent humming noise as the power supply to the device ramped to full power. Something seemed to snap, the lab lights blinked and then went out. There was a muffled thump next to him, then nothing. The Telpher had gone completely inert and the power surge had taken down all the lab lights and machinery. In the total darkness Jame could see nothing. Then he heard something that sounded like a whimper and a kind of shuffling noise next to him.

Overcoming a momentary paralysis, Jame began to remove the headset and fumbled around for the portable light he had noted earlier under the control console. Finding the light, he switched it on and swung its beam around the lab toward the floor of the Telpher cube.

Chapter 15. Dreams

Kansas City, Early Summer 2069 CE

A year had passed since Sergei's death. Sonja had renewed in earnest her research on detecting extraterrestrial signals from advanced civilizations. The mystery of the message from 54 Piscium continued to energize her, if not her colleagues. Nevertheless, despite a rejuvenated enthusiasm on her part, Mother Nature was as uncooperative and unsympathetic as usual. Amidst equipment malfunctions and distractions necessitated by other work – work that gave her needed income – Sonja made little progress in the one area of real interest to her.

At length she decided that the new apparatus – the equipment that Sergei designed for her – would need to be repowered if she hoped to intercept thoughts without the use of a large radio telescope. With the help of a couple of post-docs she accomplished this. With the greater power of the transducer, she hoped the small ten-meter dish at the university would be adequate. She also updated the neural network coding in the fMRI-based headgear she wore. Some recently published brainwave research had suggested to her a possibly more effective means of connecting with the cortical centers in her own brain that she surmised related to her own powers of mental telepathy. It was a stab in the dark, and one that she did not dare discuss with colleagues. But she was desperate for success and had an ever-increasing intuition that she was about to make a breakthrough. With continued perseverance, the missed goal of physically spanning the vast distances of space in her lifetime might be replaced by doing so mentally.

As she began testing the device in her lab she started having unsettling experiences, which she came to associate with the redesigned headgear. She experienced strange and troubling dreams at night. As the dreams became more frequent they became clearer, resolving themselves into recognizable sequences in which she was on a green-colored planet speaking with another scientist there about some problem with a spaceship. Sonja at first chalked the troubling dreams up to the stress produced by her expanded work schedule and perhaps a lingering disappointment over the events of the last year. She debated with herself over what to do. Half of her, the reasonable and practical side she associated with her father, told her to give it up -- she was possibly doing real physical harm to her brain. The other half (she did not want to "blame" her mother for this, but there it was) said to press on. And she did. She pressed on.

One night in her laboratory while she had the headset of her device on her head and the telescope pointed to 54 Piscium she fell into a strange trance. At least that is what she called the experience later. In the trance, one of her recurrent dreams seemed to come very much alive. There was a man standing in her lab in front of her. He appeared to be speaking to her, but she heard nothing. Though she did not see the man enter her lab, she assumed that to be the case until he vanished and she came out of the "trance." This both excited and troubled her. Could it be that she had achieved telepathic communication with a human being on a planet many light-years distant? Was that man responsible for the radio signals they had heard years earlier?

Sonja felt that she could not discuss these events with Dr. Spitzer, or any of her colleagues. And, mention of it to the post-docs on her team was out of the question. The phenomena were just too weird and were unsupported by any known scientific theory. To give them any scientific basis at all would require relating the phenomena to the work of Alliander. On the surface of it this would be reasonable, but it entailed significant personal risk for Sonja. It was fine to discuss extra-sensory perception in the research trials of others, but to associate it with her own research, in which she was of necessity the subject, would expose her own abilities. Moreover, it would raise questions of scientific objectivity. This she was not ready to do – at least not with any of her colleagues. But, there was one person in the world with whom she could speak about this. Someone, in fact, with whom a discussion about her mental telepathy was long overdue.

* * *

As Sonja exited the Maglev at the Eisenhower station, she wondered at the commercial development that had taken place since she had last visited with her mother. She was a bit ashamed to admit to herself that it had been over three years since she and her mom had gotten together. They kept in touch by texting or email from time to time, at holidays and birthdays and so forth. But a certain, indefinable distance had grown up between them over the past fifteen years or so. For a while, right after her father died and her mom was alone in Toronto and Sonja was in school there, they had been close – recalling in fact the special time of her childhood. But then Catherine decided she could not take living in Toronto anymore, with its many associations with happier days. And she needed something to do with herself. Catherine had a law degree as well as a bachelor's in graphic design, neither of which she had used much after Sonja and her brother were born. But armed with a new sense of purpose Catherine had one day set off on a "self-discovery journey" (as she called it) and began an extended tour of North America. Sonja had not heard from her for weeks at a time. Then one day she got an email from Catherine saying that she had "landed" in Alexandria, Virginia, and had taken a job in the North American Federation Patent and Trademark Office located there. Now retired from the PTO, she had stayed in the condominium she had purchased that was just three blocks from the Eisenhower Maglev station and equally distant from the office of the PTO.

Sonja shouldered her overnight bag and walked down Eisenhower Avenue the short distance to Catherine's condo. She passed a large new mall, put up since she was last here, which was opposite the Federation Science Foundation building. Seeing the FSF building brought uncomfortable memories of an earlier period of her career to mind – the grant she and Dr. Spitzer had received to perform studies at Green Bank. That was shortly after she had gone to CETL. The world seemed young and alive and exciting then, compared to now. Sonja wondered how she was going to approach her mother with what she knew she had to get out in the open.

Catherine buzzed Sonja into the building lobby and Sonja took the elevator to the 14th floor. Feelings of expectation and a certain weariness battled in Sonja's heart. She hesitated, then knocked at the door from which hung a large blue and red wooden geometric collage. After a moment, the door opened.

"Sonja! Dear, wayward child! Come in, come in." Catherine was a petite woman in her late sixties, and looked her native Irish to the core. A small turned up nose and rose-petal lips accentuated a round, cheery face framed in curly red hair. Hair that was beginning to show streaks of gray. She had aged well and was in excellent health, owing to both her genes and her daily regimen of health food and extended walks around Alexandria.

"Hi Catherine, it's good to see you now, at last." Sonja entered the apartment and dropped her bag in the entryway. A small kitchen was on the left. The hall continued directly into a large living area, surrounded with plate glass windows on two sides offering a magnificent view of Washington, DC, the former capital of the United States in pre-Federation days. The third wall featured a number of Catherine's graphic design works, including another collage similar to the one on the front door. It was lavender, ochre and steel gray and somehow resembled the skyline of a city. Toronto! Yes, it resembled Toronto as seen from the CN Tower. This was new, hung there since her last visit to see Catherine, and showed that she was energetically involved in her retirement activities. Catherine had returned to the graphic design of her college days after leaving the PTO.

"Sonja, child. Look at you!" Catherine took Sonja by the hand into the living area and led her to an overstuffed couch into which Sonja gratefully sank. "You are tired, dear girl, aren't you?" *Poor thing, what has she gotten herself into now? My sweet angel ...* The words crashed into Sonja's already overworked mind. Of course, she knew this would happen. At the bottom of it this was why she did not want to visit her mother very much. She still had that mental telepathy connection with her and, frankly, some of the things that Catherine thought as she was getting older were just unappealing to Sonja, to say the least. Sonja had found that engaging in direct dialogue with her mother helped to keep the other communication path shut down, so she responded immediately, cutting off the words that were likely to come after *my sweet angel ...*

"Hey, I'm okay. It was kind of a long trip this time." Sonja straightened the light blazer she wore and pushed an auburn lock back in place, a bit overly conscious of how she might appear to her mother. For an artist, a graphic design artist at that, Catherine was very neat and tidy. "The Maglev had a major breakdown in Columbus and they had to sideline us for three hours to let other trains pass while they made repairs to the one I was on. Sorry I'm later than I told you. And, oh, I'm also sorry it's been so long since I've been to see you." In spite of the difficulties that sometimes had been occasioned by her telepathy as well as the strangeness of her mom's new hobbies and friends, Sonja loved her mother very much and wanted so much to somehow return to the happier days of closeness. The days before her father died, when she was still young and full of vision and expectation of a bright future. Where had those days gone?

Catherine looked directly into Sonja's eyes at that, saying, "No need to apologize, Sonja dear. I also wish we could be closer, you know, but you have your career and I need to be doing what I am doing here. Anyway, here you are and I am glad! Can I get you a drink or something to eat?" Catherine got up and walked to the kitchen, which was separated from the living room by a small dining area and a counter over which they could still see each other.

"Just some ice water ... Catherine." She had almost said "Mom" but before she could reflect on that Sonja realized what her mother had just said. Had she indeed said something about also being closer, the very thoughts that Sonja had been thinking? Did her mother have ...? No, that was not possible, unless she had developed something recently. Sonja had long ago conducted little "tests" to see if her mom or anyone in her family could read her own thoughts. They couldn't, at least as far as she knew. Yet, her mom had certainly just picked up on Sonja's thinking. So how ...?

"Here you are," Catherine brought a tray with a pitcher of water, a bowl of ice, and a plate of small crackers and cheese. Sonja loved cheese and crackers and hungrily popped a cracker and slice of cheese into her mouth while pouring herself a glass of water. She was hungrier than she thought.

"Now, tell me what's really bothering you Sonja. I know it's something related to your work, isn't it? It isn't that one-time boyfriend of yours is it – the one who got himself killed going where mankind is not meant to go? I thought you had gotten over that."

"No, Catherine, it's not about Sergei. And the "boyfriend" business only lasted a few months in grad school – ancient history. Yes, he was a friend and colleague, though rather self-centered and strange. You may not agree with what he did, but it's the future Catherine. Humanity must go to the stars …"

"Okay, okay. Let's not go there again. We agreed last time to disagree on that and there is no need to bring it up again. I apologize for bringing him up. I was just concerned that you hadn't gotten over that … tragic event." Catherine's softened her voice to let Sonja know she was sympathetic with what Sonja went through right after the disappearance of the space ship. She had not seen Sonja since then, but they had spoken by phone once or twice. Catherine did not know the full extent of the hell that Sonja had gone through for almost a year – Sonja had never shared that with her.

"Good. I agree. We don't need to go there again." She paused, then continued, "So, to your question: It's not about Sergei but it is about something related to what Sergei was trying to do. I mean, my work in trying to communicate with civilizations that may be out there in our galaxy somewhere. I know you don't believe there are any, and that's fine. I'm not even sure myself, or wasn't, until I had a strange and very upsetting experience with my equipment in the lab. And, I haven't been able to tell anyone about. In my research group, I mean. Or anyone, for that matter. It's really weighing on me, I guess."

"Well, regardless of what I think about your work, it would probably be good to talk about. Do you want to tell me? I promise I won't be critical, if that will help."

"Thanks Catherine. But first I need to talk about something that very much relates to those experiences. At least I think it does. It's about other experiences I have had – experiences from my childhood." Sonya gave her mother an expectant look, hoping that her mom would be willing to listen, in spite of her relative antipathy toward Sonja's work. It was the telepathy part that she wanted – desperately needed – to talk to someone about.

Well, ETs or not, I'm happy you're here dear child. You're looking prettier already … Aloud, Catherine said, "Honey, I'm glad to listen to you about your work and the problems you're having. It doesn't matter what I think about outer space, stars, and such."

This was a relief to Sonja, but she still hesitated, asking herself how do I get this out in the open? What if her mom had the same reaction as her childhood friend? "Catherine, this is difficult for me, but I have to do it. Promise me you won't judge me until you hear me out?

"Yes, dear, I promise." Looks like another weird boyfriend deal, who isn't really a friend – just a sex partner. Sometimes I wonder what these kids think a real relationship is. Sonja needs a good man, like her father. She isn't getting any younger.

At this torrent of thoughts entering Sonja's mind, she could no longer resist. And, in a way it gave her the perfect entrée. She looked pointedly at her mother's gentle, smiling face and said, "No, mom, it's *not* about another weird boyfriend deal, who's just a sex partner." Catherine opened her mouth to say something. Cutting her off, Sonja continued, "Moreover, I'm glad you would like me to find a good man like father was. How I'd love to also – I just haven't, yet. I'm sorry to have let you down ..." At this, Sonja broke down in sobs. All the tension of the past few weeks burst forth in a level of weeping that, for Sonja, was so uncharacteristic. She had not meant to say that bit about finding someone or about letting her mom down. She wasn't even sure why she had said it. But there it was, and now she was crying her heart out.

The words that Catherine had been about to say disappeared. Instead, she rushed to the side of her daughter and put both arms about her trembling shoulders. "Oh, Sonja, sweetheart, I'm so sorry I said that. Please forgive me." She hung on to Sonja as her sobbing slowly abated.

Sonja turned and looked to her mother. Her emotions calmed and she regained control. Whatever had just happened inside her quickly passed, like the swiftly moving thunderstorms that sometimes traversed the prairie lands of Kansas City. "You didn't *say* anything, Catherine. You thought it – and that's okay. Don't worry about me or the man thing that I can't quite seem to get a handle on. That's not the point. The point is ..." Sonja looked into her mother's soft, blue eyes, "The point is that you thought it and I *heard* it. Isn't that the thing we need to talk about?" Again Sonja was reminded of her own culpability in this whole thing. Why hadn't she told her mother long ago?

At this, Catherine gently released her daughter and sat back on the couch. "Yes, Sonja, it is. When you started crying I was about to say, how did you know what I was thinking. But, I know how you knew. I guess I've always known, or suspected at least."

"You know about this, this …"

"Gift," Catherine finished the sentence for her. For if that is what Sonja had, it surely was a gift, and not some pseudo-scientific sounding thing like ESP or something like that. "Oh, I don't know about it, dear, in the sense of understanding it. But, I've long suspected that there was something, well, different about how you related to certain people you knew. Myself, for example. Some of your friends in school when you were young. I wondered why but could never quite figure it out. Now, after all these years, in thinking back I realize that you and I had some sort of 'connection.' I don't know what else you'd call it. Even just now, earlier in our conversation, I felt some kind of, some sort of, well some kind of mental connection with you. Not that I could read your thoughts or anything, but, I don't know … Do you know what I mean?" Catherine looked at Sonja hopefully.

Sonja was amazed. Was it really going to be that easy? She was so sure her mother would have a fit when she learned that all these years Sonja had listened in on her thoughts. Not intentionally, and usually with substantial unhappiness at having been so exposed. But, against her will, exposed nevertheless.

"It's called mental telepathy, Catherine. I have the 'ability,' some would say, to hear in my head what people are thinking. I've had this since I was a child and first learned to speak. But, it's only certain people whose thoughts I can hear. You were the first, and it was with you that I learned that I had this … . You called it a gift and maybe that is what it is …" She broke off, feeling a welling of tears about to overtake her again, whether now from joy or sorrow she didn't know. Regaining control, Sonja forced herself back into the mode of the dispassionate scientist. "It was with you that I learned I had the ability. And it was with that unfortunate incident with my school chum, Susanne, that I learned to hide it. Do you remember that time that they all ganged up on me in *Secondaria*?"

"Yes, I remember well. You don't know, and I decided to not tell you, but I spoke with the headmaster afterwards. He told me that the girls had accused you of stealing their thoughts. He thought it was ridiculous and didn't believe a word of it. I don't think he even understood what they had been trying to say. However, I kind of tucked that away in my heart and thought about it from time to time." Catherine gave Sonja an encouraging pat on her shoulder. "You see, I too am glad to get something off my chest. I didn't know how to talk to you about it at the time, but now in God's providence it has all come out."

There were long moments of silence between them, as both women put old thoughts out of their minds and nurtured the dawning of a new relationship. Sonja turned and hugged her mother. "Thank you, mom, for sharing that. And thank you for not pushing to find out why I wanted to change schools. I would not have been able to talk about it at the time. Now, I can."

"So, now can you tell me what's been happening with your work – the thing that has been upsetting you? You looked so frazzled when you arrived this afternoon, and I must say you look a lot better now."

"Yes, I think I can tell you. At least, I can try. But, you will have to suspend disbelief in 'ETs' as you call them, at least for the sake of understanding what I am about to tell you."

"Fair enough, honey." Her mother was genuinely listening now and this gave Sonja added courage. She then went on to describe the strange dreams and the trance she had fallen into. She related it to the apparatus she was using and her mental telepathy. "I'm sure it was my gift, as you call it, because the 'contact' I felt with the strange man in the laboratory trance was exactly like the feeling I get when I hear the thoughts of another person. Now that I think about it from a distance, the man himself did not speak but the feeling of connection was there. How strange!"

As she now related these events to her mother, Sonja felt that there was another individual involved in the connection. Then it burst in upon her.

"I know who I was in contact with," she exclaimed to her mother.

"I know. You said it was a man, a scientist of some kind in a strange laboratory setting."

"No. I mean yes, it was some kind of man. But he isn't the one whose thoughts I was hearing. It was a woman. And I know her name. Her name is Jana. I didn't remember this when I came out of the trance. But now, telling you about it, I remembered."

"Where was she? Did you see her too?" Catherine was getting

more interested, now that there were names of people. In spite of herself.

"No, I didn't see her. She wasn't in that laboratory place. She wasn't ..." Sonja struggled for words. "She wasn't ... *anywhere*! And, now I can't remember what she was saying, or thinking I guess. I just don't remember."

"Well, maybe it will come to you later." Her skeptical side returning, Catherine continued, "Is there anyone in your group at the university, or among your friends and acquaintances that has a name that sounds like 'Jana'? It is a strange name, I grant ..."

"No, Catherine, I don't know anyone with a name like that: Jane, Jana, or anything close. Your unbelief is showing up again. No, I am convinced that those experiences are real somehow. However, as a scientist, I must grant you that they might not have the origin that I, admittedly, am pre-disposed to think they have. But, consider this. You remember the brouhaha a few years ago about my group's discovery of so-called intelligent transmissions from outer space?"

"Yes, honey. I felt so bad for you at the time. But, you got over the exposure of the fraud, right? It was one of your grad students that perpetrated it, wasn't it?"

Sonja stiffened a bit. "No, it wasn't perpetrated by a grad student. And, I don't believe it was a fraud. That's what some of the news accounts said, but it's not the truth. The truth of the matter is that we, at least I and one of my grad students, we believe it was real but we were never able to explain it and still haven't been able to do so. Yes, I lost some reputation but I've gotten over that part of it. Here's the important piece, though, for what I've been sharing with you. You know that I use my apparatus in conjunction with a radio telescope, right? That's like a visual telescope for looking into the night sky but it receives longer wavelength signals instead of light waves." Catherine nodded. Sonja continued, "Well, that night I had the university's radio telescope imaging the sector of space from where those signals had come. Those signals that everyone thinks were a fake." Actually, not everyone she thought, remembering her trip to Caltech and Xander Abraham. And, that brought to mind something else she wanted to ask her mom about.

"Catherine, do you remember anyone by the name of Xander Abraham, someone who would have been a close friend of father's? It would have been before you and father met, but he may have spoken to you about him."

A pained look passed across Catherine's face, which Sonja noticed. "No, Sonja, I never knew anyone by that name. Your father rarely spoke of his life before we met. It was a shame, because I had the impression that he had, well, quite an interesting life. I would have loved to hear about it, but it seemed that he was perhaps ashamed of it. I think he was pretty wild in his school days. That streak was still in him and it's one of the things I loved about him. Though it never came out in public – if you know what I mean?" Sonja smiled and nodded, amused and appreciative that her mother would allude to an aspect of the intimacy she had with her father.

"That's not all of it, though, is it?"

"No, dear, you picked up something, didn't you?"

"Not really. I did not read any thoughts, that is. I just thought I saw a hurt on your face at the mention of that man's name. But I won't push you on it. Let me tell you why I asked." With that, Sonja recounted the episode on the campus of Caltech. Catherine listened intently. With a sigh, she said, "Okay, its true I never met Dr. Abraham. And, it's a shame he did not contact us after your father's death, as you say he intended to. I think it would have been a comfort to both of us. But the reason for my denial just now, and the pain at the mention of his name, is that your father's dying words to me as he struggled to speak after his heart attack were 'Tell Xander I'm sorry.' I've never told anyone. I didn't understand it, anyway. But, it hurt me at the time because I loved him so and his last thoughts were of someone I had never heard of – instead of me, or you and your brother! I'm sorry that seems so selfish – but it's true anyway."

"Mom, that's okay. Father loved you, I know for sure. I guess he felt the same guilt that Xander felt. When you're dying maybe you start thinking about all your life and things that never got settled. He was confident of his love for you, for us, and ours for him. So that wasn't an issue for him. But he regretted what had happened between him and his college friend. Anyway, it's all taken care of now, what with Xander coming to me and settling the score. Don't you think so?"

"Yes, dear, I do. Let's forget about it. Want to go out to get something to eat? Oh, I forgot to tell you something. Your brother is coming tomorrow. You'll still be here, right?"

"Oh, that's perfect!" She bounced up off the couch and smiled at her mom.

But, as they left the apartment, Sonja's thoughts were not on Tony. They were far away in the stars where there was a woman named Jana – she was sure – who wanted to speak with her about something important.

* * *

Sonja started awake, from a deep sleep. There had been no bad dreams, a welcome event. At first she did not know where she was. She looked about the strange room, then remembered that she was in her mother's home, in the guest bedroom. The events of the previous day flooded briefly into her mind, giving her a warm glow. She felt close to her mother once again. Then she remembered that her brother was coming today. What a joy! I haven't seen Tony in such a long time, she thought. He's been all over the world, travelling and doing … what? Whatever he felt like doing, I guess. He was always a free spirit, so unlike anyone else in the family.

After breakfast and a leisure morning of chit chat, Catherine suggested they walk down to the Torpedo Factory where Catherine had some of her graphic design work on display. Tony was to meet them for lunch there around noon. The walk, a few miles round trip, was one of Catherine's ways of staying active and in shape. They walked down King Street in Alexandria, toward the Potomac River. Catherine remarked that old town Alexandria had seen better days a generation ago, before the War, before she came to live there. She was a member of a civic organization that now was trying to rejuvenate the town. They were having some success. A few new establishments were open, catering to a slowly growing tourist trade. But many of the restaurants that had once been busy with visitors as well as locals were still boarded up and the streets were in disrepair. The relocation of the Federation capitol from Washington to Kansas City had put a large dent in the tourist trade. The free shuttle bus no longer ran down King Street.

The Torpedo Factory was still there, however, and still functioned as a center for local artists and artisans. So named because it had been an actual factory where torpedoes were manufactured during World War II, its warehouse-like building had been converted many years ago to house art galleries and workshops. Catherine had a little workshop there as well where she worked on her unique wood and metal collages. This was all new to Sonja as the last time she had visited her mother was still working at the PTO and had not been active in the local art community. After showing Sonja around and introducing her to a few friends and colleagues, they walked the short distance to the banks of the Potomac and strolled along the river path. The Washington Monument could be seen in the distance across the river. It was a sunny day, cool with the approaching fall. Late summer flowers still bloomed in the planters spaced along the river bank park.

"What will you do with your work, when you return?" Catherine asked. "I mean, do you think that talking through the experiences you've been having has helped you? I'm not sure I can relate to your idea of where they are coming from, but I agree with you that it is related to your gift."

"I don't know, mom. Getting the telepathy thing out in the open between us has helped me feel better. And it helps me get some perspective on what's been happening to me. For the first time last night I didn't have any bad dreams, and that is a good thing. But I still cannot bring this matter to the attention of my colleagues at work without risking my own career. Paranormal abilities in human beings is becoming an accepted field of research, but there is still a lot of prejudice and downright fear for many people. It just bothers people to know that someone might be able to read their thoughts, and that is understandable. I didn't ask for that ability and I've pretty much learned how to handle it with those people with whom I have this uninvited access. But, to come out in the open about it – that is just still too scary for me."

"So, will you just stop your researches in that area," Catherine asked, trying to be sympathetic. She wished Sonja would put it down and was aware that Sonja knew that's how she felt.

"I can't do that, Catherine. I've got to find out more about that man who appeared in both my dreams and in that trance. But, I will try to make some adjustments to my apparatus to reduce the signal intensity. Perhaps I am stressing my own cortical sensors in an unhealthy way."

"Oh, I hope you will do that, Sonja. You could really be hurting yourself without knowing it."

"Yeah, I'll do that. And, I'll do another thing. I will keep more closely in touch with you about how I am doing." She hoped that this would ease her mother's worries and indeed it seemed to. There were no more anxious thoughts bombarding Sonja from her mother after she said that.

They had made a circuit up and down the river park and had returned to the Torpedo Factory. It was just noon and Sonja looked anxiously about for her brother. Then she saw him, entering from one of the street entrances and strolling casually across the open terrace toward them.

"Tony!" cried out Sonja.

"Hey, Sis. Wow …" Tony grabbed his sister and gave her a big hug with both arms around her. "Hey, mom. Hugs for you too." Tony's curly black hair flopped over his eyes, hiding for a moment their green color. They had always teased Tony about being a Cheshire Cat on account of his eyes, a much brighter green than Sonja's deep emerald. Six years younger than Sonja, Tony was a little taller than her, a stocky build, and muscular. His given name was Antonio, but it had always been just "Tony" from early adolescence. He looked very much like his father. His speech was effusive, accompanied by an endearing way of moving his roughly sculpted hands. He stood back and surveyed the two most special women in his life.

"Well, Sis, finally we get together. How long has it been? Eight years? Something like that."

"Not my fault, bud. I've been here all that time. Well, not here, but in the middle of the country. You know, the capital of the Federation?"

"Yeah, yeah, I know. You know how it is, though. I just can't abide the politics and the arguing and bickering that goes on about how to put everything together again. So, I hide out in strange and mysterious haunts in all the forgotten places on this planet." He winked. "But, you're right. I could have come to see you. Sorry!"

"It's all right Tony. I'm just so happy to see you again." Sonja smiled broadly, her eyes twinkling as she gave him another big hug.

Tony turned to his mother and gave her another hug as well. She pecked him on the cheek but said nothing, a small tear forming in her eye. She had seen Tony more recently than had Sonja, but it had still been awhile.

"Let's eat!" Tony fairly boomed. "I'm hungry. I didn't have any breakfast and I just got off the train from New York." He had just flown to North America from Greenland, he later informed them. They found a restaurant a block away from the Torpedo Factory, one that had just opened up. It specialized in seafood, a not uncommon fare. During lunch Tony filled Sonja and Catherine in on some of his more recent adventures and there was a fair amount of reminiscing as well. When lunch was over, Catherine spoke up.

"Listen, kids. You need to have some quality time together, just the two of you. I've got some business over at my studio and after that I've some shopping to do. Why don't you just hang out together this afternoon and let's all meet again at my condo this evening. I'll do something unusual – prepare dinner for us all!" With that, she excused herself, leaving Tony and Sonja to talk over coffee and dessert.

"Now, Sis, it's your turn. "You've been too quiet, letting me do all the talking. I know you're into something big – I can see it in your mysterious eyes. Come on, spill the beans!"

"Oh Tony, you're such a phony," she teased. "You don't actually care about astrobiology and such stuff. You barely passed biology in secondary school."

"Yeah, but I do care about space. You know, *outer* space. I may not have been around when that stuff went down about the signals you heard. But I read about it and I was floored. I don't care what others were saying, I just know there was something to that. Somehow, it was real. Don't you think so too, even though others, you know ..." His normally effusive tone of voice took a more empathetic turn. "Well they put you down over it, didn't they? Did you give up? I hope you didn't."

"No, Tony, I did not give up. I always thought there was more to it than we, any of us, could explain. And lately there seems to be some sense of destiny in it for me, though I don't understand what that may be."

"Well, tell me about it. Maybe I can help you understand. I know mother doesn't believe in ETs, as she calls them. But I do. There's just got to be more out there – we aren't the only intelligent species around."

"You won't find any argument with me on that, though there are some – scientists and the like – who might agree with mother. Not out of the religious reasons that she has, but more on a logical basis. As in, 'if there are other intelligent species out there in the universe, how come they haven't contacted us,' to paraphrase a famous scientist of the last century. Myself, I'm just not sure about it. It's true that you would expect that with all the habitable planets around the millions of suitable stars just in our own galaxy alone there would have arisen life on some of them. Given the great age of the galaxy, billions of years, there would certainly have been time enough. But, then, that argument has a counter thought. Our own civilization here on Earth is just a few thousand years old. And, from appearances, it sometimes seems as if it could self-destruct any day now. In a billion years many civilizations such as ours could have come and gone. So, maybe just now, we are the only extant one. I don't know." She reached across the table and took hold of her brother's chiseled hand. "But, thank you Tony for your support. I do believe there was something there. And, I believe that I am destined somehow to find out what it was." She thought of Xander Abraham and his odd words to her.

Sonja went on to fill Tony in on some of the things that had been happening to her. She didn't mention the telepathy bit. She'd never had a "connection" with him and didn't want to complicate things at this point. But she told him about the trance she had fallen into and the mysterious man in the lab. Tony was rapt with attention, and admiration for his brainy sister. His encouragement was also a great strength for her. As they walked back up King Street toward Catherine's place, they held hands. You might have thought they were lovers at this, but if you had heard their excited conversation and seen their glowing faces you would have known they were brother and sister, happily sharing their explorations of the world they shared. It would be the last time Sonja saw Tony, or her mother.

Chapter 16. Through the Looking Glass

InterStellar Saturn Lab, Outside Verde City. May 16, 2376 GES

Still staring at what the flashlight beam revealed on the floor of the Telpher cage, Jame heard the whine of a distant generator, the lab's independent power source. Then amidst a rapid series of clicks from the closing of relays, the lights began to come back on, starting at the far side of the room. Blinking from momentary blindness caused by the sudden light, Jame tried to focus again on the lab's new occupant. There at his right, where the holographic display and spheroid had been, and were no more, he saw the source of the scuffling noise. On the floor, inside the cubical frame, was a woman lying curled up in a fetal position with her hands and arms wrapped around her head and face as if to ward off an attacker. She had a white lab coat on. Somehow, he was certain, it was the woman he had seen in the lab in the hologram. For long moments Jame just stared, unable to speak, unable to move.

Then came a rush of revelation. The strange appearance of the woman's lab in the background as he had tried to image the scene in the spheroidal hologram, the distortions at the edge of the sphere. It suddenly made sense. It was not a 3D hologram, not at all! No. It was four-dimensional, a hypersphere, a portal in spacetime! And the lab. That wasn't the InterStellar lab on earth, it was some other lab in some other place. Moreover, it appeared to be a lab in some other time. The plight of *Exeter* thundered in his mind and Forsen's worried statements about chronological sequencing skittered across the landscape of Jame's dawning realization. He was utterly floored at what he now began to understand.

Had Forsen known what his machine was? It appeared to be some kind of teleportation device. This woman had been transported here from another place and another era, an earlier era judging from her antique surroundings! As she slowly uncovered her face and looked up at him, a face full of wonderment framed by delightful auburn hair and set, as it were, with beautiful emerald eyes, he mustered his warmest smile and said, "Welcome to the 24th Century!"

Sonja was terrified at the events of the last few minutes, and even Jame's warm smile in no way calmed her fears. "Who ... who are you?" she managed, her voice squeaking. She tentatively moved to sit up, not sure whether another violent dislocation would happen to her as she did so. Jame leaned to give her his hand, from which she at first recoiled in panic. Eventually she took his still-outstretched hand and stood up, mastering the shakiness that threatened collapse.

"My name is Jame. I am Chief Scientific Officer for InterStellar Dynamics. And, who may I ask, are you?" Jame was enjoying this more than she was, probably because he had a bit more background on what had happened. Though shocked at what had just occurred he was adjusting to the fact of it. He waited, but she seemed to have not heard his question. Instead, she was looking about the lab eyes wide in awe.

"Where are we? I mean, where am I? What lab is this? Is this another part of the University?"

Jame pondered a moment how to answer. She obviously did not realize what had happened. Jame himself was still in a state of semi-disbelief. He decided to try an indirect approach to ease her into the truth, at least what he thought was the truth. "Where do you think you are? That is, can you describe where you were a moment ago and what you were doing?"

That seemed to help. Sonja folded her arms across her chest. Then she spoke, "I was in my lab at CETL in Kansas City. I was carrying out one of my experiments designed to detect signals from ..." She looked at him, hesitating. "Signals from space. There was a bubble sort of thing that appeared in my lab. As I looked it began to grow in size and it seemed transparent. I mean, I could see a laboratory in it, all distorted, and I thought it was my own lab. But it wasn't." She looked around and rushed on. "It wasn't my lab, it was another lab." She paused, realization hitting her. "It was this lab!"

"What happened next?" Jame asked, genuinely curious. He needed to understand what had happened as much as she did.

"It just got bigger and bigger. The bubble, I mean. And for some reason I was drawn to it. I heard a man's voice – not audibly I believe, but in my mind. I couldn't understand what he said." She looked at Jame then with recognition. "It was you I heard, wasn't it?" Another pause, a brief moment of panic, eyelids batting quickly. Then, "Anyway, I wanted to see that lab better. I wanted to know what I was seeing. So I, I ..." she faltered.

"You stepped into the bubble, right?"

"Yes. Yes, I did. I knew it was a stupid idea, but I was curious and I did it anyway. Now what am I going to do? Where is my lab? How do I get back there?"

"Sorry, but I'm not sure I can answer that."

"What did you say?" Sonja's face turned ashen.

"I said I didn't think I could answer your question."

"No! Before. Before, when I was still lying ... there." She cast her eyes with despair to the floor of the Telpher cage.

Jame hesitated, trying to remember. "I think I said: 'Welcome to the 24th Century!'"

Sonja sagged at that and Jame had to put out his hand to keep her from collapsing back into the cage.

"The 24th Century!" she repeated, eyes wide. "Do you mean, the Future?"

"No, not my future. But, apparently yours." He smiled again.

"Oh." Sonja just could not quite get hold of the conversation. She sat down in the navigation seat and put her face in her hands. This was all just a bad dream, she was sure. Yes, that's what it was – a bad dream. It was, in fact, just like the dreams she had been having of late. Only this time the dream seemed dreadfully real. But it couldn't be, she assured herself. It just could not be that she had somehow travelled into a far distant future. This was all just a bad, bad dream.

"Come now, it's not that bad," said Jame. "We here in this century are probably pretty much like the folks in the century you came from, whatever that was. And, by the way, you still have not told me your name." She was quite beautiful, striking in fact.

She looked up, attempted a smile, and said, "Sonja. My name is

Sonja. Sonja Bellesario." Then, in answer to his unasked question she said, "And, where ... I mean, when, I come from is the 21st century. The year 2070, to be exact. And I am ... was, I guess, an astrobiologist at North American University in Kansas City."

"Oh? You mean on planet Earth?"

"Of course, on Earth. Where else?" But an ominous sensation arose in the pit of her stomach as the truth dawned on her. "You mean this is not planet Earth?" As initial feelings of alarm gave way to an ancient (it seemed) dream she wondered: Had she really travelled to the stars? Yet this wasn't at all the way she had wanted it to happen. How would she ever explain this to her colleagues at CETL? In her animated state Sonja missed the obvious absurdity of this question and the impossibility of such a dialogue taking place.

"No, I'm afraid not. This is the planet Verde, orbiting the star Adonis, which is some 300 light-years from Sol. Your home system. I believe in your day Adonis was catalogued as Kepler 1213." Perhaps unnecessarily, he added: "Verde is the fifth planet orbiting Adonis and was settled from Earth about 100 years ago."

Sonja was mute, trying to sort through the wild kaleidoscope of thoughts cascading upon her mind. It was simply too wonderful yet too insane to get hold of. She barely heard Jame's succinct summary: "It appears that you have travelled through some sort of wormhole into a world light-years and centuries distant from your own." He did not add that it was likely she would not be able to return, for he hadn't a clue how he had managed to get the Telpher to accomplish this feat, let alone reverse it. One thing was clear: the Telpher was far more than the hyperspace communication system Hald had made it out to be. Surely Hald must have known this, yet why had he not told Jame?

* * *

The arrival of Sonja Bellesario had thoroughly upset Jame's world. Reasonably addicted to a pattern of orderliness, Jame was now faced with a series of unexpected duties and detours. In the most immediate sense, he had to attend to Sonja's care and feeding, as it were. She was an exceptionally bright scientist, he realized, and a quick learner. But over three centuries of human progress and social norms stood between the world of her birth and the galactic civilization she had now joined, albeit involuntarily. She was like a fish out of water, and there was no going back. Besides, he didn't want to. For the first time in his life a woman had caught more than just his passing fancy.

The first things were to find a place for her to stay, provide her clothing that did not bring stares and unwanted comments, teach her the rudiments of social and civil interaction in Verde society, etc., etc. Jame, the consummate manager, was up to this of course, but it pretty much consumed his thoughts and daily activities to the extent that the search for a solution to the *Exeter* disappearance had to be put on hold. A more challenging task, at least for Jame, was to disguise Sonja's true origins. For it surely would not do for anyone beside himself to know just how she had come to Verde. This would betray the existence of a machine that, if it were truly what it appeared to be, could thoroughly revolutionize human galactic commerce. Moreover, it would have profound consequences for the business of his company, InterStellar. Before going to his management, Jame needed to understand more – a lot more – about the origin of the Telpher. In particular, he needed to know how much two other people knew about it. And neither of those two people, Hald Forsen and a mysterious assistant named Pavel, were anywhere to be found.

In the meantime, Jame solved the most immediate problems associated with establishing Sonja in 24th century Verde society. Julia Friend had been Jame's first flame (and he, hers) after he returned to Verde from graduate school on Earth. She had been a pretty wild woman in those days, bouncing around from one social scene to another (and one man to another it turned out). Now she was living alone in a fashionable neighborhood near the center of Verde City. After her affair with Jame (and several others) Julia found some kind of spiritual discipline that led her into a rather tame lifestyle, at least comparatively. Owing to its liberality, Verde society was rife with a variety of religious and other non-conforming groups, all of which were tolerated with a good sense of humor – usually. Some had strange habits in public and odd dress that made them stand out. Julia's sect was normal in appearance, however, and frankly Jame could not perceive much difference at all from, say, his own lifestyle.

They were still close friends and from time to time called upon one another for a favor or just a night out in companionship. Julia was discreet and not overly inquisitive, the perfect solution for Jame's current dilemma. With no questions and only a raised eyebrow once or twice, Julia had taken Sonja in. Jame had originally considered passing Sonja off as a member of a new cult to explain her odd dress and mannerisms. However, he abandoned that idea as he knew Julia would immediately see through it, leading to even greater suspicion about what Jame was up to. Instead, Jame called her in advance to appeal to her own sense and value of privacy – all would be explained in due time he promised.

In a matter of days Sonja and Julia had become fast friends. In addition to a significant level of discretion, Julia had a gift of hospitality. Her gracious acceptance of Sonja's odd manner of speech and clumsy ways as she adjusted to her new home took an immense load from Jame's shoulders and allowed him to concentrate on some longer-term acclimatization issues. One of these was the need to get Sonja her own TASC, for without it she would not only stand out in Verde society as completely helpless, she would also be at risk for personal harm.

The TASC enabled all 24th century humans to communicate with and control their external (and even internal) environment. All humans had implanted in their visual cortex a glass-encased nanoprobe. This was usually performed at birth or soon after, though there were sometimes exceptions for medical or other reasons. The probe interfaced via miniature embedded superconductors to a subcutaneous microchip that mediated visually directed interactions with all manner of everyday devices and conveniences through the omnipresent planetary, and even galactic, man-machine interface networks. You could not function well in society without a TASC. Getting one for Sonja and then teaching her how to use it presented a major hurdle, one that Jame could not solve without revealing why she did not have one. At least, so he thought. This was the subject of an animated discussion among the three of them one evening in Julia's apartment a few days after Sonja's arrival.

Julia had just served dessert, one of Jame's favorites: Verde orange-plum compote garnished with banamint leaves. The three of them, Julia, Jame and Sonja, were comfortably situated in mag-lev chairs that floated in an informal semicircle in the center of Julia's modest living room. Fully two-thirds of the surrounding walls were transparent glass providing a spectacular panorama of Verde's night skyline – all from the 40th floor of Julia's apartment. Indirect lighting from the gallium arsenide-paneled ceiling and room climate control powered by the building's perovskite skin kept the cool autumn weather at bay and gave a sense of comfort that Sonja desperately needed. She was still very much in the throes of sensory overload and a social alienation that she had never thought possible. In lighter moments she mused over Lewis Carroll's *Alice in Wonderland* in an effort to comprehend what had happened to her. In darker moments she just stared off into space. Tonight was proving to be a somewhat lighter moment, thankfully.

To Sonja, Julia was a beautiful woman, probably a few years older than herself, though it was hard to tell. Well proportioned, even for her apparent age, she wore a shimmering, gray-green sheath that reached to the floor, revealing only the narrow, sparkling straps of delicate sandals. At the neckline of this simple yet effective gown, she wore a circlet with three bright stones. It was the only flashy aspect of her attire – she wore no other jewelry. If her face was made up, it was artfully done, showing neither age nor youth. Her hair was jet black, and cropped close, a fashion that Sonja had noticed was prominent among women of Verde – to the limited extent that she had seen so far.

The dinner conversation had been innocuous but lively, flitting from the latest fashions among the youth ("crazy!" – in the eyes of both Jame and Julia), to the weather ("unusually cool this fall"), to local civic improvements ("new skyway signage for aircars in the city is beginning to be so numerous as to present safety hazards in some places"), to the latest "shows" in vidstim ("bizarre," they all agreed, though Sonja did not have a clue as to what vidstim was). While these topics may have been light and inconsequential to her hosts, to Sonja they were occasions of one eye-popping revelation after another. The more so, because the one wall opposite the sitting area of Julia's otherwise minimally furnished home, appeared to be something like a huge, 3D TV screen. It was continually updated with vibrant moving pictures and shallow holograms portraying aspects of the conversation taking place. At that point, Sonja was unaware that those pictures were being projected and controlled by Jame and Julia as part of their animated conversation.

It turned out that Sonja's ignorance, although unfortunately evidenced, provided Jame with a segue into the subject that bore heavily on his mind. He found the opportunity to shift the tenor and direction of the conversation when Julia returned to the table with seconds of compote and fresh coffee. She gracefully presented the tray of refreshments first to Sonja, then to Jame.

Recalling the discussion about traffic congestion, Sonja summoned the nerve to speak up. "Jame, I was wondering how you drive those marvelous aircars. That is, I assume they drive themselves, of course ..." She started to add that on Earth they had driverless cars as well, but bit off the words as they were about to form on her lips. Jame had warned her not say things that would betray her unlikely origin. It was too late to take back what she had just said, so in spite of this warning, she had to follow up with something. "I mean, when we got into the car to come here, how did the car know where to go? I didn't hear you speak a command or see you enter any coordinates on the drive panel." In vain, she hoped her question would sound innocuous enough.

This was one of the few occasions in the evening in which Julia departed from her neutral stance regarding this strange woman. She shot Jame a sharp, questioning look. Clumsy as it was, this was the opening Jame needed.

"Sonja doesn't have a TASC," he announced, looking pointedly at Julia and ignoring the ensuing look of puzzlement on Sonja's face.

"Excuse me, Jame?"

"I said, 'she does not have a TASC'." At this, Jame smiled warmly at Julia with a hint of their old intimacy in his eyes, hoping that this would keep the conversation from going into dangerous territory.

"Ohh ...," responded Julia, recovering her tact. With barely a noticeable shift in demeanor, she negotiated the situation artfully. "I was wondering about that, in fact. I know you asked me to not take Sonja out and about, but I just thought she ought to see the City and besides I had to do a couple of errands. So, I ..."

"Shit, Julia!" Jame was frowning intensely.

"I know, I know – I'm sorry! Without a TASC ... Now I understand why she almost walked onto a landing ramp as an aircar was approaching. Fortunately, I caught her hand and pulled her back just in time." Julia shot an embarrassed look at Sonja, whose face was beginning to match the color of her hair. As Sonia attempted to cross the landing ramp a TASC, had she had one, would have sounded a jarring alarm in her auditory cortex.

"I'm sorry Julia," Sonja stammered. "I didn't know that's what it was. I just wanted to see the clothing in the store display on the other side and thought I could take a short cut."

"Hey, no worries," said Julia. Then, looking directly at Jame, she said, "It's your dumb benefactor's problem, not yours. He should have told me your TASC was broken. Jame, sometimes you are just a clumsy ... engineer!" She was about to use a nastier word but softened at the last moment.

"Not broken, Julia." Jame ignored the unfair insult. "She doesn't *have* one. Sonja does not *have* a TASC – never had one in fact." The repeated statement was blunt, in a tone of voice that warned Julia away from asking why and at the same time somehow let her know once again that all would be explained in due time.

"Okay, Jame. Whatever, whatever ..." Julia knew there was something very odd going on here, but with her moderate personality she just could not get up enough steam to care about the full explanation for it all. Instead, she ignored the obvious question and turned to a more practical one. "So, how are you going to get her one? She cannot possibly survive here without one, and I can't babysit her every day." Then, remembering that Sonja was listening, she turned and favored her with a soft look saying, "Don't take it personally, honey. It's not that I don't like you or anything like that. It just wouldn't be practical."

Sonja managed a small smile at that. "I understand, Julia ... I think." Then, to Jame, she almost squeaked, asking in a small voice, "What is a 'TASC'?" At this, Jame ignored Julia's audible gasp and proceeded to fill Sonja in on the details of the socio-economic technology of her new world. Having explained it in enough detail to satisfy Sonja's need for the moment, without causing more questions to arise in Julia's mind, Jame turned again to her.

"Julia, remember that friend of yours? The guy you, uh, took up with after me. What was his name ... Turnip, or something like that?"

"Tornit. Tornit Sayre." Julia stared icily at Jame. Jame gave Sonja a nervous glance, an action that was not lost on Julia. Julia continued, her voice taking on a cool tone for the first time that evening. "And, lest we bring up old wounds, Jame, why don't we leave the matter there. At just his name." She looked at Sonja and then back to Jame. Tornit Sayre had been a big mistake in Julia's life. He had been the reason for her having broken up with Jame, though she had never told Jame that. She and Jame had supposedly just revised their relationship by common consent, telling each other that they did not want to have the level of intimacy that was beginning to occur between them. The truth was that Tornit, who turned out to be a very different character than he first appeared, had momentarily swept Julia off her feet. Eventually the physical attraction between them wore thin and Julia discovered who Sayre really was. By that time Jame had moved on and it was too late to return to him in the old way. In time, after finding herself, she and Jame had entered a new kind of friendship. But it still sometimes hurt to think she might have missed something very satisfying with Jame. It was looking rather obvious that that something might be about to happen between Jame and this strange, new visitor from Earth. It was odd. Julia couldn't escape a sense of great age when she looked at Sonja, though she was clearly about Julia's own age. There was just something almost antique about her. What could Jame see in her, she wondered. She momentarily thought about Jame's twin sister, Jana, whom she had met once and who had a fascination with old stuff, like vids from the 20th century.

"Sorry, Julia. I don't want to bring up old wounds, or anything. Sincerely ..." He adjusted his tone to one of concern for her. "But, I just was thinking about what he was into. Wasn't he some kind of brain surgeon, free-lance or something?" The medical establishment on Verde frowned on free-lance practitioners, but the law permitted their practice as long as they passed annual exams.

"Yes, he was – is – an independent surgeon. She preferred the adjective independent and she knew Tornit certainly did. Not that she cared much about Tornit's preferences. He was an accomplished brain surgeon but a thoroughly incompetent human being. There was also something shady about his medical practice as well, though Julia had never discovered any evidence of wrong doing. Just a feeling, that was all. He had secrets. Then it occurred to Julia why Jame had thought of him.

"Okay, now I know where you're going with this, Jame. You want Tornit to place a TASC probe into Sonja, and do it on the QT. And, you want me to be the go-between. Right?" There was a clear hint of anger in her voice.

"Yesss ..." Jame hesitated, looking to Sonja who was showing evidence of alarm at both the rising tension between Julia and Jame and the idea of needles being stuck into her brain. Needing to say two things at once, Jame chose a brief response to Julia first then quickly attempted to assuage any fears on Sonja's part. "Sonja, it's a totally painless operation and one that is routinely performed on an outpatient basis. Sometimes the probe that is inserted at birth requires repair or replacement later. So, there are established facilities and practices everywhere to do this." As an afterthought, more to Julia than to Sonja, Jame added, "It's just that we cannot have the doctor wondering where the original probe was or why it was missing. And that is why I thought of Turnip."

"Tornit, Jame. Tornit. And yes, of course that's why you thought of him. You knew about his lack of ethics and you never approved of my relationship with him in the first place, did you, even though we had agreed to ... Oh forget it!" Flicking one of her finely molded hands in his direction, Julia turned away, afraid that she was going to lose control. There was an uncomfortable silence. Sonja did not comprehend what was going on, but understood that Julia had been hurt. She gave Jame a sour look.

But Jame was not to be dissuaded. "Look Julia, I'm sorry. Really, I am. I just need your understanding and forbearance at this point. It's not about you and Tornit. It's Sonja's safety that's at stake here, and for reasons that I cannot discuss right now we cannot go to one of the state hospitals for this. I do appreciate your taking Sonja in, and I guess this is just one more favor to ask." He tried to sound a sympathetic note at this.

There were more moments of silence before Julia turned back to them. She looked at Sonja however, not Jame, and said, "Don't worry, honey, we'll get you a TASC. I don't understand the need for secrecy here, but I understand Jame's intentions ...," she paused, before continuing, "... which are good." Julia glanced briefly at Jame and smiled weakly. Continuing, she said, "As an interesting matter of fact, I just happened to have heard from Tornit last week. He wondered if we might get together for lunch someday."

"Well, that's an obvious coincidence," Jame put in. Sonja wore a strained expression but said nothing.

"I put him off, of course. But it won't be a problem to call him back and tell him I changed my mind. Of course, it won't be just my favorable acquiescence to what he wants that will convince Tornit to not report anything unusual about Sonja when he does the procedure." She gave Jame a knowing look at this last statement.

"I understand, Julia … How much do you think?"

"I have no idea. I'll let you know after I see him, okay?"

"Okay. And thanks for the sacrifice."

At this Sonja spoke up, "Jame, I don't want to be that kind of burden to you. Is there no other way? Why don't we just tell people what this is all about? I would think it would be exciting …"

"No!" Jame cut her off before she could continue. He thought she had understood the need for caution about not revealing where she had come from – that is, when she had come from. It was okay for her to be from Earth, best in fact, but 24th century Earth and not some other time. Sonja's disorientation was affecting her otherwise excellent judgment. Although he was not entirely sure why, there was something very wrong about the whole series of events involving Forsen and Pavel. Until he found out what it was he just felt at a gut level that he needed to keep secret what he knew about the Telpher's true capabilities. Telling the authorities that Sonja had come from the 21st century Earth, assuming that anyone would even believe him, would clearly not serve the need for secrecy.

Sonja backed down and Jame turned once again to Julia. "Again, dear lady, I apologize for all this secrecy, and I thank you for your forbearance. Someday I hope it can all be revealed. When and if it is, you will be the first one I come to with an explanation. Okay?"

"Done, Jame." Julia smiled, more broadly now, having fully recovered her almost regal poise, to Sonja's surprise. "Don't have a further care. I will have lunch with Tornit and let you know the outcome."

* * *

The matter of Sonja's TASC was soon settled, though it set Jame back a bit. Luckily, with no dependents to support, he had amassed a substantial nest egg. In any event, Sonja had her own device within a week, no questions asked, and was speedily learning to use it under tutelage from both Julia and Jame. Though he wanted to turn his attention back to matters at the lab, with the Telpher and its apparent relationship to what happened to the *Exeter*, Jame realized that Sonja's arrival had given him a needed break from the tension of the previous weeks. It was a difficult decision, but in the end he decided it would be good for them both to show Sonja a little more of her new world. One day, after a stroll through one of the shopping areas of Verde, with both Julia and Sonja, Jame suggested an extended tour of the planet.

"Sonja, you've seen most of the important parts of Verde City. How would you like to see some other cities, or some of our famous landscapes in the countryside?"

"That would be wonderful, Jame. Can Julia come too?"

"Sure," he said, though he had rather hoped to have Sonja to himself.

Julia came to his rescue, however. "No, no. You guys go by yourselves. I assume you'll go in your private yacht, Jame, and you know how much I don't like flying around the planet in those things." This was true. Aircars were bad enough, but at least you had a sense of weight inside them all the time. Both aircars and transport yachts used anti-gravity engines. But the yachts drew energy from the gravitational field itself and could thus traverse long distances and go to greater heights. They were faster too. Because of the more intense field distortion associated with the operation of their engines during acceleration, which made it feel like you were on a roller coaster, pleasure yachts made some people nauseous. Julia was one of those people.

"That's fine, Julia, I understand." Turning to Sonja, he said, "How about I pick you up at 0900 tomorrow morning?"

Showing some concern at what Julia had said, Sonja was about to offer another suggestion when Jame reassured her. "Don't worry. If you get airsick we will turn around. It's a very small percentage of people that react to the a-grav engine. Unfortunately for her, Julia is one of them."

"Okay Jame," Sonja made up her mind. "Let's do it!" In truth she was excited at the prospect. All her professional life she had wondered what other planets would be like, and particularly the intelligent species that may have evolved on them, and how their "culture" (if such a word could be used of non-human, yet sentient beings) may have been impacted by a physical environment that was different from that on Earth. Here was a world rather different from Earth in its geology, its flora and fauna, its weather, and so forth. Yet no sentient species had evolved here. She wondered why. She held no illusions that one journey about the planet would yield an answer to that question – it would take years of research perhaps. Research, no doubt, that had already been undertaken by her Earth-born successors. There would be time enough to peruse the scientific journals of this age in whatever libraries Verde had. But for now, a first-hand look at a wider swath of her new home would suffice. And though it was Earth-born beings, or rather their descendants, who inhabited this world, there was plenty about Verde society that was strange and different. The social compact on Verde had to have been in some way affected by factors unique to the different planetary environment in which it thrived, and not merely the effect of several centuries of Earth-centered social change. Jame's proposed expedition would give her a chance to at least observe and speculate on some of those factors.

The next morning began as every morning had so far – bright and clear, basking in Verde's orange-colored sun. Inside buildings, when she was with Jame or Julia, Sonja could almost forget that she was on another planet. But outside there was no mistaking it. The planet Verde was very different from Earth. The cooler sun had led to the development of a different biosphere. There was still a profusion of color in the plant life, but the colors were darker and greener. Much of the flora had more black in them – particularly the leaves. She conjectured that the solar radiation reaching the surface of the planet was richer at the long wavelength end of the spectrum. A super abundance of red light, compared to Earth, would mean that the absorption spectrum for plant chlorophyll would be shifted to the longer wavelengths. Verde flora may have evolved to make more efficient use of red light than Earth vegetation, absorbing even less of the green portion of the star's light reaching the surface and making plants greener in appearance. The greater preponderance of black was more of a mystery but she reasoned that there would be a stronger infrared component in the solar radiation than in the visible spectrum. Black leaves would make the plants more efficient in capturing the energy from their star. However, she would just have to wait until she could get to a library or whatever passed for such here to verify her guesses.

Jame picked her up at Julia's and they took his aircar to the city's space terminal – at least she reasoned that's what it was. A large vessel – a spaceship of some sort – was just landing. The odd thing was, there were no visible rockets. She was still getting adjusted to the fact that humans had conquered gravity. Of course, she recalled with a start, that was what Sergei had been working on. She realized that his failure had not been permanent and scientists coming after him had learned to duplicate what he had discovered but never shared. The sudden intrusion of Sergei into her mind left a sour taste and she pushed the memory of him away. Here was the culmination of a dream for her that once seemed to have been pinned to his efforts. Now she was here without any influence at all from him.

Off to the side of the main landing platforms was a separate field with many smaller vessels scattered about. Indeed, they looked a bit like yachts, the word Julia had used. Some even had boat-like hulls underneath stubby wing formations that protruded from crystalline bubble enclosures. The latter was the area where passengers sat, and Jame explained that some of these vessels were designed to be able to land on and even navigate Verde's many small seas. Jame's aircar expertly landed itself on a slip beside a small yacht. Her hull and stubby wings were slate gray, and glistened in the morning sun. The name *Jana's Dream* was painted in red, iridescent letters on each side of what served for a prow. The yacht was about 20 meters in length and stood 5 meters high. At a silent command from Jame, the side of the hull opened and a staircase descended.

"Come aboard," Jame motioned to Sonja. "Welcome to my expensive hobby!"

"It's very nice," Sonja demurred, trying to play down her amazement at what she was about to experience. As she ascended the ramp something was tickling her memory concerning the name Jame had given his yacht – his sister's name, she knew. But what was it about her name? She just couldn't remember.

"She's a modest vessel. As you can see," he waved his arm toward other yachts nearby, as they ascended the steps, "she is one of the smallest about. But, she's fast. And fairly commodious inside as well."

They entered a roomy cabin with four seats, two in front for pilot and co-pilot, Sonja presumed, and two for passengers. Behind the seating, there was space to stand and walk about. A small side table at one side displayed unfamiliar ports and a mug-sized recess, where she later learned, beverages were dispensed. Jame called it a refreshment center, and went on to explain that below decks and astern there were small sleeping compartments, a galley and small dining area, and a personal hygiene compartment that even sported an ion shower. Grinning like a little boy, Jame exulted, "*Jana's Dream* is quite comfortable, even for an extended journey of several days. I hope you will agree, once you get acclimated. While compact, all your needs should be met." Sonja smiled wordlessly, taking in the newness of it all. Motioning her to the co-pilot seat, Jame himself sat in the pilot seat and adjusted its straps while showing Sonja how to do the same.

"We should use these when taking off, since it can be bumpy," he explained. "Then, after we go into cruise mode we can loosen or even remove them altogether. However, I would advise leaving them on until you are more experienced at riding the waves – the gravity waves that is." He winked at her. Sonja pulled her seat straps tightly about her.

The takeoff was smooth, however, and despite an odd feeling similar to that of being on an actual sea-going boat, or an elevator that was descending rapidly, Sonja had no problem with the yacht's method of propulsion – just as Jame had promised. They rose silently in the air for a few minutes and then accelerated in a direction toward the rising sun. There was a mild sensation of an up and down bobbing as they picked up speed.

The glass-enclosed cockpit afforded Sonja an excellent view of the terrain below them as they sped over the low mountains that circled Verde City on the south and east. Jame pointed out one of the peaks they passed over as the site of Saturn Lab. All around the mountains was forest with a shaggy, gray-green appearance. "Greenwood forest," Jame stated. "That is what we call it, and you can see why. It's a very distinctive characteristic of our planet. And those are the Arcadian alps," he said, pointing to the south where rose in the distance a row of peaks with whitened tops that sparkled against the yellow-orange hued, early morning sky. "They aren't Alps like those you have on Earth, though. Not as high and rugged, I'm told, though I've never seen those Alps – just pictures. But there is snow on them pretty much year around. We'll fly over them on our way back. First I want to take you into the northern hemisphere of the planet. It's still not very much developed and there are wildly beautiful mountains and meadows and streams that are still just as pristine as when man first came to this world. With the social compact we have on Verde, we expect that to remain the case. Unbridled development of natural resources and unchecked population growth merely for the sake of feeding the capitalist enterprise was contrary to the spirit of the people who colonized Verde. And by common agreement to this day, it's not allowed." Jame's voice bespoke a pride that was not his alone but one that had been true of all the generations of his forbears on Verde. Sonja exulted in Jame's words, seemingly too good to be true. Had she truly reached the place of her dreams?

In all, they were gone for a week. It was a glorious journey! Sonja had seen majestic cataracts plunging into deep gorges, and vast and softly glowing fields filled with what looked like flowers but turned out to be a kind of floating membrane that hosted butterfly-like creatures. There were arid deserts scored by the remains of ancient waterways and rocky-shored seas. There were no large oceans, just many small seas and large lakes. The sunsets were deep russet in cloudless skies. The overall green caste to this world was nevertheless punctuated by a variety of colors uncommon on Earth. The fauna was likewise odd to Earth-born eyes, though not abundant as far as Sonja could notice during the times when they landed *Jana's Dream* and camped for the night or made a short walking tour. One creature that tickled Sonja with its odd behavior looked like a cross between a large rabbit and a small kangaroo. They traveled in packs and followed Jame and Sonja at distance, while chirping noisily among themselves as if to comment on the strange beings they had found.

Verde was an old world. The volcanism that had formed the continents in its early life was gone, or nearly so. Jame mentioned that there were perhaps two known active volcanoes in the far north and there was still a modest amount of seismic activity in those regions. But the southern hemisphere, where most of the population was, was geologically quiet. The mountains in the south, such as those where the Saturn Lab was, and even the Arcadian Alps, so-called, were worn down from millennia of wind and water driven erosion. They were more strongly reminiscent of the Appalachians in southeastern North America than of, say, the Rockies. Old mountains. Really, just large hills.

Everywhere, both north and south of the planet's equator the Greenwood grew. Here and there were cities. They visited a few of the larger cities, including Port Robis, the capitol. They spent a day in the museum there. It had artifacts of early Verde civilization, including one of the warp drive engines that had powered the first colonizing ships. There was something eerily familiar to Sonja about that engine, as if she had seen it before.

They returned to Verde city late one afternoon. Julia met them at the spaceport, by prior arrangement, and they enjoyed a fine dinner at a nearby restaurant that boasted foods from all over the galaxy. The cuisine was excellent, if a bit strange to Sonja, and the service superb. They enjoyed a ravishing sunset from the outdoor patio dining area, heated by invisible infrared radiators. Sonja gushed to Julia about the many fine sights and interesting smells. Julia seemed genuinely happy for them both. Waving goodbye to Jame in the park quad, Sonja went with Julia to her apartment. Jame promised to call upon her in the next day or two, and bring her out to Saturn Lab to show her around.

The planetary sojourn did more than acquaint Sonja with her new world. It forged the beginning of an fast friendship. She and Jame, while so different in personality, seemed to have similar aspirations and complementary talents. He analytical, she intuitive. He could be stubborn, but resourceful. She was willing to accommodate, yet knew how to stand her ground on important issues. One of those issues was the exact nature of their relationship, for it was soon clear that it was charted to be more than just a friendship, as valuable as that was to both of them. Yet she had needed to put on the brakes. She thought back on events the last night before they returned.

They had touched down beside a remote mountain lake on the equator of the planet. It was warm and Jame had suggested sleeping out under the stars. She readily agreed, excited at the prospect of seeing an entirely different celestial sphere than she was used to. As Verde's orange-red sun set, they had walked around the lake holding hands. Later, she marveled as Jame expertly built a fire, an ability that she did not associate with engineers. They cooked a simple dinner, accompanied by a robust wine that complemented their primitive surroundings. After dinner they stargazed and Jame told her stories of the founding of Verde.

Their conversation turned intimate. She lay with her head in his lap watching two of Verde's three moons marshal the parade of stars overhead – so different to Sonja, so magical! He stroked the side of her neck pushing back the lustrous auburn folds and touched her lips with soft fingertips. She felt his growing firmness beneath her head and neck. When it came time to lay out the sleeping bags, Jame zipped them together into one as she silently watched, admiring the dexterity of his hands. Jame turned out to be expert in more than one kind of fire. For the first time in her life she knew what a man should be like. In whispered words afterward Jame had acknowledged a parallel discovery. The last she remembered before falling asleep was their speaking of sharing dreams and a life together.

In the slowly growing dawn, Sonja awoke before Jame. As she came to full consciousness the passionate hues of the previous night took on a different caste – still vibrant, yet paler. There was a sharpness to her thoughts and she knew she had to make an adjustment. He awoke then and after a friendly kiss and affectionate stroke of his face, Sonja spoke.

"Jame, I know we found something last night that is special, something that has a long way to go." He was silent. She looked up at the brightening sky, its incipient orange streamers promising rain later in the day. "But I'm not ready for its fullness." Waving her arm to the surrounding wilderness, she continued, "It's just all too new and sometimes I am simply overwhelmed. Oh, I'm not denying the feelings of affection and respect, nor the mutual attraction we have. Can we just slow down …?" She turned to him, hoping he understood, hoping that she would not destroy something precious.

His expression gave her the answer she needed before he even spoke. "I know, Sonja. I know. Before falling asleep last night, I found myself fantasizing a journey into the far future and tried to imagine what I would feel like landing on a strange planet in a society far advanced from my own. I found I couldn't imagine it. I was simply lost for points of reference." He cradled her head in his arm and looked affectionately into her emerald eyes. "I won't deny that I want you, that I want to spend eternity with you. Nor, that I want that now. But, it's easy for me to say that. I haven't travelled the great ocean of spacetime. You have. I need to let you catch up, so I will whether I like it or not."

She breathed a sigh of relief and leaned over to kiss him again, this time more deeply. She felt him respond and she made a quick decision. Rationalizing that the night was not fully past, she encouraged his advances. It would be the last time for a while, so best to enjoy it.

Later, over breakfast, her practical side asserting itself, and as if continuing an unspoken conversation, Sonja said, "Besides, Jame, there are more important things for you to attend to right now. And, for better or for worse, I think I am destined to help you. And, that means remaining objective." She used her most assertive voice.

Jame blinked at this but acquiesced. "Yeah, you're right. The puzzle of the Telpher and Jana are ever on my mind. What we will need would demand more devotion than I am probably ready to give."

The serenity of Jame's smile seemed to seal the matter for Sonja. It was a difficult choice. One side of her wanted so much to bask in the attentions of this sensitive man, throwing caution to the wind and burrowing deeply into the comfort of the protected life she intuited he could give her. But it was not to be, at least not yet. So, from that moment she began to take up Jame's burden as her own personal project.

Somehow, though she could not place it, the name of Jame's sister was a key. Jana. She felt that she had heard that name before, possibly even before she had come to the 24th century. However, try as she might, she just could not make the connection. The 21st century was beginning to fade in her mind alarmingly. What had first seemed a bad dream had become hard reality, and where she had come from was now beginning to seem a dream. Who had she been in that former world? Could she trust herself to this new world? Did she even have a choice?

* * *

Jame got Sonja a position at InterStellar, working on biometrics associated with space travel. Even though interstellar journeys were reasonably short, some people experienced a severe sense of dislocation upon arriving at the distant world. Many had another kind of difficulty, that of getting "space-sick" during the transition in or out of warp drive. These phenomena were still not well understood and InterStellar had initiated a pilot program in basic research in this area. Sonja's background was not a perfect fit, but Jame convinced the department director that she was a quick study. Besides, Derik owed him a debt of sorts from a long-ago favor Jame had done for him that had boosted his career. Derik was happy to clear the books on that, and did not even question Sonja's rather odd mannerisms and approach to laboratory science. She seemed a bit, well, "old-fashioned" was the only word Derik could come up with.

However, it was evident that she was sharp and caught on easily to the experimental procedures he was trying to perfect. She had, in fact, even suggested the novel approach of using an old magnetic resonance imaging technique to image parts of the brain during the stress of space travel. Magnetic resonance imaging had been replaced long ago by neutrino spectroscopy for the study of brain function. But as Derik thought about it he realized it would be far more useful than modern techniques for what he was trying to do, because it mapped and averaged rather large areas of the brain. Neutrino spectroscopy was much too pin-point for that. He was amazed that Sonja knew exactly how to build the device she suggested. She called it an "fMRI," whatever that meant.

Sonja was happy in her new work and was acclimating to life on Verde. There was the occasional faux pas and she sometimes misunderstood the language. "Universal," as the English she knew had evolved into, was not so different, allowing for a lot of new words that mostly related to things and experiences that she had not known in her previous existence. Allene was a big help in this regard, as well as in so many other ways. Jame introduced her to Allene on her first day at work and Allene had promptly adopted her as "her daughter." Sonja was a bit put off by her nosiness, but appreciated having an older woman to talk to about her progress in learning to live on Verde. There were plenty of other women in the lab and she enjoyed working with both men and women there. But to admit her discomfort or ask questions about social practices in the new world with people that were her professional equals was difficult for Sonja. Allene, despite her tendency to be a bit mawkish as well as pushy, was a reasonable solution. Jame had sensed this and Sonja was grateful for the understanding that both of them bestowed upon her.

Chapter 17. Return

Saturn Lab. June 7, 2376 GES

Jame went out to the lab early, bringing Sonja with him and intending to continue her education in 24th century science by going through some of the basic laboratory capabilities. He had convinced Sonja's new boss, Derik, that his tutoring of her would benefit her own performance in Derik's group. The real reason was Jame's desire to spend time with her. After an hour Sonja was exhausted and begged to be spared any further technical exposure. On the way to the Lab that day she had noticed a trail leading to a stand of Greenwood forest a short distance from the Lab park quad. Now she asked about it and wondered if it was safe to walk there.

"Of course, Sonja. As you learned on our tour, this planet has no dangerous beasts, as does Earth. Are you tired of scientific stuff?"

"Yes ..." Sonja wanted to be honest, but she did not want to offend Jame. "I mean, yes, I am fascinated by what mankind has come up with in the last three centuries – it is all so very good and interesting. Especially, I guess, to an ancient scientist like me." She managed an ironic smile. It was still so difficult to adjust to what had happened to her. She wasn't sure which was more disconcerting, the scientific advances from three centuries of progress or the cultural abyss between her own time and this era. As far as the science went, she could learn in time, but it felt like entering graduate school with only a junior high school science education. With respect to the cultural differences it was not likely she would ever fully adjust.

186

Except there were some encouraging advances in human relationships and social engineering that mankind seemed to have achieved. Continuing, she said, "But, you can only put so much water in a sponge before it gets soft and squishy and can't accept any more fluid. I need to get squeezed out some. I think getting close to nature would help, even if the nature here is itself very different. Yet, it has a different texture than a laboratory ambience and should have a healing effect on my frazzled mind. Can I go there? Is it safe?"

"Yes, you can, and I will accompany you to ensure your safety." Jame was not overly excited about this. He wanted to get back to the Telpher and trying to understand the HyperNav malfunction. But, he was a good host and wanted very much to help Sonja get adjusted to her new life. Despite her periods of disorientation, Sonja showed no sign of wanting to return to her own Earth. This was to Jame's liking and he was working out in his mind how he could get her established as a scientist in her own right within InterStellar.

"Thanks, Jame," Sonja responded. "But, I'd really like to be alone. I hope you understand. If you say it is safe, then I am not afraid. I want to go there and see what it is like." He repeated his intention to go with her, but equally yielded on it as she held her ground. He gave her instructions on how to get to the forest and used a portable scanner to program the lab reentry codes into her TASC. As she parted company with him she gave him a promising smile and a kiss.

* * *

About an hour later, while deeply engrossed in studying the coding for the HyperNav, Jame heard the lab door actuate. This surprised him and he looked up immediately. It was too soon for Sonja to return – unless she had run into some difficulty. Ruder had said he wanted the day off and he was the only other person with a code to enter this part of the facility. Instead, to Jame's complete surprise, it was Forsen's assistant who came through the door. Pavel approached Jame with a big smile. Jame rose immediately from the table over which he had been hunched.

"Hello, Dr. Anders. It's been a while since we've seen each other. What brings you out to Saturn Lab? This is your first ever visit is it not?" Pavel was a bit surprised to find Anders here, and earnestly hoped that Forsen had not already spilled the beans on the Telpher. That would significantly complicate matters. "Is Hald here?" Pavel looked around, trying to hide his anxiety.

Jame looked intently at Pavel for a long moment, and then responded with a question himself. "Pavel, where the hell have you been? We have needed you here to explain some things, yet you've been gone for almost three months. I know you had a sick relative in Port Robis, but don't you think it would have been appropriate to alert the company of your need for an extended stay and how we might get in touch with you?"

"I'm sorry, Dr. Anders. I guess I was too distraught with my brother's illness and sort of forgot all about my work," he lied. "Hald was on vacation when I was unexpectedly called away so I could not tell him where I would be should he need me." It was a lame excuse, Pavel knew, and he hoped Anders would not pursue it.

"Well, that's all right. At least you're back now. I have some questions about this," he motioned toward the back of the lab where the Telpher stood. "And I gather that means you haven't heard the news about Forsen?"

Pavel's heart leaped within his chest at this. "Forsen? What news?'

"Why, that he resigned. Resigned while he was on his vacation on Earth, in fact. Seems odd. You sure everything was all right between the two of you?" Again, Jame looked penetratingly at Pavel.

"Sure!" he bantered, shrugging off any suggestion of difficulties between himself and Forsen. Pavel was relieved. He covered his surprise at this seeming good news. It meant that his secret was probably still safe and that only Forsen knew about the Telpher capabilities. Realizing that he needed to preserve his cover, he said, "But what a shock! I had no idea that Hald would do that. Did he say why?" He wanted to ask where Forsen was, needed to know in fact. But Pavel wanted to keep the conversation on a low key lest Anders become suspicious. One step at a time, he counseled himself.

"Not exactly. But what he did say has left me puzzled. I debriefed him right after he resigned. The disappearance of the *Exeter* and what he said left more questions than answers."

"Disappearance, did you say...? What disappearance?" Again, Pavel's heart beat more rapidly upon hearing that Anders had debriefed Forsen. But what was this about the disappearance of a starship?

"You mean you haven't heard about it? It's been on all the vids, all over the galaxy. How could you have not heard?" Jame was growing more and more suspicious. Pavel was acting a bit too nonchalantly in respect to all that had happened. He should have been more upset about Forsen. And, now, not having heard about the *Exeter* ...

Pavel was caught without an answer. A starship had disappeared – something that had not happened since the early days of space travel. It had happened during the three months he was gone, and he had not, of course, known of it. He thought of using the "overly distraught" excuse again, but something warned him to avoid it. He just stared at Jame, who stared back.

Abruptly, Jame changed the subject. "What do you know about the new Gen 4 HyperNav? My sister was on that ship and it was the maiden voyage of the Gen 4. The ship disappeared when it was in the vicinity of a large star and I suspect some kind of anomaly in the navigation computer." Pointing at the pile of flex-screen files on the table beside him, Jame continued, "I've been going over the coding for the metric calculation to try to find a problem. But, it's beyond me." He had forgotten all about Pavel's recent dereliction and was giving vent to weeks of emotional stress over Jana's disappearance.

"Well," said Pavel, "The HyperNav was mostly Forsen's creation. When you debriefed him, didn't he say anything about it?" He needed to find out just what Forsen had told Jame.

"Yes, in fact, he did. He used a very strange phrase, 'chronological sequencing,' to describe a concern he had. He became quite distraught over that. At the time it made no sense to me at all, but when they found the *Exeter* I began to suspect why the ship got transported back in time."

"Back in time, did you say? What do you mean?"

"Oh, I forgot you've been out of the loop for the last few months. Yes, back in time as well as to an entirely different sector of the galaxy than the intended route." With that, Jame gave Pavel a brief rundown, without revealing much detail. Much of what he knew was company secret and he was not at all sure of Pavel's allegiances at this point. "Anyway," Jame continued, "What about this 'chronological sequencing' stuff? Do you know what Forsen was talking about?"

"Not at all," Pavel lied. "I have no idea what he was talking about. You know he is a bit wacky about old-fashioned stuff, don't you? He uses an antique timepiece instead of the net – a "watch" I believe he calls it. Maybe that device was losing its calibration."

Jame stared at Pavel, marveling at the obvious irrelevancy. What was he trying to hide? Did he not know what this Telpher device was? Had only Forsen been aware of its true potential? He needed to find out more from Pavel, whose behavior so far inspired anything but confidence. Jame knew he would have to be circumspect with Pavel to learn what he knew without telling him what he already suspected. Aloud, he said, "Look, I know that you and Forsen worked closely together. And when I spoke with him back in KCMetro he indicated that you could fill me in on the details of the Telpher. So, let's get down to it and have you go over this device in detail and what exactly it does and how it does it. I want to know everything about it." Then he added before Pavel could speak, "And, just remember who you are working for."

But Pavel was silent. Jame had given him the last bit of information he needed: Forsen was on Earth and had clearly not filled Jame in on what the Telpher was. All Pavel had to do at this point was go to Earth and carry out his plan with Forsen – one way or another.

"Well …?" Jame demanded.

"Oh, sorry! I was just thinking about the best way to help you out. Could we start tomorrow? I just got back from Port Robis and I need to settle some of my affairs in Verde City before the end of the business day today."

Jame waved his hands in a sign of exasperation and was about to object when he thought better of it. "Yeah, I guess that would be okay." He was relieved to put this off for the rest of the day. Perhaps by tomorrow his irritation with Pavel would subside and he would be more likely to gain his cooperation. He certainly was a strange character. And Sonja should be back any moment now. Jame did not want to have to afflict her with this turkey just now. "Let's meet here tomorrow and oh-nine hundred. Okay?"

"Sure!" Pavel managed what he thought was a friendly smile even while his thoughts were turning on how he could manage to avoid this. Jame had told him about InterStellar having shut down all commercial passenger travel until the *Exeter* mystery was cleared up. On the one hand that just played into his hand and gave him needed time to establish the new company. On the other hand it made travel to Earth to find Hald problematical. The company had small, space-going corporate cruisers equipped with warp drives, but there was no way he could hope to get one of those. He just hoped that un-manned freighters would still be operational, and that tomorrow he could bribe his way aboard one headed for Earth. Once aboard, he would need to gain entry to the navigation cubical where he could make some adjustments to guarantee a safe passage to Earth.

* * *

The forest was immense with wide spaces between the massive trees making long aisles that faded into the distance. Or, tree-like things, Sonja mused, as they were not quite like trees on Earth. There were no branches as such and no leaves that she could make out. The trunks, or stalks, reached to a canopy that must have been more than a hundred meters above the forest floor. The canopy must be some kind of foliage, she thought, for little light from Verde's sun penetrated and the sky was not visible from where she now stood.

The Greenwood Forest, it was called. From the ground, however, it did not appear green. From a distance outside the forest, as she traversed the stubble field between it and the outer lab buildings, the sides of the imposing growth had appeared an indistinct grayish color. Now within she could see that the smooth, gigantic trunks, most of which were ten to twenty meters diameter at their base, had a faint, celadon sheen. For some reason, the subdued light within the forest made it possible to perceive the true color of the trees. Looking off into the distance the appearance of green intensified, to a deeper jade tint. And above, the light that filtered through had a distinct green caste. Sonja now understood why the forest appeared to be a shaggy emerald carpet upon the planet surface when viewed from above. On their tour of the planet the week before she had learned that much of the planet's surface was still covered by Greenwood and conservation laws made it difficult if not impossible to clear these magnificent trees. Urban growth on Verde was restricted to the natural open spaces, often occurring in the lowlands around the many inland seas. Verde's seas were really just large lakes. For even the largest of these so-called inland seas was considerably smaller than, say, Lake Ontario on Earth.

Suddenly, thinking of trees and lakes on Earth, Toronto, her youth, Sonja was overcome by a crushing sense of dislocation. It was a deeply ingrained, unreasoning fear. How had she ever wanted to get off Earth, go to the stars? Why was she here? This world, the culture, this time period – so removed from her own – was overwhelming at times. Dwarfed by the large, majestic trees, a sense of being caught in a waking dream came once again to Sonja. She thought back to the first time. That time in the now-seeming safety of her lab at CETL on Earth, in Kansas City, that the dream-like sensation had come over her. She had been wearing the headset that she had designed to enhance telepathic signals from outer space. On that fateful night she had sensed a presence followed by the appearance of a shimmering bubble a couple of meters in diameter. Inside the bubble was the image of a man – Jame, she now knew. But, at the time she believed that she had somehow fallen into a waking trance, a hallucination, and was only imagining what she saw and felt. Now, here in this thoroughly other-worldly forest, she began to succumb again to that same trance-like feeling. It was oppressive, and Sonja struggled in her mind to shake it off, lest she encounter an unknown fate.

Then, just as she was about to fall to the ground, the feeling passed. Slowly she regained her equilibrium and began to sense again the joy and utter ecstasy of having travelled to the stars. And not just to the stars, but to the future! All the strange new technology and customs continued to amaze and enthrall her. And Jame. Well, there was something there that went beyond any relationship previously on Earth. She had hesitantly allowed herself to yield, just a little. But now it must wait. She felt, and shared, Jame's consuming mission to solve the mystery of the Telpher and the loss of his sister and an entire starship. But how to help him was impossibly beyond her understanding at present.

Sonja began walking down one of the wide, tree-lined avenues, taking care to observe landmarks lest she become lost in this magic wood. The silence of the trees grew as she moved into the forest. The quietness was palpable, and even the sound of her feet on the bracken floor was imperceptible. A sudden movement on her left caught her attention. A brightly colored bird flitted away and darted back and forth over a large leaf plant of some kind a few meters away. A bird, yet not a bird, she saw. It had two sets of lace-like wings that fluttered continuously, reminiscent of a dragonfly. Yet it was covered with what appeared to be iridescent red and purple feathers. And it had a beak of sorts. Darting to and fro, with no sound, it made an almost comical show of pretending to be afraid of her. Sonja smiled, and then broke into a soft laugh, remembering a time in her childhood in Spain when she and her mother had gone on an outing and had come upon a field of flowers. There were honeybees in abundance and they had watched in fascination as turquoise breasted, rosy-capped bee-eaters swooped here and there to make a meal. Like her childhood Spain, Verde was truly a magical world!

The moment passed and once again Sonja thought of the mystery of the Telpher, and Jame's urgent need to understand what had happened to his sister. Sonja did not understand how that would help get her back, but maybe just understanding better what had happened would help Jame process his grief. She felt badly for him though the strangeness of this far-advanced culture and difference from her own time made it difficult to establish any kind of real empathy with Jame over his loss. She walked slowly on, noting a large, rock-like outcropping on her right and its relationship to a singularly large Greenwood tree – the two landmarks pointing the way back from which she had come.

As she came out of the Greenwood and headed down the path back to the lab, she noticed an aircar accelerating from the park quad and heading off toward Verde City. It must have been a visitor since it was only mid-afternoon. She wondered who might visit such an out of the way place and whether the visitor had come to see Jame.

Chapter 18. Revelations

Jame arrived at Saturn Lab earlier than usual. He wanted to be prepared for the meeting with Pavel. He got out and went over the notes he had made and the list of unanswered questions, planning a strategy of debriefing Pavel that would minimize Pavel's understanding of what Jame already knew to be true. He had to find out if Pavel knew what the Telpher was and whether Forsen had also known.

Jame's TASC buzzed him that the time for their meeting, 0900 hours, had arrived. Jame did not expect Pavel to particularly be on time, but was pleasantly surprised to hear the lab door actuator just then. He was not in the least prepared for who walked through the door.

"Hello, Jame," said Hald Forsen, in a somewhat apologetic tone of voice. "I was hoping you would be here today."

"Hald! What the hell ...? Where have you been? Why did you bale out on me back on Earth? What is this business all about that you and Pavel have been working on?" The questions flooded out of Jame. Then, as an afterthought, "And how did you get in here? Your company ID was revoked when you resigned."

"Take it easy, Jame. I will explain everything in due time. First, I owe you an apology because I did not tell you all that I knew when we met on Earth. Now I will and answer all your questions if you will hear me out. Perhaps the easiest question to answer is your last. I have rejoined the Company. In fact, when I came back to corporate in KCMetro some weeks after you returned to Verde they seemed more than happy to accept my offer to reenlist. On one condition, however: that I return to the work I was doing here at the lab on Verde. They seemed most anxious to be able to report to the public that I was working on a solution to the *Exeter* problem."

"But, that must have been back in April some time. Where have you been since then? And how the hell did you get here, with the embargo on commercial galactic travel?"

"Easy enough to say how." Hald adjusted his glasses and smoothed back a lock of graying hair. He took a seat next to Jame and continued. "I got the company to let me use one of the corporate cruisers – one of the older ones that uses the Generation Two HyperNav. I didn't want to take a chance on, well ... I'll come to that in a minute. Anyway, those older cruisers take longer to travel the distance. I got here on the 20th of May but I went down to Port Robis immediately. I just wasn't sure what had happened here while I was gone so I made a few, ah, discreet inquiries before coming here. In particular, I wanted to know what Pavel was doing. I found out that he had disappeared sometime after I left for Earth on my vacation. Do you know anything about that?"

"As a matter of fact I do," answered Jame. "It's true he disappeared for a while – Allene said he told her his brother in Port Robis was ill and he had to go there to help him out. That was almost three months ago and no one had seen or heard from him since. Until yesterday."

Hald looked up, sharply. "He showed up again?"

"Yes. Yesterday afternoon he walked into the lab here just cool as a cucumber, acting like nothing was amiss. I was annoyed with him having been gone so long, what with trying to figure out what was going on here with this device of yours," he motioned to the Telpher, and continued, "and trying to figure out what happened to the *Exeter* and the possible connection to this thing. You know, Hald, that was where our last conversation was broken off by your own sudden disappearance!" Jame's anger at both of these men was beginning to get the best of him, so he stopped, and just looked at Hald.

Forsen cleared his throat and was clearly embarrassed. "Jame, I'm sorry – truly I am. I'm especially sorry about the way I jumped up and left right in the middle of our debriefing session. It was just that the disappearance of the *Exeter* and the troubles we were having with the Telpher here began to seem like the same thing, and I just lost my objectivity – thinking about all those lives lost and the possibility that I was somehow responsible for it. I just got on the next suborbital launch for the West Coast and walked on the beach for days on end. They were rebuilding the coastline after centuries of rising ocean levels and erosion had wiped out all the coastal villages south of San Francisco. As I watched the restoration I realized that I needed to come back and help put things back together, if possible. Please forgive me if you can. I know that your sister was on that ship."

"Well, thanks for saying that Hald. Sorry for my own anger, too, although I am hoping that you will be able to help bring Jana back." Surprised, Forsen shot a questioning look at Jame at this. Jame noticed this and continued, "You know they found out what happened to *Exeter*, don't you?"

"No, I don't. When I went back to Corporate I asked Ibsen, but he clammed up. I knew something was wrong, but I decided not to press it. He just told me to get back here asap and get busy in the lab – wouldn't even say what I was to be busy on, though I assumed he meant the work Pavel and I had been pursuing. I was prepared to give him a report right then and there about what we had found out, but his manner with me was so abrupt that I told myself to just forget it. He can be a real prick sometimes. Anyway, what did they find out?"

"They found a 350-year old colony on a planet that orbits a star in the Constellation Pisces, some 36 light-years from Earth. And ..." Here, Jame choked and continued with some difficulty, "And it was apparent from records and equipment found in an isolated cave on the planet, as well as from testimony from the inhabitants, that the colony had been founded by the crew and passengers of the *Exeter*." Jame went on and filled Forsen in on other details that were known only to him and a few company executives. However, he avoided providing Hald with his own speculations at this point. He still wasn't sure how much he could trust him.

Though Hald was astounded at this news, an immediate realization settled on him and he nodded to himself at what now became a clear truth. The Gen 4 HyperNav had an anomaly that created time dislocations when it was used in conjunction with negative matter. Apparently, the stronger the matter – negative matter interaction, the greater the time dislocation.

"Well, you are obviously not too surprised, Hald. So what's the story? I think you owe me a full explanation at this point."

"Yes, I do. And you'll get it. But first, one more thing I would like to know from you. About Pavel. You said he showed up yesterday. Did he tell you anything about the Telpher?" Forsen nodded to the ominous machine behind Jame.

"No, he didn't. I pressed him to do so and he begged off saying it was late in the day and could he come back today. So, we agreed that we would meet here at 0900 this morning." Glancing at his chronometer, he continued, "He's half an hour late at this point but I'm beginning to suspect he won't show up."

"You're probably right, Jame. Pavel is not to be trusted. Now I need to tell you all that we were doing. However, just in case he should show up while I am doing so, let's go into the privacy of my office." Hald stood up, motioning Jame to follow him to a cubicle at the far side of the lab.

Once inside, and comfortably seated, with a coffee for each of them, Hald told Jame all that had happened since late the year before when they had first begun to suspect that what they had created was far more than a superluminal audio-visual communication system for ships travelling in space warps. He told them of Pavel's insights into quantum wormholes and of his own work in constructing the machine. He told him how Pavel discovered the truth of what they had and then deceitfully attempted to conceal it. He told him of the arguments they had over what to do with the discovery. He described the experiments of teleporting small objects between Saturn Lab and the downtown lab. Lastly, he recounted to him the outrageous suggestion that Pavel had made – that they should try teleporting a human being. That they should try it out with Pavel himself. Hald muttered to himself, "He was always too reckless. What has he gone and done now?"

Now it was time for Jame to be astounded, but like Hald he did not appear so stunned as Hald expected him to be.

"Well," Forsen cleared his throat and took a sip of coffee, "You don't seem to be so surprised yourself, Jame. Had you already guessed what this machine was? Notwithstanding being a corner office guy the last decade or so, I always knew you were sharper in the lab than you let on."

"You're right, Hald, I'm not too surprised. But not because I figured anything out. It's more like I stumbled on the truth, or rather that it stumbled onto me. But until your explanation now there were some missing pieces. Still are in fact, but at least one big piece has fallen into place. Since you have leveled with me on all of this I think I can trust you and tell you how I found out about the Telpher."

Just then, they heard the lab portal energize indicating that someone was entering. Expecting Pavel, they looked at one another with a silent agreement to discontinue the conversation for now. Together they got up and walked out of Forsen's office into the lab. Then, for the second time that morning, Jame was surprised at who walked through the door.

"Jame, hi!" Sonja smiled warmly as she walked briskly up to them. Seeing his surprised expression, she said, "Oh, I'm sorry – was I interrupting something? I just got an urge to come out and visit you today. Derik said he didn't need me today and I just felt like, well … I guess I interrupted an important conference?" She looked at Forsen and then back to Jame.

"Sonja, it's okay. In fact, you are right on time." Jame returned her warm smile and taking her arm affectionately he said, "Sonja, I would like you to meet Hald Forsen."

"Oh, I am so pleased to meet you Dr. Forsen. I've heard so many good things about you from Jame."

Jame continued his almost mock formal introductions, for the effect he intended to produce. "And, Hald, I would like you to meet Dr. Sonja Bellesario, an astrobiologist from Earth, from the Center for Extraterrestrial Life – at the North American University."

"Pleased to meet you as well," intoned Hald, adjusting his glasses as if to see her better. He had a puzzled look and shifted his weight from one leg to the other. "I'm sorry, however, that I've not heard of the Center for Extraterrestrial Life – though come to think of it, that name is vaguely familiar …"

At this, Jame cut in because Hald was going to remember where he had heard the name and Jame wanted the coming surprise to be from him. "That's because, Hald, the Center does not exist anymore. Dr. Bellesario's Center was established in the early 21st century and was disbanded, if memory serves, soon after the first galactic colonization wave of the 22nd century."

Forsen's puzzlement grew for a moment more until the light of recognition began to dawn on him. "Then, she is not …"

"From our time." Jame finished his sentence. "Sonja has come to us from the year 2070. And she has come to us via *that*." He pointed decisively at the Telpher right behind Hald, with an expression that relayed both a sense of helplessness over something that could not be undone and of hopefulness over the possibility that a new door that might be opened for them all.

Hald slumped. Looking about for something to support him he found himself squarely in the cockpit of the Telpher. With a look of despair, he surveyed first Sonja, then Jame. Sonja wore a politely demur look, but Jame was grinning like a Cheshire cat.

After some moments of awkward silence Forsen suggested they return to his office, with Sonja to join them. It was growing more apparent that Pavel was not going to show, for whatever reason, and Jame wanted to brief Sonja on all that Forsen had just revealed to him. Then they needed to try to understand what Pavel was up to.

They sat around a circular table in Hald's office, each sipping fresh coffee from Hald's dispenser. Jame had rehearsed to Sonja all that Hald had told him earlier that morning about Pavel and the discovery of the true nature of the Telpher. He had also filled Hald in on some of the details of Sonja's coming to Verde and her adjustment to her new world. Hald was fascinated to meet someone from the 21st century. Through the ensuing discourse with her he made Sonja comfortable with his knowledge of the culture and doings of the century from which she had come. She developed a prompt liking for him, as she might have for an uncle. They soon came to a first name basis with each other.

Once everyone was comfortable, Jame shifted gears into a weightier subject. "As of now we still do not know what Pavel did with the Telpher after you left on vacation Hald, nor where he is now. But there are other mysteries as well. At the risk of proposing something wacky I want to bring up another missing piece I am puzzling over. Hald, what do you know of the history of the Frankel-Spinoza Drive? Were those two guys the ones that first invented the hyperdrive?"

"Yes, of course. Why do you think it is called that?" Forsen was a bit incredulous at Jame's question. Unnoticed by the two men, Sonja straightened in her chair, eyes wide.

"Just this: Company archives, which I recently researched, show that before the developments by Frankel and Spinoza there was some guy named Sergei Levkov who invented both a hyperdrive and navigation system. He founded a company, HyperDrive, to build a prototype, tried it out and was killed in his first attempt to warp space. Frankel and Spinoza, according to the archives were his assistants and carried on the work after him. But I had never heard of the guy."

At this turn of the conversation Sonja audibly gasped, and both men looked sharply at her. She had said nothing to Jame about Sergei Levkov and in fact had hoped to never think of him again. That his name should come up now in this conversation was shattering.

"Sonja!" exclaimed Jame. "What was that about?"

At almost the same time, Forsen remarked rather more calmly, "You know, come to think of it – though strangely I had forgotten this fact until now – there was a brilliant scientist named Levkov who did some of the initial pioneering work. But I believe most of his work was lost when he perished."

Sonja turned pale, not wanting to rehearse the past, but realized that she needed to speak up at this point. "Yes, Hald, you are correct. In fact, I knew Sergei personally and I was there, along with millions of others, on the day that he died trying to prove his invention. It's a very unpleasant memory for me that I prefer not to call up. But if needed, I can provide you both with a lot more particulars. I don't know much about Frankel and Spinoza, though I knew of them. They were a couple of propulsion engineers whom I think Sergei hired from another company – Aerospace something or other. He put them to work on aspects of his project – the navigation system I believe. But whatever they might have done after Sergei's failure – it seems so weird to say this – must have happened after I left Earth to come here. However, I don't see what the connection is with what you've been talking about – I mean with Pavel and what he was trying to do."

Jame stared at Sonja, at a loss for words at first. "You ... you knew this Sergei Levkov?"

"Yes, Jame, I did. We attended grad school together in Toronto and later he came to North American University where I was, using the university as an initial incubation site for the company he founded, HyperDrive." She hastened to add, "He was ... just a professional colleague, Jame, that's all, and a not very pleasant one at that. But he was brilliant and his ideas for building a ship that could go to the stars captured my attention for a while since I so wanted to go there myself." Sonja criticized herself for not being fully truthful about her relationship with Sergei. But this just wasn't the time for it – she would tell Jame later.

"Hah!" Forsen slapped his knee, chuckling. "I guess you beat him to that with no help from him at all." Then, noting Sonja's sour expression, "Sorry, Sonja. I didn't mean to offend."

"It's all right, Hald. Sorry for my reaction, which was uncalled for. It's just that anything related to Sergei brings back difficult and hurtful memories that maybe someday I'll relate." She said this looking earnestly at Jame.

Jame came back to the subject of the F-S Drive development. "Hald, Sonja doesn't know much about Frankel and Spinoza since she wasn't there when the Drive was finally perfected. Do you have anything you can recall from your own perusals of history?" He was still puzzled about the different accounts he had read.

"Nothing, Jame. Nothing that comes to mind. What Sonja has recounted now seems to me to be accurate. Frankel and Spinoza must have gone on to pick up the pieces left by Levkov's untimely death and by the end of the century they had succeeded in building the warp drive that we essentially are still using today.

With that the conference seemed to be over for the moment. To Sonja's great relief, Forsen suggested lunch in town, and Jame acquiesced though partially formed questions still swirled in the back of his mind. They left the Lab and headed for Verde City in Jame's aircar.

* * *

Verde City Spaceport. June 8, 2376 GES

Pavel carefully threaded the maze of outbuildings surrounding the Freight Dispatch Center of the Verde Spaceport. It was just before midnight and he hoped that the changing of the shift for the traffic coordinator would give him the opportunity he sought. The InterStellar freighter, *Ceres-XI*, was due to lift off at 0700 the following morning for its regular, unmanned flight to Earth. Commercial flights carrying only cargo were still permitted in spite of the company moratorium on passenger travel that was in effect until the anomalous behavior of the HyperNav navigation system could be understood. Normally, freighters such as the *Ceres-XI* would carry a nominal crew of two or three, but the ships could be auto piloted from satellite-based control centers in an emergency. InterStellar was managing to keep itself afloat financially by continuing unmanned interstellar trade, its core business.

This upcoming flight, however, would have more than the usual manifest of the fruits of Verde commerce: exotic foods, stylized furniture from the wood of the Xebo tree found only on Verde, TASC-responsive entertainment systems from Verde's nascent high-tech sector, and the like. The ship would also be carrying a single "crew" member, himself. Pavel had greased the skids with a generous bribe to the shipping agent, and signed a waiver of responsibility as well, in order to get himself officially listed as crew on the journey. It wasn't really stowing away on the ship, but it was close to that. Part of the deal was that no one else was to know. Thus, the need for stealth tonight to board the ship unseen. He adjusted the strap of the small bag slung from his shoulder that carried a change of clothing and some personal items. He needed to be prepared for the cold weather since it was winter in North America at this time. Such a sudden departure was inconvenient, he thought. It would have been better to plan his encounter with Forsen, but this was the only way to avoid the probing of Anders. He would just have to take his chances on finding Forsen when he got to KCMetro.

Checking the time, Pavel prepared to take the last leg of his approach to the ship at a sprint. It was a minute before midnight and the swing shift traffic coordinator should be finishing her rounds in preparation for the shift change. It would be while both she and her replacement were in the dispatch office together executing the handoff that Pavel would make a dash for the gantry that was still in place at the base of *Ceres-XI*. One of the first responsibilities of the night shift coordinator was to lock down access to the gantry and secure the spaceport aux-power infrastructure in preparation for the early morning lift-off. Pavel had to get aboard her before that happened. Spotting the night shift gal approaching the shed that served as an office, Pavel tensed. They would only be together in the building for a minute or so and he had to cover about 100 meters from his hiding place to the foot of the gantry during that time. The door of the dispatch office opened, splashing a yellow panel of light on the tarmac and closed again, shrouding Pavel's successful run in darkness. He gained the gantry and was inside the ship before the dispatch office door opened again.

There was another reason why Pavel had to get to the ship a few hours before lift-off. Although there had been no repeated instances of ships disappearing, like the *Exeter*, Pavel was taking no chances. He would gain entrance to the Navigation Cube and make the necessary changes to the Alcubierre metric algorithm that had been the culprit in the case of the *Exeter*. For, he was sure that was what had happened to the *Exeter*.

Gaining access to the Navigation Cube, Pavel set about making the needed changes. In a matter of 15 minutes he was done and, leaving the small cubicle, he took the lift to the crew quarters to settle in for the night. It had been a long day and the stress of his meeting with Anders and then having to hastily and innovatively find a way to get to Earth had exhausted him. He immediately fell into a dreamless sleep, with silent words of self-congratulation upon his lips.

What Pavel did not know was that one other level of systems check was normally carried out in the hours immediately before departure of the ship. The ship's engineer routinely accessed the ship's HyperNav and ran a systems check on the navigation routines to ensure that there would be no surprises. This extra level of flight security had been put in place since the *Exeter* incident because, although there were no human passengers, the value of the cargo was significant and not to be carelessly treated. This night the ship's engineer, Henrik Glaston, boarded *Ceres-IX* earlier than usual. He wanted to get home to his mate for she had just returned from a month-long vacation with her girlfriends at a resort in the Arcadian Alps. At the moment that Pavel entered the Navigation Cube Glaston was on the flight deck signing out, having just completed his systems check. It was with some alarm that he noted Pavel's entrance, seeing him on the ship video surveillance cameras, and he was about to call Spaceport Security to report a stowaway. Before doing so, on an impulse he called up the ship's manifest and flight plan. Surprisingly, it revealed that on this journey the ship would carry a Navigation Specialist, an individual named A. Pavel. Doubtful of this, however, he at first thought to call Superintendent Manris of

InterStellar Shipping, a brusque man who should have retired years ago and who had a bad temper. Glaston had an unpleasant run in with Manris a couple of weeks before on a matter that he, Glaston, thought should have been of concern. Recalling this, and noting that it was after midnight, he decided against the call.

In any event, Glaston was curious about what a "Navigation Specialist" would want to see or do in the Navigation Cube. So, from the flight deck he logged into the HyperNav UI and set up an auto-logging program. The program would record any activity by this guy related to the HyperNav and that way, if anything went wrong, Glaston could not be held accountable. He arranged for the auto-logger to transmit the information to his own data store in a computer in his Verde-based office. Private, and shielded from company snooping, but instantly available should need arise. Having done so, he departed the ship at peace with himself and headed home, anxious for the intimate reunion with Bekka.

* * *

Saturn Lab. June 9, 2376 GES

The next day, Jame and Hald were again in Hald's office at Saturn Lab. The rift between them resulting from Forsen's panicked flight from the debriefing session on Earth had been healed. They were reunited now in a common pursuit. Jame asked the question that was on both their minds. "Hald, what did Pavel do with the Telpher after you left on vacation? You said that you locked the power supply for the negative matter accumulators that give the Telpher its spacetime warping capabilities. However, it's apparent that he hacked your password because I was able to inadvertently power it up and bring Sonja here."

"Well, as you know, I told you that he wanted to try teleporting himself. If he tried that and succeeded, he could have only gone down to the City Lab where we had set up a tachcon beacon to help position the receiving end of the device. It was the accidental teleporting of my glasses there that revealed the truth of what we had discovered."

"What I don't understand, though, is why the Telpher was tuned to Earth when I first turned it on. It is as if it had been left in that state when Pavel disappeared."

"Well, there was one other place where we had thought of

aiming the device: the tachcon beacon satellites orbiting Earth. Ultimately, using those and Earth-based GPS, we had planned to communicate with I-S headquarters on Earth to convincingly demonstrate superluminal, long distance audio-visual communications. But I, at least, had forgotten that goal when the teleporting capabilities of the Telpher became apparent." As the import of Jame's words settled upon him, Forsen became agitated, his left-eye nervous tic asserting itself. "Could Pavel have attempted teleportation to Earth?" he wondered aloud. Privately, he began to suspect just that.

"That's crazy! Surely he wouldn't be that reckless or irresponsible." Jame stood up and began pacing the room. After a few moments, he continued, "Though upon reflection I suppose he could have had time to do that and get back here by yesterday. Except, there is no passenger travel allowed just now, so how could he get back to Verde? Unless of course he got a corporate cruiser like you did, Hald. No, I don't think he could not have done that, though perhaps it bears checking out. We could query Verde Spaceport for all private ship arrivals over the last couple of weeks. What do you think?"

Hald said, "No, I agree with you. Company officials didn't trust him and he'd never have gotten a ship to bring him back here. But, he could have tried stowing away on a freighter. It wouldn't have been too hard for a sneaky guy like him.

Chapter 19. Reunion

Verde Spaceport. Mid-July, 2376 GES

Pavel stepped out of the freighter *Ceres-IX* onto the tarmac of the Verde Spaceport and hurriedly crossed to the parking quad where he had left his aircar. He was still angry at having taken a useless journey to Earth to find Forsen, only to find out that Forsen had left Earth even before Pavel had departed Verde. Luckily, the *Ceres-IX* was still in port in Chicago City and he was able to wangle a return to Verde in the same manner as his outbound trip. Now, however, weeks had passed and Forsen would no doubt have had an opportunity to confer with Anders about the Telpher. That is, if Forsen had indeed returned to the Lab. Of that Pavel was fairly certain. Though he knew from Anders that Forsen had resigned, his informants on Earth had told him that Forsen had been reinstated and had returned to the I-S Lab on Verde where he was supposed to be working on a solution to the missing *Exeter*.

Pavel fingered the small weapon, a CNS interrupter, he had in his jacket pocket as he grimly approached the aircar for an immediate trip out to Saturn Lab. Though he hoped not, things might get messy, particularly now that Anders would be privy as well to the truth about the Telpher. Pavel was not given to violence by nature, and as a younger man had abhorred the use of force. But much had changed in the preceding months. A slow, yet relentless moral erosion had now escalated into a condition in which whole foundations in Pavel's character were crumbling within him. What had started out as an unrequited quest for recognition had progressed in stages through self-pity, envy, and avarice to outright hatred. A reckless character that could, on its good side come up with daring scientific insights, had on its negative branch been corrupted by self-seeking and greed. Pavel was now a man haunted by shadows, relentlessly pursuing a dream that threatened to escape him at every turn. If it came to force, then so be it. An understanding that he was trapped on the treadmill in a world of his own making fully eluded him.

* * *

Saturn Lab. Mid-July, 2376 GES

In the weeks following Forsen's return to Verde, Jame and Hald continued attempts to determine what, exactly, Pavel had done with the Telpher. Jame had to return to duties in the City, while Hald continued to direct activities at Saturn Lab. Thus, they had to pursue their project during moments of time off from normal responsibilities, and separately for the most part. By mid-July, as the cooler weather of Verde's southern hemisphere mild winter began to set in, they had made some progress. However, mysteries remained. They agreed to meet again at the Lab to discuss findings and theories.

Forsen had gone over the lab database recording Pavel's movements, Telpher power consumption, video surveillance records and so forth. He learned some things, such as that the power surge the night Pavel disappeared was of the same magnitude as the one that occurred when Sonja had come forward. There was no video surveillance of the area around the Telpher, however, so there was no direct evidence that Pavel had used the Telpher.

Seated comfortably in Forsen's office they compared notes. Forsen began: "Jame, it has become increasingly clear to me that somehow Pavel teleported himself to Earth. Moreover, I suspect that upon landing on Earth the wormhole collapsed, evidenced by the power surge that took out all equipment in the Lab. The Telpher became unstable when a large mass was transported through such a large spacetime rift and overloaded the Lab's power source. That also could explain the Telpher being left in a slightly different spacetime orientation."

"So, that meant the only way to get back here was to stowaway on a freighter, or possibly bribe someone to take him on a corporate cruiser."

"Exactly." It all seemed to hang together, yet Forsen felt that something was missing.

"So, we're at a dead end with Pavel, I guess." Jame said.

"Unless he comes back here to tell us what he has done," affirmed Hald.

Though not in full agreement on Pavel's actions and potential role as architect of the conditions they now faced, Jame and Hald turned to the problem of the HyperNav itself. They were again in Hald's office a few days later and had been discussing how they might find the programming error in the HyperNav that caused the chronological skewing. For that is what Forsen felt it must be – a sort of sideways sliding down the "side" of the spacetime bubble, along the time axis, instead of remaining on a fixed space-like course. After some moments of silence, Jame spoke up.

"If only Pavel were to come back to debrief us on the Telpher. He did not seem disinclined to do so that day he was here. Although he did seem more interested in finding you than in speaking with me."

"Well," responded Forsen, "We might get lucky and he will come back. From some of the things he intimated before I left on vacation, he had bigger ideas than conducting human experiments in teleportation. He was still rankled over the Company's supposed failure to give him credit for inventions and insights he has had. Of course, I know he also was angered over my appointment to the directorship, instead of him. But I assured him that he would get credit for the Telpher, as soon as we could confirm that it worked properly. With that he seemed satisfied, so I don't see why he would not come back to obtain that which was promised him."

"Then, if he comes back we need to have a plan to confront him. Because, if he did successfully teleport himself to Earth – and we still don't know that he did – then he must have figured out the problem with the chronological sequencing. At a minimum we need to have his knowledge on how to fix the anomaly in the HyperNav – the financial fate of the Company hangs on it." Privately, Jame also hoped for another, more personal outcome that would somehow return his sister to him.

Jame continued, as Forsen drew them both seconds on coffee, "If we do confront Pavel, how shall we do it? Would Pavel be able to deny that he travelled to Earth? Would he want to deny it?"

"He might," countered Forsen, "Possibly because the exposed behavior could lead to his dismissal. Particularly if he had known how to correct for time dislocations but had failed to warn company management before the *Exeter* set off on her fateful voyage. He could be held responsible either directly or even indirectly for the loss of the starship."

"Then we should confront him in a way that he would not deny it, perhaps by offering him immunity from prosecution."

"Which," protested Forsen, "We have no real authority to do. Nevertheless, we could point out that InterStellar is losing money on this thing and that he could be a hero if he were perceived to be the one who comes up with the solution rather than the one who caused the problem. We *can* offer him that – by just remaining silent on what he did with his knowledge."

At that they heard the lab portal energizing. Looking at each other, they wondered if they might have come up with an approach to Pavel at just the right moment. As Pavel entered the Lab and called out Forsen's name, they knew they had reached a decision point.

Chapter 20. Pavel's Story

Verde City. Mid-July, 2376 GES

It was a weekend and Sonja slept in. It had been an exhausting week, with obligations to meet that she promised Derik in her day job and evening reading up on the ecology and biology of Verde. They were beginning to see some positive results in relieving space sickness thanks to Sonja's fMRI. Using an a-grav engine stripped from a space yacht and a mockup of a space liner cabin, simulations of warp engagement/disengagement with volunteers were undertaken with the fMRI in place on the subject's head. The control group was placed in an identical space liner cabin with all the attendant sights and other sensory perceptions, except that there was no a-grav engine. Brain function pattern was clearly different in the two groups. Derik was pleased with the results, which he said were almost ready to turn over to the biomedical group for investigation of possible treatments. Derik's group, of which Sonja was part, was the "hardware outfit" as he liked to call it; he cared only for innovative devices to build for others to use in more fundamental research.

The past week had also been something of a watershed for Sonja. For most of her adult life she had wanted to go to the stars, to be part of a new civilization of mankind. A society that had learned to overcome the moral relativism and anarchy that had led in her own time to environmental and political disasters. Upon arriving in the 24th century, she at first thought that she had indeed come to Utopia – with all the wonderful advancements in medicine, living standards, and sensible tolerance for cultural differences. Now the honeymoon was ending. The stories that Jame and Hald had spun about the misdoings of Pavel and the tragedy associated with the *Exeter* had shown her that all was not perfect in Utopia. She was beginning to realize that human weakness was still prevalent with consequences for both the good and the bad. Jame and Hald were struggling to pursue a just course of action with a character who seemed intent on the opposite. She still had not met this Pavel, and wondered how she would feel about him if and when she did meet him.

A soft chirping, almost like the sounds of birds from her childhood, began to penetrate Sonja's troubled dreaming. As she slowly awakened to the sound of the alarm, her conscious mind began to put recognizable fabric on the subconscious currents in which she had been caught. In her dream she was on a boat on the ocean. It was an ocean on Earth, not one of the many inland seas of Verde. It was a small boat with a single sail. It was her boat, a catboat of some three to three-and-a-half meters in LOA. She had started sailing in fair weather. Then, as the winds increased in their intensity and the waves grew in strength, she began to lose confidence in her ability to manage the boat. The water turned jet-black and foreboding. Leering faces fleetingly formed on the restless waves. Indistinct voices seemed to call out to her from the increasing gloom.

Paradoxically, there were shafts of bright yellow light penetrating the darkness. They alternated in their intensity as they swept across the bow of the boat, making her alternately happy and sad as the light beams came and went. She realized they were coming from a lighthouse on a nearby shore. As the lighthouse came into focus she saw that it was the CN Tower in Toronto. Then she was no longer in the boat but atop the Tower, inside its glassed observation area. Sergei was there. The floor opened under her and she fell. She looked up to Sergei as she fell, hoping he would reach out to prevent her fall, but he only leered at her. She braced herself for the coming impact with the earth beneath, which never came. Instead she was swept into a raging river that rushed headlong to the sea. Then she was back in the boat, only this time it was a space yacht, like Jame's, and they were travelling about the planet, exploring and talking about the upcoming reunion with Jana, Jame's sister. She was to arrive later in the week aboard a space liner that someone said was named *Exeter*.

Upon hearing the name *"Exeter"* she saw an orange-colored star around which orbited a planet called Mycenae. There had been a colony on Mycenae, but now she saw that it was abandoned. She wandered about the forgotten colony until Sergei, his face indistinct in shadow, approached her and told her that she was in the wrong universe. She awoke, grateful to hear the birds of Spain singing.

It took Sonja awhile to come fully awake, so strong was the attraction of the dream state. When she did she went immediately into the privacy cube of her small apartment and splashed cold water on her face. Over coffee and pastry, she mulled over the parts of the dream she could still remember. The idea of being in the "wrong universe" was disturbing. The more so, since it was so suggestive of the thoughts she sometimes had of being in the wrong time zone. It was barely two months since she had arrived and although she had adapted to much of the new world, there were still occasional moments of panic. This morning was one of them. The panic was heightened because of the dream about Sergei.

Back on Earth Sergei had died, and his dream with him. Back on Earth, Sonja had put Sergei out of her life, and when he died, out of her mind. How is it that he should now come back in this new world? For that is what has happened, she thought. Jame's bringing up of the history of the development of space flight in her own time had done it, because it was Sergei who had been responsible for so much of it.

She hadn't seen Jame in several days and in fact hadn't wanted to, given his obsession with finding out what Pavel had done. She wanted to help him but didn't know how, so she stayed away unless he called her. It was a weekend and Sonja had planned to visit one of the botanical parks in the City, to rest and be refreshed. The dream seemed to have changed everything. She felt compelled to see Jame. So, after a light breakfast, she made arrangements to get out to Saturn Lab where she supposed he would be.

* * *

Saturn Lab. Mid-July, 2376 GES

Three men were seated around a table in a small conference room that stood to one side of the laboratory that housed the mysterious invention that had catapulted the three of them into the present confrontation. The truth about that invention was known to all three of them and each of them now knew what the other two also knew, though not everything as was soon to become apparent. Two of the men hoped for a peaceful resolution in which business could return to normal and bruised egos restored. Even, possibly, a return to former times. The third man was of a different cast, and held out for a personal gain that ignored the greater good the other two hoped to achieve.

"How can you say, Pavel," said Hald Forsen, "that we don't have your interests at heart? We have offered to remain silent on what you have done, though we know little about it – how you teleported yourself to Earth when I expressly forbid you from trying such foolishness and how you returned. And you claim that you know how to fix the anomaly in the HyperNav in the *Exeter*-class space ships though you have admitted no wrong doing in not alerting company management before the tragedy."

"I am neither denying nor affirming anything, Hald, except what we both know to be true – and now Anders here also knows: The Telpher represents an amazing breakthrough to propel humanity into the next stage of galactic civilization and we have the opportunity to make it happen. Without the oppressive and trade-inhibiting practices of the Company we work for. And by the way, for which we would be handsomely rewarded," he added. "I'm offering you both the chance of a lifetime. Join with me and we will start a new company that offers …"

Jame interrupted, "Pavel, we told you our answer to that already. It's not going to happen. You're inviting us to be thieves, not entrepreneurs. Moreover, you cannot possibly succeed. The Telpher relies on exotic matter engine technology and other trade secrets that you do not have."

Pavel sneered, "Don't be so sure I don't have the needed technology. Nor that I need you. I don't, and I am prepared to go it alone if you will not join me." He tentatively fingered the weapon in his jacket. Things were not going as smoothly as he had hoped, and the complication of Anders' involvement was making him jittery.

Jame was about to respond when they all heard the sound of the lab portal opening. Once again someone unexpected came through that door. Sonja called out as she entered the lab, "Jame, Hald – Are you here?"

The three men stood and Jame walked to the conference room

door. Waving to Sonja, he called out, "We're over here. Come join us." He figured it was about time for Sonja to meet the troublemaker. Perhaps she could help break the impasse.

Sonja crossed the lab floor and entered the room, following Jame. She looked around and was about to greet Hald when she saw Pavel. Their eyes locked.

"Sergei! What ...?" Words failed her in stunned disbelief.

"Sonja! How did you get here?" Pavel was equally stunned though he recovered more quickly. "So, I see. You spurned my offer and found your own way here." Looking then to Jame and Hald, he said, "I see also that you also know how to use the Telpher. Or was it an accident?" He looked again at Sonja, an unasked question in his expression. A nasty smile indicated that he had guessed the answer.

Sonja sagged against Jame's shoulder, not believing, willing herself to think she was dreaming, yet failing. Jame put his arm around her and spoke, firmly and with considerable passion, "So Pavel, or is it 'Levkov'? What a revelation! Though I guess we should not be too surprised. You would neither affirm nor deny, yet the truth comes out despite your duplicity. Damn it! What have you done? Don't bother to answer! You did in fact teleport yourself to Earth, but not the Earth of our century. Isn't that so – you cannot deny it!" Jame's fears and suspicions came crashing to the fore as he pointed a shaking finger at Pavel. "You went back in time, you created a time paradox, and in doing so you have produced this twisted new world that we find ourselves in. The *Exeter* lost, interstellar travel shut down ..." He could not continue, his emotions boiling to the surface at the enormity of what Pavel/Levkov had done.

Sonja buried her head upon Jame's shoulder, and wept silently. However, Pavel was not to be shamed. He tried again to remonstrate with Sonja. "How is it that you would come here at another's invitation yet refuse to come with me, Sonja? These men ..." He looked disparagingly at Forsen and Anders, "These men do not have the fortitude or dreams that you and I share. Remember how you wanted to go to the stars? Remember how you once thought I was your ticket to do so? Yet, when I offered you the chance, you turned it down." He softened his tone further, still hoping for a resolution without violence. "But, it's still not too late. We are on the verge of a climactic paradigm shift for humanity. The ability to instantaneously transport ourselves to anywhere in the Galaxy. An opportunity to break the stranglehold of an antiquated and overbearing company that inhibits trade and expansion so that it can reap a maximum profit."

At this point, Hald spoke up, trying to bring a spirit of peace to what was becoming an increasingly bitter scene. "Pavel, please. Let's be reasonable. Yes, we may agree with you that the Company has its failings. But to steal its property and start another company is ultimately to invite a similar fate. Let's change course in this discussion, if we can. Now that it has become clear that you did teleport yourself to 21st century Earth, let's not be bitter about it. Yes, it is a great victory for mankind. Yes, you were the one to prove it. Why don't you tell us how you did it and maybe we can find a solution that will benefit us all?"

Jame frowned at Hald, but said nothing. It was clear to Jame that Pavel must be stopped, whatever the cost. But he figured that maybe it wouldn't hurt to have more details about what he had done. At the end of the day, they needed to get the fix for the HyperNav out of him. Hald's approach might help.

Pavel grudgingly acceded to this request. Either they would all join him in his proposed venture or it wouldn't matter what they knew anyway. Pacing back and forth in the small conference room, he told his story speaking slowly, deliberately.

* * *

"Okay, yes, I did continue to work with the Telpher after you left, Hald, to see if living things could be teleported. I went slowly with this, first using small animals from the forest. Then I myself went into the hypersphere, first to the City Lab and then to Port Robis to prove it out. These trips were successful, so I proceeded to the ultimate goal. I attempted to transport myself to Earth. But, Earth in our time … not earlier." His countenance darkened as he remembered the event, recalling his reckless crawl into the hypersphere and rehearsing what happened next.

"Unlike previously, everything at first went black. When I awoke I felt the brief remains of the stomach queasiness and guessed I had momentarily lost consciousness in the passage. There was a strange sensation of timelessness, but that was all. As expected, I had fallen from the hypersphere opening, landing on my knees. They were still throbbing a bit from the fall, but the kneepads provided some protection. To my amazement, it wasn't a hard building roof on which I landed. It was grass! I looked around for the hypersphere opening of the wormhole and was just in time to see it vanish with a brilliant orange flash that rapidly constricted like a gigantic camera iris to a small blue-white spot. The spot lingered a moment and winked out. Beyond was an inky winter sky with the Constellation Orion rising in the east. It was cold.

"'Well,' I said to myself, 'There goes my way back to Verde.' I realized I'd have to find some other way since the wormhole stability problem was still not fully resolved. But I still didn't realize that things were about to get much worse." Pavel paused and looked around at his audience. He saw only two stern faces and one weeping. Shrugging impatiently, he continued. "Okay, so I figured I had gotten displaced a few hundred meters in the transit. It was a good thing I landed in a field and not inside a concrete wall! Anyway, I began to look in which direction lay the company headquarters. I was in what appeared to be the central quad of a university campus. Across the field there appeared to be the ruins of a tower, as if something or someone had broken off its top half. This did not look at all like the surroundings of company headquarters and I began to wonder if my navigation was further off than a few hundred meters.

"I had a vague recollection from a company history brochure I had once seen and the name North American University associated with its early history came to mind. Along with that there was something about the Company having been built on land donated by the University, land that had been the site of an ancient war memorial – World War One, I think. But, as far as I knew there was no university there now, in the 24th century, and I couldn't recall ever seeing ruins of a memorial on previous visits to headquarters.

"I wound my way down some steps and onto a grassy hillside, at the bottom of which was a large, deserted street intersection and, beyond, an imposing building from which emanated the lights I had seen. It was quite cold and I began to think of food and a hotel room. I hadn't planned on being trapped outside. I still needed to know where I was and how to get to Company headquarters.

"There was a squat kiosk sort of structure near the corner of the intersection. I thought it was a booth from which food or holovids were sold, and maybe had a public terminal I could access with my TASC. As I approached, I noted a glass-front display behind which was a white fabric with printing. I had never in my life seen a "newspaper" but I was conversant enough with Earth history to realize that this is what I was looking at. Across the top of the pale linen sheet were the large, black letters spelling the words, "The Kansas City Star." I knew at once that I had arrived in the right city but at the wrong time, because under the newspaper head was the date: 'Wednesday, March 15, 2045'."

At this point Pavel shuddered. The scenes of that night were still etched on his memory. He wouldn't tell them about the news story he had read on the front page. It was a story that should have produced in him penitence. Instead, in Pavel's already diseased heart, it led to greater anger.

The heading of the lead story read: "Modern Re-take on the 'Ides of March.'" It was a piece about a local theatre company makeover of an old-school "movie." Compelled, somehow, to read the entire blurb, his head swimming with disbelief, Pavel noted the concluding words: "While the play is a tragedy, in the Aristotelian sense, where profound consequences result from a small mistake, the North American University Players have performed wonderfully in driving home the playwright's intent, to leave the audience without surcease or a message to take home."

Too late, Pavel recognized the tragic immediacy of Forsen's concern about the problem of chronological sequencing. Forsen had directed him to investigate this in his absence and now, with a solid certainty, Aleksandr Pavel realized that he had first-hand evidence of its existence.

Pavel continued his monologue. "So, as you suspected Hald, there were indeed problems with the chronological sequencing. Much as I hate to admit it, you were right." He paused, awaiting the expected 'I told you so,' which did not come. He resumed his pacing and measured account. "I realized my misfortune and that I was trapped. After a period of disillusionment and despair, I vowed to find a way to return to the 24th century and to Verde. Being trapped in the world of 300 years ago was simply unbearable. I came up with a plan, a plan that I suspected might be dangerous in the sense of creating a paradox. But it was my only recourse. So, to avoid any time discontinuities, I adopted a different name so that history would record me as a different individual. Levkov is an old family name, and for a first name I didn't have to use the one my parents gave me, which I hated.

"I disliked the culture and most of the people of 21ˢᵗ century Earth. And most of those I met were impossibly slow intellectually and had no real interest to me. But there was one who attracted me." He looked meaningfully at Sonja. She avoided his gaze. "She was attracted to me as well and I thought that we had an understanding …"

Sonja started. "Sergei, I was not attracted to you. You assume too much!" She let go of Jame and made as to approach him, but he turned away.

"Whatever, Sonja. But you liked me to tell you about my plans for space travel. And you understood them. At least I thought you did. I guess you were just like the others – only interested in what you could get out of me without wanting to give me any credit." Sonja started to answer but recognized a certain truth in what he said. She bit her lip as she felt Jame's hand on her arm. Pavel continued.

"I had a hard time adjusting to the ways and means of your Earth," he glared at Sonja, "but eventually through some hard knocks I was able to get a job to support myself. I left KCMetro, I mean 'Kansas City' as you called it then, and went to North Carolina. There I enrolled in university, starting at the bottom because I had to have a credible history and I knew that it would be in the universities that I would find the necessary talent and equipment to do what I needed to do. UNCC in Charlotte had a program in tachyonics that was fairly advanced for its time – developed out of their earlier advances in optics. Of course, they knew very little about it and I had to suffer through their ignorance without tipping my hand. Anyway, I got through their undergraduate programs in little over two years and ended up at Toronto for my PhD. For once in my life, people were recognizing my abilities and rewarding me accordingly."

Turning to Hald and Jame, Pavel said, "Sonja knows a lot of the rest of the story, how I ended up back in Kansas City at the University there. And how everyone was eating out of my hand, to use a 21ˢᵗ century expression, because the success I was having in developing the warp drive. I was able to start my own company, spinning off from the Space Sciences group there …"

Jame again cut in, "HyperDrive, you mean. That's right, isn't it?"

"How … how do you know that?" Pavel was stunned. "By my

planning there should be no record of that company in this century. It was important that the Drive technology be seen to have been developed by Venture Star, the progenitor of InterStellar."

"You can confirm it for yourself, Pavel, because the Company archives record it so." Jame stopped there, not ready to elaborate further.

"Okay, so I failed in that regard. But it doesn't seem to have created any paradoxes as we are all here, just as before. Except Sonja, of course, which is not my fault for sure. Anyway, fortunately for me, I landed on Earth at a time when the science of both exotic matter and tachyons was in place, however rudimentary. If it had been necessary to bring people up to speed in those areas, there could have been real difficulties with time paradoxes. My collaborators had no reason to question the source of my understanding. They just thought I was a brilliant scientist, which was true of course. Nonetheless, I had to be very careful about who I chose to help me and what information I left behind."

Jame interjected, "So, what about Frankel and Spinoza? As you know, they were the inventors of the Drive as far as we knew."

"Oh, that's very sharp, Anders." His tone belied the words. "That was exactly one of the key pieces I had to put in place. I knew the history, of course, so I had to set things up so that they would in fact go on to invent the 'F-S Drive' after I left. I knew, from the time period I had ended up in, that they were alive and the right age to understand the physics and celestial mechanics of warp drive technology. After a search of universities and space exploration companies I tracked them down at some outfit that was building fusion rocket engines for interplanetary travel. It wasn't hard to convince them to join my team, with the promise of interstellar travel being a big step up for them. I hired them both and put them to work on the tachyon guidance system. But when I left I had to destroy enough of what we did so that there would be a real and independent development effort by them.

"That was my main contribution, you know. The tachyon guidance system. What the people who were researching tachyons did not realize was that tachyons are not superluminal particles. Rather, they are ordinary bosons travelling through quantum-sized wormholes. This I knew from the work I had done here, before going back. Knowing that, of course, enabled the next step of figuring out how to enlarge the wormhole to classical dimensions so that a person could go through – also work that I did here in this lab with Forsen. A big problem that I had to overcome, however, was the source of the anomaly in the guidance system, the HyperNav, that was creating the time dislocation. Unless I learned how to navigate when in warp drive I would never be able to return here and now." He paused, reflecting again how he had managed his successful return.

"After completing graduate work in Toronto, it took months of excruciating calculations and testing to get to the bottom of the problem that had led to my being transported back in time. I eventually located the problem in the Alcubierre metric algorithm of the HyperNav. Of course, I had to construct a HyperNav as well as a negative mass accumulator and warp field projector. But for that I had able helpers, whom I also kept in the dark about the true purpose of the device we were building. Fortunately, negative mass particles as well as tachyons had been discovered by the time I arrived on Earth. The real problem was finding the anomaly. The rest was just a matter of fast-talking and utilizing insights that were beyond the scientists of that day.

"There were other concerns, as well, affecting others. I was very careful not to introduce any significant changes in the course of history in the 21st century. Whether or not there was a so-called "chronology protection clause" in the founding charter of the universe, I didn't want to find out. I could have potentially arrived back in a very different 24th century. But, as you see, I was successful in fixing the anomaly."

Hald leaned forward, eagerly. "Pavel, that's great. I'm not surprised you could solve the problem. Tell us how you did it."

"Hah! Very tricky, Hald. You would like to know, wouldn't you, so that you don't have to deal with me. But there is only one way you'll find out, and that's by joining me in my new venture. Even then, it would be a long while before I'd trust you."

Jame interjected, "Okay wise guy, go on and tell us how you got back here."

"I thought you had it all figured out, Anders. Once I had a prototype of what would become the HyperNav, I secretly adapted it to enable spacetime travel through the same kind of wormhole that brought me to Earth. To do this I hid a series of secret control algorithms in the code that the guidance system uses. It took several iterations to get this right, but I succeeded as evidenced by the fact that I am here – in exactly the time period I planned.

"By good fortune, I had first tested the Telpher by a teleportation from Verde to Port Robis. That meant setting up a navigation beacon in an unused storage locker of InterStellar's Port Robis office there, and fortunately no one had yet discovered it. That's where I aimed my return. The first thing I did was query the local network for the date. If I had done my calculations right it should have been May 16, 2376 GES. It was. I only needed be sure that it was *after* I left, that is after March 7, 2376. Very uncomfortable things could happen if I arrived before I left – assuming that was even possible."

He paused, again reflecting on something inwardly. Then he said, "For your benefit, since you have always thought me a second-rate physicist, I will admit to another error I made. Inadvertently, of course, but one that seems to have produced difficult consequences."

Softly, and wanting to encourage any hint of remorse, Hald asked, "What is that Pavel?"

"Well, you remember that I said it took several iterations to get the guidance system right and also that I had destroyed all the records of our work when I left. When I got back here, however, I learned of what happened with the *Exeter* and I thought about the source of the time dislocation problem. I asked myself how the Gen-4 HyperNav ended up with that problem? I now believe that it was because Frankel and Spinoza must have retained the plans for an earlier version of the system we were perfecting and ended up using it in their subsequent work. That earlier version has errors in the Alcubierre subroutine that only manifest themselves at greater than quantum scales when large masses are involved."

"How can that be?" asked Jame. "Forsen informed you of a chronological problem with the Telpher guidance system that existed *before* you went back in time and changed the course of history." Again, Jame held back information that he had, which suggested that what Pavel suspected is exactly what Frankel and Spinoza had done. He had his reasons, though he had to admit to himself there remained a seeming puzzle. In any event, in Jame's opinion, Pavel's boast that he had fixed the Telpher's guidance system to get him back here was empty. He was just lucky – and so were they. However, with Pavel's knowledge, they could truly fix the HyperNav and maybe even figure a way to get Jana back.

"I don't know, Anders. Why don't you tell me? You seem to be the smart guy here."

"Sorry, Pavel. I'm not falling for that. Maybe in time we will better understand it." His sardonic pun was intentional but Pavel only shrugged. "Meanwhile, continue your story. How did you get back? The history books say that you went out alone in a retrofitted interplanetary vessel and that it exploded. And you died." Jame was beginning to wish he had but for the fact that they needed what he knew about the anomaly.

"That's easy and I'm surprised you haven't figured it out. That retrofitted interplanetary vessel was in reality a cleverly disguised version of what sits out there in the lab. I just laced the ship with plastic explosives timed to go off after I entered the hypersphere to return here."

* * *

Hald and Jame looked at one another. Sonja was mute, an expression of alarm on her face that would have been visible had Jame taken time to notice. Pavel rejoined them from his position at the other side of the room. He spoke, quietly, yet as forcefully as he could, with a pointed glance at Sonja: "Now gentlemen, and lady, it's time to make up your minds. Are you going to accept the very generous offer I am making you, to join the new company I am going to form, or not?"

Jame shot back, "There will be no new company, Pavel. In fact, if you do not go along with our very generous offer you could find yourself indicted and possibly convicted for your role in the disappearance of the *Exeter*." Jame knew this was a bit far-fetched, but he was grappling for a means to bring Pavel around to some sense of responsibility. "But if you cooperate with us and show us how to fix the HyperNav, then, as we have said, we will ignore such a charge. Instead you will be the hero. Something you've always wanted, right?" Jame was goading him a bit and did not realize the danger he was putting them all in.

At this Sonja tugged on his arm and leaned to whisper in his ear. Pavel was backing away, putting his hand in his pocket. Jame pushed Sonja away and leaped at Pavel, who made to pull the weapon from his pocket. It caught on a seam and he momentarily lost control of it. Jame was upon him in an instant, wrestling him to the floor. Sonja put both hands to her face in a silent scream and Hald looked helplessly on as the two men rolled about on the floor. There was a loud pop and a hissing sound. Both men went limp. Sonja screamed again, this time audibly, and rushed to Jame. Hald joined her as she implored, "Jame, are you all right? Speak to me, speak to me!"

There was a muffled groan and Jame, who had ended up on top of Pavel, rolled off him and lay still on his back on the floor. He had a dazed expression, his breathing shallow. There were light colored burn marks on his tunic. Pavel on the other hand was clearly dead, a surprised yet pathetic expression upon his face. Hald leaned over to close his eyes while Sonja tried to revive Jame.

"Hald, please get me some water!" Meanwhile, she held Jame's head in her hands, saying to him softly, "I'm sorry, I'm sorry. I should have told you sooner, but I was so shocked by the revelations of what Sergei – Pavel – had done that I was … I just couldn't speak or move."

Hald returned with the water and together they helped Jame to a sitting position from which he could take the water. Hald stated that Pavel's weapon had gone off pointed at himself instead of at Jame, but that Jame had been close enough to experience the beam flashback. It had stunned him but he was apparently unharmed. He was lucky.

Yet, they were all unlucky. For with Pavel dead the secret of how to fix the HyperNav had died with him.

Chapter 21. Parallel Universe

Saturn Lab. Mid-July, 2376 GES

The next day, after the authorities finished interviewing them and left the lab, Jame and Hald tried to relax in Hald's office. They avoided the conference room where the confrontation took place. Needing to process all that had happened, they were reconstructing again the events the day before. Forsen recalled something Jame had said.

"Jame, what did you mean when you accused Pavel of producing, I believe you said, 'this twisted new world that we find ourselves in'? You related it to his having created a time paradox, but what were you getting at?"

"Well, it's an idea that I am a bit reluctant to share with you. But I guess I must." Jame leaned toward Hald in a gesture of entreaty. He still held out hope that, somehow, they could undo the events that led to the *Exeter's* mishap. This, he knew, was grasping at straws. In thinking over some of the things that had happened, and particularly the different accounts that he had read of the history of the F-S Drive, a desperate idea had formed in his mind. He decided to risk sharing it with Hald.

"Do you remember that a few weeks ago when you first met Sonja and we were here in this office discussing Pavel's doings, that I asked you about the history of development of the F-S Drive? I said that I had recently investigated the company's archives to learn more about it and found out to my surprise that someone named Sergei Levkov had been involved in it early on. Then Sonja dropped her bombshell telling us she had known Levkov and his research activities."

At Forsen's affirmative nod Jame continued, "Well, the reason that I was pursuing the subject and the reason for my surprise at the appearance of Levkov in the historical record is that I had previously read an alternate history." At this Forsen raised an eyebrow, but Jame pressed on. "Let me explain: Back in late February, during my journey to Earth to meet with you, I happened to peruse the history of the Drive as recorded in my ship's library. That was before the disappearance of the *Exeter*. Though many details are identical, the shipboard version did not agree as to the role of someone named Sergei Levkov. In fact, he was not mentioned at all. Nor was his company, HyperDrive. When I later looked at the version in our corporate archives here in Verde and discovered the difference I at first didn't know what to think about it. But then learning that Sonja knew Levkov served to whet my appetite to get to the bottom of the mystery. The *Draconis*, the space liner I took to Earth back in February, was then in port. So, I flew out to the Verde Spaceport and obtained permission to go aboard to check the library. I fully expected to find the record to be as I had remembered on my journey to Earth – no Levkov. To my amazement, the ship's library had the full story of Levkov's early achievements, his death, the relationship between him and Frankel and Spinoza. The ship's library archives now agree with and say exactly the same thing as the corporate library archives. Yet, there is no way I would forget such a lurid story as that concerning Levkov. That I could be mistaken in my memory is just not reasonable. So, Hald, how do we explain this?"

Hald was silent, a slight frown on his face being the only evidence that he had heard Jame's question. Jame continued, "Well, the only way I know to explain the disjuncture between my memory of what I read on that trip to Earth aboard *Draconis* and what I have now just read from the same shipboard library is that the two space ships are in fact not the *same* ship. Or, more precisely, one is an almost but not quite identical copy of the other. If that is the case then this present universe – the one inhabited by me, by you and by the ship I just investigated in the spaceport – is not the same universe that you and I and the ship were inhabitants of earlier this year.

"If that was true I conjectured that the source of the parallel universe as well as the disappearance of the *Exeter* were caused by one and the same event: Pavel's spacetime travel to an earlier age in this galaxy. The *Exeter* disappeared on March 7, which is the very same day that the Lab database recorded Pavel's entrance to the Lab but no departure. Is it possible that by going back in time Pavel accidentally caused a parallel universe to emerge? Did Pavel, by his time-defying choices, inadvertently drag all of us into another world, one with just a slight offset from the original, one in which we all now find ourselves? A parallel world nearly identical to the one he started in, but this one having a spaceship navigation system with coding errors that in certain circumstances lead to spacetime dislocations? That would explain the different accounts of the F-S Drive history."

"Jame, you may be getting close to the truth of what has happened, but I'm not so sure." Seeing Jame's face fall, he hastened to add, "That's probably because I have not had such compelling and personal evidence of it. I mean, you've had the experience of reading two different accounts of the history of the F-S Drive. Anyway, as you know, the idea of parallel universes has been around for a long time. Unfortunately, the idea has been judged by most reputable researchers to be unscientific – that is, outside the realm of science – owing to repeated failures to find experimental evidence for it. Or even by definition, since a truly 'parallel' universe would not intersect with our own – at least at greater than Planck-length scales. Moreover, how is it that we seem to remember the other universe? Is there some sort of quantum entanglement going on at the molecular level of our brain function?" He paused, scratching a non-existent itch on his chin and musing silently for a moment as Jame tensely waited for the wisdom he knew Hald possessed.

"However, we now know that Pavel did indeed inject 24th century scientific knowledge into an earlier century and that would certainly constitute some sort of paradox. The world he went to – and changed – could not have evolved into the world he left since by his own admission he brought to it knowledge from the future. Such actions would inevitably change that future and possibly preclude his travel back to the past and to accidentally change the future. A logical impossibility. So, by application of Occam's razor, we may come around to your ideas about parallel worlds as the simplest explanation. As bizarre as it seems to me, you could be right about a "slightly shifted" universe that is mostly, but not entirely, the same everywhere."

Jame began to relax but Forsen hadn't finished. "Still, I still think there might be some other explanation. One point your hypothesis does not seem to explain is that before Pavel made the time leap there were chronological sequencing problems in the Telpher guidance system. How do you account for that?"

Jame smiled, his confidence in Hald reconfirmed. "Yes, I know that and have thought about it quite a bit. I might have an answer, but it's pretty wild."

"Well, before you stretch my brain any further," Forsen interjected, "Let me give you a fairly non-controversial idea. It is simply that the Alcubierre navigation metric has always had a potential bug, but one that had not surfaced until now. Perhaps some aspect of the *Exeter's* flight metric exposed the weakness in the algorithm." He paused and winked at Jame. "But I'll give you this: Such an explanation would not be inconsistent with your parallel universe idea and the two different company history accounts remain unexplained. So, now tell me your less civilized approach."

Jame stood and slowly paced about the room, looking back and forth between Forsen and a wall-mounted data screen on which he called up some crude diagrams. "Okay. It occurred to me that at a quantum scale in any universe there are virtual quanta of information popping into and out of existence. Multiple universes may potentially exist side by side at the quantum level, with each universe unique in its own right yet slightly different. It occurred to me that owing to the closeness of the universes, there may be a quantum tunneling effect wherein so-called 'virtual' information from one universe could 'tunnel' into a nearby parallel universe. The virtual information from one universe would pop into and out of existence in a neighboring universe."

Jame pointed to the data screen on which were little ovals, each embedded with the letter 'I' and subscript "T_P" together with curly arrows up or down. He continued, "Although such information from a 'host' would create a time paradox at classical scales in a 'guest' universe, its virtual, Planck-time existence, T_P, would not result in an actual paradox. Unless, however, there occurred some action or event in which the virtual information is captured and brought into classical realms. You know that negative mass accumulators are thought to work by such a tunneling and capture mechanism.

"Now here it gets a little wilder. We are dealing with information, not dark matter. Quanta of information, in fact. So the capture mechanism is not a machine, but human acts of choice. And the process is governed by the laws of probability because human beings are free agents. Human beings freely and randomly use information and the human brain interacts with the virtual information quanta in such a way as to affect the probability that an inconsistent, or paradoxical, information set would be captured, so to speak, and descend to classical scales. At this point a chronology protection mechanism, if such exists, might operate. It might do so by segregating the inconsistent information and all the potentially paradoxical events, and associated human beings, in a new, emergent parallel world that was the same, or similar, in all other respects.

"So, let's suppose, as you point out, there is a pre-existing bug in the Alcubierre algorithm. Let's call it a design feature or weakness, and one that occurs in two universes – ours and a 'potential' other universe. I say 'potential,' because from the perspective of anyone in the original universe all other universes are emergent, not yet having been concretized by human choices. Let us further suppose that the design flaw is virtual and at a quantum scale, with a net zero probability of a paradox occurring across the two universes. But Pavel's plans to use the Telpher for his own greedy goals then began to connect the two universes in a potentially paradoxical manner. The small chronological discrepancies you noted with your glasses were an indication of that but the consequences of such discrepancies were not significant enough to invoke a chronology protection mechanism. Pavel's actual journey through the Telpher to an earlier time, on the other hand, amounted to a full-scale capture of the potentially paradoxical information, a collapse of the wave function in a sense, such that a paradox would occur in the 'original' or host world. That resulted in a separation of the universe we now inhabit, the guest world, from the former host world, thus avoiding the paradox. And somehow, as far as we know, only those people who were in some way connected with Pavel were affected. To his credit, Pavel managed to find the design flaw in the navigation algorithm and fix it, but the understanding of it died with him. Unfortunately."

Forsen shifted his not inconsiderable mass in his chair, the mag-lev mechanism responding subtly to maintain a steady level, and

228

raised both eyebrows at that suggestion. But he remained silent. Apparently, there was no further place to go in the discussion. As crazy and as improbable as that seemed, and notwithstanding Forsen's skepticism, the parallel universe idea gave Jame a ray of hope. If true, then possibly those choices Pavel made, and presumably acted upon, might conceivably be reversed – or, amended. And if that were possible, he thought, maybe they would all get out of this nightmare world they found themselves in and return to the one in which all was whole and without the grief he now experienced over his sister. But Jame knew there were problems with this idea, not the least of which was the fact that in the world to which he wished to return, there would be no Sonja – at least not in his time frame. He had to admit to himself that were he to have the power to make a choice in this regard, it would be a difficult one.

Chapter 22. Gen-4 HyperNav

Verde City. Late July, 2376 GES

Ship's engineer, Henrik Glaston, sat at morning breakfast with his love, Bekka. They were watching the early morning news vid on the 3D mounted to the wall next to the eating nook in their small apartment. It was mostly the same old news until something came up that arrested Glaston's attention. It was a bit of investigative reporting about the ongoing revelations coming from InterStellar about problems with the navigation system of their galactic fleet. They had resumed operations with a couple of older space liners brought out of retirement. These used an older version of the HyperNav guidance system that the company claimed to be free from the defects in the newer version that had shut down all interstellar passenger travel. The company still had not made public how they knew that the older system was safe, nor even how they knew that the Gen-4 had problems. He remembered having observed some strange character – what was his name, anyway? – having seen him making changes to the navigation computer of the *Ceres-IX*. He wanted to forget that incident, however, for he still felt guilty about not reporting the fellow.

Then the special report took on a new twist. They were announcing that InterStellar had let out more information about the problems with the HyperNav, saying that an I-S scientist employed in the Verde City offices had been convicted, post mortem, for crimes related to making unauthorized changes to the HyperNav system. The scientist had died in an attempt to bribe company officials.

InterStellar, the reporter said, was searching through laboratory records left by the scientist to see if it could determine the changes that were made. Glaston noted, somewhat cynically, that the tone of the report made it clear that InterStellar was at pains to shift blame for the debacle from itself to this hapless scientist. Having worked himself for the company all his life, Glaston had no illusions about the motives of his company. But it was a living to him and he needed to stay employed. The report ended with a picture of the deceased scientist and gave his name: "Pavel." At that, Glaston sat bolt upright in his chair.

"Honey, what's wrong?" Bekka was alarmed at his sudden movement.

Glaston recovered himself. "Nothing, lumpkin. I just got a cramp sitting in this slouched position. You know you're always telling me to watch my posture. Well, I guess you're right this time."

With that, Bekka went back to planning the renovations to their small living quarters that they had agreed to do with Henrik's coming bonus. She detested the news programs and wished Henrik would turn it off. Surprisingly, he did just that, getting up while stuffing the last of a honey-sweetened gluten wafer into his mouth and gulping the remains of his coffee.

"Honey, what's up? Where are you going?"

"Got to get to work."

"But, it's early yet!" Even though she didn't like Henrik's news addiction, she cherished these morning times, before he went off to the Spaceport. He often didn't come home until quite late, usually after she was asleep.

"Sorry, dear. I promised the old fart – you know, Superintendent Manris – that I would run some performance statistics on unmanned flights for him. I need to get there early to do that." It was a fib, or maybe a white lie, but close enough to the truth for Glaston to feel justified in deceiving his love. No use in upsetting her unnecessarily. If he did not take care of what he now knew he must take care of, then she would be more than deceived.

Glaston was worried that he could be disciplined for not reporting Pavel's unauthorized access to the HyperNav on that supposedly authorized trip to Earth. They were sure to continue to research all of Pavel's moves in the attempt to find out what he had done. It was only a matter of time before they discovered his journey to Earth. That was okay, he supposed, until they found out that Glaston knew about it and did not report it. The ship's log, which he had signed, would show that he was aboard at the same time as Pavel.

Glaston was in a bit of a torment. To admit that he had seen Pavel tinkering with the navigation computer on *Ceres-IX* without reporting it could subject him to discipline. He could not afford to lose his job – especially not now with the plans Bekka had. On the other hand, it was quite possible that the changes Pavel was making would give a clue to what the company was looking for. And he had a full recording of what those changes had been. In that case, if he came forward with that information he could be seen as a hero, and get a promotion. In the end he felt he must come forward. He would report what he had observed, and he would turn over a data chip that showed the results of the auto-logged changes made by Pavel prior to his journey.

Chapter 23. Confession

Though weeks had passed, the trauma of the encounter with Pavel, his violent death and their near escape still weighed heavily upon them. Adding to the stress, though in a more positive vein, had been the stunning revelation of Henrik Glaston, the ship's engineer on the *Ceres-XI*. Glaston had shown them the coding changes to the HyperNav that Pavel made to correct the navigation anomaly. It was a bitter victory for Jame. Yes, he could claim some credit for helping InterStellar escape the financial disaster it faced from the paralyzing shutdown of manned space travel. But of what use was this new knowledge for his sister, Jana? She was permanently lost to him, in another time and space.

Hald had disappeared again, but was probably hanging out in his apartment in the City. Sonja and Jame agreed to meet each other for lunch one day. Lunch with Sonja offered Jame a respite, which he now began to savor with a renewed hope. There had been that brief liaison during the whirlwind tour of the planet in Jame's yacht. But Sonja had pulled back, requesting that they put things on hold for a while. Though disappointed, he had empathized with her situation. Then what had been put on hold had been all but buried in the cascading events surrounding the return of Pavel and revelation of his 21st century sojourn as Sergei Levkov. Now, Jame thought, he could start to rebuild his fractured life. Perhaps, this beautiful woman from the past of Earth would become a part of that rebuilt life.

Jame locked his apartment behind him and strode down the hall to the elevator tube. A short tram ride brought him to the City center. Descending from the tram landing to street level, he walked out into the brilliant light of Verde's orange-tinted sun at midday. The weather was unusually mild that day for mid-winter Verde. The Aqua trees along the pedestrian way glistened, their tiny green and yellow blossoms freckling the undersides of elongated leaves. Jame strolled leisurely along the shaded way provided by the trees, and began to hum a tune that arose from somewhere in his past. The faint swoosh of aircars some stories above combined with the snatches of conversation of passersby to give a sense of busyness that helped Jame to momentarily forget his responsibilities. This was the City of Verde, his birthplace, his home. He knew its byways and bylaws well, one of which was to let the rest of the universe go its way. Verde was its own reason for existence, and was its own source of life. Terra, "Earth-home," was distant in both time and space, and was to be forgotten in the minds of most native Verdeans. Except that InterStellar, Jame's employer, had all too great an interest in keeping up the connection. The remembrance of his job, his place in Verde society, tempered Jame's reverie.

The tree-lined avenue descended some 500 meters in a gently sloping arc from the central business district of Verde to the plain of the Galene, the inland sea that bordered the city and gave to it so much charm. Halfway down this way Jame turned left into a narrow alleyway, accessible only by foot. Balconies protruding from shorter, squatter buildings here on either side of the alley shielded pedestrians from the insistent sunlight. Profuse waterfalls of blue-green Alanthus blooms appended to sinuous, fragile vines descended from planters that the residents of this sector of the city meticulously cared for. A sudden breeze sent flutters through the shimmery veil of flowers.

There was a not-so-well-known restaurant a hundred meters or so down the alley that Jame often resorted to when he wanted to take a break from normal routine. A shaded patio at the back overlooked the river and lake, providing an almost empyrean vista that he hoped Sonja would appreciate. The nice thing about this particular bistro, something that would help Sonja relax, was that it was decidedly "old school." The owner was enamored of Earth culture from the 21st century and had created an eating and drinking establishment that one could have found in any major European city of the time – Paris, for example. In the spirit of this creation, there were actual human waiters instead of bots, and there were menus on hand-held flex-screens instead of the more modern table consoles that via their personal TASC devices allowed patrons to bring up virtual menus. Of course, the flex-screens were electronic, and one could make direct selections if desired. Most of the patrons, however, kept to the old-style practice of speaking their dining choices to a human waiter. Jame enjoyed the place and felt that Sonja would as well.

Jame had given her suitable directions, as she would be coming from the other end of the alley if she walked from her apartment as he now did. He hoped that he had managed his time well enough to arrive before her and to pick a table with a perfect view. Sonja was still adjusting to Verde culture, and Jame wanted to not overly stress her pilgrimage. They needed to be able to talk, frankly and openly. It would be advantageous to meet in an environment that provided sights and smells that were at least somewhat similar to the time and place from which she had come – and would now never return. Although, knowing how to fix the navigation module, they could in principle use the Telpher to transport her back. But it was dangerous. Would it be the same world for her and what would happen in his own world? Besides, she had shown no desire to do so, quite the opposite in fact.

As it turned out, they arrived at the restaurant simultaneously. Jame saw her approaching from the other direction just as he arrived at the bistro door. With a broad smile on his angular face, he awaited her. Overhead, an old-fashioned sign suspended upon a horizontal wooden beam announced the name of the place: Orange Haven Café.

"Hello!" Jame called out enthusiastically. "I see you found your way."

"Hi Jame," replied Sonja somewhat shyly as she strolled up to him. "How could I miss with such precise, such engineering-like directions?"

"Well," Jame grinned sheepishly, "I don't know about that." Then, taking her hand, he lifted it to his lips to kiss. "Welcome to one of the best-kept secrets of Verde," he said as he motioned with his free hand. Sonja blushed, but allowed Jame to guide her into the darkened interior of the bistro, his hand place lightly in the small of her back. She felt instantly at home, with smells of coffee and pastry, which though slightly different than on Earth, were still familiar enough as to make her forget for a moment where she was.

"Bonjour, Dr. Anders! What has kept you away so long?" A roly-poly maître d' approached them with outstretched arms and large, toothy smile. His pale orange tux-tunic was a bit rumpled, matching a face somewhat wrinkled with age. He walked with a slight limp, Sonja noticed, making her feel even more at home in this place.

"Good afternoon, Andre. Yes, I guess it has been awhile. Lots going on and, you know, just too busy to unwind. Which is what we are going to do today." Turning then to Sonja, he said to Andre, "Please let me introduce Miss Bellesario, Doctor Bellesario, a colleague recently come from Earth."

"A colleague, eh, Mon Ami?" Andre expostulated good naturedly, shrewdly appraising the auburn-haired beauty in front of him. Then to Sonja, and resuming an official posture, he said, "It is a pleasure to meet you Dr. Bellesario, and especially so since you are a good friend of Dr. Anders." He seemed to emphasize without undue pointedness the words "good friend." Continuing, he said, "Welcome then to the Café Orange Haven, and may it truly be a brief haven for one so far from home!" Jame was inwardly amused at Andre's choice of words and wondered what he would say if he knew just how far. Andre continued his semi-official banter. "Your usual place, Jame?"

"Yes, Andre. And the table with the unique view of Galene please. If it's available, that is." He knew it probably would be. There were so few customers at the Orange Haven and that particular table seemed always to be free. Jame wondered how Andre made a living on the sparseness of traffic to this hidden jewel.

Andre led them to the patio in the back and seated them at Jame's table, handing each a menu and retreating. Sonja was agog. "Oh my!" she exclaimed softly. "What a beautiful view!" Jame was impassive as Sonja took in the expansive vista. The sea sparkled turquoise below them, some several hundred meters distant. Ranks of rather ordinary looking (by 21st century Earth standards) buildings fell away on either side, giving way to the treed meadows and pathways of the city's parks that fringed the seashore. Jame was glad that the more "modern" metallic spires and plasticene skyways of 24th century architecture were not much in evidence from this perspective. The few aircars that passed silently to and fro like sleek birds without wings above the verdant parkland would be just a minor reminder, he hoped, of the strangeness of her new world.

"I'm glad you like it."

"Oh, look! Across the lake." She still thought of these bodies of water as lakes. "The large mountain in the distance. Is that …?" Sonja hesitated.

"Yes," Jame affirmed, wishing she had not noticed, "That is Saturn Mountain. Where the lab is." His normally bright countenance shaded. Catching the slight shift in tone in Jame's voice, Sonya looked over at him.

"Hey!" she scolded. "Stop it. I'm a big girl. I can handle this … this new world, what has happened. Look, I always wanted to go to the stars. And after Sergei's ship exploded ... I mean, Pavel," her brow wrinkled and she tapped her finger nervously on the table. "Anyway," she continued bravely, "After that happened I thought I would never make it. But now, look at me! Some 300 light-years from Earth. And in an instant, too. No space sickness, no G-forces to contend with, no time effects …" She paused. Then, "Well, a few time effects I guess."

"I know," responded Jame, his face brightening a bit to see her resilience. "The time thing, that's the hardest thing I guess. I know about that."

"Oh, Jame, I'm so sorry. I reminded you of … of your sister, didn't I?"

"That's okay. It doesn't take much to remind me of it. To be truthful, though, I was hoping to forget about it for a while and just enjoy …" He broke off, unwilling to complete his sentence. He did not want to rush things with her. She looked at him with an indecipherable expression, perhaps guessing what he had been about to say. Looking then again to the magnificent vista she graciously finished his sentence for him, "Yes, let's just enjoy the beauty here."

At that point, Andre returned to take their order. He prided himself on knowing just the right time to interrupt the intimate conversation of two lovers. Okay, they possibly aren't lovers yet, he told himself, but Merci! What possibilities here for his friend Jame! The poor man seemed to have a succession of "femmes fatales" all of whom delighted to have him treat them to a night out, and none of whom were worthy of his personal caliber. But, this Sonja! She was different, Andre felt.

"Ah, Andre. I was beginning to wonder if you had taken a siesta," Jame winked with a grin.

"I am sorry, Mon Ami. I've been so busy with the others," he motioned behind himself to the mostly empty seats in the restaurant. Andre's self-deprecating sense of humor always charmed Jame.

"Yes, Andre, I realize that," Jame retorted in mock seriousness. "But, I am, you know, one of your oldest and most faithful customers. And, this young lady," he continued, with a slight gesture of his hand toward Sonja, "This lady from Earth is here for the first time and gaining first impressions that ..." Jame broke into a hearty laugh, unable to keep up the charade. Andre, not for a moment deceived, joined him with a sort of bubbly chuckle.

Even Sonja, catching on, joined in the fun. "Yes, Andre," she said laughing softly, "When I get back to Earth I will certainly want to bring a good report of the wonderful eating establishments here on Verde, and I'm sure you would want your fine bistro to be among those I cite. In my memoir, that is, for I think I shall not soon return." She surprised herself how easily she had added the afterthought, had mentioned and then abandoned Earth. Perhaps her enculturation was progressing faster than she realized.

The brief interlude of good fun dispersed the heavy atmosphere of talk about time. They ordered a light lunch with some varied samplings, Jame pointing out items on the menu that both characterized the planet's cuisine yet were not too strange to an Earth-borne palate. Not that he knew anything about Earth cuisine of the 21st century. But he guessed well, for Sonja enjoyed everything except the fish soup. It was a local species of fish, quite unlike anything found on Earth, sporting what looked like tails on both ends and no visible mouth. It was an experiment, Jame knew, and the one thing he thought might stretch Sonja a bit. She had said she did not care for fish anyway, but was willing to try anything once – especially since Jame had said it tasted nothing like Earth fish. And, indeed it did not.

After lunch they ordered coffee (the one Earth heritage item on the menu, it seemed, that the 24th century had not forgotten). Sipping quietly, each of them were lost in faraway thoughts, just enjoying the peaceful presence. Jame's feeling that they needed to have a serious talk had waned. Earnest conversation about the future could wait. Then Sonja spoke, breaking the soft silence.

"Jame," she began resolutely and bravely, for this would be only the second time in many years that she had spoken of this. "There is something I need to tell you. I'm taking a risk in doing so, but I feel somehow that something in the future will depend upon you knowing this about me."

Anticipating some revelation about an Earth side relationship, Jame glanced up at her. Intuiting his unspoken concern, she said, "Hey, relax! This is not about another guy. And, anyway, what we started a couple of months ago is still very much there." She reached over and reassuringly touched his hand, winking as she did so. There was a hint of remembered sensuality in the touch and he relaxed. "But I'm still not ready for something deeper. And neither, I think, are you," she said more sharply than she intended. "Oh, gosh … sorry, Jame. I didn't mean it to sound that way. It's just that …"

He cut her off. "Hey, it's okay. I need to be more sensitive to your situation and I'm sorry I miscued on you."

"Apology accepted. So, here's what I was going to say. And please don't get blown away by this. Let me explain first and then we can soberly discuss any questions or concerns you have."

"Okay, fair enough."

"Okay. So, you remember how I told you back there in the lab in that confrontation with Pavel, that I knew he had a weapon?"

"Yes, I wondered about that at the time, but everything was happening pretty fast so I didn't focus on how you knew. I guess I figured you had somehow seen it." In truth he had forgotten it.

"I'm a telepath." Sonja spoke meekly and quietly, looking away from him lest she discover his displeasure.

"You're a what?" Jame asked, surprised and not sure he had heard correctly. But, his voice was gentle. He leaned forward a bit as if to catch something he had missed.

"I'm a telepath," Sonja repeated, daring now to look him in the eyes. "I can read other people's thoughts. Oh, not everyone. And not yours," she hastened to add, being sure to note any alarm that would appear in Jame's face. But there was none. Jame, a scientist at heart, just like her, was clearly interested with an almost academic posture.

Sonja continued, "That's how I knew that Sergei, or Pavel, had that weapon. His angry thoughts were bombarding my mind in a torrent I could barely handle. He had originally planned to kill

Forsen if he wouldn't go along with his plan. That is why he returned, you know. But during the argument I heard his thoughts that now he would have to kill all three of us. I knew I had to tell you about the weapon, no matter what the consequences."

"What do you mean, consequences?" Jame asked.

"I mean ... Oh, it's such a long-ago story and maybe it doesn't matter anymore."

"What ...?"

"I mean, that I was afraid that you would reject me if you found out I could read minds. Because that is what happened before, when I was a child. And I lost all my good friends because of them finding out. I had told my best friend and that was a mistake, but I was young then and didn't understand how people might feel. I have never told anyone else since then. Well, except my mother, just before I came here. And now, you."

"Wow! Well ..." Jame was momentarily at a loss for words. He sat back in his seat, the fingers and palms of his hands steepled together in front of his chin. Then he continued, "Sonja, I don't know what to say. Except, I'm glad you have enough confidence in me to speak of this. It does seem strange to me, but in no way would I reject you." A few moments of silence between them passed, with just the faint tinkle of glasses and soft laughter from inside the restaurant to remind them of where they were.

Sonja continued, relief plain in her voice, "Okay, so now you know, and now I'm not carrying around this heavy burden of secrecy anymore. None of my colleagues at CETL or friends in Kansas City knew, even though I sometimes knew everything they were thinking. But I developed a way to ignore the incoming thoughts when they got in the way of genuine relationship or work."

Suddenly, Jame realized there was a disconnect somewhere. He asked, "Well, what about Pavel? He was Levkov to you, of course, though his true identity was Pavel. And you knew what Pavel was thinking there in the lab, as you just said. So, you must have been able to read Sergei's thoughts as well. Didn't you?"

"No. That's the strangest thing. I never could read Sergei's thoughts. I always thought there was something odd about him – mostly how he could be so smart. Now, I know why. But to read his thoughts – no, I could not. In fact, since coming to Verde, I seem to have completely forgotten that I had the ability to read minds. I guess

I've been so astonished with all the newness that I'd forgotten something of who I was on Earth. I haven't had any experiences of telepathy since coming here. So, there in that conference room, I wasn't even thinking of reading Pavel's thoughts. But something happened during those last moments of the confrontation. Something snapped inside and a whole forgotten realm of my former life reopened. After I accepted who Sergei was, Pavel that is, and made the connections as mind-boggling as they were, I began to hear angry thoughts from him. I wish I hadn't, they were so spiteful. I had always sort of admired Sergei, I guess. Maybe falsely, because I selfishly saw him as my only hope for the stars. But it all came crashing down on me when I saw the real side of him, the cruel and greedy side. It had been there all along, with Sergei I mean. But I hadn't seen it. Pavel was the true man, not Sergei."

They sat in silence again, finishing their coffee. Finally, Sonja asked the question she was most afraid to ask. "Jame, does it bother you? That I can read people's thoughts? Please be truthful."

"Can you read my thoughts, just now? I know you said only certain people were "open" to you and that I wasn't one. If you could read my thoughts you would know that I have nothing but admiration for you. Your telepathic ability doesn't faze me in the least." Jame hesitated, and then continued, "However, you would be well-advised to keep it our secret. The history of Earth society, some one hundred years after your time, shows that there began to be a large number of telepaths. Experts suggested that the gene pool had been altered through increased cosmic rays from the IK Pegasi B supernova. Sadly, they were persecuted, hunted down, and ... Well, let's just say that the gene pool out of which they arose became extinct, or nearly so. In our own era there have been isolated instances of human telepathy. I would like to believe that our society, at least here on Verde, is more enlightened than 22nd century Earth. But from what I have heard people with that ability are generally shunned." He looked upon her benignly and spoke from his heart when he said, "I am truly sorry for you, Sonja, for the torment of "hearing" angry thoughts from such as Pavel and for the difficulty you had as a child." Then, as if he had just spoken to his sister, he added, "I wish she were here. You and Jana would instantly bond to each other, I'm sure."

At this last statement Sonja was shaken to her core. For as Jame said the name of his sister a brilliant image of a woman with long, straight blond hair and angular features very like Jame's came into her mind. And she heard in her mind a voice, a woman's voice, saying just one word: "Jame." Then it all came back to her. The trance-like vision she had of the strange man in a laboratory that had happened to her a few weeks before she had entered the hypersphere and come to Verde. And the sense that this vision had involved "contact" with a woman named Jana. How could she have forgotten this? A second time. For now she remembered having related the same thing to her mother. What did it mean? Why, after all that had happened in the last few months since she had come to Verde, after all the involvement with Jame in trying to reverse the fate of his sister, why would she now remember the visions she had back on Earth? Sonja was floored with the enormity of the realization that whole realms of her former life could be forgotten. Was there more that she no longer remembered? And what of this latest revelation? With Jame's fragile state of mind over his sister, dare she tell him what was happening to her?

Then, before she could say anything to Jame, Xander Abraham's words came thundering back to her: "Remember 54 Piscium." Time collapsed as she was taken back in her mind to that encounter on the campus of Cal Tech. At the time she had sensed *destiny* somehow embedded in those words. Even the name, *Jana* – that too had the ring of destiny back then, though she didn't understand it at the time. Now it all began to make sense, though not in a way that could have been understood at the time. Her longing for the stars. Her chosen field of research. Her "gift" of telepathy. Then her "accidental" coming to Verde via the Telpher. The fact that they had found a 350 year old colony on a planet that orbited 54 Piscium, the very place where Jana had been marooned and from which those radio signals had come – in Sonja's time. And Jana was Jame's sister, calling to Jame somehow through Sonja. This was why she was here. This was the destiny that Xander had foretold!

Sonja felt like she was looking at the cosmos through the opposite end of a telescope, with history reversing itself into a white point of light. She forgot where she was, forgot that she was with Jame in the Orange Haven, forgot what they had been speaking about. She stared wordlessly at Jame. Though only moments passed it seemed an eternity.

Jame noticed that she had blanked out and asked, "Sonja, what's wrong? Are you fearful for what this society may do to you? Was it something I said?"

Sonja looked at Jame in wonder, hearing again his name upon the lips of a woman – clearly the inner voice of his sister, Jana. Then, as quickly as it had occurred, the thought wave passed. She came to, managed a response, bringing herself under control.

"It's ... it's nothing, Jame. I suppose it was the realization of what a burden this "gift" of mine has been over the years, and now the sudden lifting of that burden." She forged on, willing that he not know the real reason for her reaction. "Until now, I have had to hide it from everyone, at least everyone who could possibly understand it from a scientific point of view. And now, here, in this strange world – thank you for your understanding ..." Sonja let her words trail off. She did not want to tell Jame what she had heard. At least not until she could process the meaning of it. Greatly alarmed, she wondered what had just happened. Was she actually hearing the thoughts of his sister, from the past? How could that be? Yet, she was sure that the words she heard were not coming from Jame. His mind was closed to her, opaque. The only thing she could read – in the worried expression of his face – was his obvious concern for her. And that was enough for now.

* * *

Four weeks had passed since their lunch at the Orange Haven. One day Sonja dropped by Allene's cube during a coffee break, just to chat a little. She had been working hard on Derik's project and needed some mental relief.

"Sonja!" exclaimed Allene. "Naughty girl, you," she play-acted a hurt pose. "It's been too long since you came by. I've missed you." It had only been a week or so and Sonja was about to say so, but thought better of it. Play-acting aside, she suspected Allene really was hurt.

"I'm sorry, Allene. I've just been too busy. So I told myself to chill a bit and come down to chat with you. So, here I am. What's new?" 'What's new' was one of Allene's favorite expressions, whether she wanted to know or not. Sonja hoped this would ease the tension.

Allene visibly relaxed and said, "Oh, not much. How's it going with you? Have you seen Jame at all? I know he's real proud of you, the way you've tucked into things. I heard you invented some device for Derik – something out of the history books, Derik said. Where did you learn such things?"

Sonja would not take the bait. Unlike Derik, Allene was intensely curious about Sonja's past and made no bones about it. She also was obviously trying to play match-maker between her and Jame. She avoided both questions, and asked a question back instead, smiling sweetly.

"Allene, can you explain to me the sizing convention for women's apparel here on Verde? The clothing on Verde, as you probably know, is different than on Earth." This was literally true, but not nearly so different as what Sonja had in mind. Men and women both wore a kind of two-piece tunic that fit their bodies closely. The style would have been depressingly uniform were it not for the fact that the color and sheen of the fabric could be changed at any moment. Using their TASC implants people could adjust the appearance of their garment at will. Some more advanced garments, she had learned to her horror, would change without direct control in response to strong emotions felt by the wearer – even becoming semi-transparent. That particular brand of apparel, she learned, was the current rage among the youth and twenty-somethings on Verde. Sonja was thankful she was past that age.

Allene immediately launched into the arcana of women's sizes, amazingly complex for such a simple set of garments. Arm and leg length, chest size, torso length, etc., etc. were all specified by what seemed a complex algorithm. Sonja caught most of it and was grateful to have diverted Allene from her original intent. Unfortunately, not for long.

Finishing her discourse on clothing sizes, and assuring herself that Sonja was on the same page with her, Allene changed the subject for no apparent reason.

"Has Jame spoken to you about his sister? Poor thing. I feel so bad for Jame, the dear man. She was such a beautiful and smart woman. And they were so close, too, like two peas in a pod." Did Allene just wink? Sonja asked herself. "You and she would have instantly liked each other. Straight blond hair meets wavy red hair. Hah! I was young like you girls once, though you are both prettier than I was. And brains, too – the both of you. When I think about Jana … oh, what a shame! She was smart, smarter than Jame I'll say

– but don't tell him I said so!" She stopped abruptly at that, wishing she had not said that last about Jame. Allene was a kind soul, and though extremely busy with the affairs of others, she wished no harm on those into whose lives she so vigorously inserted herself. Seeing the alarm on Sonja's face she apologized profusely, thinking that Sonja had been offended by her comments about Jame.

Sonja, however, was light-years away at that point, unaware of her facial reactions. For at the mention of Jana, it had happened again. Not since four weeks ago, in the Café Orange Haven, had this occurred. There it was again: She heard the original word, and more: 'Jame. Jame, I need you.' The image of a woman's face, too, stunning in its likeness to Jame's, and framed by long, straight golden blond hair – the same color as Jame's. It was so similar to her experiences of telepathy with those with whom she had a connection. Yet different, with a visual component she had never experienced. What was happening to her? Somehow she had a connection with Jana, and Jana was calling for help! But, how could that be? Then it was gone and Sonja returned to the present.

She caught the last few words of Allene: "... so sorry, Sonja. I truly admire Jame. He's a great man. And I did not mean to ..."

Sonja cut her off, somehow able to regain her composure in spite of the intensity of what she had just experienced. "It's all right, Allene. I know it's a sensitive subject with Jame so I don't usually speak with him about it. Your bringing it up startled me, since I know he doesn't like to talk about Jana."

This seemed to pacify Allene, and Sonja begged her leave, backing out of Allene's cube with expressions of gratitude for the interesting discussion on clothing sizes. Reluctance or not, Sonja knew she had to talk to Jame about Jana, and her experiences. It was time. She resolved to do so at the earliest opportunity, though in truth she did not know what she was going to say. One thing she was sure of, however, was that the thought waves from Jana were real. The thing she could not explain was how. Sonja wondered how she could be in telepathic communication, at least one-way, with someone who no longer existed – at least not in her present world? Was Sonja communicating with a parallel world, something that Jame believed in? Which brought up an even weirder question as to how someone who had been born Jame's sister in this world had, in fact, lived out her life and died three centuries ago on a planet hundreds of light-years away? In another universe. Or had she?

Sonja puzzled over this for the next few days. A big part of the puzzle (or was it a hint of a solution?) was that she had found no evidence of the fact that Jana had settled on Mycenae. Even though Jame had spoken little of events surrounding the disappearance of the *Exeter* and the subsequent discoveries, Sonja had done some additional sleuthing. To help Jame, she had tried to better understand the anomalous behavior of the *Exeter's* HyperNav system and the connection to Sergei/Pavel's duplicity. Unbeknownst to Jame, Sonja had found the report on the *Exeter* that had been sent to Jame from InterStellar's Jack Ibsen. Jame had mentioned it to her, so one day when he was gone on an errand she went into his office to look for it. She felt a bit guilty in doing so, but if she found something helpful she could point to the successful results of her search to allay any ill feelings. Unfortunately, she found nothing helpful about navigation system issues, but what she did find was eye opening.

Jame had not mentioned an appendix to the report and she wondered later if he had even read it. The appendix had included rather detailed inventories by Captain Wrain and his Exec of the items they had found in the cave on Mycenae. Among these was a detailed birth and death record of the first few generations of the settlers from the *Exeter*. First, second, and even third generations were recorded. Captain Tang's name was there as were the names of some of the *Exeter's* crew. But there were notable omissions from the list. Since the list of names purported to be thorough, Sonja had understood it to be authoritative and complete. Upon comparing it with the original crew list for the *Exeter* there were several names of crew that were not in the cave records. Among those were the names of Commander Jana Anders, Chief Navigator; Lieutenant Joss Sommers, Pilot; Rolfo Hardy, First Mate; Serene Jackson, Chief Medical Officer, and a few others. Sonja had wondered at the time about this, but had dismissed it. Now she was beginning to suspect something, an explanation so weird that, as a scientist, she could scarcely credit it.

Oddly, at just this juncture, she recalled once again the words of Xander Abraham that day in Pasadena. He had said, "Sonja, the story of the stars is not yet over. Don't forget that! Or, 54 Piscium!" Since that traumatic experience in the Orange Haven a few weeks ago she had now come to understand the source of those signals from 54 Piscium that her post-doc, Latya, had fatefully picked up in their lab at CETL. They were the signals from the crew of *Exeter* after they had disappeared back in time. She had done the calculations and figured out that the distance of the star from Earth and the approximate date of the founding of the colony on Mycenae all worked out to a reception of those signals on Earth in the year 2065. And Sonja had been almost the only one to believe in them. Now those signals were being corroborated by the other kind of signals that Sonja had always hoped to find: thought waves of sentient beings coming from the stars.

Chapter 24. Voices From The Past

Verde City, September 2376

It was a week before Sonja could get together with Jame again. Sonja had left a message for him that she needed to talk to him, but he had made a trip to Port Robis to settle a personnel issue in the field office there. During that week, and engaging the assistance of Hald, Sonja had done some research into a subject she knew very little about: time. So, by the time they were able to sit down and talk, Sonja felt she had a reasonable handle on what might be happening to her with the presumed telepathic communication with Jana. If she was right, she had a plan on what they could do to rescue Jana and the other *Exeter* crew members – at least those who had not been recorded as having died on Mycenae. It was, she admitted to herself, a crazy plan. All the same, she was now ready to engage Jame in it.

They met again in the Orange Haven Café. Though it was early Spring in Verde's southern hemisphere, it was a cloudy, gray day with a fine mist rising over Galene. There was a chilly breeze on the patio where they sat before. Sonja suggested they sit inside, tucked away in a booth where they were assured privacy. Not that there were many people there, but Sonja had not wanted any interruptions. She had adroitly explained this to Andre beforehand, who after taking their orders pointedly left them alone.

"What's with the secrecy bit?" Jame asked her as Andre departed. It had been mostly small talk up to that point, Jame filling her in on his trip to Port Robis, and Sonja telling him how much she was enjoying the work supporting Derik.

"It's not secret, Jame. But … well, I guess you would say it's a bit wacky. And I'm not sure about what I am going to propose, so I want your undivided attention." She took his hands in hers, affectionately.

"Okay, you've got it."

"Well, let's see … where to start? Okay, I'll try this: Have you ever heard of a mathematical philosopher by the name of Kurt Gödel? He lived in the 20th century, and is best known for a mathematical theorem he proved, the so-called Incompleteness Theorem."

"Sorry, it doesn't ring a bell. Philosophy, even mathematical philosophy, is not on my skills chart. Or, interest either."

"Well, that doesn't matter, because there is something else he proved that has, I think, a direct impact on some things that have been happening to me. I'm going to tell you about those things, but I need to set the stage first."

"Okay, doctor, lead on," Jame smiled warmly at Sonja, but a bit too benignly.

"Jame, please! This is serious. And I'm a little unsure of myself here. If you laugh at me I'm not going to be able to get through this."

"Sorry, sorry, sorry!" exclaimed Jame. "I apologize. Please go on and if I do not understand something I promise to politely ask. Okay?"

"Okay. Hey, I'm sorry too that I am so sensitive on this. We need to trust each other. Especially if we go through with a plan I have."

"Wow. Now you've got my attention. What's the plan?"

"Just wait. I have to set the stage and I have to make another confession as well. First things first. So back to Kurt Gödel. You've heard of Einstein, I dare say." Jame nodded. "Well, Gödel and Einstein were good friends toward the end of Einstein's life. They were both at the Princeton Institute for Advanced Studies, and they spent a lot of time talking about physics and philosophy and sharing their mutual heritage of pre-war Austrian science. Gödel was not as well known to the average 20th century man on the street as was Einstein, but in his own field of abstract mathematics he was notorious. He had upended the universe of thinking about mathematics as much as had Einstein in the field of cosmology. They also shared a similar conviction about the unreality of time –

but with different results. To Einstein, time was relative, and flowed differently for every observer. For Gödel, time did not exist at all."

"Just a minute," interjected Jame. "I understand Einstein relativity, but as far as I know whether it is relative or not, time still exists. What did this Gödel guy mean that time did not exist?" He leaned forward and hunkered down a bit as he spoke, as if to try to divine the answer himself. Then, before Sonja could answer, he asked, "And, by the way, how does an astrobiologist get mixed up with relativity?"

Sonja laughed softly. "Well, I confess I had some help on this. I started thinking about time – you know, that subject has been rather prominent amongst us the last few months. Anyway, I decided to ask Hald to help me understand relativity and simultaneity because of some things that have been happening to me ..." Seeing Jame about to interject again, she said, "Just wait, Jame, I'll get to those things. So, where was I? Oh yeah, Hald. I asked Hald for some help and he put me onto Gödel; apparently, in keeping with his fixation on 20th century culture, Hald also reads up on odd characters from that period. By all I've read, Kurt Gödel was certainly an odd character.

"However, he was brilliant, too. Hald has tutored me in some of this, so if I am not too sure of some things or can't explain it right, we can ask Hald for help. Anyway, after he and Einstein became friends Gödel began to look at his friend's theory of relativity, the General Theory that is, and to apply some of the same reasoning he had applied to the abstract mathematics of his day, when he had come up with his Incompleteness Theorem. According to Hald, both Einstein and Gödel were riding against the tide of philosophical idealism in their day that was infecting the world of Western scientific thought with Eastern concepts. In short, they were materialists in an age when the "politically correct" or at least popular interpretation of modern scientific discoveries, such as quantum theory, cast doubt upon the ultimate reality of the material world. It seems, however, that Gödel went even further, being a closet Platonist. As such, he was also skeptical of Einstein's desire to discover a 'unified field theory' that would deterministically encompass all known forces."

"Help me out on that one. What does being a 'closet Platonist' mean?"

"Well, Plato had posited that the material world, though real, is nevertheless ephemeral, being a shadow of eternal realities, which he labeled Ideas, or Forms. The examples that are often given for the eternal realities are mathematical abstractions, such as perfect geometric forms, or concepts such as beauty. A triangle that I might draw upon a sheet of paper, for example, would be the material, yet ephemeral manifestation of the eternal idea of triangleness, to coin a word. To Plato, and to Gödel, mathematical abstractions that could be intuited by the human mind existed independently of the mind, having a timeless and perfect existence."

"Okay. And 'closet' …?"

"'Closet,' meaning that Gödel was afraid to publically state his Platonism. Such ideas in philosophy would have been laughed at in his day. To the mathematicians of Gödel's world, mathematics was to be practiced as a symbolic exercise using scientific methods. They wanted to establish mathematical propositions and make them provable by systems of logic with known, agreed upon rules. Gödel burst the bubble of their aspirations by showing, using their own logical system of rules, that simple arithmetic 'truths' – for example '2 + 2= 4' – that were intuitively obvious could not be completely proven by logical systems. Or something to that effect – his Incompleteness Theorem. I'm not a mathematician," she said with an apologetic look. "So this is just what I gathered from Hald's tutoring. Anyway, Gödel believed in logic but he also believed in intuition. It seems he believed that you could know abstract mathematical reality by a mathematical intuition – by a kind of extrasensory perception."

"Well, I don't know. Haven't thought about it much, but the idea of eternal realities kind of appeals to me …"

"I'm glad it does, because where I am going with this is going to require some sensitivity to Gödel's ideas on time."

"Yes, what about time?" Jame asked, bringing the conversation back to its original tack.

"Well, in short, while Einstein exposed the Newtonian fiction of absolute time, Gödel exposed the fiction of time altogether."

"Wow! I guess he was a wacky character. How could he say that time itself does not exist? I guess that is what you are saying he said? Seems to me that time is still very much present with us. Notwithstanding some of the recent surprises about it that you have suffered." Here, Jame winked at Sonja, but she was nonplused.

"Speaking of time, I wonder where our orders are?" He

continued, looking in the direction of the kitchen. "Seems like a long time since we sent Andre off with our choices."

"Jame, you have just hit on one of the things that has also confronted me. I think I understand what Hald has told me about Gödel's ideas, but thinking about this I have concluded that there is more than one kind of time. There's the time, t, which we use in the formulas of physics, and so forth, for example. But, there is also a subjective time. Call it capital T. And subjective time, as its name implies, is subject to individual states of mind and emotion, while the time of scientific equations of motion for example, little t, is not subjective. It is something that is externally measured, by clocks for example, and there is common agreement on its quantity and duration -- as well as its relativity a la Einstein. Not so with subjective time, T. Here's the proof: I've been so busy talking about Einstein and Gödel that I had not noticed much passage of time at all -- that is, since we placed our orders. That was my time, capital T. But you aren't so caught up in this subject as I am, so the time has dragged on a bit for you. Your time, T, has been longer than mine and you are getting hungry. You see what I mean? Time, the time we call "t" in equations – 'little t,' to give it a name – does not apply to what you and I have just experienced while waiting for lunch. The clock time that has passed, let's say twenty minutes, has been the same for everyone in this restaurant, including us. But our waiting for lunch, capital T, has been subjective, and different for each of us. Anyway, I'm sorry! Maybe we'd better take a breather on this and have something to eat. I confess, I had asked Andre to hold off on the food so that I could get the meat of what I wanted to say out before the distraction of eating!"

"Hey, that's okay. I do want to hear this. But having something to eat would probably make things go down easier at this point."

With that, Jame waved to Andre who, ever attentive to his special customers, appeared immediately with their orders. Jame wondered how he had managed to have hot food ready at just the moment when the conversation on time had momentarily paused, yet without any sign that it was time to serve them.

After dinner, and over a rather sweet liqueur, Sonja continued her explanation. "The reason I was taken up with what Hald told me about Gödel was, as I said earlier, that he had conjectured that the kind of time that is used in physical formulas, little t as I have called it, did not have an objective or 'real' existence – in the Platonic sense of reality to which he was committed. That is, the "time" of physics, the "time" of clocks and calendars, while measurable and thus apparently 'real' to us in this world, has no concomitant Form in the Platonic realm of ideas. Geometric forms such as triangles do, but time, little t, does not. Just as he did in arriving at his Incompleteness Theorem in mathematics, he proved his assertions by using the accepted mathematics of General Relativity. He proceeded by finding a solution to Einstein's equations for a particular universe, called a Gödel universe, in which it would be possible to travel in a space ship outward on a certain path, yet at less than the speed of light, and return to a time before you started. A universe in which this could happen is one that is rotating and not isotropic. Admittedly, the universe he conceived in which this could occur does not conform to the universe we live in. As far as we know, anyway. Here's the key point, though. The very fact that a rationally conceivable (and therefore possible) universe, one that did not disobey any known laws of physics, could be so structured in such a way as to permit travel backward in time to a point before you started, meant for Gödel that time, the 't' in the Einstein equations, had no real meaning. In the universe that we know clock time, little t, flows in just one direction as implicated by the 2nd Law of thermodynamics. One cannot conduct an experiment the results of which are to go back to an earlier time. Thus, clock time, little 't' in a Gödel universe, has no meaning – such a concept is illogical. Gödel then reasoned that if time is not meaningful in one possible universe, it is not meaningful, or real, in any universe. I guess the fact that, in our universe, we think clock time is real is only an artifact, so to speak, of the limited understanding – or, consciousness – that we presently have of that universe.

"But what if, for the sake of argument, our four-dimensional universe is but a subset of a higher dimensional reality – one in which time, t, as we conceive it does not exist? Many of Gödel's later admirers thought that he had proven that time travel was possible – in this universe, that is. But that was not his point. To himself, Gödel had shown that time was unlike geometric forms, mathematical abstractions, and concepts like beauty – all of which had an eternal existence in his Platonic world view. We can use time, little t, to talk about physical events in our world of sense perception but according to Gödel it has no reality outside of our ephemeral spacetime world. However, after thinking about it, I would amend his view to: 'it has no reality in any higher dimensional realm'."

"Well, I guess you and Pavel for that matter, have given the lie to his ideas. The recent events in our lives have shown all too clearly that time travel is possible – including travel to the past."

"No. Not if you admit to the existence of parallel worlds," Sonja corrected him. "Remember that you have hypothesized that the only way to understand what Pavel did, without creating logical paradoxes, is to conjecture that his choices created a parallel universe – at least for himself and those whose lives were bound up with his. On this view Pavel did not really go back in time only – he went to a parallel universe. And, you have certain proof of that, too. For example, the different 'histories' of the development of the F-S Drive and the evolution of your company, InterStellar Dynamics. The interesting thing is that some of us remember both histories. You, Hald, and Pavel – each of you remembered something of the other history."

"Except you. Right?"

"Yes, except me. But that may be because my history is (or was) the same in both worlds – at least up to the time I stepped into the hypersphere and came here."

"Yes," agreed Jame, dropping his eyes momentarily, "You are right. I guess I'm trying to have it both ways – to live in both universes, to experience both histories. Sometimes I think I am still in the same universe as Jana ... was. Actually, she is – or was – in the same universe as me, the one we are in now. Because of that colony on Mycenae. What I mean, I guess, is that there is no way to go back to the old universe. Not that ..." Here he stopped, not wanting to continue the thought. He was torn between his love for his sister and his enchantment with Sonja. Sonja would not be here now with him if he were to somehow set things right and go back to that conjectured "other" universe – the one in which Jana lived in the same time as did he.

Sonja smiled sympathetically, and placed her hand first on his forearm and then in his hand.

"Jame," she said softly, "I'm not sure, but I have a feeling that all is not lost. Gödel's Platonic ideas about time have provided me an answer to the puzzling things that have been happening to me, which

I now want to tell you about. There is a realm of experience, and of communication between humans, which exists outside of this four-dimensional spacetime we all are so caught up in. Call it a fifth dimension if you like, but it is a realm in which time does not exist, neither the time of science nor the subjective time. So, here I have to make my confession."

Jame looked up at her, expectantly, savoring the warmth of her hand in his. He said, simply, "Okay."

"It is this: You remember our conversation some weeks ago, here in this café. I told you of my telepathic abilities and you accepted me. I am still so grateful for that, by the way. You may remember that at one point in our conversation the subject of your sister, of Jana, came up. You began to speak of her and think about your loss."

"Yes, I remember," said Jame, not looking at Sonja.

"Well, you may also remember that I reacted rather strongly at your mention of Jana."

Jame nodded in the affirmative. "You seemed to have blacked out momentarily."

Yes, it was like that. Because at your mention of Jana's name I heard a voice, a woman's voice, in my mind that said, 'Jame'. And I saw a clear image of a woman who looked very much like you, with long, straight blond hair. She looked your twin. Are you and Jana twins?"

Jame stared at her, unable at first to speak. Then he said, "Yes we are … were twins – and very close, as you know. What do you mean that you heard her voice?"

"I mean that it was just like when I hear people's thoughts with whom I have a telepathic connection." Jame started to speak but she continued. "Please, let me go on. It happened again, a couple of weeks ago while I was visiting with Allene. You know what a busybody the dear lady is. Anyway, she got around to bringing up Jana and how you missed her. When she did so I again heard the voice and received the image of a blond woman. I have never received images like that with people with whom I am in telepathic communication. Maybe that is because they are always right next to me. At first I thought that this was just some kind of hallucination I was having, but it seemed so like what I have known all my life that I couldn't put it down."

"But, how you could be hearing the thoughts of someone who is … who is dead," Jame forced the words out from a clenched jaw. This was so difficult, and he wondered where Sonja was going with it. Sonja sensed his discomfort and again took his hands in hers.

"Jame, I know this is hard for you. And there is more I need to confess. But please do not judge me until it's all out on the table. While you were gone one day I went into your office to find the *Exeter* report that you had mentioned. I was trying to learn more about the anomaly in the navigation system and thought the report might shed some more light on it. However, while looking in it, I discovered the appendix. Did you ever read the appendix, the list of things they found in the cave?"

A mixture of emotions swirled within him. He pulled his hands away and was about to speak. Instead, he shook his head to indicate he had not read the appendix. Involuntarily he stroked his forehead in a display of puzzlement. Sonja pressed on, telling him of the list of names of those who had lived and died on Mycenae and how his sister's name was not among them. Jame listened in silence until Sonja finished. Then he said, "So what?"

"The 'so what' is that I believe … Oh, this is so hard, Jame, and I know you are hurting with this. Please try to bear with me on it – I am so hopeful of my plan. What I believe is that I have a 'timeless' telepathic connection with Jana, through you, a connection that transcends the ordinary time of this world. Gödel's ideas have suggested to me that there is a realm beyond this in which calendar time does not exist, but in which human minds do exist and which human minds can comprehend. It is a realm through which people who seem to be separated in both space and time can nevertheless be connected. And I have been given that ability, a gift I now realize, at least for your sister." Sonja again recalled the prophetic words of Xander Abraham.

For the first time in many minutes, Jame visibly relaxed. Something had taken over in him – perhaps a new hope, or at least a growing trust in Sonja's intuitions. Perhaps she was on to something. He would listen and try to understand, even go along with her plan.

"What do you propose to do?" he said.

"Just this: I want to try to establish, through you, a reverse telepathic communication with Jana. I have never done anything like that before. It's always been just one way, toward me from another.

But I don't believe it must be one way, particularly because when you think of her, her thoughts come to me. Perhaps because you are twins, you also have a type of mental telepathy with each other that you are not aware of. And if that is so then maybe I can communicate to her, through you. In short, I could communicate the 'fix' to the Alcubierre metric algorithm that Glaston showed us. I could impress upon her mind to carry out that fix and to bring the *Exeter* back to this spacetime."

"But, she's dead! How can she …?

"No! She is not dead. Not in the timeless world of mind."

"How can you be so sure of that?" Jame asked. "How do you know such a thing could work?" His voice took on a desperation-tinged hopefulness.

"Jame, the reason for my hope is that list of names of people who lived and died on Mycenae I told you about. Jana's name was not on that list. Why wasn't it? It must be, it can only be that you and I carried out this plan and successfully communicated with her. And that, acting on what she received, she turned the *Exeter* around and returned to our time." With that, Sonja slumped back in her seat, exhausted. She could go no further.

There were long moments of silence, not even penetrated by the sounds of other customers in the café. It was as if there was a bubble of mysterious hope surrounding them and their table. The churning thoughts in Jame's mind slowly subsided until he could look once again into Sonja's face. Her eyes were closed, as if asleep, her breathing steady, hands resting peacefully in her lap. The anxious look of concern had eased and her face seemed to glow with hope.

"Okay." His voice, breaking the ethereal silence, startled them both. "Okay, let's try it," he said.

257

Chapter 25. Jana's Dream

Planet Mycenae, Apollo System. Local Date: Circ 1, Early Fall.

Jana carefully re-read what she had just written: "Captain's Log, GES time unknown, local time "Circ 1, Early Fall. Captain Arun Tang was buried today on the planet Mycenae, with full honors. He died of apparent heart failure, brought on by a sickness from a local micro-organism. He did not suffer, succumbing quickly to the infection. The crew of the *Exeter* mourns his passing." A tear formed in her eye as she closed the log. Not usually given to morbid thoughts, this day Jana was truly down. She thought of her brother, Jame, and wished he were there. They had so many fun times growing up together, each supporting the other when a difficulty or personal reversal came to either one of them. Why couldn't Jame be here now, she thought. Of course, she knew why, but that did not help. "Jame," she intoned, under her breath, "I need you."

The burden of command had fallen upon Jana, yet there would soon be no *Exeter* to command. Preparations continued apace for shuttling to the planet surface the vital equipment they would need. Included in this was Rolfo's emergency beacon. They had shut it down yesterday and packed it up. The solar panels that would provide a long-lasting low power source for it were already in place. Jana went into the Navigation Cube to complete the programming of *Exeter's* micro-fusion drive to keep it in orbit for as long as possible. She wasn't sure why she bothered with this -- there would be no one aboard and no need to have *Exeter* remain in orbit after the last of the crew and equipment were taken planet side.

Entering the Cube, Jana saw the plastext notes she had been

making in her attempts to discover the problem with the Alcubierre metric calculation. It had been such a fruitless effort! She picked them up and thought, idly, to have one last try. But at that point a sleepiness overtook her. It wasn't surprising -- they had all been working long hours with little rest. There was a couch in the Cube and Jana lay down, placing the plastext notes on the deck beside her. She fell into a deep sleep.

* * *

"Jana! Wake up! You all right?" It was Rolfo. Jana awoke with a start. As she did so, numbers and figures swirled in her mind. She looked at Rolfo -- looked right through him in fact.

"Jana, what's up? You look like you've seen a ghost or something."

"Where are the notes?" Jana ignored him, looking around desperately for the plastext notes. Finding them on the deck, she grabbed them up and pushed roughly past Rolfo to the small desk at one side of the Cube.

"Jana ...?"

"Rolfo, sorry, please don't interrupt me! I just figured it out. That is, I think I figured it out. No, that's not right. I did not *figure* it out. It just *came* to me – I see it all so clearly right now and I've got to put it down before I lose it." She took a stylus from the desk and began scribbling some numbers. Then, activating the computer terminal, she called up the Alcubierre metric model and compared what she saw with what she had written down. Slumping back in the chair, she exclaimed, "Yes, that is it! I believe I've found the problem with the metric calculation that led to the spacetime anomaly."

"Are you sure, Jana? That would be great! That is, I guess it would be." To Rolfo the deal was done and they were going to spend the rest of their lives on this strange planet below them. But, if true, then he could only look on proudly at this beautiful woman who was so much smarter than he.

"Yes, I think so. No ... I'm not sure. But, yes, it has to be right. I'm just having a hard time believing it. How is it that suddenly it came to me, in my dreams of all places, when all those months I couldn't figure it out?"

"Does that mean we can reverse what happened, somehow?" Rolfo was still not at all clear about what she was getting at.

"No, we cannot reverse it. What's done is done. But we may be able to direct the future into a different path. At least for some of us." Jana was already thinking logistics, announcements, preparations. She wondered if it was even possible. So many of the crew had resigned themselves to living on Mycenae – even seemed to be enjoying it. Arun was dead. How could she command the ship, she wondered. Would Lieutenant Sommers be willing to pilot *Exeter* in such a dangerous maneuver as Jana knew would be necessary? All this had to be planned out and managed – and in fairly quick order. Their supplies were running low and the timing had to be just right for the move. Jana knew, also, that she would have to make some complex calculations and that the lives of anyone who chose to go with her would depend upon the accuracy of those calculations.

* * *

It was a farewell party aboard *Exeter*. To break the news and ensure both a level of secrecy and a spirit of unity, Jana proposed the gathering. All the crew were invited, but none of the original passengers. She wanted to be able to explain to them what she had found and to propose to them the dangerous mission she had in mind. She hoped that by being all together one last time there would be mutual support and good will between those who chose to stay on Mycenae – as she was certain would be the case – and those to chose to try their luck with her. She believed Sommers and Jackson would sign on, and Rolfo of course. How many others, she was not sure. Even with no others she hoped that the four of them could manage the flight.

For what could have been a somber celebration, it was turning out to be pretty joyful, even raucous at times. Drinks flowed freely and the food was good. Here and there were conversations of the good times on previous journeys. All was going well in Jana's eyes and she knew it was time to make the announcement. She got Rolfo to go about the crowd clinking a champagne glass, while she stood up on the dais at the front of the mess deck.

"Fellow *Exeter* crew members, brothers and sisters, in fact," she began with an almost motherly tone. "I have an announcement of considerable import and one that I hope will give you hope." The room grew instantly quiet. "I'll get right to the point. I believe I have found the answer to the navigation system error that brought us here. I have found the error in the Alcubierre metric algorithm and made what I believe to be the necessary adjustments to it to ensure a correct chronological sequencing. And I have come up with a plan to take us back to the 24th century." She paused while the silence grew deeper. Some were not prepared to hear such an announcement, after months of failed hopes. Others did not believe it, she could tell. She did not blame them. However, there were a few for whom hope springs eternal. It was not surprising that Serene Jackson was the first to speak up.

"Jana, do you mean that you found a way to go back through the worm hole?" Her eyes glistened brightly, a tear showing.

"No, Serene, not *back* through the wormhole through which we came. That, I am sure, is forever closed to us. Rather, creating a new wormhole, or more exactly a spacetime rip, that would – if all goes well – provide a channel through which we can return to our own time." She did not say, our own world, for she suspected that the world from which they had come was forever lost to them. At the same time, she believed somehow that if they were successful, the world to which they returned would not be terribly different. She fervently hoped that whatever differences there were, that people like Serene would find the same husband and young children whom she had left. Privately, she also fervently hoped that her twin brother Jame would be there and be the same person she had always known.

Jana continued, noting the tentatively growing hopefulness on the faces of some. "I want you to know that such an attempt that I have in mind will be dangerous in the extreme and may not succeed. In essence we are going to deliberately navigate as close as possible to the star around which this planet orbits and then, taking advantage of the very strong spacetime curvature in its vicinity we will actuate warp drive. I have re-programmed the HyperNav to project us forward in time and back to the trajectory on which we were travelling when we got lost. For some of you I suspect the better choice would be to stay here. But the offer is open to any of you who want to join me. Oh, and we are leaving day after tomorrow – the *Exeter's* normal space propulsion system is nearly out of fuel and we dare not wait longer." With that she sat down, exhausted.

There was a low murmur of conversation, some speaking to their neighbors, while others sat in silence. Then, one by one, each member of the crew made his or her choice. As she had expected, and hoped, Joss Sommers signed up as well as Jackson, Rolfo, and a few others. Most, however, judged it too risky and elected to stay.

Nevertheless, also as Jana had hoped, those electing to stay had nothing but well-wishing and prayers for the success of those who would go. And conversely the farewells and good luck wishes flowed from the departing crew to the new citizens of Mycenae.

They would have a skeleton crew to man the ship, but Jana and Joss judged they could do it. Immediately after the party the two of them got together in the ready room to go over Jana's plan. Joss understood her role in piloting the ship as close as possible to Apollo and the need to be ready at exactly the right moment to engage the hyperdrive engine. As they were about to separate and make final preparations, Joss had a last question for Jana.

"Jana, I get it what you are trying to do and it makes sense, sort of, now that you've explained it all. Yet, you spent months trying to figure this all out with no success. How did you finally do it?"

"I dreamed it, Joss. That's all I know. It just came to me in a dream."

Chapter 26. *Exeter* (Epilogue)

October, 2376, GES. Earth: Inter-Federation Space Station Five

Space Flight Controller Lukos Manteel eased into his controller's couch in the navigation pod of IFSS #5, having just returned from break midway through his first six-hour shift. The geosynchronous satellite in which he sat silently orbited Earth, doing its part in monitoring all space travel – both within Sol's system and without. Lukos adjusted his TASC to reduce the volume of the regular pings from interstellar ships as they traveled in hyperspace from Earth's sector of the galaxy to other distant regions. A virtual screen floated a few inches from his face, depicting visually each ship's position. With the recovery of information from that rebel scientist on Verde on the unauthorized changes he had made to the HyperNav, InterStellar's space fleet was once again in full operation. It was Lukos' first day back on the job as they had laid off many of the Controllers during the embargo. He was glad to be back.

Tonight, in fact, he was assigned to monitor that same sector of space in which the unfortunate space liner, the *Exeter*, had been making her maiden voyage. That had been the event that had brought the whole interstellar trade business to its knees, and Lukos had been the one to have first reported the demise of the *Exeter*. "Poor souls," he murmured to himself as he dedicated himself afresh to the chores of a Space Flight Controller. Satisfied that all was well, he was tempted to indulge in a little game of Space Marbles. Thinking better of that, and on a whim, he brought up the Narrow Field Array that showed any selected region of space within a 5 parsec radius. Lukos chose not just any region, but the region in which *Exeter* had disappeared. He didn't know why he did that, because he knew there were no planned flights in that sector. Company officials were still leery of letting ships travel as close to massive stars as *Exeter* had been allowed to go on that fateful journey. He still remembered with unusual clarity the view he had on the NFA that day. A blinking green triangle had represented *Exeter* in the display, mimicking the periodic transponder signals. Lukos had watched the blinking icon with a mixture of satisfaction and ennui. Then it had disappeared.

Well, he thought, that was all over now. As expected, the NFA showed empty space tonight. He was about to switch it off and activate his portable Space Marbles game when something happened that shouldn't have: A blinking green triangle suddenly appeared in the display, mimicking the periodic transponder signals of an interstellar flight. Lukos watched the blinking icon with a mixture of incredulity and awe. For, the transponder vessel identifier indicated that it was the *ISS Exeter*.

Acknowledgements

First of all, I want to acknowledge the profound assistance and contribution of my wife Barbara, my muse and best friend, who first encouraged me to write this novel, inspired the core ideas of the plot, and helped with every phase of publication. An author in her own right, she also reviewed and edited every major draft and tutored me in good writing habits. My son-in-law, Brian Miller, an avid sci-fi reader, provided many edits and suggestions. My granddaughter, Sara Anne Miller, an amazing artist, did the cover art (see more: https://paperbirdfineart.com/).

Some of the science ideas in the novel came from contemporary scientific literature, including in particular Kip Thorne's book, *Black Holes & Time Warps,* from which I drew the idea of scaling up quantum wormholes to classical dimensions as well as other background for wormholes and time travel. I want to thank two professional colleagues/friends for their technical contributions. Dr. Paul Grant, retired from IBM and the Electric Power Research Institute (EPRI), suggested connecting the discovery of the axion particle with the theoretical understanding of dark matter. This led me to imagine the existence of negative mass, dark matter antiparticles in a "nearby" parallel universe, which could be "captured" or accumulated for use in an Alcubierre warp drive. Dr. William Hassenzahl straightened out my description of the visibility of the star, 54 Piscium, from which Jana's distress signal originates. Bill also provided other helpful edits.

I am indebted to beta version readers, Debra Chan, Bill Hassenzahl, Jr., Joel Rickert, and Randy Shaw, who made suggestions regarding language, character description and plot sequence. Thanks also to colleagues and enthusiastic supporters from my career in the field of superconducting power transmission, Ms. Sue Butler, Associate Director of Public Affairs at the Texas Center for Superconductivity at the University of Houston (TcSUH), Dr. Alan Lauder, Director of R&D for DuPont (retired) and Executive Director of the Coalition for the Commercial Application of Superconductors (CCAS), and Randy Shaw, Business Development Manager for Sumitomo Electric, USA. Besides giving me great edits and insightful comments, they are also enthusiastic readers who tell me they can't wait for the sequel. I'm working on it …

About the Author

Steve Eckroad recently retired from the Electric Power Research Institute where he culminated over 40 years' experience in the research, design, and deployment of advanced power delivery technologies for the electric power industry. He has a degree in physics from Antioch College and did graduate work in Electrical Engineering at the University of Missouri-Rolla. He has several patents and numerous technical publications in the areas of superconducting transmission systems and energy storage. Steve currently resides in Southern California with his wife, Barbara Eckroad. *Telpher* is his first novel.

Made in the USA
Middletown, DE
13 January 2021